As Far as the Eye Can See

Clarise Rivera

Cover design by Zach Starr.

ISBN-13: 978-1545409947
ISBN-10: 1545409943

For my family, and my friends who treat me like family…home is where the love is.

I would like to thank several people for their love and support for this novel:

Peyton, who has been my encouragement for almost twenty years and who provides me quiet time to write when the writing mojo beckons; Sandy, whose passion for the written word, copywriting, and a good ole' fashioned love story helped in the editing of the novel; Zach, whose creativity and patience allowed for cover art that made me feel like the characters were coming home; David, who patiently explained hay farming and horses too many times to count over the last three years; Val, who knew I was five chapters away from finishing the book and would remind me nightly to push through the resistance; and my numerous family and friends who always offer to read and talk about characters to help make them more believable—thank you for being my tribe.

CHAPTER ONE

Emily Mitchell drove up a long stretch of gravel road until she reached a blue farmhouse with a wraparound porch. She parked and watched the dust settle around the '87 Honda Civic she was driving and let go of the death grip on the steering wheel. The car definitely needed new tires. And brakes. She rolled down the windows, because at 9 a.m. it was still cool in western Ohio in June, and she was burning up from nervousness. She gave herself a once over in the rearview mirror, patted down her short, dark hair, and tried to rub away the black circles under her eyes in vain. She looked like hell, the toll of the last few months resting solely on her face. She picked phantom fuzz off the pink shirt and the black slacks she was wearing. She hated this outfit, but this was the best she could find, rummaging through her Aunt Margaret's clothing on such short notice.

A tall, broad-shouldered man walked out onto the porch of the farmhouse with a mug of coffee. He was dressed in Wranglers, a green button-down shirt neatly tucked into his jeans, and a Tennessee ball cap, curved heavily at the brim. He looked like he was about early fifties. He squinted at her car with some uncertainty and wore a very serious and annoyed look on his face.

Oh, great, she thought. She smiled nervously at him and got out of the car, clutching her purse like a shield.

"Ms. Mitchell?" he asked. He had a slow, Southern drawl, his voice deep and soothing.

"Mr. Shaw?" She prayed he couldn't smell the fear on her.

"Come on in. Coffee's ready." He propped open the screen door with his left hand.

Emily walked past him into the dim vestibule of the farmhouse. It took a few seconds for her eyes to adjust, but when they did, she saw the house was decorated with a woman's touch— white, laced curtains hung on the windows, and dated, flowered wallpaper hung on the walls. He led her to a large, oval, oak dining room table with matching chairs. There were little hand-sewn pillows on the seats.

"So, where are you from?" he asked as he poured her a cup of coffee.

"Originally? Texas. But I lived in New Jersey for the last ten years." She took the hot cup of coffee and thanked him.

"Whereabouts in Texas?" he asked, sitting down.

"Dallas area."

"How did a Dallas gal end up in New Jersey?"

Emily took a long sip of coffee. "Got married. My husband was from New York." Mr. Shaw nodded.

"Has your family always owned this farm?" she asked.

"No. My wife was in the Air Force, and we ended up in Ohio. We bought it a few years back. We met when I worked on her daddy's ranch in Karnes City, Texas. We moved around a bit, but always knew we'd end up back on a farm eventually."

"Is she still in the Air Force?"

"She passed away over five years ago," he said softly.

Emily felt the coffee burn her throat. "I'm so sorry."

Mr. Shaw drank his coffee and changed the subject. "So, did your husband transfer to Columbus for a job? I'm sorry to say I can't remember exactly what was printed in the church bulletin."

"Um, no . . . my husband also . . . he recently passed away," Emily said, clearing her throat several times just to get the words out.

Those words, those God-awful words, no matter how many times she uttered them in the last three months still stung and caused her to tear up and cry. It was like a knee-jerk reaction. She tried to blink back the tears, unsuccessfully. Mr. Shaw handed her a tissue from the buffet that was next to the table and frowned at her.

"I'm sorry." She cleared her throat several times.

"Quite all right."

"Look, Mr. Shaw, I'm going to come right out and level with you. My husband worked on Wall Street, and apparently was in several shady deals. When the feds were alerted and he knew he was going to be arrested, he committed suicide. I had no idea about any of this. All I was told was that he killed himself, and then a few days after the funeral, federal agents came and seized our home and pretty much everything we owned. The only family I have is my crazy Aunt Margaret who lives in town—and believe me when I say she is borderline insane. None of our friends would help us, because they all lost money when Aaron stole it from them. I have a 7-year-old son who is deaf, and I am willing to do anything for work to get back to some sense of normalcy. I can cook, I can clean. I can muck out stalls, I can run errands. I am not afraid of hard work. I just really need to support my son."

He leaned back in his chair and looked at her, a crumpled mess, clutching balled-up tissues in her hands.

"I know I sound like a lunatic," she mumbled.

She blew it. She shook her head, disappointed that she could not even get through an interview without falling apart.

"A little. But you mostly sound like a mother who is trying to do right by her boy. I can appreciate that," he said. Emily wiped away more tears.

"I'll give you a shot. You say you can cook? Well, I need one. We are about at harvesting time. I need someone to cook for the six hands we have on deck for the harvest. Let's start with that."

Relief flooded Emily. "Are you serious? Thank you, Mr. Shaw."

"Gavin. Call me Gavin. No one calls me Mr. Shaw."

"Emily. My name is Emily. My son is Sam," she said.

"All right, Emily. Let's get to work."

CHAPTER TWO

It happened just a week before spring break. Emily had been trying to get Aaron to commit to a time they could all go to Cape Cod for the summer, but he kept putting her off, saying that work was busy, and that he was unsure if he would be able to get away at all that summer. They had an awful fight the night before he did it.

"*You have lost your focus since you got promoted. All you care about is your damn job!*" Emily yelled.

"*My damn job puts food on the table and pays the bills. You should be more respectful of it,*" Aaron hissed at her. His blonde hair was wet, and beads of sweat had started to pool on his brows. His appearance had changed drastically in the last six months. He had lost about 20 pounds and was popping Pepcid like it was Tic-Tacs. She had mentioned more than once that he needed a physical check-up with their family doctor, but he was always backing out of every appointment she made for him.

"*You are hardly home anymore. Sam barely sees you during the week, less and less on the weekend. It's not right, Aaron. He deserves more of your time, not just your paycheck!*"

"*I'm doing the best I can, Emily. And if you can't appreciate that and shut the hell up, then maybe I should just leave and be on my own,*" he yelled.

Emily sucked in her breath. "*Maybe you just want me to be so damn miserable that I want to leave you. That way you look like the martyr, like always. Well, you can forget that. You can go to hell,*" she said.

"*What you don't know astounds me,*" he said. He walked out of the bedroom, out of the house, and drove his car back to the city. That was the last time she saw him alive.

The local police department drove up the next morning. She saw them park and walk up the long driveway, and she knew he was dead. All she could say over and over again was

No. No. No. No. No.

She was numb from disbelief. Numb from guilt. When she told Sam, he threw up and cried, his mostly unused voice squeaking in a heartbreaking sound that knew no language, only sadness and pain. Emily closed her eyes every night and heard that cry, and that horrible sound shredded what remained of her heart.

She moved in slow motion as she sat in a daze at the funeral home making arrangements. Friends and neighbors came by with food and offered to help with Sam. She hardly remembered the service or the burial. She remembered holding Sam's hand in the limo ride over to the funeral home. She remembered at least 200 people at that service. There were flowers galore from clients, college friends, and fraternity brothers. Lilies and irises gave their fragrant perfume. Random people shook her hand, hugged her, and encouraged her to be strong. All during this time she blamed herself for pushing him too hard. How did she not see he was on the brink of something drastic? He was her best friend; she could read him like a book. But the last year was filled with behavior that she couldn't figure out, and after time, grew tired of trying to figure out.

She was lying in bed with Sam four days after the funeral, napping. The mourners had finally left them alone when she heard a pounding on the front door. When she opened it, ten men in dark suits appeared, handed her a search warrant, and declared that her house belonged to the U.S. Government. She tried desperately to call their lawyer, but he refused to take the call. He was one of many who Aaron had swindled. Of the 200 people who were at the funeral a week earlier, not one would return a phone call or offer a couch when she and Sam were put out on the street.

***

Gavin moved deliberately, favoring his right side. Old

5

injury, she guessed. She followed him into a decent-sized U-shaped kitchen with a small island in the center.

"You will probably have everything you need to cook here. These boys are mostly used to meat and potatoes, but a lot are putting on the spare tire and would probably benefit by some healthier fare, if you get my drift. I wouldn't try anything like tofu but try to throw some fruits and vegetables in the mix if you can."

Emily glanced at Gavin. He was about 6 feet 2 inches and a little on the thinner side, probably not even breaking 200 pounds. She wondered what he ate, or if he was more like her these days, focusing so much on surviving that eating was never high on the list of priorities. She was the thinnest she had ever been in her life, but still on the higher range of "normal." Having her life shattered was the best diet she had ever been on.

Emily opened up drawers to see what kind of pots and pans she had to work with. She opened the fridge and saw that it was pretty bare. A six-pack of microbrew beer, milk, various jams and jellies, eggs, condiments were about all that was in there.

"I have hens in the back. The Borg. You can get your eggs there. I planted tomatoes, sweet corn, spinach, lettuce, some berries, and various other things. Feel free to take from that as you will." Emily smiled at the *Star Trek* reference.

"What kind of budget are we working with?" she asked. She took out her notepad and started scribbling down ideas.

"Two hundred dollars a week."

Emily tried to hide her surprise.

"Trying to save up for a new barn," he explained.

"Understood. Six men, three meals a day. Five days or seven days a week?"

"We work every day until the work is done, sometimes late into the evening."

"Seven days then," she said. She calculated that averaged to about $10 a meal. That would be very tight, but she liked a challenge.

"What time is breakfast? Should it be heavy? Protein based? Lighter lunches? Dinners heavier?"

"Usually start at 6 a.m. We don't break for lunch until noon. So, it should be a heavier breakfast. Lunch, probably a little lighter. On the days we are baling, sometimes the sun can wreak havoc on the appetite," he said. "Dinners should have some variety. Some like a bigger dinner. Some just want a sandwich and a beer."

"Are we buying beer with this money?"

"No. I provide the water and drinks off a separate budget. Like to buy those at Sam's Club."

"Whew, thank God," she mumbled.

He looked at her taking notes and peeking into cupboards again. "Can you do it?"

"Yes, sir. Or die trying," she muttered. He smiled into his coffee cup.

"Would you like to try my cooking? I could whip up something for you for lunch. I would need a few more things from the store, though," she offered.

Gavin looked intrigued. "Can you do it for $10?"

She looked at him then opened the pantry. She saw flour, cornmeal, and most basic spices. She opened up the freezer and saw frozen beef, chicken, and pork, including bacon and sausage.

"Show me your garden," she said.

He escorted her outside, past his barn. She could see that most of his produce, which rested on about two acres, was starting to peak. The rest of the land was soft, green hay as far as the eye could see. She pulled off some rosemary and crushed it, releasing its pungent, woody fragrance. The basil was peaking, too. Tomatoes were still a little green, but that gave her an idea.

"I can do it for $7," she told him. She squinted at him in the sunlight. Gavin reached into his pocket and pulled out $7 and handed it to her. She shoved it into her front pocket.

"Lunch at noon?" she asked.

"Sounds good."

She walked back to the kitchen to fill the sink with tepid water, then opened the freezer and tossed a frozen, cut-up chicken in water to defrost. She wiped her hands on a dishtowel, grabbed her purse, and sprinted down the stairs. She met Gavin at the porch.

"Chicken is defrosting. One hour. I'll be back."

Inside Kroger, Emily quickly grabbed a small basket. The cool grocery store was a relief from the morning sun, which was starting to raise the temps to the mid-80s. She would have to change clothing before going back to Gavin's because she didn't notice any air conditioning in his house, just like Margaret's. With her $7 she picked up a lemon, red potatoes, garlic, a small container of cream, and a small box of iced tea. The final tally was $6.15. She was so excited that she practically ran to the car with the remaining change in her pocket.

Gavin emerged from his barn when he heard her car drive up the gravel road an hour later. She had changed into a gray t-shirt, dark blue shorts and expensive running shoes. He couldn't help notice that in these clothes she looked much younger and completely in her element. She smiled at him when she saw him.

"Well, by the looks of it, it seems like I would have lost had we made a gentleman's wager," he said.

She handed him the receipt and the change. "I'm impressed with your calculations. This gives me hope."

"I know my way around a grocery store," she said.

She walked back into the kitchen and set the bag down on the counter. Gavin lingered behind at the dining room table pretending to read the local paper while watching her buzz around. She poured water into two big pots, put them on the stove to boil, and grabbed a plastic bowl. She disappeared out to the garden and returned with sprigs of rosemary, spinach, and three green tomatoes.

Back in the kitchen she put tea bags in one pot of boiling water and let it steep on the counter. She drizzled a roasting pan on the stove with oil and zested the lemon. She pulled the firm leaves off the wooden stalk of rosemary and chopped it up fine with a butcher knife. Curiosity got the best of him, so Gavin walked up and leaned against the kitchen doorway, lured in by the wonderful smells.

"Your wife liked to cook I see," she said.

"She did."

"I can tell. Lots of gadgets." She smiled warmly at him. He walked into the kitchen, pulled a stool from underneath the island and sat down.

"She liked to buy tons of stuff from catalogues. William-Sonoma and another one that had Table in the name."

"Sur la Table," Emily said.

"That's it."

"I have bought many a gadget from that place." She paused then shook off a memory. Her mouth turned down sadly for a second.

Gavin inhaled deeply as the lemon zest and the rosemary hit the hot oil. He loved the smell of rosemary, growing it just so he could sniff it during the summer months.

"Were you a professional chef?" he asked.

She smiled, showing off her dimples. "Define 'professional.' I was never trained formally, but I did run a catering business for a bit before Sam was born."

"Now I feel I should pay you more," he said.

"Well . . . considering we haven't discussed salary, feel free to up the amount if you'd like." She winked at him and continued to work. He chuckled.

She patted the chicken pieces dry with a paper towel and added them to the lemon zest and rosemary cooking in the pan. He couldn't remember when his house smelled so good.

After a few minutes of cooking, she placed the chicken in the oven, then washed her hands and wiped them on a dishtowel tucked in the belt loop of her shorts.

"Do you have any children?" she asked.

"I have a son in college at Tennessee. Joshua," he said.

"Volunteers! A college man. Wow. You know, I have such a hard time imagining Sam as a grown man."

"Well, it happens as fast as they say. I swear we just brought him home from the hospital last month."

"That I feel all the time. I remember Sam being born like it was yesterday. Now he's 7, almost 8. Time does fly." She nibbled on the spinach. "This is amazing, by the way. You have talent for growing things. I can barely grow tomatoes and herbs."

"Thanks," he said. She poured them both a glass of iced tea and she sat by him at the island.

"So, you grow hay, that's your primary crop?" She took a sip of tea and crossed her legs, patiently waiting for an answer.

Gavin sipped his tea. He was amazed at her ease in a new kitchen and with him. He was even more amazed that lunch was in his oven with only ten minutes of prep time.

"Yes...and corn. Not the sweet corn, but corn used for feed," he said.

"I wasn't aware there was a difference."

"Field corn is planted and pretty much dries up on the stalk. Then we harvest it, chop it all up, and combine it with hay. Dairy cows eat various types of feed, hay and corn products, called silage, and other things."

"So, you are harvesting hay starting next week. And your corn at the end of the summer? Do you sell your produce at farmer's markets?" she asked.

Gavin shook his head no.

"That's too bad. Columbus is near here, right? Yuppies love them some fresh, organic produce. You can practically name your price. I only say that because I'm an ex-yuppie and know of such things." Emily joked.

"We thought about it. But that was going to be Natalie's domain after she retired," Gavin said sadly.

"Was she ill? I'm sorry, I shouldn't be asking this . . . it's none of my business." Emily shook her head, obviously embarrassed the question slipped out.

"It was a car accident. Bad weather. On I-70 outside of Columbus . . . multiple fatalities." His eyes got a far away look as he remembered the accident— the rain, the impact, the fire, the screams, and the ultimate darkness that followed. He snapped out of it when he saw her studying him. His face and ears felt hot, and she quickly looked away and bowed her head.

"I'm sorry," she whispered.

He lowered his head and drank some more tea. He never talked about the accident and wasn't sure why he decided to tell her this story. She stood up and opened the oven to look at the chicken to break the tension in the room. She trimmed the spinach and cut the tomatoes in big slices, placing them on paper towels, sprinkling salt on them.

"Are you making fried green tomatoes?" he asked, clearing his throat. Emily nodded as she seasoned the cornmeal with paprika, garlic, salt, pepper, and cayenne.

"I probably should've asked you what you like to eat before I made anything, but to stay in your budget I want to use the things you have at hand. Hope that's okay."

"Of course."

"It's been a while since I've been in a proper kitchen. I forgot how good it feels."

"What happened after you were out of your house in New Jersey?" he asked.

Emily sighed as she crushed garlic with the butcher knife.

"Well, it was a hotel at first, then money started running out. Credit cards were frozen, bank accounts frozen, everything frozen—like Antarctica-frozen. I didn't have a car, because that was included in the assets pile."

"What did you drive?"

"A 5-year-old Mazda 9. Hell of an asset, right?" Gavin shook his head.

"My best friend Mary had just read that book *Eat, Pray, Love*—ever heard of it? Oprah talked it up and they made a movie with Julia Roberts. Anyway, Mary is currently in Bali trying to find love. Shut down her life here in the States and moved to Bali. When I finally got ahold of her, because she was the only friend who would help us, we were staying at the YMCA with my last hundred bucks, and I was looking into moving into a shelter. Mary had one of her sisters wire me

11

enough money to get here to Margaret. She offered to take care of us in Bali, but there is still some sort of investigation going on. I didn't feel I could leave the country..." Emily fried the tomatoes silently as she remembered that conversation.

"Come here. I'll get you enough money for you and Sam to come here," Mary said.

"Mary, I can't run off to Bali when the freakin' feds are watching my every move. What the hell would that look like? Like I am part of this insanity that Aaron was a part of."

"Who gives a crap what people think? These people who haven't helped you and allowed you and your DEAF child to be on the streets? Screw them. Come to Bali. I can take care of you both in Bali," Mary yelled.

"Mary, please. Please. I just need money to get to Ohio. I just need to get out of the city. I need to be in a place where I don't turn a corner and expect to see Aaron," Emily whispered. She huddled in the awful stink in the telephone booth in downtown Manhattan and felt so exasperated, she wished someone would come and kill her dead right there where she was huddled.

"Okay. Okay. I understand, Em. And I am truly sorry I'm not there. I'm going to get Robin to get you some cash. Hang tight. It should be tomorrow at the latest."

"I'm sorry," Gavin sympathized. He looked at her with a truly sorrowful expression. She shrugged.

"On to brighter things now." She handed him a small plate with a fried green tomato and a fork. He smiled and accepted the plate. She watched him intently as he tasted it, eager for praise.

"Reminds me of home," he said. Emily exhaled deeply, pleased.

A few minutes later she served him roasted chicken with rosemary and lemons, creamed spinach, garlic smashed potatoes, and more fried green tomatoes. Gavin looked at the plate of food in front of him and paused. He stood and grabbed another plate from the cabinet, filled it with her creations, and handed it to her. It was a simple gesture but spoke volumes to the type of man Gavin Shaw was. She gratefully took the plate.

"Thank you."

They sat by each other in silence and ate, their silverware clinking on the blue willow plates. Gavin closed his eyes after every bite. She really did have an amazing talent with food.

"Not bad for being out of practice for a few months," she mumbled.

He put down his fork and looked at her. He hired her first out of pity, but felt he needed to make it worth her talent and effort.

"How's $400 a week sound?"

"Fair. Extremely fair. Thank you, sir."

Dillon "Shakes" St. John knocked while walking in Gavin's front door around 8 p.m. that night. He was Gavin's farm hand, and although he lived in a small house on Gavin's land, he spent most nights hanging out with Gavin watching TV.

Shakes was a tall, almost scarily thin man with a dark brown mullet, covered by a dirty Cincinnati Reds ball cap. A Winston cigarette dangled from his lips. He carried in a pizza from Pizza Hut and a six-pack of pale ale beer.

"What's the score?" Shakes asked as he walked into the kitchen to put the beer in the fridge.

Gavin, who was lounging in his big, brown recliner, was immersed in a movie he had streaming from Netflix and didn't answer him.

"Holy shit, where did all this food come from?" Shakes asked from the kitchen.

"I hired a girl to cook for us during the harvest. She made me lunch."

Shakes walked into the living room with a drumstick in one hand and a fried green tomato in the other.

"You hired a cook? Seriously? No more KFC and McDonald's? Damn, I was kinda looking forward to the three months of the shits, followed by persistent heartburn," Shakes said in a deadpan voice.

"She made all of that in there for $7. With the money I save feeding your sorry asses, I may be able to have the down payment for the new barn next spring."

"Jesus, this food is fantastic. Who is she?"

"Some gal from Jersey. Down on her luck and needed a break," Gavin said simply. Shakes nodded. He was all too familiar with that scenario, having been down on his luck and needing a break on several occasions, mostly caused by his love of women and tequila.

Shakes suddenly realized the Reds game was not on Gavin's TV.

"What the hell are you watching? Is that Julia Roberts?"

"*Eat, Pray, Love*. Ever seen it? Not a bad flick."

Shakes looked at him like he was crazy. "Fuck. That. Shit. Give me the remote. Game's on." Shakes flopped on the couch.

Gavin switched it over to the game and stood to get another beer. As he popped open another cold one, he looked out the kitchen window to the setting sun. He was not sure he would have picked Champaign County over Bali, but he was certainly glad Emily did.

CHAPTER THREE

The next morning Emily sat in Gavin's big Ford F-250 and accidentally gunned the engine instead of hitting the brake. Thankfully the truck was still in park. He gave her a patient smile, and she sighed. She hated feeling like an incompetent female, and she could tell he was nervous having her drive his truck into town for errands.

She shook off her fear of driving such a big vehicle, put the truck in reverse, and waved good-bye to Gavin, faking fearlessness. Gavin waved back, exhaling without breaking that patient smile from his face.

Once Emily got on the main road from Gavin's gravel road, she found her groove and began to drive the truck with ease. She had to admit she liked the feeling of being about five feet higher than most vehicles. Once she got into the Kroger parking lot, she managed to park it perfectly away from every other person and cart. She didn't want to risk any dings on that vehicle. She grabbed a cart, tossed her purse in it, and wrestled out her coupons, her list, and her pocket calculator.

An hour later she filled the cart with whole chickens, family packs of thighs and legs, pork chops, bacon, sausage, a pot roast, skirt steak, several packs of butter, large tortillas, pasta, milk, rice, beans, sugar, flour, oats, cheese, bread, tortilla chips, creamy peanut butter, yeast, and lemonade. With coupons and store deals, she had only spent $170 and was flying high.

The clerk whistled when he saw the final price. "Impressive savings. Feeding an army?" he asked.

"Yes, sir," she said.

She got the change and receipt and shoved it in the front pocket of her jeans. She knew that this was only half the battle. She still had to cook it all and see how the men would accept her food.

She walked out with the bags in her cart and put the items in the backseat of the truck when she caught sight of her wedding band. For a split second she felt that she was back in New Jersey, shopping like she normally did, preparing a meal that Aaron would come home to that night. She had to remind herself again that he was dead, and she would never cook for him. She paused at the grief swelling in her chest and leaned against the truck as the flood of emotions overtook her. She was most angry that she could never anticipate when grief would rear its ugly head. In these moments where she was caught off guard, left weeping in a parking lot, she hated Aaron for his selfishness. She hated him so much.

"What about Sam's boxes of baby things?" Emily asked the agent. She was a middle-aged woman. Her name badge read "Barnes."

"You can tell us which boxes they are, and we can tag them as non-liquidated items," the woman replied.

"Can I take the photos?" Emily asked.

"No frames," a man's voice said. Emily looked up and saw Marcus Stanton, the lead agent in the case.

"There could be expensive frames," he said and smiled wickedly at Emily. She bit her tongue until she tasted blood.

Stanton was a short man, heavy set, with a ruddy complexion. He made no bones about it that he was convinced that Emily knew all about Aaron's scheme and was his accomplice.

"The wives are usually in on it," he said over and over again. She wanted to punch him in the throat every time he spoke to her. His condescending voice grated on her like nails on a chalkboard.

"My grandmother's pearls? My mom's jewelry?" Emily asked Barnes.

"It's communal property and will be included in the inventory," Barnes said sadly. Emily felt sick.

"Can we at least take some clothes? I have a son. He needs clothes and his asthma inhaler," Emily said.

"Mrs. Mitchell, I don't think you fully understand the situation. Your husband defrauded dozens of people out of $30 million dollars. All assets are frozen. You are not allowed to take anything," Agent Stanton yelled at her.

"I do not understand how a damn asthma inhaler and kids' clothes are assets, Agent Stanton," Emily yelled back.

Agent Barnes looked sadly at her. Emily refused to cry. She would not give them the satisfaction.

"No furs, no jewelry. Check her wedding rings, I want those too," Stanton said. Emily fingered the thin, platinum band.

"I don't even own furs. I drive a 5-year-old Mazda 9. I cook for my family and clean my own home. I don't know where the hell the $30 million dollars is, but I can tell you that it's not in this house," she snapped.

In the end she packed two suitcases each and stored three boxes with baby memories, photos, and personal papers and journals. She was told that after the investigation she could remove any other personal effects, but she already knew that she was never coming back to that house again.

Barnes helped her load the suitcases into a cab and handed her a small envelope that included Emily's heirloom jewelry as she sat in the cab. Barnes shook her hand while secretly handing Emily back her wedding ring. She looked at the agent with questioning in her eyes.

"This is not my first rodeo, Mrs. Mitchell. I can tell who's guilty after the first ten minutes of meeting with them, and I'm rarely wrong. Listen to me, as we don't have a lot of time. Your bank account with Mr. Mitchell is already frozen, as are your credit cards. I know you have a second bank account and a credit card that is only in your name, and an account that is for your son's savings. Those will be frozen by close of business tomorrow. Check into a hotel and go to the bank first thing. Get the cash out of everything and hang out someplace safe and cheap. Hopefully we can clear this up before the end of the month, but don't hold your breath. Stanton seems to have a hard-on for you. Good luck," Barnes said.

"Are you working at the Shaw farm?" a woman asked,

17

bringing Emily back from her memories.

Emily turned and saw a blonde woman look at her with territorial daggers in her eyes. This woman was overly made up and dressed up for a Saturday morning run to Kroger. She looked about mid-30s, like Emily.

"Yes ma'am," Emily said. She closed the truck door, wiping tears.

"I thought I recognized Gavin's truck." Emily quickly put the cart back in the return stall.

"Well, you must be new in town. Because I know everyone here," the woman continued.

"I am," Emily said.

"I'm Sue Ellen Richter. My husband is Darryl Richter," Sue Ellen paused. Emily assumed that she was waiting for her to acknowledge Darryl's prestige and rank in Champaign County.

"Nice to meet you Sue Ellen," Emily said.

"And you are?"

"Emily Mitchell."

"Emily Mitchell. Well, Emily Mitchell, welcome to Champaign County. Please give Gavin my regards," Sue Ellen said and walked off. Her pink high heels clicked and clacked as she pushed a cart to the entrance. Emily noticed that Sue Ellen shook her toned rear as she walked. With her white, skin-tight capris and floral top, she looked like a peacock strutting her stuff for the world to see.

Emily started the truck and chuckled. Sue Ellen reminded her of several of the women where she used to live in Watchung, a suburb of New York City on the New Jersey side. Emily and Aaron had purchased a house there ten years ago, before the housing boom, mainly because it was close enough to the city for Aaron's commute and it had good schools. As Connecticut became passé, Watchung inherited several high and mighty socialites who should have remained in Manhattan but were either persuaded by their husbands or peer pressure to move to the suburbs. As Emily and Aaron enjoyed their modest life, massive mansion-sized dwellings were popping up along with several Sue Ellen-types who thought they were queen of the small suburb. Emily never succumbed to the hype, preferring to live within their means, saving for rainy days, taking vacations to Aaron's parent's nearly falling-down house on Cape Cod, while everyone else jet-set to Cabo or St. Thomas. Emily cooked dinner for her family every night. She didn't even have a maid. The horror!

She drove down to the local feed and supply store and pulled into the area designated for order pickups. A young man wearing an Ohio State University shirt and ball cap came to her window.

"Can I help you?" he asked.

"Picking up for Gavin Shaw," she said.

"Okay, go ahead and drive on up between those two poles. We'll load it up for you," he said and walked back to the warehouse.

Emily did as she was instructed and waited patiently. She saw three more young men come out carrying various bags of feed and supplies to the back of the pickup truck, causing the truck to move slightly from the additional weight added.

The first young man came back with a clipboard. "Go ahead and sign for it."

Emily signed the sheet and was taken aback at the amount, weight, and cost of what was in the truck bed. Who knew running a farm was so damn expensive?

"Have a nice day, ma'am," he said and handed her a copy of the receipt. She drove back to the farm, even more carefully than before.

When she pulled up to Gavin's, there was a red truck next to her Honda. Gavin walked out to the porch with an older gentleman.

"Hey," she said.

"Any trouble?" Gavin asked.

"I just ran over several small hybrids who tried to get in my way. But other than that, nope." The older man laughed.

"Emily, this is Will McCoy. He is one of my balers," Gavin said. Emily shook his hand and smiled.

"Emily. Pleasure to meet you," Will said. He spoke with a

gentle voice and had a mane of silky white hair peeking from his tan cowboy hat. His eyes were sky blue, and he had a full white beard and moustache that covered his very pink lips. He was shorter than Gavin but had a build that showed strength.

"Nice to meet you, too."

Both Gavin and Will began to gather bags from the backseat to carry to the house.

"So, how much did you spend at Kroger?" Gavin asked.

"$170."

"Wow! You're a hell of a bargain shopper," Will said.

"Well, let's see if I didn't forget anything. But I obsessively planned for most of the evening last night. I think I covered everything," Emily said.

They walked into the coolness of the kitchen. She had to admit that the house was designed well and kept cool in the summer heat despite the lack of air conditioning downstairs.

"Oh, I forgot to tell you that I bumped into someone at Kroger who recognized your truck," Emily said as she began to put away items.

"Oh?"

"Sue Ellen Richter."

"Oh . . ."

Will shook his head. "Darryl's wife. God bless that man for having to deal with a woman like that," Will mumbled.

"What did she say to you?" Gavin asked.

"Not a whole lot. I think she just wanted to say hello. And to make sure to tell me who she was," Emily said. She gave Gavin a knowing look and he shook his head.

"So, you guys hungry? I can whip up some fried egg sandwiches."

"Well, that sounds nice," Will said.

Gavin politely declined. "I'm going to unload the truck."

He walked out and silently fumed about Sue Ellen. He backed up the truck to the barn and began to angrily unload bags, thinking about Sue Ellen's fake nails, fake breasts, and her fake smile. He wished he had the balls to tell Darryl Richter that his wife was nothing but a two-bit whore who begged him to bed her on every occasion that they ran into each other. *"I'll make you come like no other woman you've had. You can do whatever you want to me. I take direction well."* He knew that if Natalie were still alive, she would have chewed Sue Ellen up and spit her out. He never appreciated how much Natalie shielded him from the horrible man-eaters that roamed the earth. Being in the Air Force put a protective shield around the family, and no one dared to mess with Colonel Shaw's husband, children, or property. He missed so many things about her, but that was one of the big things.

Will walked out to the barn and handed him a wrapped-up sandwich.

"Emily insisted I bring one to you. If you don't want it, I'll eat it."

Gavin sat on the edge of the truck bed and pulled off his gloves to unwrap the sandwich. She made it like a true sandwich with lettuce, tomato, and cheese, but with a fried egg. Interesting, he thought as he tried it. As expected, it was delicious.

"I ate two. I would've eaten another but heard your nagging voice," Will said.

"Someone's gotta look after you, Old Man."

"That's for damn sure. My useless sons won't," Will said, and hopped up on the truck bed.

"They're just young. After this summer, they'll be changed men," Gavin said.

"I had them when I was too old. Hell, I was 43 when they were born. Too old and tired to discipline them right. You and Nat were smart to have children in your 20s."

"We didn't know any better and it wasn't exactly planned," Gavin said, polishing off the sandwich. That had to be one of the simplest, yet most delicious things he had ever eaten.

Will started handing Gavin bag after bag of feed and supplies.

"What was Emily doing at the house?" Gavin asked after a few minutes of silence.

"Making bread. Or dough. Or dough for bread. Is there a

21

difference between bread and dough?" Will asked.

"Not sure."

"How lucky is it that you found someone who can cook like she can?"

Gavin shrugged it off. "I'm just helping her out. Her husband died a few months ago. Government took all her earthly possessions because he was in some shady Wall Street deals. She shouldn't suffer because her husband was a thief."

"That's awful. Poor woman. Does she have any children?"

"A 7-year-old son who's deaf."

Will shook his head. "Well, it was real decent of you to give her a job. I think you may get your money's worth. She was talking about dusting and scrubbing your windows," he said.

Gavin laughed. "Well, you can't beat that."

An hour later, Will and Gavin walked back into the house and the smell of fresh bread hit them. Emily had opened the blinds of the living room, filling it with beautiful light, dusted all the tables, and was sweeping cobwebs off the corners with a broom.

Will whistled. "Haven't seen this house this clean in years," he joked.

"I wanted to make sure I stayed busy. Hope you don't mind," she told Gavin.

"That's perfectly fine. Know your way around horses?" he asked.

"It's been a while, but I think I remember," she said.

"Come with me."

He had four beautiful horses—two sorrel Quarter Horses named Elliot and Grace, a black draft mare named Lily, and a chestnut Pinto gelding named Bob. Bob was a bit of a stubborn horse, refusing to leave the stable to go to the pasture to graze.

"I think he's secretly a mule," Gavin said lightly.

Emily looked around the barn and could see why he wanted to replace it. There were holes in the roof, and she swore that one whole side was leaning.

"It's not going to collapse, is it?" she asked, looking up.

"Not without a bulldozer or a tornado to help it," he assured her. He grabbed a wide shovel. "So do you remember how to muck out a stall?"

"Fortunately for you that is not something that one easily forgets," she said.

Gavin pointed out the rubber boots in the corner, pitchforks, and where he kept the fresh hay.

"If you can come after breakfast and let them out to walk, that'll help me out. But don't do it if you see a storm coming. They are not fans of thunder and will get wild—kick and all. I don't want you to get hurt," he said.

"Understood," she said.

"Everything should be good for a couple of days. Shakes took care of this last night."

"Shakes?"

"My farm hand."

"Interesting name," she said.

"He's an interesting fellow," Gavin said.

"So, you have Shakes and Will. Who else helps you?"

"Shakes, Will, and Paco Ortiz are my three normal hands. Will's twin sons Ian and Wyatt are helping out this summer. They just graduated high school and are a bit . . . lost."

"Will has boys in high school? Wow," Emily said.

"Third wife. That was a disaster. Never ask him about her or you'll be there all day hearing how she did him wrong."

"Gotcha," she said.

As they walked back toward the house, Emily mustered up some courage.

"So, I saw that you have laundry needing to be done. I would be happy to do it for a small barter?" she asked.

"And what would that be?"

"That I could use your washing machine. My Aunt Margaret's machine is broken, and spending time at the Laundromat may not be the easiest thing to do with this new schedule. I would bring my own soap . . ." she said.

"All right. Sounds fair."

"And one more thing."

"Go on," he said.

"I fully intend to use your leftovers when possible and plan accordingly, but I wondered if you would mind me taking a plate of dinner home to my son in the evenings."

Gavin stopped walking. "Of course not."

"Okay, thank you, sir."

"I'm surprised you asked me that," he said as they continued to walk.

"Some people would consider that stealing. I just wanted to make sure you knew my intentions were only to feed him," she said softly.

"You take what you need to keep you both fed," Gavin said.

"Thank you, sir," she said.

"You can call me Gavin."

She smiled politely. "I promise I will try, but that will take time . . ."

CHAPTER FOUR

Emily arrived at Gavin's at 5:30 a.m. sharp to start the official first breakfast of the first harvest. She decided on simplicity—biscuits, eggs, and sausage gravy. She had other ideas and thought about being fancy, but in the end, she just wanted to do what was easy and natural for her instead of trying to make a false impression. Failure was not an option.

Gavin told her he had been up since 4:30 and was already on his second pot of coffee. He slid over a big, yellow mug and poured her a cup, saying that she looked like she could use it.

"How much sleep do you get?" she asked him.

"About five hours if I'm lucky."

"I'm about the same. I can't turn my mind off at night, no matter how hard I try."

"Maybe with the long hours it will improve," he said.

"Fingers crossed," she said and lifted her coffee mug. She took three big gulps of strong coffee and jumped off the stool and began to cook.

She measured out the flour, milk, butter, baking powder, and salt for the biscuits, using Natalie's pastry cutter to make a wonderful biscuit dough.

"You don't use shortening?" he asked.

"I prefer the taste of butter."

"Interesting."

"You sound unsure," she said and smiled.

"I'm a Tennessee boy. I know my way around a biscuit."

"Oh, ye of little faith," she joked.

She pulled the wet dough onto a floured surface, formed it into a workable dough, then used a biscuit cutter to cut about three dozen biscuits. She popped those in the oven and started frying up three pounds of breakfast sausage.

"Now that's a smell I could come to work to every day of the week," a voice boomed.

Emily looked up and saw a short, dark-skinned Hispanic man walk into the kitchen.

"Hey, you must be Emily. I'm Paco. Paco Ortiz. Nice to finally meet you," he said and held out his hand.

"Nice to meet you, too."

Paco was about two inches shorter than Emily, stocky with square shoulders, with a thin moustache. He wore a Dallas Cowboy's ball cap and t-shirt.

Emily pulled the biscuits out of the oven, all browned and heavenly looking, and put them to cool on the center island. Both Gavin and Paco surrounded them, waiting like impatient children.

"What are we looking at?" Shakes walked up to see what was going on. "Oh, hell yeah, biscuits."

He pulled one off the pan and juggled it, trying to cool it off enough to handle.

"All right, savages. Out of the kitchen! I'll bring your breakfast in five minutes. Go! Go! Go!" Emily shooed.

"She's a bit of a ball buster," Shakes said, mouth full.

"Hey, give me some of that biscuit," Paco said.

Shakes pulled off pieces and shared with both Paco and Gavin.

"Yeah, I'm eating about five of those," Paco said.

Emily brought the biscuits out in a bowl covered with a dishtowel. "Miss the shortening?" she asked Gavin.

He swallowed what he was chewing. "I will never doubt you again," he said. She smiled.

"I'm Emily," she said to Shakes.

He shook her hand. "Shakes."

"Nice to meet you. You grab my food like that again, I'll take a cleaver to your hand," she said and winked. She walked back into the kitchen.

Shakes looked at Gavin. "Is she serious?"

Gavin laughed. "God, I hope so."

Emily carried out a platter of scrambled eggs and a pan of sausage gravy to Gavin's large oak table. She stacked plates on the corner, along with a bunch of bananas, sliced nectarines and plums, two types of jam from Gavin's ample collection that he had in his fridge, and coffee. The men grabbed the plates and started to pile on food like they had not eaten in weeks.

She was washing dishes a few minutes later when she heard voices outside the kitchen window.

"Stayed up too late playing that damn Xbox, and now you both are dragging your sorry asses to work. How are you supposed to hold a proper job if you are pulling crap like this?" Will scolded.

Emily saw two apathetic young men, both on the chubby side, with long blonde hair hanging in their eyes, walking up the stairs. Will was harping on them the entire walk from the truck to the front door.

She slowly made her way to the dining area and saw that Gavin, Shakes, and Paco were done eating and drinking their coffee when Will and his sons walked in.

"You're late boys," Gavin said.

"Sorry," one of the twins said quietly.

"You know what that means? They get to walk out to the back fields first and look for dead animals," Paco said.

"Don't we get to eat first?" one of them whined.

"Breakfast is for those who show up on time," Gavin said and stood up. Paco and Shakes followed suit, gathering their dishes and piling them in a neat pile on the counter by the kitchen sink.

Will sighed as everyone, including his sons, followed Gavin out to the barn. Emily scooped a couple of biscuits, made impromptu sandwiches for Will, and wrapped them in a paper towel for him. She winked as she made the handoff.

"You're an angel," Will whispered and smiled, shoving the biscuits into his morning paper. She suspected he was hiding them from his sons, not from Gavin. She watched as they climbed into two separate pickup trucks and sped off, leaving her all alone.

She kept herself very busy that morning, gathering eggs from the Borg, letting the horses out, and picking fresh produce. Gavin had several things ripening on the vine and in the ground including cucumbers, radishes, various greens, and strawberries. It took her almost two hours and four trips back and forth to carry everything in. The kitchen was in disarray as she tried to cross reference her original list for meals with the produce that was now ready to eat. She saw that there were about nine biscuits left. She decided on strawberry shortcake for dessert for lunch with the calzones and a stone fruit cobbler with the remaining fruit that was leftover at the breakfast table for dessert at dinner. While the chicken was stewing for the calzones, and the dough rising, she managed to organize the rest of the pantry and iron out the plan for the rest of the week. The sheer volume of eggs surprised her. Gavin had thirty-two chickens, and almost every one of them laid an egg. She saw quiches and savory tarts in the rotation just to make use of the fruits of their labor.

"Ever thought of an egg box?" Emily asked Gavin at lunch. They were in the middle of a clover hay field, sitting around the tractors eating.

"What's that?" Gavin asked.

"You put a cooler at the end of your road with a few dozen eggs and a lock box for the cash and let people stop by and drop the cash for the eggs," she explained.

Gavin thought about it for a minute.

"There is some risk, as it's an honor system. But I would be willing to check on it during the day. But your hens are laying almost three-dozen eggs in a single day. If they keep it up, that's roughly twenty dozen a week, $5 a dozen, that's almost half your grocery budget recovered."

"Not a bad idea," Paco said.

"Hell, I saw one of those egg boxes in Union County last time I was there. Man was charging $8 a dozen," Shakes said.

"Ideally you want to charge just a little more than the stores, because it's farm fresh, but not so much that people think you've lost your mind," Emily said.

"If you're willing to man it, we can try it, why not," Gavin said.

"Great. Okay. I'll try to find a way to set it up in the next few days," Emily said.

She began to gather dishes and load them in the back of her Honda. Will's boys were playing on their phones by their dad's truck, not engaging with anyone else, not even each other.

"Calzones were awesome," Shakes said. He had eaten three whole ones while everyone ate one or two. For someone as thin as he was, Emily was surprised by the amount of food he could put away.

By the end of the day, Emily had successfully fed all the men without too much hiccup, corralled the horses back in, pre-cooked some of the next day's breakfast, and finished Gavin's laundry. By 8 p.m. she was exhausted and ready to pass out.

"We're headed back out there to deal with an issue, but you can go on home. I'll see you bright and early in the morning," Gavin told her.

"Sounds good. I packed a strawberry shortcake, half a calzone, three eggs, two cucumbers, and a plum for Sam," Emily told him as they walked to the door.

Gavin stopped and turned around.

"Emily, I don't need a list every night. I trust you," he said and looked her in the eyes.

"Right. Right. I'm sorry. It's just given the last few months, it's just a habit trying to justify most of my actions."

"You've proven yourself in more ways than one. Let's just say that I'm beyond impressed and think I am one of the luckiest men in the world for stumbling upon you," he said.

She swallowed and blushed. "Thank you, sir."

"It's Gavin. I'll see you tomorrow morning."

CHAPTER FIVE

Emily loaded up the trash and serving dishes back into her car after a lunch of pot roast sliders, homemade chips, and fresh lemonade. The humidity was already at 75%, and she had pulled her short hair up into a ponytail. That afternoon Gavin lingered while the rest of them climbed back on their respective machines to try to finish working before nightfall. He was still sipping on lemonade that she poured for him at the start of the meal.

"Did you get enough to eat?" she asked.

He only eaten one slider and nibbled on a few chips while the others grabbed four or five. Shakes grabbed seven, but because he was so damn thin no one blinked twice about it. Now Gavin nursed a lemonade while the others took their third glass with them back in their red Solo cups.

Gavin looked over at her. "It was really good, thank you."

His formality was beginning to frustrate her. He was so polite, but she knew he was thinking a million things. That combined with his picking at her food was causing the obsessive-compulsive side of her personality to kick into overdrive.

"If you tell me what you like to eat, I could make it for you. Or attempt a try..." she said cheerfully.

"I'm really enjoying what you are pulling together," Gavin said.

"If you say so," she muttered and slammed the trunk down. She tried to shake off his vacant stare and lack of enthusiasm for her cooking as not anything personal, but still, it ate at her. She wished he enjoyed her efforts like the rest of them. She really wanted to make a good impression on him.

She got her keys out of her pocket and she felt a burning sensation in her neck. "Owww! Dammit," she said and grabbed at the pain. In her fist she saw a bee.

Gavin walked over and touched her neck. "Ah, bee gotcha," he said.

Emily squinted her face up from the pain. "God, I freaking hate those things," she muttered.

"Hold still. Stinger is still in you," he said.

Gavin's hot breath was on her neck as he focused in and carefully pinched out a tiny stinger from the wound. She felt the roughness of his strong hands on the smooth curve of her neck, pressing down slightly.

"Wow, you're really starting to swell already," he said. He quickly got her some ice in a leftover plastic grocery bag.

"Me and bees are not friends. In fact, if there is one in a ten-mile radius it finds me."

"You're not allergic, are you?" he asked.

"Not as of yet," she said.

He held the ice to her neck, and she instinctively put her hand over his and looked at him. He paused at first, then startled slightly at her touch and at the closeness of their faces. His breathing slowed and he slowly removed his hand from hers. He nervously licked his lips and cleared his throat several times.

"When you get back to the house, I have plain aspirin in the medicine cabinet in my bathroom. Take two tablets out, and mash them with a drop of water to make a paste and put it on the sting. It'll take the swelling down. Just keep that ice on until you get to the house."

"Okay..."

He eased back a safe distance from her, casually picked up his lemonade glass, and drank it all down in one long gulp.

"I'm headed back out there. Thanks again for lunch. We'll see you for dinner." Gavin walked quickly back to his truck and drove away.

Emily held the ice to her throbbing neck and leaned against the trunk of her car trying to figure out what just happened then. She felt an unfamiliar sensation in her chest, something that she felt had died long ago when she met Aaron. Gavin was a strong, competent figure in her very chaotic life. She appreciated the calm and strength that he represented. But, for a brief moment in that hot June sun, she allowed herself to think about Gavin the man— the way he walked with a slight limp, his smooth-as-leather Southern drawl, his green eyes that shifted to the spectrum of blue when he wore the right clothes, and the right mood struck him. She imagined, only for a second, what it would feel like to have him towering over her, making love to her.

Horrified, she quickly shook the thoughts out of her head, guilt spraying all over her like freezing cold water, and drove back to the house, struggling to put other thoughts back in her head. The chicken needed to be grilled, the salad needed to be tossed, and the strawberry tarts needed to be assembled.

When she walked back into the house, she headed to Gavin's bedroom, located at the far-right corner of the first floor. She had never been in there, never really having a reason. She left his laundry on the couch, folded neatly in the basket. He never asked her to put away his clothes, so she assumed he wanted to keep his room, the place he and his late wife shared, private.

The room had sunlight spilling onto the red patchwork quilt, pulled up messily over yellow with white-flowered sheets. The room smelled of him, a mixture of hay and aftershave. Pictures in various-sized frames lined a tall dresser and another wide dresser. Emily walked up and saw a much younger version of Gavin, posing with what she assumed was his wife. Both had hair reminiscent of the 1980s, feathered and draping at his collar on him, big blonde bangs and perm on her. She smiled at the memories that she saw. There was an older picture taken at a portrait studio of Gavin, his wife, and *two* children—a son who was about seven and a baby girl, dressed in beautiful white ruffles, with her little blonde hair pulled into two adorable, threadbare ponytails. He had only spoken of his son. What happened to his daughter?

Emily pulled the ice pack off her neck and sat on the bed, suddenly realizing that Gavin not only lost his wife, but his daughter in the car accident. *Multiple fatalities.* The news weighed heavily on her shoulders and felt like a punch to the gut.

That revelation explained so much about his life and his house that was wiped sterile clean of any sign of them, except what was in that room—a mini shrine to when life was right and made sense. It was his sanctuary, and she suddenly felt like she was trespassing.

She quickly walked into his small bathroom and grabbed the aspirin out of his medicine cabinet. She shook two in her palm, replaced the cap, and walked quickly back to the kitchen where she belonged.

She made his concoction in a small yellow bowl, and the pain and swelling went down immediately when she applied it to the sting. The heaviness in her chest remained.

As she whisked the salad dressing, she struggled to remember the last time she and Aaron had made love. It had been months before he died. That in and of itself should have been a warning sign. Aaron would always come home and no matter how late or how tired he was, make it a point to reach for her. She would wake to feel his arms wrapped tight around her waist, his gentle kisses on her neck.

"You awake?" he'd always ask.

"I am now," she would joke.

"I missed you, baby," he would say. She would turn to face him and with one kiss they would maneuver out of clothes and into the familiarity of each other's body. She loved everything about Aaron, his shoulders, his gentle hands that caressed her body in the darkness of their bedroom. She loved the way he kissed, always passionate, always with love and adoration. She loved how he stroked her face when he made love to her, and how he always said he loved her when the moment was over.

She wondered when the feds walked through her house if they even looked at her pictures, the snapshot of the life she had with Aaron. She wondered if anyone cared that the life the people in the pictures shared was real and held purpose and meaning. If they knew that the people who remained from those pictures deeply mourned a life that was taken from them without warning. Did they give a damn? Gavin knew what she was going through. He was one of the few people on the planet who knew exactly how she felt, and exactly what she lost. She almost cried from realizing that she was not alone on this horrible journey.

Gavin called the house at about 6:30 and said that they were wrapping it up and would be headed to the house by 7:00, but Will's sons were heading home because they were going to Columbus to see a concert. She set up a table on the wraparound porch and had all the food laid out and waiting for them. She lit citronella candles to keep the bugs away and used real plates. She managed to throw together some appetizers out of leftover dough, cheese, garlic and spinach. When the trucks started pulling up to the driveway, she was pulling the last of the chicken off the grill. The corn, salad, pinto beans, and Spanish rice were already set. She set out iced tea and moved the cooler of beer closer to the table.

"Oh, my, GOODNESS, that smells delicious," Paco said. He was covered in tiny pieces of hay, and his dark skin had a thin sheen of white dust on it.

"Gavin, you let her use your grill. You never let me use your grill," Paco said.

"Paco, the last time you used my grill you damn near burned my house to the ground. I have utter confidence that she knows how to use it," Gavin retorted. He came up from his truck with Will riding with him.

"Evening, ma'am," Will said and smiled at her.

"William," she said.

"Wash up fellas. Food is hot," she said. Shakes moved straight to the table and popped four appetizers into his mouth. Instinctively Emily swirled her dishcloth and popped him on the leg.

"Wash your hands, mister!" she barked. The men hooted and Shakes hustled to the kitchen to wash up.

"Gavin said you got stung by a bee. Are you okay?" Will asked. He reached in for a Yuengling beer and sat at the table. Gavin, who was within earshot, pretended he didn't hear anything.

"Yep. Mixed up some magic aspirin concoction Gavin suggested and good as new," she said. She saw Gavin smile.

"I got stung on my ear a few years back. That was some horrible pain," Will said.

Shakes came back out and showed Emily his hands. "Happy, warden?" he said.

"Ecstatic," she said and smiled. He rolled his eyes, grabbed a plate and piled it full. She wondered again where in the hell he put all that he ate.

Paco came out wiping his face and arms with several wet paper towels. "Wooo, it was hot out there today," Paco said. He reached down and grabbed a beer and sat by Will. Emily hung back on the windowsill of the living room windows watching them all unwind and relax.

"Slow down, Shakes, you'll choke," Will said.

Shakes ignored him and picked a chicken leg clean. Paco tasted the beans.

"Wow, Emily. Who taught you how to make beans?" Paco said.

"My friend's mom. When I was 14, she pulled me into the kitchen and shared her secret with me. Stuck with me all these years," she said.

"Did she teach you how to make chicken mole? Please tell me she told you how to make chicken mole. Oh my goodness, if you could make chicken mole, then I would be your best friend forever," Paco said.

"She did. I'll make you a batch next week," she said.

"Gavin, she's going to make us chicken mole!" Paco called into the house.

Gavin walked out, checking his cell phone. "Uh-huh," he mumbled.

"What's wrong?" Will asked.

"Nothing, I think I did something to this damn phone. I should've stuck with my flip phone. Who the hell decided all phones should be smart phones?" he said.

Emily went and looked over his shoulder. "Here, let me,"

she said. He handed her the phone.

"Go on and eat," she said. She gave him a look like she was not messing around.

"Yes, ma'am," he said. He went through the line, picked up two chicken legs, a huge heap of salad, a small scoop of beans, and a small scoop of rice. He pulled up next to Shakes and started to eat slowly. Shakes stood up and started in with the strawberry tarts. She learned pretty quickly to make the food for ten, or she would never be able to take any of it home.

"It was just a system update. Phone is rebooting now," Emily said and put the phone by Gavin. She poured herself a glass of tea and sat by Paco.

"Thanks," he said, pocketing the phone.

"How's your son doing? Gavin said he was around 7?" Will asked.

Emily wondered what else Gavin told them. "Good—all things considered. Yes, he turns eight in July, actually," Emily said.

"You should bring him by. We'd love to meet him," Will said.

Emily smiled, but she was apprehensive bringing him into an environment like this where she was working so much and could not supervise him.

"Paco can use sign language," Shakes announced, as if he could read her thoughts. He leaned back in his chair, sufficiently full, drinking a second beer.

"Really?" Emily asked. Her curiosity was piqued.

Paco wiped his hands with a napkin. "Yeah, I use it with a few of my students at school. And my son seemed to respond well to it when he wasn't talking at first," Paco said.

"You're a teacher?" Emily asked.

"Special education. My son is autistic. Both me and my wife were elementary school teachers, but when Xavier was diagnosed, we went back to get certified in special education, just to make sure he got the best care," Paco said.

"Wow, that's really amazing. Truly, what a wonderful commitment to your son," Emily said.

"Was your son in a regular school or a school for the deaf?" Paco asked.

"A school for the deaf. He is pretty good at reading lips, but since he's non-syndromic, it made sense at the time," Emily said.

"What does non-syndromic mean?" Shakes asked.

"That Sam is only deaf—sometimes deafness comes with other mental issues, learning delays, vision loss. His deafness is genetic. My husband and I carried the gene for it. It affects the little hairs that move sound in the ear canal. The hairs don't move, so he can't hear. But he also has never really talked. Made sounds, but no words. Maybe someday," Emily said sadly.

She felt all eyes on her and suddenly became self-conscious. She almost forgot how nice it was just to sit and talk to people without them automatically passing judgment on her for Aaron's transgressions.

"Wow, look at the time. Did you all get enough?" she asked and started clearing plates. Gavin stared at her and took in what she said. He didn't look away right away when her eyes met his. He chewed on a morsel of what she said, and only when he was satisfied with processing it, he looked away.

"It was all delicious, Emily. Really delicious," Will said.

"Awesome meal. I haven't eaten this good in years," Shakes said and rubbed his non-existent belly.

"I'm glad. Pigs in a blanket are planned for the morning. You all continue to relax. I'm going to start cleaning up if that's okay," she asked Gavin.

"Sure," he said. Paco and Will stood up and started pulling plates together and followed Emily in the house.

When he thought Emily was out of earshot, Shakes said, "She's definitely a keeper."

"She's been really good at keeping us on budget so far. That new barn is becoming a reality next year," said Gavin.

"Yeah, that's not what I meant," Shakes said and gave him a look. Gavin looked sternly at him, and exhaled, angry. Shakes had broken a cardinal rule.

"You like her. What's the harm in liking her, G? She's a decent, hard-working woman," Shakes asked.

Gavin stood up noisily and grabbed his beer. "I'm checking the horses," he said. Shakes shook his head.

***

On Friday night, after successfully serving ribs for dinner, Emily wiped down the last of the pots and set the crockpot's timer to start cooking at midnight.

Gavin was in the living room with the television on low. Emily walked in the room with her purse, a bag of laundry, and her car keys.

"Goodnight, sir. The crockpot is set for midnight. Trying an apple spiced oatmeal for the morning."

He looked at her and smiled politely. "Looking forward to trying it," he said.

She was a bit proud that most of her creations were well received by the crew. They all seemed eager for mealtime just to see what new thing she had laid out for them. All of them agreed that her cooking was fantastic, and they had never eaten so well.

"Well then, I will see you in the morning," she said.

"I'll walk you out. Wanted to check on Lily one last time. She was acting like she was off her feed this morning," he said.

Emily walked to the Honda and tossed her purse in the open window. She opened the back door and placed her bag of laundry in the backseat. "Goodnight."

"Goodnight. Drive safely," he said.

She sat in the car and turned the key. The engine would not turn over.

"Crap," she said. She tried to crank it again. The engine complained and whined, but the car would not start.

Gavin walked back to her and leaned in the open window.

"Won't start?"

"No, sir."

"Hop out, let me take a look at her," he said.

Emily obliged and stood obediently by the car with her hands in her jean pockets.

"Sounds like the alternator," Gavin said and hopped out. Emily frowned at that word.

"How much do those run?"

"Depends. I'll have Ray in town look at it in the morning."

"He'll probably find a lot more things. I don't think Margaret has had this car serviced since she bought it," she said.

"We'll know more tomorrow. I'll give you a ride back into town. Let me get my keys and wallet," he said.

"Okay, thanks," Emily said, but deep down was dreading that. She reached in and grabbed her bags and rolled up the windows, leaving the car keys in the passenger side seat. In her bag she had leftover rolls, baked potatoes, and strawberries. She was sad she did not have any meat tonight—the guys ate every last rib she made. She prayed that they still had peanut butter at home. In a few more days, she would get her first paycheck and make Sam and Margaret a feast. Chicken fried steaks, or roast beef with garlic bread and mashed potatoes. They would love that.

Gavin came back out of his house and hit the button on his keychain to unlock the door. The Ford F-250 lit up in the evening sky, and Emily followed quietly to the passenger side of the truck and climbed in. The diesel engine revved and Emily put on her seatbelt and glanced sideways at Gavin as he maneuvered the truck into gear.

They were quiet as they drove down his long, gravel road. As they drove onto the main county road, he looked at her and smiled a short, friendly smile.

"I'm not quite sure where Margaret lives," he said.

"Right, sorry. Off Avenue B. You take a left at the Dollar General and follow it on down," Emily said.

There was an awkward pause.

"Thank you for giving me a ride. I'll try to find someone to fetch me in the morning."

"I'll come get you."

"Are you sure? That's a long ride out both ways," Emily

said.

"Yes." Then he looked at her. "I'm sure."

Emily fidgeted a little in the seat. She had never really spent any time alone with Gavin since the bee sting incident and she was suddenly feeling shy.

"This is a nice truck," she said.

"Thanks."

She exhaled and shook her head. What the hell was she doing? She hated acting this way.

"Something the matter?"

"No . . . Yes. Since this happened to me and Sam, I live in perpetual fear that I will say the wrong thing and be on the street again. It's an awful way to feel," she said looking directly at him.

Gavin stopped at a stop sign and looked at her.

"Are you speaking in general or specifically about me?" he asked. He arched his dark eyebrow at her.

"Both. But in this instance, I am talking about you. I don't know if I can ask you questions, make small talk, make jokes, or just stick to talking about the weather around you. You are one of the hardest men to read, you know that?" Emily said.

Gavin chuckled. "Emily, I think you should say whatever you need to say. Not doing so is a terrible way to live," he said.

"So, I can ask you questions? And you won't fire me?" she asked.

"Now, I can't promise that, but every day, run-of-the-mill questions should not invoke the need to terminate employment," he said and began to drive again.

"So, I guess I should put off asking religious and political views until we know each other longer than a week," she joked.

He smiled. "Probably." Emily laughed.

"What do you want to know?" he asked.

"How old are you?" she asked.

"Forty-five," he said.

Her eyebrows went up and she made a surprised face.

"Seriously?"

"Why, how old did you think I was?" he asked.

"Fifty . . . ish," she said.

Gavin bit his lip. "Well, that's it. You're fired," he joked.

Emily laughed, and then looked pensive.

"What?"

"It's just been a really long time since I've laughed," she said, looking out the passenger window. Gavin turned left at the Dollar General.

"Me, too," he said. They looked at each other and smiled.

Gavin drove down Avenue B, slowly taking in the street. The houses were rundown and very small.

"The second house on the left." She pointed to a small white house with light blue shutters. Gavin parked off to the side, as the driveway could not support his two-ton truck and shut off the engine. The house couldn't be more than a two bedroom. The lawn desperately needed cutting. The backyard looked like it was filled with its fair share of rusted junk.

"Thanks again for the ride. I'll see you in the morning," she said. She wanted desperately to get him out of there, before he could take anymore of the situation in, but he grabbed her laundry bag, opened his door, and walked toward the front door, much to her horror. She fumbled for the door handle and quickly ran after him.

The door flung open and a little boy with her eyes and dark hair ran out.

"Mommy!" the boy signed with his small hands. Emily hugged him and kissed the top of his head.

"Sam, this is Mr. Shaw. He is Mommy's new boss," she signed back to him. Sam waved at Gavin.

"This is my son, Sam," Emily told Gavin.

Gavin smiled and patted Sam on the head.

"Good-looking boy," Gavin said.

"Takes after his father," Emily said, sadly.

"He favors you," Gavin said, matter-of-factly.

Light from the house spilled onto the front porch, and Gavin caught sight of the inside of the house. Emily's face fell.

Margaret was a "collector," or at least, that's what she

called herself. In reality, she was a classic hoarder. She collected a variety of things from newspapers to plastic soda bottles, but in classic hoarding splendor, she did not throw anything away. When Emily and Sam arrived on her doorstep three weeks ago, the house was so bad that she almost vomited from the smell alone. It took her almost a week to clear out the kitchen, the source of the smell.

"Let me walk you to your truck," Emily said firmly. Gavin ignored her and walked in.

"Good evening, Ms. Margaret. How are you doing this fine evening?" Gavin said in a loud voice in the direction of a pile of papers and boxes in the living room. He stumbled along the narrow pathway that was semi-clear of clutter.

"Hello?" Margaret said, emerging from around a corner of trash.

"Gavin Shaw. From Grace Methodist Church." Gavin shook the frail woman's hand.

Margaret was a small woman, no taller than 5 feet tall. Her long, silver hair was pulled back into a tight bun. She wore a green housecoat and looked bewildered that Gavin was standing in what should have been her living room.

"Of course, Mr. Shaw. So nice to see you again. I am so grateful that you were able to hire Emily at the farm. She's a hard worker. She's been helping me around the house. As you can see, I have not been well and have fallen behind on my chores," she said.

"Yes, ma'am. I heard you were not feeling your best. I'm going to bring my boys out tomorrow and help you with this yard. How's that sound?" Gavin said.

"Oh, I don't want to be a burden, Mr. Shaw," Margaret said.

"Oh, it's no burden. It's the least I can do since you recommended Emily. She's working out just fine. Saving me all sorts of time and money over at the farm. She'll be an asset, I'm sure. Just want to repay the favor," he said.

"That's awfully kind of you, sir," Margaret said.

"And I think Emily brought you and Sam home a little

dinner. You just let me know if you need a little more to tide you over. I got plenty of fresh veggies and eggs this year. Hens are laying like crazy," Gavin said.

"Thank you, Mr. Shaw, much obliged," Margaret said, holding Emily's bag. Gavin smiled kindly at her.

"Could I trouble you for some water?" Gavin asked Emily. Emily complied, knowing full well he just wanted to see the rest of the house.

The kitchen was less crowded. When she arrived, she could not even step foot in the kitchen. The sink was filled with dirty plates, from God knows when. The stove had not been used in years. The refrigerator was filled with rotten food. Almost a month later, the sink, fridge and oven were clear and clean. The table still needed some work, but at least the fridge was clean. Pretty bare, but clean.

Emily pulled a blue plastic cup from the cupboard and poured some water from the tap in the glass. Gavin took the glass from her, but she avoided his eyes. He took a sip and continued to walk around. Out from the kitchen was a sunroom. In it he saw two cots and two suitcases in the corner. The place was tidy and neat. There were toy soldiers and Hot Wheels, the type that were a dollar at the grocery store, on one of the cots. He also saw a stack of books and workbooks for fourth grade reading, arithmetic, and science.

"I'm trying to get him ready for school in the fall," Emily said softly. She wrapped her arms around herself, trying to suppress her shame. Instinctively he lifted his hand to touch her but dropped it quickly.

"Walk me outside," he said. She nodded and followed him.

Sam and Margaret were going through Emily's bag and dividing the food. Margaret pulled out two small plates for the baked potatoes, rolls, and the strawberries and poured Sam a small glass of milk.

"Good night, Margaret. I will have my crew out tomorrow to see about that lawn. Feel better, ma'am," he said. Margaret smiled. Gavin waved at Sam and Sam cheerfully waved goodbye to him.

He walked through the minefield that was the living room and Emily had a hard time keeping up with his long strides. Once outside he leaned against the driver's side of his truck. Emily stood across from him with her hands still folded across her chest. They were silent for a while. She heard the neighbors watching *CSI: Miami* and a dog barking in the distance.

"You never really realize how alone you are in the world until something like this happens to you," Emily told Gavin.

He exhaled deeply. He understood it all too well.

"Don't get me wrong. I am grateful to have a roof over my head. There were days where even that was iffy. I'll take a house full of trash versus the streets any day," she said softly.

He reached into his pocket and pulled out a money clip of cash.

"Put your money away, Gavin Shaw," Emily said firmly.

Gavin paused. "I want to help," he said.

"You are helping. You gave me a job. I get paid on Monday," Emily said.

"Consider it an advance then," Gavin said.

"No sir."

He looked at her closely, her chin was jutted up and defiant, arms crossed across her chest. He pocketed the clip.

"All right then. Monday it is. I will be by at 6:00 a.m. to pick you up for work," he said.

"Yes, sir. I'll be ready."

He climbed into his truck and closed the door. He rolled down his window. "Bring your boy with you." Emily opened her mouth to protest.

"That's not up for negotiation," Gavin said, and rolled up his window. The truck started with a thunderous rev, and he drove away.

Gavin drove back into town after stopping at the IGA to pick up another six-pack of beer and more beef jerky. He pulled his truck up beside the Honda when he got back home and placed his beer and small bag of groceries on the roof of the car before opening the door and popping the hood. He reattached the wires at the distributor cap that he had pulled earlier that day while Emily was driving his truck into town to run an errand. After talking with Will that morning about the rumored condition of Margaret's house and the fact that Sam was with her 12 hours a day, he wanted to check it out for himself.

"How bad is it?" he asked Will.

"Well, she's had a couple of notices to condemn the house if she didn't clear it. I'm not sure of the condition now, but the yard is a jungle, and the backyard probably has more junk than grass," Will said.

Gavin tried the engine after he reattached everything, and it purred like a kitten. Satisfied, he killed the engine and took her keys inside with him, grabbing his beer and groceries.

CHAPTER SIX

Emily had been awake since 4:30, jarred awake by nonsensical nightmares that seemed to haunt her since she arrived in Ohio. She lay awake on the cot on her side facing Sam. She heard his soft breaths of a deep sleep and decided not to move too much to wake him. Even though he was deaf, her movements could startle him awake. She struggled to remember what the dream was about but could only remember it was about Aaron. She could not stop dreaming about him, her mind fluttering, pasting all her memories in some psychotic scrapbook that terrorized her when her defenses were down. Sam was glad to be going to work with her this morning. It pained her every morning to leave him the past week, but she saw that Margaret was committed to getting the house in order more so when Sam was around. Emily came home every night to a bit more space, and more on the back porch for Emily to take for Goodwill, or to dump in the dumpster behind Dollar General in the cloak of darkness.

When Emily showed up before Memorial Day on Margaret's doorstep, she walked in and was so overwhelmed by the mess she almost cried.

"Margaret, what happened?" Emily had asked with her hand to her mouth.

"I don't know. I just haven't been myself these days."

Margaret was her father's only sibling, eccentric and wild. Her father always complained about his crazy younger sister, but in reality, loved and adored her. Everyone did. She had the knack to make anyone feel warm, welcome, and included. Margaret was always around when Emily was a child and would keep her for several weeks in the summer at her small house in Galveston, Texas. They would spend hours at the beach, take long naps, and hike down to the ice cream shop for double-scoop cones that would be half-melted by the time the

46

clerk handed them over in the intense Texas heat. Margaret preferred to be called Margaret, thought it to be more exotic and defined than Maggie or Peggy. When Emily's parents decided to move to Dhahran, Saudi Arabia, for a once-in-a-lifetime opportunity, and to earn four times their current paycheck, they enrolled her in boarding school near Dallas and listed Margaret as next of kin, 4 hours away. Margaret would call a few times a week and write weekly. Her own parents only called quarterly, preferring only to send money.

Margaret dated interesting men, marrying a handful of them. She called herself a serial romantic, said she loved being married, but as it turned out, not staying married. There was Fritz, the coffeehouse poet, or at least he tried to be, although his poetry left much to be desired; Alvin, the ballroom dancer, who had a ridiculously thin moustache and dark comb over; Fred, the computer repairman, who managed to break more computers than repairing; and Craig, the Air Force Major, who was almost twenty years her junior.

Craig was true love. She was completely smitten by the dashing officer, following him all the way to Dayton, Ohio. She loved being a military wife, shopping at the commissary, meeting with other officer wives, doing anything to support her man. Then 9/11 happened, and the wars in Iraq and Afghanistan broke out. The beautiful Major was sent into Tikrit and was one of the early tragedies in Operation Iraqi Freedom.

Margaret never fully recovered from Craig's death. She had told Emily at the funeral that her spirit had been forever broken. Craig was her soul mate, and she could never see loving another. Emily herself had only been married less than two years when the shattering news came and was Margaret's only family in attendance at the extremely grand military funeral. Emily's parents were still in Saudi Arabia at this time, and she was filled with constant worry for their safety with the dissention for Americans abroad increasing. Her worry would be short-lived, however. The following year her father was diagnosed with virulent prostate cancer and chose to come home for treatments at M.D. Anderson in Houston. Two long, miserable years of chemotherapy and enrollment in two clinical trials for newly developed drugs added just enough time for him to witness his grandchild being born. He lost his battle shortly after Sam's first birthday. Emily's mother, whose sole purpose in life was to be a devoted wife, and not so much a mother, never recovered from the loss of the love of her life and followed her husband in death six months later. Emily was devastated.

Margaret and Emily were alone in the world and had no one else but each other. Emily tried to get her to move to Watchung with her, Aaron, and Sam, but she would never agree to it. Margaret followed a man, who was less charming than the previous men, to Urbana, Ohio who drained her savings of Craig's insurance money and what little dignity and pride she had left.

Craig's Social Security and military benefits were still paid out to Margaret but were pissed away with the Home Shopping Network and frequent trips to the Goodwill. Emily took over the checkbook when she got there and hid Margaret's credit card in hopes she could get Margaret's life back to a version of normal. Oh, how Margaret fought her, calling her every name in the book, but slowly she fought her less and less, realizing that Emily and Sam were more than just mere visitors. She seemed to have more purpose in her life, and Emily would catch glimpses of the aunt she once knew. There was hope.

Emily rinsed off her face and hair in the bathroom. The shower did not work, so they took their baths outside at night where no one could see them. Emily was hesitant to call a plumber to fix the tub that had not been working for years until the house was somewhat approachable. She feared that the city would be called back, and the house would be condemned. She managed to get the kitchen sink working, and they took bucket baths on the back porch. She had to get it together before winter, when that would no longer be an option.

That first night in town, she and Sam slept in a fleabag motel, and the next day Emily came back with four gallons of bleach, masks, gloves, and garbage bags and cleared the kitchen. She sat Sam in front of the TV watching the Family Channel in closed caption, surrounded by the ceiling-high piles of boxes and clothing, praying that watching Toy Story 1, 2, and 3 would distract him long enough to clear up the mess. By night's end, the kitchen was clear, the refrigerator completely empty, dishes put away, and one small space in Margaret's colossal mess was cleaned. She fell asleep on a pile of clothes, exhausted and stinking to high heaven. The remaining days followed suit, with more and more dumping and clearing that Margaret would let her do. She cleared the sunroom, which had less junk than the spare bedroom, attic, or basement. Margaret found two cots buried under pounds of boxes in the garage, and Emily made a makeshift space for them that was comfortable and clean. It was a proud accomplishment. They celebrated that night with the Dollar Menu at McDonald's while Sam climbed on the playground.

"I need a job, Margaret. Eight hundred dollars a month won't keep this family going," Emily said, sipping a Coke.

"It's almost harvest time. Lots of farms around looking for help. Maybe I can get them to post an announcement at church," Margaret offered.

And so, she did, and a few days later, Gavin Shaw called saying that he could use some help this summer. Emily felt like crying when she got off the phone with him, finally feeling like she was shaking off this horrible luck that plagued her since March 10th.

As the clock pushed 5:25, she wondered what Gavin thought now knowing her secret. She wondered what else he would offer and wondered how much she could continue to refuse. Pride was a fickle beast when there was a threat of starvation and a life of being surrounded by a million plastic soda bottles.

Emily shook Sam awake, and he sat up, groggy. She pulled out fresh clothes from the laundry bag and marched him to the kitchen to brush his teeth. She pulled on a gray Air Force t-shirt from Margaret's collection, a pair of jean shorts, and ankle socks before shoving her feet into her Nikes. She pulled on a red bandana as a headband on her short, dark hair.

She measured out cheap dollar store coffee for her and Margaret for the small coffee pot and filled the container with water. Gavin had better coffee, because she bought him better coffee, but she still needed a jolt in the morning with sleep eluding her for weeks.

Sam wandered back to the sunroom and pulled on a simple blue t-shirt and too-big blue shorts. She noticed him trying to shove his ever-growing feet into his shoes. She sighed knowing he was going to need shoes ASAP. He ran a small black comb through his hair that desperately needed cutting and sat sleepily on the cot while Emily chugged her black coffee.

They were waiting on the porch, the sun starting to peak out from the east, when she heard Gavin's truck driving down Avenue B. It was quiet that morning, as most people were sleeping in on Saturday. She briefly remembered her Saturdays before all this, waking up way past 9:00 with Aaron snoring softly beside her. Sam was usually awake watching whatever was on the Nickelodeon or the Family Channel eating his third bowl of cereal. They usually made love before going downstairs, and Emily would make them all a big breakfast with eggs, bacon, and pancakes.

She grabbed her bag, which included a few workbooks and toys for Sam, and slung it over her shoulder. Gavin smiled at them as they walked over toward the truck. Sam waved as Emily put him in the backseat and buckled him in before she climbed into the front seat.

"Morning," he said.

"Morning."

She closed the door and buckled her seatbelt.

"Nice shirt," he said.

"Thanks. I wanted to give a shout out to our troops," she said in a deadpan voice.

"Boo-yah," he mumbled. She couldn't help but smile.

"House smells fantastic, by the way. I had dreams I was baked in an apple pie," he said.

"Were you being eaten?"

"No, I woke up wrapped in my sheets, a hot sweaty mess, though."

She laughed and shook her head. She glanced back and saw that Sam's eyes were already drooping with the smooth truck ride.

"How did you sleep?" he asked.

"Got a full four hours," she mumbled. "You?"

"About the same."

"I fiddled with your car this morning. Seems like some wires shook loose. Seems to be all better."

"That's a huge relief," she said. She relaxed a little. They rode the rest of the way in silence. The sun was already peeking through the clouds as Gavin turned down his county road toward his gravel driveway.

"The land looks strange with the hay cut," she said.

"It'll come back up, God willing," he said.

Emily toasted big slices of buttery bread in the oven when she got to Gavin's. She heard Paco, Will, and Shakes walk in laughing at some story Paco was telling. All the men stopped suddenly when they saw Sam.

"This is my son, Sam," Emily said, suddenly nervous.

"I'm Will."

"*W-I-L-L*," Emily signed.

"Hey, little man, I'm Shakes."

"*S-H-A-K-E-S.*"

Sam began to move his hands. Emily laughed. So did Paco.

"What'd he says?" Shakes asked.

"He asked vanilla or chocolate," Paco said and signed. The men politely chuckled.

"*You can use sign language? Cool! Do you have a deaf kid, too?*"

"*My son has autism. He doesn't use his voice, but likes to use sign language to talk,*" Paco signed.

"*A few kids back at school had that. Some talked, but no one used sign language. What's his name?*" Sam asked.

"*X-A-V-I-E-R.*"

"*Does he like video games?*"

51

"More than anything," Paco said and smiled. Sam grinned. Emily exhaled, unaware that she had been holding her breath.

The men ate every last bit of the apple spiced oatmeal with buttered toast and fruit. Sam sat at the table with everyone, and Paco chatted with him about the tractor and what they were doing in the field that day, his teacher persona shining through. Gavin walked in from outside and took off his gloves. He hardly ever ate breakfast with them after the bee sting incident. Emily tried to not make a big deal out of it.

"Looks like rain is coming this afternoon. Best be getting the baling finished ASAP," Gavin said. The men instinctively stood up and took their bowls to the kitchen.

"Something for the road?" Emily offered Gavin.

"Coffee. And maybe some of that toast."

Emily poured him coffee into a thermos and wrapped up two pieces of toast in a paper towel.

"I planned on washing your sheets on your bed today and cleaning your bathroom. Any objection?"

Gavin paused and looked at her. The question threw him off guard. "No. Of course not. Thank you," he stammered.

"Should I dust?"

Gavin swallowed. "Mind the photographs."

"Of course," she said, but he quickly disappeared.

Emily put Sam to work, clearing and washing dishes while she stripped Gavin's bed. She found clean blue sheets in his hall closet and took the quilt outside to shake it out with Sam's help.

"Can I see the barn?"

"In a little bit. I have to get lunch started, and we can walk out to get eggs and veggies."

Emily started a small load of sheets and towels in the washer while she had Sam sweep the kitchen.

They walked out to the barn to look at Gavin's four horses. Sam smiled as they sniffed him. He placed his small hands on their long muzzle, and they bumped him playfully. She opened the stalls to let them out to the pasture, and they all eagerly walked, enjoying their short chance of freedom. The sky was overcast, but she saw no storm clouds, like Gavin warned her to look out for. She had Sam fill up the water buckets, while she mucked out Lily's stall and threw fresh straw down.

Sam stood by the barn door, looking out at the pasture.

"There's a lot of nothing out here," he signed.

"Some people like it like that."

"Do you?" Sam signed.

"Sometimes. But then sometimes I miss New York."

"I like it. It's calm. New York was too crazy for me," he signed.

"What about Watchung? Do you miss our house in Watchung?"

"I miss Daddy," Sam signed quickly.

He didn't make eye contact with her, rather looked out to the land of cut hay and got lost in a memory. She hugged him, tears burning in the corners of her eyes. She missed Daddy, too.

She gave Sam a reprieve from chores and let him watch TV in Gavin's living room. Sam tucked his long, lanky legs under him on the flowered couch. Emily brought him a glass of milk and some peanut butter cookies she was baking. He looked happy to be there, which calmed her troubled heart down somewhat. While the broccoli cheese rice casserole was baking, she decided to clean Gavin's bathroom and dust.

She lifted each frame and carefully dusted underneath, trying hard to not to not disturb the pattern in which they were placed. She scrubbed his tub, which desperately needed it, as well as the toilet. She wiped the sink and paused. His wife's toothbrush was still in its slot by the sink. She sat on the edge of the tub and stared at the pink thing, her chest burning with emotion. She put her face in her hands and sobbed. His room gave her a glimpse that this pain she felt all the time in her chest did not lessen with time, and she was so desperately counting on it to.

Gavin noticed her somber mood when they took a break for lunch. She had set up a simple meal in the dining room with little fanfare. Sam was still watching TV and she stuck around in the kitchen instead of sitting down with them and talking. It started to drizzle outside.

"I'm going to bring the horses in," she announced. Gavin waited a few minutes then followed her out to the pasture. He watched her carefully corral in Lily and Grace, then reach for Bob, but Bob was being his usual stubborn self, refusing to take orders. Elliot had walked back to the barn himself, hating to get wet.

"Here let me," Gavin said.

"I can do it," she said in a stern voice. Gavin backed up. She tugged on Bob, making the horse understand she was dead serious about moving him back into the barn. Bob begrudgingly moved and Emily walked him back into the stable. Gavin made a move to go back to the house to leave her in peace.

"Tell me something, because I need to know," she called out to him. He stopped and turned around.

"Are you still living in this hell that I feel on a daily basis? Because it seems like you are, and that scares the crap out of me, you being over five years into this journey," she said.

The words hung in the air cartoon-like above them. Gavin leaned against the barn door jam and let them float above them for a few seconds.

"The hell has lessened over time, but the guilt is what still gets me," he answered honestly.

"Guilt?" she asked.

Gavin looked down and took a minute to think about what he was about to say. He'd never talked about this before with anyone, but for some reason he just let the rest of the words spill out of him, laying them down at Emily's feet.

"The accident. It was my fault. I was driving. I was pissed off. I didn't want to be taking that trip to Columbus. It was some stupid Girl Scout thing that Natalie dragged me to. I was driving mad. Some asshole comes up behind me, passes me aggressively, and I speed up to teach him a lesson. The car blows a tire, and I spin out of control, and I cause this chain reaction accident that kills my girls, the asshole who passed me, and two other teenagers who were behind us. Yet I survive it. It was like karma wanted to teach me a lesson I'd never forget," Gavin said.

The rain started to pick up as he told his story. A cold wind blew beside Emily in the barn, and she felt herself shiver. She leaned against the door to Lily's stall and chewed on what he said. Lily poked her head out and Emily instinctively rubbed her muzzle. Gavin waited patiently for any response at all.

"Aaron and I had a vicious fight the night before he killed himself. I told him I didn't want him anymore. I told him to go to hell. Yet I am the one who is conveniently living there."

"He was wound tight because of the investigation," he offered.

"The tire probably blew because of debris in the road. Doesn't make the outcome less horrific, or us any less guilt-ridden," she said.

"Touché."

They were quiet as they both watched the rainfall.

"I will tell you this—there are more good days than not as time moves on. Sometimes I do actually catch myself enjoying life without desperately missing the one I had," he said softly.

"Well . . . that's something," she whispered.

CHAPTER SEVEN

Emily was at the table Sunday afternoon writing out her grocery list for the morning run to Kroger. Outside it was gray and raining for the second day in a row. She had all the ads and the coupons spread on the table. Sam was playing quietly, and Gavin was in the living room watching ESPN, catching up on a week of scores. The rain gave everyone a reprieve, and although Gavin grumbled about the rain making him fall behind, he seemed to pass the time just fine with TV and a cold beer. Emily was grateful everyone had a chance to take a break since the harvest started. For the first time in a week, she had a chance to breathe. Sam came running down the stairs and was smiling. He was holding a silky brown teddy bear.

"Where did you get that bear?" Emily signed.

"I found it in a secret room.".

"A secret room? What secret room?"

"Where did Sam find that bear?" Emily turned around to find Gavin in the dining room with a look on his face that she had never seen before.

"He said he found it in a secret room," she said. Gavin was at the table in two short steps and took the bear out of her hands with such force she almost fell back from her chair. He stared at the bear in disbelief, gently touching the silky, light brown fur with his thumbs.

"Where did he find this bear?" he growled.

"Show me where you found the bear," Emily signed. Sam looked afraid as he slowly walked to the side of the house where Gavin slept and showed them a side panel behind the stairs. In that area there was just enough space for a small child to play, and there were several toys packed in there—pink tea sets with Disney princesses on them, several stuffed animals arranged in a circle, and plates with pretend cookies and cakes on them. Dust covered the tea party, a snapshot of a simpler,

happier time. Gavin's breath became labored as he knelt down and held the teapot in his hand. His hand went to his mouth to try to keep the grief at bay, but Emily saw the pain on his face at seeing his daughter's secret hiding place, the one place that he failed to scrub clean the memory of his old life, and it was all he could do but to slump on the ground. Emily moved toward him.

"You need to give me a minute," he said firmly.

Emily recoiled at the tone of his voice. She quickly led Sam to the front porch.

"What's wrong? What did I do wrong?" Sam signed over and over again.

Emily fought back tears, tears of illogical anger toward Sam, sadness for Gavin, and fear that he would put them out on the streets for invading his privacy in such an intimate way. She paced around the porch.

"You should not be snooping in other people's houses," she signed and spoke at the same time, her voice shaking.

"I wasn't snooping, I was just playing!"

"Sam, you should not play with things that aren't yours," she said.

"But I don't have any toys. I was being careful with it!"

Guilt combined with her fear finally released a small stream of tears. Sam looked at her completely confused. He looked like such a young adult to Emily just then. She could remember holding him as he slept as a baby, the curls of his hair along the nape of his neck, and how she always wished he would stay that little. She wanted so desperately to keep him young; to be unaware of the horrible things that life could throw at you. He already knew way too much.

"What, Mom? Tell me!" Sam demanded. Emily paused and exhaled loudly.

"Mr. Shaw had a daughter your age. The bear belonged to her," Emily began.

"What happened to her?" Sam signed slowly.

"She died. In the same car accident that killed his wife—her mother," Emily whispered and signed.

Sam's mouth turned down sadly. He looked back at the front door and back at his mother. He finally ran back inside.

"Sam! Sam!" Emily called out in vain, chasing back after him.

She saw Sam walk slowly back to Gavin, who was still kneeling in the hallway with the bear in his hands. Gavin looked up at the small boy, his eyes red from crying. The sight of him like that tore Emily apart, and tears sprung to her eyes. She had a soft spot for men's tears.

Sam rubbed his right fist over his heart several times, trying to communicate with Gavin.

"S..s..s . . . ry," Sam squeaked.

Emily choked back the tears of amazement as she finally heard a word come from Sam's mouth. He smiled sadly at Sam through his tears and hugged the boy's neck. Emily and Gavin looked at each other, his eyes piercing through her chest. She wanted to hug him, tell him that she understood, that her heart broke for him, that she cared. Something. Anything. Instead, she prayed Gavin could get that message through her son. He stood up and handed the bear to Sam.

"Are you sure?" she said, touching his arm. He turned to face her, inches from her face. He allowed her touch to linger before pulling away.

"Yes. The boy hardly has any toys."

"I'll take care of it, I promise," Sam signed.

"He said he would take special care of it."

"I know he will," Gavin said, and walked past her to his bedroom. The sound of the door closing was the saddest sound she had ever heard.

She left soon after, braving the rain, taking Sam to eat at McDonald's with a scrap of change she found at the bottom of her purse. She really just wanted to allow Gavin the space he needed and to walk away from the intensity of that moment. After shopping for the week and putting away the groceries, Sam worked on his math at the dining room table while Emily baked, her go-to stress relief. She made loaves of chocolate zucchini bread and mulberry cobblers. The mulberries were turning her fingertips and everything in the kitchen a deep purple, but she did not care.

He walked into the kitchen from the barn, talking on his cell phone, stopping suddenly when he saw she was immersed in a crime scene of hulled mulberries, tiny green stems in a haphazard pile on the island, and purple juice bleeding all over a cutting board.

"She'll have to call you back—she's elbow deep in a project right now," he said. He paused and hung up.

"Wow."

"Who was that?" she asked.

"Paco. Well, Celia, his wife. He called; she took over the phone. She wanted to invite you over for Sunday dinner tonight. I said you'd call her back."

"That's nice of her."

"I've never seen anyone use mulberries to bake. I've only seen the birds eat them."

"Well, baked in a gossamer of cobbler crust, they are fit for human consumption, I promise," she said.

"No doubt. It looks delicious."

Emily finished hulling the fruit and began to clean up the mess.

"Can I try this chocolate loaf?" he asked quietly.

"Of course."

Emily saw him slice a bit of the loaf and close his eyes as the flavor reached his taste buds. She smiled when she finally realized his food weakness. Chocolate.

"This is amazing. What's in it?"

"Cocoa, flour, eggs, oil, cinnamon, and about a pound of your zucchini," she said.

"Are you kidding me? Tastes like cake."

"Healthier cake."

He cut a bigger slice. Emily pulled a small plate down, pulled out the milk, and poured him a glass. He sat at the island and broke the cake off in smaller bites, chewing and drinking slowly.

"I wanted to apologize for earlier," he said.

"There is no need to, Gavin. Seriously," Emily said.

It was the first time she called him Gavin. It finally felt right to call him that.

"Sam's a really good boy. You've done well with him."

"I appreciate that, but he came from the womb that way. Gentle. Loving."

Emily poured the cobbler crust into a baking pan. Gavin watched as she sprinkled mulberries on top of the wet batter in a beautifully random pattern.

"What was your daughter's name?" Emily asked softly, not looking at him.

"Melissa. We called her Sissy, though. Named after Natalie's grandma," Gavin said.

"What was she like?"

"Wonderfully girlie. Pink everything. Princess everything. Fairies, tutus, and unicorns. So different from Natalie. She almost didn't know what to do with a girl that feminine," Gavin smiled sadly. He allowed the vision of his beautiful daughter in her tiara, wielding her wand at him as he came in from the fields each night, to come and rest at the forefront of his mind.

"Abracadabra!" Sissy said.

"What are you doing, Princess Sissy?" Gavin asked.

"Magically making you less stinky," she said.

"I know saying I'm sorry doesn't say enough about your loss," Emily said, looking him in the eyes. Her true sorrow formed a lump in his throat. He swallowed it away.

Gavin went back to eating his chocolate loaf. "It comes close," he said to his plate.

***

Paco lived four streets over from Margaret, but in a neighborhood so vastly different it may as well have been in a different town altogether. Everything on that street was fairly new construction, with clean, beautiful houses with well-manicured lawns. Paco's house was nestled in a cul-de-sac with his black Ram truck and a red Nissan Sentra in the driveway. As Emily strolled up the walkway with Sam in tow, carrying a cobbler and chocolate loaf, she felt somewhat envious of the idyllic neighborhood, and missed her life back in Watchung so much that it made her near weepy.

A Hispanic woman with a mane of crazy curly brown hair opened the door and smiled a warm, brilliant smile at her. She was about Emily's height, but was voluptuous, built with more curves than Emily ever prayed to have, complete with an ample chest and backside. Her nails were painted a steel metal color, and she wore a beautiful red shade of lipstick, making her attractive in a 1930s pin-up girl kind of way. Emily smiled to herself, thinking Paco was a *very* lucky man.

"Hi, Emily and Sam! I'm Celia. So nice to finally meet you!"

Emily smiled and Sam handed her the treats in his hand. Celia made the sign for "*thank you.*" Sam signed, "*You're welcome.*"

"Please come in. Paco is in the back cooking a brisket. It should be close to being ready. He's been out there all day," she said.

They walked into the house, down a small hallway into a very open living room where there were nice couches, all in a neutral brown, and a 50-inch flat screen television set with an impressive speaker set around it.

To the left of the living room was a dining/kitchen area, accented in bold red walls, beautifully ornate crosses, and a collage of family pictures done tastefully in black frames.

"These desserts look amazing. Paco said you were a wonderful cook," Celia said. She put the cobbler and loaf down on the table that was set with tortilla chips and various dips, including a seven-layer and something with hot cheese and tomatoes.

"You have a beautiful home," Emily said.

"Thank you. I'll freely admit that I'm obsessed with HGTV. Paco hates it because I change it up every year, I swear. Do you like the red walls? Those are my newest idea. I think they're nice. He thinks they are too bold."

"No, I like it. Bold and all," Emily said.

"So, we have drinks in the cooler by the patio. I have Capri Suns for the kids, or milk. We have beer, wine, soda. What can I get you?"

"Coke if you have it," she said.

"Would you like a juice?" Celia signed to Sam.

"Sure," Sam signed back.

Celia walked out to the patio, and Emily noticed that she had a tattoo of tiny footprints on her right shoulder blade, peeking out from her black, bedazzled tank top.

"Babe—Emily and Sam are here," Celia said.

Sam looked around the house and Emily wondered if he was also feeling envious of the space, remembering that not three months ago he lived in a place much like this, with a room full of toys and video games.

Paco walked into the house. He looked different in a gray Cowboys t-shirt and jean shorts. He wore no hat that day, showing his short, dark hair.

"Hey, welcome! Welcome! Glad you could come," he said and hugged her and high-fived Sam.

"Thanks for inviting us. I'm amazed you managed to cook out in the rain."

"Hell, man, we're Mexican. Rain, snow, sleet, hurricanes. We cook out no matter what!" Paco joked.

"Xavier is in the basement playing video games. Why don't we take Sam down there to meet him?" Celia suggested. She opened a door near the kitchen. They walked down the stairs into a nicely finished basement that was designed with children in mind. Video games were neatly stacked near another large TV; various PG-rated movies were in a bookcase by the TV. There were building blocks, toy cars, an art center, and table with short legs and four short chairs around it.

Xavier was playing Mario Kart on the Wii, flicking the Wii-mote with great precision. Sam clung to her, finding himself suddenly shy around another kid, like he usually did.

"Zay—this is Sam and his momma, Ms. Emily. Say hello,

please," Celia said.

Xavier was a small boy, light skinned like Celia, with dark brown hair and chocolate eyes. Like most autistic kids Emily had met, he did not really make eye contact with them.

Xavier signed *"Hello. I'm playing a game."* He was like Sam, mostly non-verbal.

"Do you play Wii?" Celia signed to Sam. Sam nodded.

"Xavier, can you please let Sam play with you?" Celia asked. Xavier handed the Wii-mote to Sam and Sam cautiously took it.

"We can play two-player," Sam signed.

"Okay," Xavier said.

Emily watched with pride as she saw Sam cautiously observe the situation and attempt to talk to Xavier with sign language. Celia smiled. Emily understood the simple happiness that came when a special needs child found a friend. It just made a mother's heart happy. For a brief moment, life was "easy" and somewhat "normal," and they got a glimpse of what other people must feel like on a daily basis.

A few minutes later, Celia and Emily sat at the dining room table with a glass of wine exchanging stories, eating snacks, and getting to know each other. Paco mostly stayed outside, allowing the women their time, patiently babysitting his smoked meat.

"We lost our first baby, a girl, Rosa, in 2003. We don't know what happened. I was set to deliver a few days before my due date and she stopped moving," Celia said.

"I'm so sorry."

Celia's eyes teared up at the memory. She inhaled and exhaled a few times. "I got pregnant again within six months, and we were finally blessed with Xavier. But we knew pretty quickly that he was on the spectrum. When did you find out about Sam?"

"At birth. He failed every hearing test. And we were pretty much sure that he was going to be deaf. It was just a matter of preparing for it," Emily said.

"We did the same thing. Being teachers, we already saw so

much of it that we knew what we had to do. Early intervention was key," she said.

Emily remembered how terrified she felt when the doctors came in as a group while she was nursing Sam hours after he was born. They looked so somber trying to tell her that it could be nothing, but Sam was going to need more follow up testing to make sure. Aaron held her hand and was so calm when they left, telling her that no matter what they found, everything would be fine. He kissed her and kissed Sam's forehead as he slept in her arms.

"So, I want to ask—but I don't want to pry..." Celia started.

"About Aaron?" Emily took a drink of wine.

"Did you know what he was doing?" Celia asked.

"No. Nothing. Just assumed he was having a hard time at work. Stress and all."

"Girl, I hear you. Sometimes these men we love can hide the deepest of secrets. They're like a fortress."

"Part of me can't even believe that he was capable of it— that's not the man I knew. I sometimes wish I could have had just one conversation with him. Just to get his side of it. There must have been a reason," Emily said.

Paco walked in with a pan covered with foil. "Let's eat!"

"Finally! I'm starving! I'll go get the boys," Celia said.

Celia walked downstairs and Emily helped Paco slice the meat in the kitchen. She was impressed with the tenderness of the brisket, and when the smell hit her, she was instantly back home in Texas about to partake of some excellent barbeque.

"I know I kinda sprung this on you last minute, but she really wanted to meet you. She's had a hard time finding women to be friends with who get what it's like having a special needs kid, you know? I mean she has her sister who lives next town over. But with me working on the farm in the summers, and she spends all her time with Zay, I think she gets really lonely," Paco said softly. Emily saw the pain that he had from witnessing the pain Celia felt flutter across his eyes. He really was such a good, kind man.

"I'm glad we came over."

Celia came up alone from the basement. "Apparently they are playing a sudden death tournament and cannot be interrupted," Celia said.

The three of them ate dinner while the tournament continued, and the conversation moved toward Gavin.

"Gavin's never had a woman work for him, right babe? I was totally shocked to hear that he hired you," Celia said.

"Not in the four years I've baled hay for him. He doesn't usually interact with women very well. He usually avoids them like the plague," Paco said.

"It's probably because he doesn't want to, you know, diminish his wife's memory or something. Some men are like that when their loves pass on," Celia said matter-of-factly.

"That and the ladies around here are either batshit crazy or ugly dogs," Paco said and howled. Emily laughed out loud.

Paco grinned. "Not y'all of course. Y'all are the exception to the rule," he said and winked.

"So, you didn't know his wife, Paco?"

"No. I came on board after she passed. Will knew her, though. He said she was a nice lady, but a bit of a ball buster. Exactly what you would think from being a Colonel in the military," Paco said. Emily tried to imagine Gavin and Natalie together and wondered what kind of relationship they had.

"Paco says he likes you a lot," Celia said.

Paco gave Celia a shocked "*Sssshhhhhh woman!*" look. She looked confused.

"What?" Celia asked.

"Babe. Seriously? Oh my God," Paco muttered. Paco shook his head. Emily raised her eyebrows to him. "I just mentioned that he seems to enjoy having you around. I have no idea what this woman of mine is thinking beyond that," Paco mumbled, giving Celia a look.

Emily chuckled. "On that note, we should get some food into these kids."

She walked down the stairs and saw that Sam and Xavier were no longer playing a video game but sitting on the floor quietly. Emily saw that Sam was signing the end of a sentence.

". . . *he died*."

Xavier rocked back and forth a little bit and thought for a few seconds. *"Sad. Very sad,"* Xavier signed.

"Yes," Sam signed.

"We are friends now. Maybe you're not so sad anymore. We can play games and have fun and you won't be sad anymore," Xavier signed.

Sam smiled a patient smile at Xavier and nodded. Emily felt emotion catch in her throat.

Xavier was right. With friends you aren't so sad anymore. Emily was grateful that she was making new friends and that Xavier reminded her of that.

CHAPTER EIGHT

The hay team was reduced by two during the second week of baling. Gavin relented and decided that having the twins around was more of a liability than an asset when Ian nearly flipped over a tractor and Wyatt whined so much that Will lost it and slapped him out of frustration. Ian found work at the Domino's pizza and Wyatt became a bagger at the IGA, which was a far better fit for everyone. The small, but effective team began to make different-sized bales of hay to allow it to dry. That week Sam got to ride in the tractor and watch the process, riding with Paco after they all had lunch, bouncing up and down the whole time. Emily took that time to drive with Will into town to run errands with him.

"How did you meet Gavin?" Emily asked.

"I used to own the farm next to his. I wanted to retire, so I sold it to him after Natalie passed, and we worked a deal that I got to live in my house and work with him in the summers for salary."

"So, how much land did you own? Are we on your old land now?" Emily looked to the horizon.

"The Shaws only owned about 40 acres, and only grew hay for their own horses. I sold them close to 600 acres, minus the lot my house sits on. All of this used to be mine," Will said.

"You owned 600 acres? Wow! That's impressive."

"Eh, not really. I made a decent living on it growing corn and soybeans. But the weather is so unpredictable around here. Always nervous the first of spring. Never knew if we would be able to get the seed in the ground. Then it became obvious my boys were not farmers—as you witnessed, so I really didn't want to hold on to it for much longer."

"And their mother? She's not around?"

Will sighed deeply. "No. She ran off with some musician when the boys were babies. She begged and begged me to give

67

her children. I was in my 40s, and she was only 25. Well, we go through this *in vitro* thing, and surprise we get two babies. And then after they were born, she changed. When they were about six months old, I walked in from the back forty and there was a stranger in my house babysitting them. There was a note saying she changed her mind, and she was sorry."

"That's awful, Will. I am so sorry."

Will shrugged. "I did the best I could. But children need their mothers," Will said.

"They need their fathers, too," Emily said softly. She looked out the window and thought of Aaron.

"That's true too," Will said quietly.

"Well, they aren't serial killers, and they are now gainfully employed. I think you're doing a great job," she said, shaking the memory away.

"You're a sweet lady, Emily, but..."

"No, I mean it. It takes about from the age of 20 on for a boy to realize his father isn't full of it. So, they're 18 now—in two years, mark my word, they will be waking up from this teenage fog."

"Here's hoping."

Will stopped at a stop sign. They were quiet for a little while.

"Is Shakes from around here?" she asked.

"Shakes and Gavin go way back, about 20 years or so. They met when Nat was stationed at Keesler Air Force Base in Mississippi. Lot of history there."

"Two men in their 20s. I'm sure," she joked.

Will smiled as he drove. "Not that kind of history. Shakes was in a bit of trouble back then. Gavin helped him out and Shakes is forever indebted to him."

Emily didn't ask for elaboration. She felt it wasn't Will's place to tell her the story.

As soon as the clover hay was cut, dried and baled, it was time to start on the alfalfa fields. On the sixth of July, the crew began chopping down that hay to begin the drying process. Emily tried more innovative ways to use Gavin's vast produce crops, especially his squash and zucchini, which were growing by the barrelful.

Emily walked up to Gavin, who was working in the barn, after everyone but Shakes had left for the evening, carrying a folder of paper that she had printed from the local library.

"I have a proposition for you," she said and smiled.

"You're not selling Amway on the side, are you?" he joked.

"Ha. No. But I do want to have a talk about your other crops. Can we sit down for a minute inside so you can hear me out?" she asked.

"Sure," he said and followed her inside.

She poured him a cup of coffee and opened her folder. "I took some time yesterday to investigate the farmer's markets in the surrounding area. I found one in Dayton that is open on the weekends and everyone is already peddling most of what you are growing, but I had an idea. They allow you to showcase foods that are made from the crops you are growing. I thought that I could make some of the baked goods that I already make, maybe throw in some tomato tarts, some quiches from the Borg laying so many eggs, and we could sell those things at the market. It would be a good way to add revenue to the farm and use up the produce that I haven't already used or squirreled away for you later in the winter."

Gavin leaned back in his chair and thought for a little while. Emily could see him churning the idea over in his mind. She continued.

"The initial investment is the $100 farm registration fee and about $100 for the first weekend baking. I think I can make all of that back and add a small profit of about $200, assuming the money for gas is taken into account. The next weekend would probably be all profit, and I am assuming up to an extra $500 a week. The market lasts until the end of September, so there are about 12 weeks left—so maybe a profit about $5,000."

Gavin looked at the numbers she had calculated and was impressed with her notes in the margins about the cost of flour, disposable pie tins, and bakery boxes.

"We could just try a test run. If it all goes to hell you could just fire me," she said.

He noticed a drawing on the opposite side of the page.

"What's this?" he asked.

"I didn't know if you had a logo for the farm, but I was doodling something fun that could be printed on those Avery labels with the Shaw Farm name and address on it," Emily said.

The logo was simple. It said Shaw Farm and Bakery, and there was a cup of coffee next to a slice of pie, drawn in a modern style.

"If you don't like it, we can search for another one..."

"No, I do like it. It's nice," he said.

"So, that's my presentation. What do you think?" she asked.

"Do you always get your way?"

She looked shocked. "Um, no, I don't think so."

"Well, I think you can sell ice to an Eskimo," he said and laughed. He handed her back the paperwork and stood. He pulled out his wallet and dropped two $100 bills on the table.

"So, this is yes?" she asked.

He drank the last of his coffee and put his cup back on the table before walking back out to the barn.

"Yes," he said.

Celia kissed Xavier, despite his multiple attempts to wriggle away. "Y'all are going to be late," Paco singsonged.

It was about 7 a.m. on a clear, beautiful Saturday morning. Emily and Gavin loaded the back of Paco's truck with breads, pies, tarts, and quiches. Gavin also loaded collapsible camp chairs and a small ice chest full of water and soda. Emily had her bag filled with business cards, invoices, pens, paper, four ham and Havarti cheese sandwiches, and various snacks.

Emily looked at Sam. *"I'll be home for dinner,"* she signed.

"It's all cool, Mom." He really was such a laid-back kid, so much like Aaron. She hugged him and knew that he was in capable hands with Gavin and Paco.

"Love you," she signed.

"Love you more," he signed back and winked.

"All right, girl, you ready?" Emily asked.

Celia kissed Xavier twenty more times. "Mommy loves you, Mijo," Celia said. Xavier finally moved towards Paco.

"Well, if I fail, you all will be eating pies and quiche for the next week," Emily said nervously.

"You'll do fine," Gavin assured. He gave her one of his positive looks, silently offering her some encouragement. She inhaled and exhaled deeply. She smiled to show she was confident, although she was completely terrified, she was going to fail miserably.

"Break a leg. Or sell a lot . . . what the hell do you say in this situation?" Paco asked.

"Thanks, Paco," Emily said. Celia hugged and kissed her man.

"Finally, I get a kiss!" he said.

"Take care of our boy," she said.

"Babe, get in the truck, please, you're embarrassing me," Paco said.

Emily climbed in the driver's side and started the engine.

"I-70 to I-675," Gavin said.

"Got it," Emily yelled. Celia finally got in the truck, eyes still blurred with tears, and waved until it looked like her hand would fall off.

They arrived in Dayton less than an hour later and found a parking spot in a Kmart parking lot where the farmer's market was to be held. The location left a lot to be desired, but Emily knew that it really didn't matter where they were, as long as they had a table, good product, and customers. She remembered selling her cakes in some shady places in New Jersey trying to drum up business when Aaron was a young broker, and they could barely make their rent payment.

"At least it's a nice day," Celia said as she hopped down from the truck. She was always trying to find the silver lining. Gavin called her Molly Sunshine behind her back. Emily pulled out the paperwork for the registration and proceeded to walk up to the check-in booth.

"Good morning," an older woman said.

"Morning, ma'am. I'm Emily Mitchell of Shaw Farms."

"Ah, yes, welcome. Glad you made it. I have your tables. I set you up by the Wingate Jams and Jelly booth. Booth number 29."

Emily took the small map and thanked the elderly lady. There were only 30 booths in all, and she wondered if there would be anyone coming out at all to this thing given the number of vendors there.

Emily showed Celia where they were supposed to set up and Celia jumped back into the truck to park closer to help unload. Each booth had an awning, which she was grateful to see, and three long tables. Celia backed up as close as she could to the tables and started handing Emily bags and coolers.

Gavin had packed everything up snug, and they thankfully made the trip down with minimal damage.

"Oooh, is that a tomato tart?" a voice asked.

Emily looked up and saw her booth neighbors, an older man and woman evaluating the products that she was arranging. They reminded her of her neighbors back in Watchung.

"Yes ma'am."

"I'm Gertie Wingate. This is my husband Roger," the plump woman said and shook Emily's hand.

"Emily Mitchell," Emily said.

Roger walked over the front of the booth.

"Wow, look at these pies, Gertie, and the quiche!"

"Made fresh with organic produce grown in Champaign County, and our hens laid the eggs," Celia chimed in.

Emily smiled and thought of Gavin's earlier comment. He was wrong. Celia was the salesman—she was the one who could sell ice to an Eskimo. Paco told Emily that Celia was the primary fundraiser for the Academy where they both taught. She had local businessmen donating tens of thousands of dollars for the children at the school every year. In the last year alone, local Columbus businessmen donated brand new playground equipment and fifty new computers, all because of Celia's power of persuasion.

"And her rockin' tits and ass helped."

"Paco!" Emily said and laughed.

"Lucky for me I get them for free," he said and winked.

"Now Gertie and Roger, I'm going to let you sample this pie and you tell me if you don't think this is some of the yummiest dessert you ever had," Celia said.

Celia had cut up a berry crumble pie and put out little samples on the table and handed some to both of them.

"Very nice," Gertie said.

"Emily, our head baker, used to run a catering business in New York. She is self-trained and has an impeccable palate for ingredients, don't you agree?" Celia continued. By then, a small crowd gathered, and Celia continued on with her pitch while passing out samples. People walked up and started buying product. All were reasonably priced at $12 a pie. They sold two-thirds of their products in an hour.

Emily took a break and walked around the other booths, looking at handmade soaps, fresh produce, yarns, honey, and the Wingate jams. They really had a nice spread with about twenty different varieties.

Emily sampled the habanero apricot, on Roger's insistence.

"It's really not hot. It's sweet with the taste of the habanero but no heat," he said.

Emily tasted the cracker with the pale jam with red flakes in it and smiled. Roger was right. It was sweet like apricots with the taste of a pepper minus the heat.

"How much?" she asked.

"I'll tell you what. I'll swap you a tomato tart for two jars of jam," he said.

"Deal." She picked out the apricot habanero for Gavin and the strawberry rhubarb for Sam and Margaret.

Emily walked over and pulled the last tomato tart out of the cooler and handed it over to Roger. Roger bagged up her jam and handed her the small, brown bag.

Celia handed her a sandwich and bottled water, then fanned herself, her curly hair in little ringlets around her face.

"Eat and drink up girl. One more hour and we are done with this place. I'm going to sell the rest of these pies," Celia declared.

"Go girl. Do it. Sell it. Own it," Emily joked.

"I will. But first, I need to hit the little girl's room," Celia said and ran off for the Kmart bathroom. Emily laughed as Celia sprinted across the parking lot.

Emily took a bite of her sandwich, which had gotten melty from sitting out in the sun.

"Oh, my. Look what we found here, girls," a voice said.

Emily looked up and saw Sue Ellen Richter and her entourage of friends from Champaign County standing in front of the booth. She swallowed the sandwich in her mouth.

"Afternoon, Mrs. Richter," Emily said.

"Wow. I am truly shocked that Gavin Shaw would be selling at a farmer's market in Dayton of all places," Sue Ellen said.

Emily sat quietly, opting to be a selective mute. The three other women with Sue Ellen were dressed to the nines in their summer attire from Talbots— white capris, fancy floral shirts, flip flops with big flowers on them, and big sunglasses. Emily felt a little plain in her blue jean cut-off shorts and blue t-shirt.

"So, Shaw Farms is selling *pies*? How adorably cute is that?" Sue Ellen said, voice condescending.

"Best damn pies in town," Celia said, suddenly reappearing.

"I'm sure. I'm sure. Too bad we are all on diets. Preparing for the beach. Two weeks in the Caribbean. Want to look good in those bikinis, don't we girls," Sue Ellen said.

Emily glanced at the other women who were on the plumper side and probably would be covering up those bikinis with a t-shirt. She smiled politely.

"Another time, then. Enjoy your vacation, ma'am," Emily said.

"Keep up the hard work, ladies. Maybe someday you'll be able to take a vacation, too," Sue Ellen jabbed before walking off.

Emily smiled sweetly at her. One of the friends lingered over the pies.

"Betty, like you really need a pie? How many calories did

you eat at breakfast?" Sue Ellen hissed. Betty looked at Emily and Emily smiled sadly at her as an attempt to ask "why are you friends with this woman? Be free! You are wonderful! Eat dessert!"

"Take care," Emily said softly to her. Betty secretly grabbed a business card and snuck it in her purse before walking away.

"Oh. My. God. That woman has some nerve," Celia said. The "salesman" Celia was gone and the "Latina ready for a fight" emerged.

"You know her?" Emily asked.

"Honey, everyone knows Sue Ellen Richter. The Richters own half of Champaign County. She's a plastic surgery *puta* who thinks she's God's gift to men. That *perra* thinks she can come talk smack to you. I don't think so."

"Easy there, Killer," Emily said.

"You know she's madly in love with Gavin, right?"

Emily arched an eyebrow. That bit of news turned her stomach. "No. Really?"

"Oh, yeah. Paco told me that she's always trying to bump into him in town. Follows him. Once Paco caught her trying to dry hump Gavin in the barn."

"And what was Gavin doing?" Emily asked carefully.

"Girl, he was trying to pull her off him. He can't stand that ho," Celia said.

Emily exhaled and felt vindicated. She swallowed a long drink of water.

"Gavin is Champaign County's most eligible bachelor. But that man is shut down emotionally. I think when his wife and daughter died, he died with them," Celia said.

Emily frowned. She did not want to think that he was dead inside. That made her incredibly sad.

"Oooh, more customers. Do I have anything in my teeth? How's my breath?" Celia asked.

"You're fine."

"Ladies, please come and try some delicious baked goods," Celia called.

They arrived back on Gavin's land close to 5 p.m. that

night. Gavin and Sam emerged from the barn when they heard the truck doors slam shut. Sam was carrying a small orange and white kitten and petting it. Gavin had about 4 stray cats that slept in the barn to keep the mice at bay. She would catch him playing with the cats whenever he let the horses out. He liked the orange tabby, named Spike, the best. Spike was actually a girl, much to everyone's surprise, which was revealed when Gavin found her in the hayloft surrounded by a litter of kittens two weeks ago.

"Hey there. How did it go?" Gavin asked, walking in his usual slow, calm gait up to the truck.

"We kicked so much ass," Celia declared, so proud.

Emily looked at him and smiled a tired smile. "It went well," she said.

Gavin pulled her bag off her shoulder and smiled. "Good. Glad to hear it!"

"Well? It went better than well. We sold out in three hours, and we got fourteen pre-orders for next week," Celia said. She pulled empty coolers out of the back of her truck.

Sam walked up to her and showed her the kitten. *"We named him Stripey,"* Sam signed.

"We?"

"Well, Gavin wanted Tiger, but I thought he looked more Stripey than anything," Sam signed. Emily smiled and hugged him.

"You look beat," Gavin said.

"Yeah, mostly from this woman dragging me shopping afterwards," Emily joked.

"We had to celebrate our success!" Celia said.

"Did you buy anything?" Gavin asked her.

"No, of course not."

"You should have," Gavin said.

"I don't need anything, really," she said. "But I did do a horse trade for something I thought you'd like." She reached into the bag he was carrying and pulled out the jam. "I tried it. It was good. You can add it to your collection," she said.

Gavin turned the jam over in his hand and smiled. "Thank you. That was very thoughtful."

"You're very welcome. When we unload, I will show you what you netted today."

"Why don't you come in and have some dinner first. I have a stew cooking in the crockpot."

Emily raised an eyebrow. "You cooked? I'm impressed," she joked.

"Don't be until you try it," he grinned.

Celia slowly jumped off the bed of the pickup truck while watching Gavin and Emily walk toward the house. She folded her arms across her chest and smiled at the scene she was witnessing. *That's what Paco meant*, she thought, watching Gavin walk with both Sam and Emily up the stairs like a family.

"There is something about her that gets to him," Paco said.

"Gets to him in a good way or a bad way?" Celia had asked.

Paco smiled. *"It's a good way. I think he really likes her."*

"Really babe? Wow. Well, good for them! Both widows. They would be good for each other," Celia said.

"Celia, you coming?" Emily called.

"Yeah, be right there," she said.

Celia pulled out her phone and sent a text to Paco that she was home and added. *"Gavin is totally into Emily."*

Paco texted back *"Told ya…"*

"This is so exciting!"

"Stay out of it, babe," Paco texted back.

Celia pouted, put her phone back in her pocket and walked into the house.

CHAPTER NINE

Emily was walking Elliot out to pasture a few days later when she saw Shakes jump the metal gate.

"Hey, Shakes," Emily said.

"Hey, Em."

"What's shaking?" she said and smiled at her own joke.

Shakes took a final puff of his cigarette and stomped it on the ground in front of her. "We heard that it was Sam's birthday on Sunday," he said.

"It is."

"Well, the guys were talking and thought we'd chip in and take him to a ballgame in Cincinnati, to see the Reds. What do you think?"

"Just the boys or am I invited?"

"All of us. Thought we'd take the day off and spend the day at the ballpark. They're playing the Cardinals. Should be a good game," Shakes said.

He grabbed Elliot's reins and playfully smacked his backside to get him to walk.

"That's really nice of you guys. I think Sam would love it. He used to love to see the Yankees," Emily said.

"Great. We'll set it up then," Shakes said.

"Thanks, Shakes."

Shakes walked back to the truck where Gavin was waiting in the driver's seat.

"She said that was cool."

"Good."

"Why didn't you want to ask her yourself?" Shakes asked.

Gavin didn't answer.

It was a clear, blue day on Sunday, with a high in the mid-70s. A perfect day for baseball, Shakes said. Sam was beside himself with excitement waiting through all the morning chores, asking constantly if it was time to leave yet. Emily had gotten him up at the usual time that morning but greeted him with chocolate chip smiley face pancakes like she had done for all of his past birthdays. Margaret sung and signed him "Happy Birthday" in her beautiful soprano voice and handed him a big box wrapped in leftover Christmas paper. He tore open the package and smiled when he saw a beautiful baseball mitt nestled inside.

"From me and your mom," Margaret signed slowly, getting more and more proficient with sign language over the passing weeks.

Sam smiled and put the glove on his left hand, bending the fingers of the brand-new leather down trying to break it in. He brought it to his face to inhale that fresh leather, new glove smell.

They ate breakfast around the small table, Margaret piling mounds of whipped cream and strawberries on Sam's pancakes. Emily slid another gift over to him.

"The glove was enough, Mom," he signed.

"Something else. From Daddy," Emily signed. Sam looked at the small white box and opened it slowly.

Inside was a watch. Aaron's 1940s Rolex that Emily bought for him in celebration of his first promotion ten years ago. It had a black military-style dial, chromed steel case, and a very worn black leather strap. It was the only expensive thing that Aaron ever really owned, and he loved it. Emily found it in the envelope of heirloom jewelry that Special Agent Barnes gave to Emily the night when they were kicked out of their home. Agent Barnes probably assumed it belonged to Aaron's grandfather based on the antique look of it. Whatever the reasoning, Emily was grateful to have it to pass on to Sam, even though she came damn close to hocking it when things were tough.

"It's a handsome piece. Your father would be so proud of you, working so hard with your mom," Margaret signed.

Sam looked carefully at the watch. He was sad and wistful all at once.

"Can you put it someplace safe? I don't want to mess it up when I work out at the farm," Sam signed and handed her back the watch.

"Of course."

Sam went back to eating, but Emily could tell that he was sad. She wished she had waited to the end of the day to give him the gift. Margaret saw Sam's sadness and smiled playfully. She leaned her head back and squirted a big shot of whipped cream in her mouth from the can. Sam smiled. Margaret motioned for him to lean his head back. Sam did and Margaret squirted a big blob of whipped cream in his mouth, much to his delight. Emily decided to do the same, and soon all of them were laughing with mouths full.

Margaret passed on the ballgame for a date with a handsome older gentleman from church. They were going to lunch and to see *Transformers 3*, at her insistence. Emily could never quite get a handle on Margaret's quirkiness but was happy that she was going out and seeing people again, despite her taste in movies.

Gavin stepped out of the shower close to 11 a.m. after morning chores, smelling clean and fresh like Brut aftershave mixed with the manliness of his deodorant. He wore a Reds t-shirt and his Wrangler jeans.

Emily was putting chocolate frosting on a cake for Sam so they could enjoy it when they got back that night.

"Looks great," he said. She handed him one of the beaters from the mixer. He paused.

"You know you want to." He smiled and took it.

Sam ran into the kitchen, and she handed him the other beater, and she watched both of them enjoy the simple joy of licking the beaters clean.

Shakes and Will walked in both carrying a gift bag. Sam noticed the gifts and smiled shyly.

"Happy birthday!" they both said, handing him their bags. Sam made the sign for thank you and looked to see what he got. Shakes bought him a large Lego set and Will bought him a model airplane and a set of modeling paints. Sam smiled and signed thank you twice, very taken with the gesture.

"You can make different spacecraft if you want to," Shakes said, kneeling down to Sam's level, pointing out the feature at the back of the box.

Emily caught a wisp of something in the way Shakes showed Sam the toy. Familiarity? Yearning? She wondered if Shakes had a child or helped raise a child in one of the past numerous relationships he had. The thought that he could not be with that child any longer made her a little sad.

"We'd better get going. Game is at 2:00. There might be traffic," Gavin said.

"*Go get your glove*," Emily signed to Sam. He ran to get it, excited that they were finally leaving.

They all piled into Gavin's truck, Will, Shakes, and Sam in the back and Emily in the front with Gavin. Paco and Celia intended to go, but Xavier had caught a summer cold and was recuperating at home. Earlier that morning they had opened a gift from the three of them and a nice card that Xavier had drawn with Mario and Luigi in impressive detail. They bought Sam some new Nikes and a Transformer.

"We noticed his feet were a little squished in his old ones. And every boy loves Transformers," Celia said softly.

The men chatted about the weather, the game, and the traffic while Emily looked out the window at the changing scenery.

"You okay?" Gavin asked softly.

"Yeah, I'm good."

The Cincinnati Reds played in a ballpark located right by the Ohio River in downtown Cincinnati. Emily could see the river in the background from their really nice seats located on the lower level behind first base. They filed into the fourth row of section 132 with plenty of time to see the Redlegs warm-up. Sam sat in-between Shakes and Emily, teetering at the edge of the seat. Gavin sat by Emily and Will.

Emily thumbed through the program while the men chatted about various players like Brandon Phillips and Jose Arredondo, the Cardinals outfield, and how equally the teams were matched this season.

"I'm going to get a beer — anyone hungry?" Shakes asked.

"I'll go with you," Gavin said, standing. "Would you like something?"

"A Coke. And maybe a Cracker Jacks for Sam. We can share the drink," she said.

Gavin returned a few minutes later with three trays of goodies: a mass of hot dogs, two nachos, sodas for Sam and Emily, two bags of Cracker Jacks, three bags of peanuts, beer for the men, a pack of Twizzlers for Will, and various other candies.

"Lord, did you have to take out a loan to pay for that?" Emily joked, taking one of the trays from him.

"It's a special occasion," he said simply.

Sam grabbed one of the hot dogs and waited impatiently while Emily smeared mustard on it from a packet. She balanced the rest of the tray on her lap while she opened up the Cracker Jacks and fished around for the prize.

"Don't you remember when the prizes were more than tattoos and stupid paper things that went on top of pencils?" she sighed.

"Hell, back in my day, there were actual metal toys in them," Will said.

She shared her Cracker Jacks with Will, leaning over Gavin to pour some in his hands. Gavin closed his eyes as he caught wind of her vanilla scent. She offered some to Gavin, who politely declined, happily sipping his beer.

The game was an exciting one, and Sam stood through a lot of it, eagerly hoping for a foul ball to come his way.

"Why don't the two of you come with me for a bit, before the seventh inning stretch?" Gavin asked. Emily nodded and tapped Sam to come with them.

They followed Gavin to a nice fan shop, with a lot of choices of caps, jerseys, and various toys with Reds logos on them. Gavin walked them up to the wall of ball caps.

"I would like to buy him a cap for his birthday, if that is okay with you," Gavin said. Emily was moved by the kindness that both he and the crew had shown Sam on that day.

"Gavin would like you to pick out a hat," Emily signed.

Sam turned to face the sea of choices. He carefully looked through all the styles while he narrowed down his choices. He looked every bit as young and precious in his white Adidas over-sized man's t-shirt and blue shorts that came up right above his knobby knees, scavenged from Margaret's collection of clothing, as he did when he was a two-year-old toddler wearing an oversized t-shirt and a diaper.

Sam finally settled on a vintage-looking hat, faded red with the Cincinnati "C" on the front of it. He pulled it off the rack and showed Gavin timidly.

Gavin shook his head in approval. "Try it on," he said.

Sam put the hat on his head. It was way too big for him. Emily looked at the size. "These are fitted. What's the smallest size they make? Should we try for a kid's hat?"

Gavin looked at the size of the hat in her hands and started thumbing through until he found the smallest one they had. He handed it to Sam.

"Try this one," he said.

Sam put it on, and it was only slightly loose on his head. Gavin smiled and gave a thumbs up. Sam smiled.

"He'll grow into it before you know it," he told her. She looked at him wistfully. How she knew that to be true, down to the marrow of her bones.

They all walked to the counter to pay for it.

"Your son has your wife's eyes," the cheerful clerk said.

Gavin paused with his Mastercard in his hand. Emily blushed at the comment and looked down.

"He sure does," Gavin said politely.

They walked back to their seats, Sam sporting his new hat. He ran down to show Will and Shakes, who smiled with their approval. Emily touched Gavin's arm.

"If I forget to tell you later, thank you so very much for today," she said.

"Glad to do it."

The rest of the game went by quickly. The Reds won by

two, much to Shakes' delight, who pumped his fist in the air and clapped loudly when the last fly ball was caught for the third out. Before they knew it, they were loading up in Gavin's truck, navigating the crazy traffic of downtown Cincinnati.

Emily fell asleep on the ride back, curled up on her left side, her tanned legs tucked under her. Content and happy that Sam was able to have a nice day despite the insanity that he had endured over the last few months, sleep finally found her.

Gavin snuck looks at her sleeping peacefully while he was driving and felt a strong urge to touch her face. He looked in his rearview mirror and saw that Sam was dozing off between the men. Shakes raised an eyebrow to him and looked at Emily. Gavin focused back on the road, annoyed that Shakes knew weeks ago that he liked this woman, even before he could admit it to himself.

He drove quietly on I-75 and tried to think about other things but felt himself migrating back to the curve of Emily's body, the delicate form of her hands, the slight overbite in her smile, and the way her hair curled in the heat. He stopped fighting the thoughts by the time he got on I-70. Thoughts were harmless, he reasoned. They were safe.

CHAPTER TEN

On the way back from the farmer's market the following Saturday, Celia insisted that they stop for coffee, even though Emily was eager to get back home. It was unbearably hot that day, and Emily endured several customers who were extremely critical about her products.

"Is it all organic? Even the butter? And is it all local? I only want it if everything is local, and organic, including the flour and the spices."

It took the full six hours to sell their inventory, leaving Emily near baked in the heat wave and extremely punchy at the arrogant people who grilled her about the ingredients. She kindly told one couple through gritted teeth that vanilla was only grown in tropical regions like Madagascar and there was no way every ingredient could be propagated in the State of Ohio. Celia and Emily outlasted Gertie and Roger Wingate, who called it a bust and left shortly after noon for their air-conditioned house in Greene County. Emily was regretting not following their lead, feeling worn out and a little sick from sitting there all day.

"Come on. I'll buy you one of those frozen yummy thingies at Tim Hortons," Celia coaxed.

Emily relented, as it was easier to grab a coffee than to hear Celia begging her to stop for another hour. She put the signal on Paco's truck and took the next exit.

They both walked into the small doughnut shop and were hit with a refreshing blast of air conditioning and the sweet smell of doughnuts. Celia ordered them frozen coffees and a small box of Timbits while Emily used the restroom. She splashed cold water on her face after she washed her hands and tried to calm herself down. Her face was red and flushed despite drinking a ton of water and slathering with SPF 50 sunscreen.

She walked back out and Celia handed her a drink, and they sat for a few minutes. Emily took a sip of the frosty beverage and felt a little better.

Celia took a sip and played with her straw, pulling it out of the cup and licking the whipped cream. She still looked great, and very well put together, only looking slightly flushed and ever-so-slightly less coiffed. Emily wished she got a little bit of luck in that department. When she was tired, she looked every bit as haggard as she felt.

"So, Paco made a phone call to Dr. Taylor, our dean, to talk about possibly getting Sam a spot in the Academy this year," Celia said. She looked at Emily with her big brown eyes and waited for her reaction.

"And he said?"

"She. She thought it would be a great place for Sam. Especially given the fact that he's 8 and non-verbal. We have a lot of excellent speech therapists that work with our deaf students. We told her that he seems exceptional in math, and she thought he would be a fine addition."

Emily was stunned. "That's amazing! Thank you both so much for doing that."

Celia frowned a little. "There's a small catch."

"What's that?"

"Tuition. Dr. Taylor seems to think you could qualify for financial aid; however, those packets are usually based on tax returns. And since your last tax return was linked to your old life with Aaron, she doesn't think she can get a waiver for the first semester."

Emily's heart sank. "How much is tuition?"

"Ten thousand a semester without any financial aid."

"Well, that blows that plan," Emily said dryly.

"Wait, maybe not necessarily," Celia started.

"Celia. There is no way in hell I can come up with ten grand. I can barely keep the lights on and keep food on the table with what I make now."

Celia stirred her coffee with her straw. "What if Paco talks to Gavin about it?"

"No."

"He really seems to care about you and Sam. I'm sure he would loan you the money."

"No, Celia. Come on. We've known each other like two months. I can't go asking for a $10,000 loan. I just can't. It's not right. No."

"I just hate the idea that Sam will be in public school," Celia said, and pouted.

"He's a resilient kid. I promise you. If he can survive his father's death, living with Margaret, and working the farm for twelve hours a day, he can survive public school."

"You're right. You're right. Sam is a strong little boy. But will you consider registering him for the Academy once you're eligible for the waiver?" Celia asked.

"Of course. I'll consider all possibilities presented to me that don't cost money I don't have or cannot get right now."

Celia looked relieved. "Okay, great."

Emily drank her drink in silence, the sweetness finally becoming too much, turning her stomach sour again.

"Do you mind driving back? I'm feeling a little worn out from the sun," Emily said.

"Of course. Are you ready?" Celia asked. Emily stood and felt like falling over.

"You okay?"

"Yeah, just tired," Emily said.

On the ride back to Gavin's, Emily was quiet, feeling bone-achingly tired. She remembered a trip to Whidbey Island outside Seattle that Aaron surprised her with for their seventh anniversary. He rented a cabin overlooking the Sound, and they ate lobster and crab dinners every night and had chilled champagne and strawberries waiting for them each of the four nights they spent at that cabin. They soaked in a bathtub for two and made love in front of a potbellied stove, the only source of heat for the cabin. She had never been so relaxed and calm in her life. How much was that vacation? Five thousand? More with the tickets and the souvenirs she bought, including a nice art piece from a gallery in Langley, Washington, which hung in their foyer at their house in Watchung, and a suitcase full of toys and books for Sam, who was only 3 years-old at the time. She closed her eyes. On most days she could wage the war against fair and unfair and be quite philosophical about it. However, on the drive home she grew more and more upset about the life that was taken from her.

Gavin and Sam greeted them like always when Celia drove up. He arched an eyebrow when he saw them.

"Tough day at the office?" he asked.

"It was so hot today. And people were so difficult. But we sold everything. Just took longer," Celia answered.

Gavin continued to stare at Emily as he helped unload the truck. Emily could feel herself getting overheated again and excused herself. She walked into the cool kitchen, ceiling fans on ultra high and the window unit Gavin dragged out of storage for the heat wave buzzing in the background.

Sam walked in. *"Are you okay?"*

"Yes. Just very tired. Too much sun. I think I should take us home so I can rest," she signed.

Gavin walked in a few minutes later with Celia close behind him. "Celia said you haven't been feeling well. Why don't I drive you home?" he said.

"I can drive. But I do think I should go get a bath and rest up. This was a brutal day," she said. Gavin still looked concerned.

She opened her bag and handed Gavin the receipts and cash. She suddenly felt cold and clammy, like ants were crawling on her neck. She felt herself fall over. Gavin caught her.

"Celia, go into the kitchen and get me that jar of pickles I have in the fridge."

"Come again?"

"Pickles. Fridge. Now!" Gavin barked.

Gavin carried Emily to the couch and laid her head down on the embroidered pillows. Celia ran and returned with the jar of dill pickles. Gavin screwed off the lid and lifted up a groggy Emily to drink the pickle juice. Emily tasted the brine and resisted drinking more.

"You're dehydrated and your electrolytes are out of whack. You need to drink more," he ordered her.

She sat up and drank more, frowning at the vinegar taste. Soon she felt better, less jittery and nauseated. She held the jar and looked down into it. She fished a pickle spear out and started eating it. Gavin relaxed.

"Heat exhaustion. Seen it a million times," he said as he sat on the coffee table across from the couch. Sam came and sat next to her. She offered him a pickle spear to calm the fear in his eyes.

"That is the weirdest thing I have ever seen you do, Gavin," Celia said amazed.

"Old farming trick. Salt from the brine helps bring everything back to normal."

She looked at Gavin. "Thanks. I'm not usually so faint," she joked in an attempt to hide her embarrassment. She wanted to crawl in a hole and die. She handed him back the pickle jar.

"You need to take a day off. You're working too damn hard. You need to get some rest."

She slowly stood. "Negatory. I just need to go home now and take a bath," she said.

"But our bathtub is broken," Sam signed. Celia arched her eyebrow. Emily held Sam's hands gently and moved her head in the direction of the front door.

"I'll see you all in the morning," Emily said.

Gavin looked unsure but really had no say in the matter. He stood with Celia on the porch and waved as they watched Sam and Emily get in the old Honda and drive down his gravel path.

"Sam said the bathtub was broken," Celia told Gavin.

He shook his head. "That damn house should be bulldozed to the ground," he mumbled.

Celia frowned then waved goodbye with her keys in her hands, skipping down his stairs.

He went back to the living room and picked up the invoices and cash where Emily dropped them. There were fifty invoices neatly written in her cursive script, and $600 in cash, held

Clarise Rivera

together with a rubber band. He pulled the money out and placed it in a locked drawer in his desk in an envelope on which he'd written "Emily." There was already over $2,000 in there. He still didn't know what he was going to do with it yet, but part of him knew that it was her money that he was keeping safe for her until she really needed it.

Emily sat in the kitchen at midnight in near darkness trying to handle the heat that was penetrating the house. She was wearing only a tank top and her underwear drinking a glass of ice water, nibbling on another pickle. Living with a hoarder was a lot easier in the winter, Emily decided, as the ninety-five-degree heat hung on every box, bag, empty container, and memento in that house like a blanket. Even with fans, it was still a miserable existence. She was glad she and Sam only had to endure it in the evenings.

Margaret walked into the kitchen to get a glass of water and jumped when she saw Emily.

"Lord, girl! Are you trying to give me a heart attack?"

"Sorry."

"Why are you up so late? Don't you work in the morning?"

"I work every day," Emily said softly.

Margaret raised her eyebrows and reached into the cupboard for a glass. She poured water from the pitcher in the fridge and put it back, her white, thin-laced nightgown gently moving ghostlike in the darkness. Her long hair was pinned up on top of her head.

"How are you feeling?" Margaret asked.

"Tired. Worn out. Mad. Hopeless. Pick an emotion. I'm feeling it right now."

Margaret sat at the table across from her and put her glass down. "All right, I'll bite."

"Do you know how much I had in my savings account in March? Almost $150,000. My house was paid off, my car paid off. We lived within our means. We took vacations, we ate nice meals. We didn't go without. I cannot wrap my head around why Aaron would want to steal more. We had four

90

people's yearly salaries saved away."

"Four *middle* class people's . . ."

"All to be taken away by the feds. I wish I had spent it. Bought a boat I'd only use twice a year, or a BMW or Ferrari. I should have shopped Neiman Marcus instead of Target. Bought Sam $80 t-shirts. Why not? Aaron made good money. I should have flaunted it."

"Got too much of your daddy in you. Your father was a miser, to a fault."

"Jesus, don't remind me."

"I wish I could tell you why he did it, Em. Maybe he was in some trouble. Tried to fix it this way. Made a bad choice, and it got out of hand," Margaret offered.

"What I hate most is that he did this to Sam. That he put us in a position to not offer him the best education, considering he is already going to be at a disadvantage because of his deafness. It's the reason he took that job and I stayed home. For Sam. We were committed to Sam to make sure he would be able to be okay in the world that he could not hear," Emily sighed and drank her water.

"Now I have to worry that he'll fall through the cracks, that teachers will think he's retarded and incapable of learning just because he can't hear and can't speak. Can I even stay on top of everything if I'm working 14-hour days to barely make ends meet? And what happens when the summer is over? Minimum wage at a fast-food place? How will we survive this, Margaret?"

"We will find a way."

"When? How? All I see are opportunities I can't take advantage of because I'm poor now."

"Such as?"

"I can't enroll him at the Academy Xavier goes to. Costs ten grand a semester. May as well be ten million. Seven months ago, that would have been nothing. I had that squirreled away. It was saved for this very purpose. To help Sam. Now I have to enroll him in public school where there is bare minimum special education help. In a room with 25 other kids. Where he will never learn to speak. Where I will never

91

hear him say 'I love you' or 'Mommy,'" Emily said. Her voice caught with emotion.

Margaret's eyes became teary, and she rubbed the corners with her fingertips. Emily inhaled and exhaled. She drank the rest of her water.

"I'm exhausted. I'm going to try to sleep," Emily said, and went back to the sunroom to her cot. Sam was lying on his cot wearing only his Spiderman underpants with a fan blowing full blast on him. She could see the outline of his pale chest moving up and down slowly in a deep, deep sleep. She was grateful he was resting.

Emily woke up at her usual time of 5 a.m., despite the fact she wasn't expected at Gavin's until 10 a.m. He went to church most Sundays, as did Paco and Will. Shakes took the morning to sleep off the previous night's hangover. Emily usually made breakfast for the three of them before Margaret went off to the same service Gavin attended then drove out to Gavin's house to inventory and prepare the shopping list with his Sunday paper and coupons.

She tried to go back to sleep, to no avail, and decided to take advantage of the darkness to bathe in her makeshift bathhouse on the back porch, which was walled off for privacy with lattice Emily scrounged up discarded at various places in town and contained a blue kiddie pool she got for $5 at Kroger. The one good thing about the heat wave was that the water was still warm. Every time she cleaned Gavin's bathtub, it took everything in her power not to climb in it for a good, long, hot soak.

After she dressed and combed her wet hair, she pulled down a box of cereal. She woke up starving, having skipped dinner after feeling so terrible.

A half-hour later she felt tired again and decided to lay back down on her cot with the fan blowing on her. The coolness of her wet hair combined with the lull of the fan put her back into a deep sleep, and the next things she knew it was 9 a.m. and Sam was shaking her out of a sweaty nightmare.

"Some man is here," Sam signed. He was dressed in a large

man's t-shirt and no shorts. His hair was in ten different directions.

Emily stood up and rubbed her eyes, smoothed out her hair, and walked out to the living room. She saw a man she had never seen before, standing on the porch.

"Hello?" she said as she opened the door.

"Hi, Emily? I'm Miguel Cavazos, Celia's brother-in-law. I came by to check your bathtub." He was tall and dark-skinned like Paco and wore a similar thin moustache.

"Oh, okay . . ."

Miguel noticed her concern. "Celia already prepared me for the house. No worries," Miguel said and smiled.

Emily shook her head and silently cursed Celia's ability to use sign language. She opened the door and let him in, then walked him to the bathroom.

"I'm just going to take a quick look and try to see what the problem is. Does the water run in the bath?" he asked Emily, kneeling by the tub. She was grateful she had just cleaned that bathroom two days before, and then laughed at her reasoning, as the rest of the living room and bedrooms still looked crazy.

"It's never run as long as I've been here. Sink runs, toilet runs, but no water in the tub," Emily said.

Miguel turned the knobs on the shower, and nothing came out.

"Hmm," he said.

Miguel then unscrewed the spout where the water should come out.

"It looks like galvanized pipes."

"What does that mean?"

"Galvanized pipes eventually corrode over time. That's why newer houses use copper. The pipes aren't letting water through to the shower," he said.

"So, you replace the pipes? How do you do that?"

"Tear down the wall and put in copper. Then repair that wall. Pretty simple fix," he said.

Emily shook her head. All she could see were dollar signs. Miguel examined a few more things, and actually went outside to look at the water lines.

"We can knock it out next weekend," Miguel said.

"How much?"

"Celia said whatever it cost, no worries."

"Ballpark, then, Miguel."

"Not that much. A few hundred for the pipes and to repair the wall," he assured.

Emily exhaled and extended her hand. "Thanks for coming by." He smiled and shook her hand in return.

When Miguel left, she walked back to the kitchen through the wider path that Margaret had cleared the day before. Sam was sitting at the table eating cereal.

"*Who was that man?*" he signed.

"*Celia's brother-in-law. Here to help fix the tub.*" Sam continued to read his comic book.

"*Do you want eggs or is cereal enough?*"

"*We can have eggs for lunch at Gavin's. It's too hot here when you cook.*"

She relented, because he was right. "*Get dressed. We can go when you're ready,*" she signed.

Gavin did not show up immediately after church, which was a little unusual for him. She fed Sam and Shakes egg salad sandwiches and chips after she wrote a shopping list. Gavin walked in close to 1 p.m.

"Where you been, Hass?" Shakes asked.

"Helping out an old lady at church," Gavin said and winked.

"Is that code for something?" Emily asked Shakes.

"Not sure," he mumbled.

Emily stood to make Gavin a sandwich. He gladly accepted the plate and sat at the head of the table where they were all sitting.

"So, what's on the menu this week?" he asked.

"Anything but squash. Please, dear Jesus," Shakes mumbled.

"Hey, I thought the San Antonio casserole went over well," she pouted.

"That was tasty," Shakes admitted.

"Well, if Gavin feels like splurging, we can do a lobster bake one night," Emily said. "I can show you how we do it Cape Cod style."

Gavin made an intrigued face and looked at Shakes. "Tell you what, we can do that after the last corn harvest next month. A celebration. Sound good?"

Emily grabbed a bunch of reusable bags from the pantry. "All right, we're off to the store. Any last requests?"

"Nope."

"We'll see you in a couple of hours," she said.

Gavin watched her leave and stood to put his plate in the kitchen. Shakes stood and walked toward the porch to get a smoke.

"Don't go too far. I need you for something," he said.

Shakes turned his hat brim facing backward, his universal sign that he was ready to go to work. He puffed on his Winston until Gavin came out in work clothes. Then he put the cigarette out on his work boot and pocketed the butt, a habit Natalie made him start several years back.

"Where are we going?" Shakes asked.

"Margaret's house. She needs a favor."

Shakes had never seen a garage packed so full in his entire 44 years of existence.

"Margaret, sweetheart, what the hell do you have in here?" Shakes asked. He picked up small trinkets and boxes to attempt to get past the first layer of stuff, and a small avalanche of boxes fell. Gavin shook his head, terrified about what he just signed up for.

After church Margaret had walked up to Gavin in a matter-of-fact way and told him she needed him for a mission involving Sam and Emily. Gavin immediately agreed and followed her home, where he sat in her hotter-than-hell kitchen drinking an iced tea.

"In the garage I have a 1966 Corvette. I need to pull it out and sell it for Sam to attend the Academy in the fall," Margaret said.

Gavin remained silent, and a bit confused.

Margaret took a sip of tea, paused and tried to find her words. Clearly she was not accustomed to asking for help.

"I have a lot of things in the garage. I can't seem to get to it on my own. Can you please help me with this," she said simply.

"Sure, Margaret. I'll grab Shakes and we can try to unearth it this afternoon." Margaret smiled, pleased with herself.

"How attached to this stuff are you, Margaret?" Shakes asked, lighting another cigarette.

"Most can go. I just ask that I do a quick scan of items before they are dumped."

"We need a dumpster, G. We can't do this just with just the truck."

Gavin stood and chewed his bottom lip. He was trying to figure out the best plan of action. "Why don't we move the first layer out and put it in the truck. Then I'll call Waste Management for a dumpster tomorrow," he suggested.

Shakes took a long drag and blew out a smoke. "All right," he said. Shakes left the cigarette dangling in his lips and he began to pull boxes, placing them in front of Margaret. Once Margaret looked through them, Gavin stacked them in his truck for disposal. In an hour Gavin had stacked about 20 boxes in his truck. They could see the front of the Corvette, covered in a cloth.

"How long has it been here?" Shakes asked as he gently lifted the cover.

"Ten years, give or take. It was my husband's. I just put it away when he was killed in action," she said.

After almost three hours, they only made it as deep as the front tires, and the truck was overflowing with garbage.

Shakes pulled back the cover and saw a peek-a-boo of the metallic blue car.

He whistled. "That is a thing of beauty," he said.

"Have you researched what you could get for it?" Gavin asked her. He wiped his brow with his sleeve, soaking wet from the beating sun. Margaret handed both men cold water in her light blue tumblers.

"I know Craig took a while to restore it. I think he said once it was worth about thirty grand," she said.

"Depends on the condition. Hopefully the cover kept the rodents out. But in pristine condition, these bad boys can go as high as $45,000," Shakes said. He gulped down the water. He was also soaking wet with sweat.

"I need at least $20,000. That should buy us some time," she said matter-of-factly.

Gavin gave Shakes a signal that they were through there. Both men handed her back her glasses. "We will be by tomorrow, hopefully with reinforcements," Gavin said.

"Could we not tell Emily? Not just yet?" Margaret asked.

"Sure thing, Miss Margaret," Shakes said. Gavin nodded in agreement. Margaret smiled, relieved.

Gavin and Shakes climbed in the truck and slowly drove out of her neighborhood toward the city dump.

That night the heat wave broke, sending a torrential rainstorm through Champaign County. Emily and Sam had just reached the front door when the ozone was wafting in the air, the thunder rumbled, and the lightning flashed in the dark sky.

Margaret greeted them, and Emily noticed that Margaret had cleaned out the entrance to the front door. There were no boxes in sight.

"You've been busy today," Emily said.

"Took the mind off the heat," she said simply.

Emily walked toward the kitchen and placed the bag of greens and an egg carton on the table.

"Your choice tonight is egg salad on whole wheat or a BLT cobbled together with what was left in Gavin's fridge."

"You both eat something. I'm beat. Going to turn in with a book and the rain," Margaret said. She kissed the top of Sam's head and walked off to her room.

After a quiet dinner of BLTs and ice-cold veggies and dip, Sam yawned really big and asked if it would be okay to turn in early. He wanted to lay in bed with the fan and watch the rain. The house was already feeling cooler with the 20-degree drop in temperature and the gusts of wet wind through the house.

Emily made a small tray of fruit, iced tea, and a peanut butter sandwich and walked over to Margaret's side of the house. She knocked on her door.

"Come in."

Emily walked into Margaret's room, which was still filled nearly to the ceiling with things. Her bed was cleared, with the help of Emily, and she had a romance novel on the left side by her nightstand.

"Thought you may be hungry," Emily said, and sat on the foot of the bed. She nearly fell over a stack of papers, but thankfully kept her balance of the tray.

Margaret grabbed the tray from her and put it on the clear side of the bed. Emily looked around slowly and saw Margaret's attempt at order. Bags of clothing with the tags still on them stood in a heap on the north side of the room, papers in boxes with books on the east side, and various gadgetry on the west. Her bed and end table sat on the south side of the room. Emily tried not to focus too much on the mess, because the thought of it completely stressed her out. She was grateful she was allowed to clean the kitchen, the bathroom, and the sunroom. It made her feel somewhat in control of the chaos she lived in.

"Are you all right?"

Margaret drank her tea quietly and got a far-away look. Her long, silver hair rested almost down to her waist. She looked very much her 60 years, and then some.

"Do you know how I met Craig?" Emily shook her head.

"We were at a club where they were teaching ballroom dancing. I was there with a fellow I'd been dating for a few weeks. Sergio was his name. Very Latin, with his shirt halfway unbuttoned down his hairy chest. Spoke with a heavy accent. You know the type."

"I made a deal with Sergio that if he took ballroom dancing lessons, I would take salsa lessons. So we went to these classes that were taught by this old man and woman. They had been doing this for years. And even though they didn't look like it, when their arms went around each other, they were transformed into this magical dancing duet that glided across the floor. He could move her in any direction, and she could sense what he wanted her to do before he led her to do it."

"How did Sergio dance?"

"Ha. Like a horny Latin man. He was like a puppy humping me. It was ridiculous," Margaret squealed. Emily laughed.

"At the second lesson, there was this dashing man with this young thing dancing next to us. He had the most amazing blue eyes. Clear, like the water in Maui. He kept staring at me. I swear he made my blood run hot the second I'd laid eyes on him. We were doing this ballroom dance step where you switch partners, and he was to my right. When we connected hands, it was like we were like those instructors, caught in this wonderful ballroom step, and he would twirl me and I instinctively knew what to do. It really was magical," Margaret said, and smiled at the memory.

"We dumped our dates and found a justice of the peace the next day after spending all night making love. That was it for us."

"Wow." Emily could hardly imagine running off to marry someone after only a day. She and Aaron were together almost five years before they decided to get married and were married almost four years before they brought Sam into the world. She always took her time with men, or any big decisions she had to make in her life.

"We only had three years together before that goddamn war came calling. Three beautiful years of getting to know each other. We would go out to nice dinners, take long drives in his '66 Mustang, watch movies, sleep in late some weekends after staying up all night talking. He was my best friend. He knew everything about me. I knew everything about him. We talked so effortlessly. We were so in love."

Emily bowed her head and felt so sad for Margaret, but she felt sad for herself as well. She was describing a lot of what she and Aaron had in their marriage. They used to talk for hours every night. There was so much to say, so much to learn about each other.

"It's been almost ten years since he's been gone. He's been gone three times longer than I was with him, and yet here I sit with my thoughts of him spinning me around in his arms. It's the only thing that keeps me going me these days."

Emily held on to Margaret's hand and watched a silent tear fall down her wrinkled face.

"It's late. Best be getting some rest for work tomorrow," Margaret said.

Emily stood slowly, feeling sad and grief-stricken. She bent down and kissed her aunt's cheek very quickly before leaving her alone.

The house was quiet except for the sound of rain. Emily walked out to the back porch, passing the sunroom. Sam was asleep when she checked in on him, lulled to sleep by the cooler weather and the rainstorm on the windows. She stood on the porch and watched the rainfall. She covered her face with her hands and wept.

Gavin and Shakes were gone most of the morning for five days straight. Emily didn't realize they were not out in the fields until Will accidentally let it slip over lunch on Friday.

"Well, when you're done with Margaret's, we can talk about when the corn should come down," he said to Gavin. Gavin gave Will a stern look and Will grimaced, realizing what he had done.

"You've been at Margaret's? Why have you been at Margaret's?" Emily asked Gavin.

"She'll have to be the one to tell you that," Gavin said.

That night Emily drove up and saw a shiny, metallic blue Corvette in the driveway with a "for sale" sign. Margaret told Emily the dumpster on her property was for the neighbors who were doing a kitchen renovation and offered Margaret to use it too for exchange for the storage space.

"Margaret, no," Emily said, as she walked into the house.

"No, what? It's done. An ad's been placed in the Penny Saver, and Shakes has two men interested in it coming out tomorrow."

"We don't need money that bad," Emily said.

Margaret looked at her with a moment of clarity that she had not seen in her aunt in a long time. "It's time, Em. Sam needs that money more than I need the car gathering dust in the garage."

Emily placed her hand to her chest, humbled by Margaret's gesture. "Thank you."

Margaret winked.

CHAPTER ELEVEN

Emily sat in a small room at a long table surrounded by eight men and women, all special education staff that included an occupational therapist, speech therapist, and two people who specialized in hearing issues in young children. She hated this part of Sam's schooling. She always felt they were under a microscope, being analyzed from every angle. She could already feel the pool of sweat underneath her blouse.

Dr. Taylor, the Director of the Academy, sat at the head of the table opposite Emily. She was an older woman, with short, gray hair, dressed professionally in black slacks and a white silk shirt. She pulled out her glasses and set them on the table next to a file that contained Sam's evaluation.

"Mrs. Mitchell, thank you so much for coming out to meet with us and for allowing us to meet Sam. What a beautiful and happy boy," she said. Emily smiled shyly.

"We are going to go part by part with the evaluation and give the findings that the team found." Emily took a deep breath and sat up straight, full of anticipation.

"Mr. Cantu is our occupational therapist. Roland, if you will..."

"Sure thing. I spent about an hour with Sam and put him through some tests for strength, coordination and for gross and fine motor skills. As you know, he's a strong boy, able to climb well, balance on both legs well. We had him do some fine pinching, picking up small things like beads and putting them in small containers. Again, he did well. Cutting, holding the scissors and pencils, again, all performed well. We believe there are no issues with his gross motor and fine motor functions."

"Thank you, Roland. And Mrs. Mitchell, if you have any questions during this briefing, please feel free to interrupt," Dr. Taylor said. "Given the recent tragedy with his father, we also had him evaluated by Dr. Gibson, our resident psychologist. Gina, if you will."

Gina was a younger woman, a newer psychologist. Emily felt dread come over her.

"Well, let me just start by saying that Sam is a really sweet child, and I am so happy to have had the chance to talk to him. We discussed his life a bit before March, what he did at school, his daily activities. We eased into the relationship with his father, and with you. As expected, his father's passing was quite shocking. He's still somewhat confused about why he had to leave New Jersey after his father died. Can I ask you a bit more about that?"

Eight sets of eyes were suddenly on Emily. She felt a cold sweat on the back of her neck. "Well, my husband worked on Wall Street and was involved in some deals that were not exactly legal. After he died, federal agents came and confiscated all our earthly possessions."

"Oh, I'm so sorry," Dr. Taylor said.

"What did you tell Sam about that?" Dr. Gibson asked.

Emily tried to remember. Did she say anything specific to him as she ran to scramble to maintain what she could of value before she was placed on the streets all alone? Where was he when she was frantically calling people to help? In her memories she could not even see his face, just the panic and the rage that she had toward Aaron.

"I don't think we really talked about it. As we were on the bus to come to Ohio, I made mention that his dad made a bad business choice and we had to wait to see if we could get the house back," Emily said.

"And Mr. Mitchell passed from a heart attack? Is that correct? Sam said something about his father's heart," Dr. Gibson said. *God, please stop,* Emily thought.

Emily swallowed and tears stung her eyes. "Yes," she lied.

The looks of concern and pity around the room nearly broke Emily, but she blinked back the tears and wiped her eyes with a tissue that was passed to her.

"With time, and maybe weekly counseling sessions, we

would like to work toward getting Sam the skillset to cope with his father's death, of talking through some of the emotions that he has, to ease some of the confusion."

"Absolutely. Whatever you can do to help," Emily said.

"Well, let's move on to Justin. Justin McFadden is our audiologist," Dr. Taylor said.

Justin proceeded with his report, detailing the structures of the ear that were affected, which was something Emily had heard about multiple times from multiple audiologists.

"And Tonya Vickman is our speech therapist," Dr. Taylor said.

Tonya had clear blue eyes and dark hair. She smiled a tight smile at Emily, and Emily felt her stomach drop. She just knew she was about to get bad news.

"I know that speech was one of your main concerns about Sam. And let me start by saying that I have been a speech therapist for almost fifteen years, and in my experience, most deaf children, if they have not started speaking by age 5, well, the likelihood is that they will never speak."

Emily felt sick.

"Not to say that it can never happen, but it is something we will have to evaluate deeper when he is enrolled. My initial evaluation shows that he can make some sounds, but letter formations, vowels, consonants are all deeply lacking. He has no real basis of sound formation," Vickman said.

Emily felt the tears fall. She was not prepared for this news. She bowed her head and felt a few hands patting her on the back.

"Well, we will not give up hope that there is a chance he can use his voice. Please know that we will do everything within our power to figure out what we are working with here," Dr. Taylor said.

Emily shook her head as she tried desperately to regain her composure. He will never talk? How will he never talk?

"Let's take a 5-minute break, shall we?" Dr. Taylor said.

Everyone but Dr. Taylor stood and left the room. She closed the door and sat in the chair closest to Emily. She poured her some water from the pitcher on the table and placed it near Emily, who whispered thank you.

"My daughter Stacey is autistic. We didn't know much about it back then, really. There wasn't a real good name for it. I had doctor after doctor tell me that she was retarded and should be put in a home. I wouldn't do it. I was her mother. Why would I send her away because she wasn't like other children?"

"Stacey is 45 now. She lives with me still, but has a part-time job, and gardens and reads. She doesn't talk much, but she is happy. And that makes me happy," Dr. Taylor said.

Emily smiled sadly and pressed the tissues to her eyes. Dr. Taylor grabbed her hand.

"Don't give up hope. Not yet."

"I won't," Emily whispered.

"Good girl."

A few minutes later, the team rejoined them in the conference room, and an hour later, Emily signed no less than forty pieces of paper to enroll Sam into the Academy for the fall semester. She handed over a cashier's check for $10,000, compliments of Margaret and the Corvette that sold for just under $30,000.

Emily had promised Dr. Taylor not to give up, but it was hard not to be extremely discouraged after meeting with the specialists. Paco took her to lunch after the evaluation at a small pub over by OSU and ordered her beer after beer while she talked incessantly, wondering why she would bother spending that kind of money if he was never going to speak. After she was done crying and drinking, Paco drove her back to Champaign County, where she finally passed out, exhausted from her ugly, sniveling cries.

Celia showed up later that evening to check on her and begged her to consider the other wonderful points of the school. She tried to be encouraging.

"They said they would work with him, and there could be a chance he can talk."

Margaret agreed that hope should not be lost, but despite

their encouragement, Emily continued to have internal arguments with herself day and night, talking herself in and out of enrollment. By day two of these internal debates, she fell into a deep depression.

Gavin could tell something significant happened after the evaluation at the Academy, and finally broke down and asked Paco what the hell happened after the second day of watching Emily sleepwalk through her daily chores. Paco told him about the meeting, and how disappointed Emily was with the diagnosis, but Gavin didn't know the impact of it all until he walked into the barn after breakfast and found Emily near Lily's stall, weeping. This was not a normal sniffling, but genuinely painful sobbing, a sound that made him feel a little misty around the eyes. She was hunched over the door of the stall, Lily sniffing at her head trying to make sense of the commotion.

He paused and almost turned around to run away. Who the hell was he to offer her any comfort? He often found himself doing the same thing when life got overwhelming, near the same horse. In fact, Lily had seen more than her fair share of human tears in the last five years.

Emily's tears felt like tiny pinpricks in his mind, painful and heart wrenching. He finally walked up to her and quietly handed her his bandana, grateful he put a clean one in his pocket that morning. She took it and huddled in the corner, not making eye contact. He was at a loss for words and stood there awkwardly until he finally had the idea to saddle up the horses and take her for a ride.

She rode Lily and he rode Bob for about twenty minutes in silence until they reached a stream with two large, fallen trees by it. He and Natalie rode out here a lot and did a fair amount of skinny-dipping in that stream, cloaked in woods covered in pine trees. He did not even realize where he was taking Emily until the horses stopped, purely out of instinct.

Emily let Gavin tie up the horses, and she walked by the stream, the early sun warming the land.

"I feel like I was told there is no Santa Claus. Devastated, and so stupid for believing. What a child I was," she said softly.

"There is nothing wrong with you hoping for Sam to talk. You are his mother. Hope is what parents do. Hope is good," Gavin said. He jiggled pebbles in his hand and skipped them across the stream.

Emily shook her head, and the tears started up again. Before the second tear could fall down her face, Gavin took her into his arms, breaking all the unspoken rules he had for himself about women. She relented and relaxed into his arms, her face cradling the nook of his collarbone. She didn't know how badly she needed his hug, his strength, but with that simple gesture, the grief lessened, and she felt realigned. He only hugged her for a few precious seconds, but in his alternate mind, the one that screamed "what the hell are you doing?!" the hug lasted for an hour, all day, several days, a month, a year. And he hated and he was relieved when she finally let go of him.

They sat together by one of the fallen logs, and he handed her a peppermint that he had in his pocket. She smiled gratefully and took it.

"Bet you're wishing you hired some old man to do your cooking right about now. Way less drama," she joked, popping the mint in her mouth.

"No."

She glanced at him sideways, but he didn't meet her eyes— he couldn't. They would give away too much of what he felt.

CHAPTER TWELVE

Emily watched Sam as he ate his Frosted Flakes at Margaret's small table.

"You're staring," Sam signed and exhaled, annoyed.

"Sorry. I'm just realizing how big you're getting. Sue me." Emily wiped her eyes.

Sam wore a white polo and light khaki pants, the Academy's uniform. His hair was neatly combed and looked great, thanks to a last-minute haircut by Margaret the night before. He had grown four inches since the last school year, and he was turning into quite the young man.

"You should eat something, too. You've been running around like a crazy person these last few days," Margaret chastised. Emily ignored her and sipped on her coffee while practicing slow, deep breathing.

Paco, Celia, and Xavier pulled up a few minutes later in Paco's truck, and Emily rushed to get her disposable camera to take a picture of Sam in his uniform. He groaned and stood in front of the refrigerator with his Transformers backpack and a scowl on his face.

"Please smile for me," she begged. Sam smiled a big, toothy, fake smile and crossed his eyes. Emily snapped the picture, annoyed. Margaret started chuckling.

"Don't encourage him," she mumbled.

"Oh, hell, he's exactly like you. To the core." Emily rolled her eyes and all three of them walked to the door, out to Paco's truck.

School Paco and Celia were very different from summertime Paco and Celia. Both wore blue and white polo shirts with the emblem of the school embroidered on the left side and dark slacks. Paco was clean-shaven and Celia's wild hair was pulled back in a tight French braid. She wore very little makeup.

"Good morning, Champaign County!" Paco yelled from the driver's seat and smiled. Emily laughed. Paco could always make her laugh. Celia walked around the front of the truck. She hugged Emily and Margaret, smelling fresh and clean, with only a hint of her perfume.

"Are you ready for a great school year?" Celia signed and smiled. Sam nodded. "We should be home by 4:30, okay?"

Emily smiled tightly, crossing her arms in front of her. She shivered a little, even though it was in the mid-70s. Sam looked at her and impulsively hugged her middle and ran to the truck before she could react.

"He'll do great! No worries, my friend. It's going to be a beautiful day!" Paco assured. Emily smiled bravely and waved until her armed ached, even when the truck was no longer on their street.

"Do you want to get some breakfast? How about McDonald's? Buy one, get one Egg McMuffin?" Margaret offered.

"I should head to Gavin's," Emily said, and walked back inside. She wanted to get away so she could cry and be miserable in private.

As she drove to Gavin's her eyes teared up so much, she could not see. She pulled over on the side of the road and sobbed. She never used to react this way to Sam going off to school. What the hell was wrong with her? She tried to get it together, telling herself he was fine, that he needed to be around kids his age, and that she was more upset than he was. After a few minutes, she felt stable enough to drive the rest of the way to the farm.

Things had slowed down considerably now that hay season was winding down. Gavin was usually in the house waiting for her when she showed up, instead of working in the barn. He had her coffee and cream poured in her yellow cup the second he heard the humming of her Honda in the driveway. Today, though, she prayed he was focused on the animals, but no such luck. He sat at the dining room table with his green cup next to her yellow cup and focused squarely on her puffy eyes the second she walked through the door.

"Tough morning?" he asked gently. He stood and handed her the cup. She shook her head, taking the cup and walking to the kitchen to start breakfast. He followed her.

"Why don't we go out for breakfast? I'm not expecting anyone this morning. We could run to Columbus. Maybe hit one of those nice diners by the campus?"

"I won't be good company today," she mumbled. Gavin looked disappointed. He opened his mouth to attempt to change her mind but was distracted when he heard a truck coming up his driveway. They both looked out the kitchen window.

"Who could this be?"

He walked out to the porch and up to the white Chevy Dually truck he had never seen before.

Gavin was still selling his smaller bales of hay to local farmers, and it was common for various trucks to drive up and down the driveway, hauling away his bales of alfalfa, timothy, and clover for their livestock. Emily walked out to the porch with her yellow cup in her hands, equally curious, but mostly out of caution. There were times when she felt safe and isolated on the farm, but other times when she realized that isolation could be dangerous if the wrong people happened to drive up to your front door.

Gavin talked to the young man briefly before pointing him to the back area of the barn where his hay was kept. Emily sat on the porch swing and waited patiently for Gavin to reappear, keeping careful watch on the barn. It was a bit absurd for her to keep watch, but she did know where he kept his shotgun just in case things got bad.

The weather was beautiful this time of year, highs in the mid-70s with clear blue skies. Emily couldn't help but swing a little more, with the smell of autumn enveloping the farm, pointing her worn-out Nikes out in front of her. September was biding time, waiting for the corn to be harvested, and it allowed everyone a much-needed breather. Both Shakes and

Will took a few days off to unwind and prepare for the final corn harvest. Gavin rarely traveled, preferring to stay home and remain busy, cleaning the house and barn and preparing for the winter months.

"Winter is Gavin's time to rest. He runs ragged until he collapses and hibernates like a bear," Shakes told Emily.

During this lull in the harvest, Emily started to can and make meals for Gavin over the winter. She jarred her preserves and began canning okra, peas, and corn during the summer, which she stored in his nearly empty kitchen shelves. She made small casseroles, all labeled with ingredients and specific instructions on how to heat them up and placed them in his deep freeze. She did not like the idea of him reverting back to his beef jerky-and-eggs-only ways. She would at least give him a shot at sustenance when she was not around.

Gavin brought out several bales of hay to the front of the barn. She was always amazed how strong he was, throwing what was probably 50 pounds with little effort to the back of the truck. After fifteen bales were loaded, the man handed Gavin cash, honked, and drove off.

He walked back to the porch and sat next to her on the porch swing.

"Not a bad haul. Who was he?" she asked.

"Some new guy who was passing through from Union County. Just starting out. Has a couple of Paint horses."

"What do they paint? Houses? Landscapes?" Gavin laughed, and Emily smiled into her yellow cup.

They sat there and gently moved back and forth on the porch swing. Both were lost in their own thoughts. Emily watched Gavin looking out to the fields. He looked content and peaceful. She was happy that she could witness that part of him, as it was rare for either one of them to feel any sort of contentment these days.

"Feeling better?" he asked.

"Yes. And no," she laughed a short laugh. "I'm pathetic. A lost cause."

"Doubtful," he said. They continued to swing.

"This is nice," she said. Gavin agreed. "But I'm hungry." He stood and grabbed her hand to lift her up. "What did you decide?" he asked, still holding her hand.

"Let's go to Columbus," she said. She did not want to let him go today.

They drove for an hour into Columbus, Gavin navigating his Ford F-250 effortlessly through the University District, only having to retrace his movements once to find a proper parking place. During the ride in they made small talk. Gavin told stories about his childhood in Tennessee and Emily shared with him what going to boarding school was like.

"So, you didn't all shower together like in those bad 80s movies?"

"Nor did we braid each other's hair topless," she said.

"Well, that's a damn shame. My whole perception has been a lie," Gavin said, and chuckled. Emily punched him lightly on the arm.

"Hey, I only had that to draw from. Sue me."

He took her to a place called the Hang Over Easy, a breakfast joint that had wonderful dishes such as the Dirty Sanchez, Ramblin' Man, and chicken and waffles.

"They also have burgers the size of your head . . . if you are so inclined to eat that today," Gavin said, as they were seated at a table.

"I do like a good burger," she said, looking at the menu.

"I know."

They ordered iced teas, and the waitress came back with their drinks and took their orders.

"I'm torn between the green eggs and ham and the chicken and waffles," she told Gavin.

"Let's order one of each and share," he suggested. Emily smiled and handed the menu back to the waitress.

"It's quiet here," she said.

"Kids are probably in class right now."

"Do you come here a lot?"

"Not a lot. A few times. I like the campus feel. Reminds me of younger days."

Emily smiled and remembered her days at the University of Texas with Aaron—the feel of the vastness of the campus as she walked it as a freshman, and how she felt giddy every year when she bought her new books for the school year. She loved the feeling of belonging with the other students and the feeling of invincibility, like there was nothing she couldn't do. Hubris of the young.

"I think I know what has been getting to me the last few days." She stirred her tea with her straw and stabbed the lemon with it until it released the pulp. Gavin squinted his eyes and put his palms down on the table, waiting patiently.

"When did you really feel that Natalie was gone forever? That she was never coming back?" she asked softly.

The memory hit Gavin immediately, and it slammed against his chest, slowly knocking the wind out of him. He wasn't prepared for her question. He cleared his throat, but the words still did not come right away. Her cheeks flushed when she realized how crushed he looked.

"I really need to stop asking you these questions. I'm sorry," she said, and took a long sip of tea. He cleared his throat, inhaled deeply, and spoke.

"One day, about three months in, Josh asked me what's for dinner. I went to the fridge, and it was bare. Then I went to the freezer, and it was empty. All the casseroles the church ladies made were gone. And then it hit me that Nat was gone. She wasn't deployed or TDY. She was gone and she was never coming back." Emily sat stoic as he spoke.

"I am having that moment now. With Sam starting school, and Aaron not around to see him go through all of this." she said softly. "I've realized that my freezer is empty." Her eyes filled with tears again.

The food came before he could say anything. Emily cleared her throat and began to rearrange things, moving a waffle from her plate to Gavin's plate and scooping green eggs beside it. He touched her shaking hands to make them still. She exhaled deeply.

"Ask me what I did after I realized she was gone," he said.

113

Emily shrugged.

"I called for reinforcements," he said. His green eyes were clear and looked directly at her. He willed her to understand she was not alone. She had friends. She had him.

She smiled through her tears, gently brushing them away. She patted his hands, and gently released her hands from his.

They ate silently for a few minutes. "So, do you like green eggs and ham?" she asked him.

"I do!! I like them, Sam-I-am! And I would eat them in a boat, and I would eat them with a goat . . . and I will eat them in the rain. And in the dark. And on a train," Gavin recited while cutting his ham.

She giggled and he grinned. Her laughter melted a bit of him that had gone cold. As he sat there in the restaurant with her, watching her daintily tasting waffles covered with syrup and topped with fried chicken, he realized this was the best date he had never been on

CHAPTER THIRTEEN

Emily packed up the last of the supplies for the lobster bake in the back of Gavin's truck and checked her list before shoving the piece of paper in her back jeans pocket and lifting up the truck's gate.

"Hey, Gavin, don't forget the water, okay?" she called.

Gavin walked out of the house holding Stripey, the orange kitten, who was now considerably bigger. Gavin scratched Stripey behind his ears and gently dropped him on the porch.

"Paco was bringing it. He texted and said he was ten minutes out with everyone in tow. He may reach the stream before us."

"Great," she said.

She opened the door to the driver's side of his truck to drive, and Gavin smiled an amused smile as he opened the door to the passenger's side, never remembering a time when he ever sat there.

When he slammed the door, Emily started the engine and maneuvered the truck toward the back forty, where the lobster bake was being held. She was a thousand times more confident than that first day on the job, where the size of the vehicle overwhelmed her. He took pride that she was now a country girl, fearless and knew her way around his farm. Plus, she looked pretty fine driving his truck.

Shakes and Will were already assembling the bonfire when they drove up. Months of gathering fallen branches and old seedlings that threatened to overtake the farmland resulted in a few bonfires each year.

"Did you bring snacks? I don't think I can wait for these sea critters to bake," Shakes said. Emily handed him a crockpot with buffalo shrimp dip.

"Aw, hells yeah! Where are the chips?"

"Keep unloading," Gavin ordered. Shakes grumbled but

continued to help.

Paco drove up half a second later and honked his horn twice while Emily and Gavin waved and walked up to the truck. Paco opened the door and frowned.

"Get these THINGS out of my truck!"

"Since when do you call our family THINGS?" Emily joked.

"I swear to the baby Jesus, Em, these damn lobsters were scraping the box all the way from Columbus. Like they were saying 'Paaaaaaaaaaco, freeeeeeee us . . . Paaaaaaaaaaaaaco, don't kill us.'"

"Well, they'll be dinner in an hour. You can have your sweet revenge on them," Emily said. She hugged Sam, Margaret, and Celia and fist-bumped Xavier before walking to the backseat of Paco's truck to retrieve the two large boxes of lobsters.

She stumbled to lift them, tripping over backward right into Gavin, who instinctively grabbed her hips. "Are you okay?" Gavin breathed. Emily nodded and gently fumbled out of his arms, feeling her ears turn pink. His touch always seemed to make her blush these days.

"Lord, Paco, how many did you buy?" she asked, clearing her throat.

"All of them. I know how Shakes eats," Paco said. Everyone turned and looked at Shakes sitting on the bed of Gavin's truck with a crockpot of dip on his lap and a half-eaten bag of tortilla chips.

Everyone gathered around and watched Emily and Margaret assemble five large pots with potatoes, corn, sausage, clams, shrimp, and three lobsters in each. Margaret sprinkled all of the pots with Old Bay seasoning and handed Will and Gavin the prepared loads for the fire. They assembled them in a smaller grill fire that they had built closer to the water. When those pots were going strong, Emily passed around drinks for the adults, Cape Cods, specifically for the occasion, and the kids had cranberry coolers without alcohol.

Will brought his cornhole games, and soon teams formed to start a tournament. Will and Celia. Paco and Margaret.

Gavin and Emily. Shakes and the two kids. Margaret was a natural at the game and beat everyone by double-digit points. Shakes kept whining that she was cheating, and she kept teasing him that he was just sore that an old woman was beating him. Soon after, it was time to eat, and Celia and Shakes laid out butcher paper on the folding tables they assembled by the water. Gavin helped Emily turn the steaming hot pots over on the butcher paper, spilling out red potatoes, corn, shrimp, clams, sausage, and lobster on the 6-foot-long tables.

"I feel like crying. That's such a beautiful sight," Shakes said.

Everyone took a seat and passed around rolls and salad to accompany the lobster bake. Emily sat by Sam, who expertly pulled the claws off the lobsters and the mantle off the clams, dipping the meat in melted butter. He showed Celia and Paco the best part of the lobsters and stopped them from eating the green mushy stuff. "*It's bitter and gross,*" Sam signed.

Will struggled with a claw and Emily leaned over and helped him.

"Thank you kindly."

"No problem. I guess you have never been to New England?" Emily asked.

"Hell, I've never really been outside Ohio. Except for the places you can drive nearby—Indiana, Michigan, West Virginia."

"Really? You should travel more, Will. A history buff like you?"

Emily knew Will only watched the History Channel and always had a non-fiction book in his truck. He read about Lincoln, Carter, and the untold stories of the Louisiana Purchase during the summer. Will held a degree from OSU in history, but never got a chance to use it. His father had a sudden heart attack, and Will chose to go back home and run the farm to help his mother out.

"Go see the sights. D.C. in the spring. Or go see the leaves change next month. Vermont. Maine . . . avoid Rhode Island. Whole state smells like fish."

"She's not lying. Rhode Island does have a strange smell to it," Margaret agreed.

"It's awfully far away," he said.

"Four hours by plane, right Margaret?"

"Maybe less. It's about two hours to New York. Maine is not much farther up."

"Your boys are grown. Gainfully employed. You worked hard all summer. Go enjoy your break!" Emily encouraged.

"I'll think about it," he said, and smiled.

"So, what do you do in the winter, Shakes?" Emily asked.

Shakes smiled while peeling shrimp. "Try to find a nice warm body to share it with," he said.

"Girl, he ain't lying. Every year. A different chic. What was the last one's name? Stella?" Celia said.

"STELLA!" yelled Gavin and Will in unison. Everyone laughed.

"I'm what you call a seasonal romantic," Shakes said.

"Oh, is that what you call it?" Gavin teased.

"Yes. And I already reactivated my online Match.com account. I'm ready for love."

"Oh, boy," said Paco.

The conversations ebbed and flowed as each person focused on food and got lost in the familiarity of good friends and a good time. When each person was so full and could barely move, everyone gathered their trash in two big, black trash bags and took turns helping Emily stack the empty dishes and pots. At dusk, Shakes poured kerosene on the pile of wood for the bonfire and lit it, and everyone cheered.

The night held a chill in the air, promising the change of seasons. A few trees on Gavin's land started showing signs of color. Strong yellows and a few hints of red were in the distant tree lines. The warmth of the fire brought everyone closer together, sitting on logs, watching the gigantic flames flicker.

Emily passed around sticks for marshmallows, and each person took turns roasting them and assembling S'mores. Gavin bit into his, sending a trail of white goo down his chin. Emily smiled and took a napkin to help him remove it.

"Thanks. I can never eat these things without making a mess," he said.

"Me neither," she said, showing him her hands covered in chocolate. Paco pulled out his guitar from his truck and began tuning it.

"I'm taking requests," he said.

"I request that you don't play the guitar," Shakes said.

The evening ended only after all the beer was finished, Paco sang through the five songs he barely knew, and the fire died down to smoldering ashes. Will and Gavin took buckets and doused the final flames with water. Harvest was officially over.

The next morning, Emily reported for work, but she knew it would be the last time in a long while. Gavin had hinted she could stick around, maybe clean or cook for him and Shakes, but she knew he was just being generous. She didn't feel right about taking his money when he had saved so much to finally replace the barn. Gavin handed her the yellow cup with coffee in it and smiled sadly.

"I wanted to show you what I did for you while you were working out in the fields," she said.

She walked into his pantry and showed him the canned items, neatly labeled and stacked in a very organized fashion. She opened his deep freeze and pointed out the flat Ziploc bags. "I put the instructions on the outside. Take one out overnight and put it in the fridge. Then you just dump it in the crockpot in the morning and it will be ready for you at night," she said. She closed the freezer door. "I put them in smaller portions. If you have company, like Josh or Shakes, just pull out more to cook," she said.

As she spoke, he felt a panic that she was really about to leave his land for the last time. He had a terrible feeling he would never see her again.

"So, that's it. I'm going to finish your laundry and then, that's all she wrote," she said, and smiled.

"Well, maybe I'll have you make me lunch before you leave. For old time's sake," he said. His voice shook ever so slightly. If she caught the sadness in his tone, she did not show it on her face.

"Of course. Any requests?" she asked.

"Surprise me," he said.

"Are you going out to run errands?" she asked.

"No."

"Great, then I can put you to work," she said.

She decided on chili and cornbread. Gavin hung around the kitchen and watched her cook, offering to help, but she just let him sit there and take in her presence for the last time.

When they sat at the kitchen island, like they had back in June, they both clinked the silverware in the Blue Willow bowls and felt a sense of déjà vu. They ate in silence for a while.

"Will you come visit us?" she asked.

He smiled. "Of course," he said.

"Well, if I'm going to be at Margaret's for a while, I intend to get that house in shape before the winter," she said.

"If you need help with that, just holler," he said.

"I may take you up on that," she suggested.

"Happy to help anyway I can."

"I want to thank you for all the help you gave to me and Sam this summer. We would have never made it without you," she said.

He felt a lump in his throat. "It was my pleasure," he said.

They both finished their chili in silence, slowly, not wanting to rush the moment. Gavin took their bowls and washed them in the sink while she dried them with his green and white dishtowel.

"I will miss this kitchen. Margaret's is not nearly as sunny," she said.

"You're welcome to use it any time."

When the last of the food was put away and the last of the laundry was placed in his white and blue laundry basket, Emily stood at the doorway and paused.

Gavin walked to his desk and handed her the envelope where he kept all the farmer's market cash. She took it from him and opened it, eying her handwriting and the receipts that she meticulously wrote out. She looked at him shocked.

"I can't take this. This was for you and the barn."

"I took half for the barn. Half for you. To get you through the winter," he said. Emily did not argue. Instead, she hugged him tightly, burying her head in his chest. He closed his eyes, took in her vanilla smell, and exhaled.

"You're an angel, Gavin Shaw," she whispered.

He shook his head. This was too hard for both of them.

He walked her to her car and watched as she climbed behind the wheel. "So, back to work in May?" he asked.

She smiled. "Unless I win the lottery. May it is," she said. She waved as she drove down his gravel driveway, until he was nothing but a spec in her rearview mirror. Somewhere between his land, and Will's house, she pulled over and cried. Back on the farm, Gavin sat at the kitchen island holding the dishtowel that she used to dry dishes and prepared himself to get used to the quiet again.

CHAPTER FOURTEEN

Gavin stopped by a week and a half before Halloween with three pumpkins he had picked up when he was driving by a friend's farm in Columbus. He somehow made it to the front door balancing all three, and Emily laughed when she saw him. She handed one to Sam and carried one while holding the door open for Gavin to walk through.

Emily had done amazing work to the house over the last few weeks. She held true to her promise that if she was going to be unemployed, she was going to get Margaret's house back to a livable condition. The living room was completely clear, and a brown sofa and loveseat were facing a small TV. Pictures hung neatly on the walls, a tapestry of Margaret's life and adventures over the years.

"Place looks great!" Gavin said.

"Thanks. It's still a work in progress," she said. She led him to the kitchen and placed the pumpkins on the kitchen counter.

"Her room is still a mess, and the guest room is still covered from top to bottom. And the garage. Lord don't get me started on the garage. I almost cried when she filled it up again," she said.

The smell of Emily's roast chicken wafted from the kitchen, the one she made that first day they met, with lemons and rosemary. His mouth instinctively watered. He couldn't remember the last time he had turned on his stove. He had been subsisting on beef jerky and eggs for the last few weeks.

Emily saw him inhale deeply. "You're staying for dinner. It's the least I can do for the thoughtful gift. Plus, I can't carve these things worth a damn. Last time I tried I got four stiches after a long wait in the ER," she said.

"Well, you pulled my arm," he said, and sat down at the kitchen table. She poured him a glass of iced tea and put a small cranberry and orange scone in front of him. He took one bite and tried not to moan in pleasure.

"How have you been? It's been a while," she said.

"Busy. Crazy busy. Got the blueprints for the new barn, planning for the spring. I'm thinking of going down to Tennessee for Christmas. See my son," he said.

"I'm glad," she said.

"This is really good," he said, holding up the scone.

"Are you eating since I've been gone? Heating up those casseroles?"

"A few."

Sam tugged on his arm, hands moving a mile a minute.

"He wants to know how the kittens are doing. Stripey, Garfield, and Moose," she said.

Gavin signed, *"Getting big."*

Sam smiled at Gavin's attempt at sign language. "*You're getting good!*" Sam signed.

"*Not yet. Still learning,*" Gavin signed. Sam disappeared down to the sunroom to get something.

"Any luck with a job yet?" he asked.

"Not yet. Hard to even get an interview. I've applied everywhere—Kroger, Dollar General, McDonald's. I'm hoping with the holidays I may be able to get some part-time work," she said. Gavin sat quietly, thinking, scheming.

"I've gotten some work baking. I think I am going to try Celia's suggestion about advertising for the holiday baking season. It'll hopefully bring some income in. Keep the lights on. Give Sam a decent Christmas," she said. She stood up and started peeling potatoes.

"You can still come work for me," he said.

She smiled patiently at him. "You said it yourself. Harvest begins in May," she said.

Sam reappeared with a workbook from school. He wanted to show Gavin his high scores. Gavin pulled on his glasses and thumbed through the entire workbook very carefully.

"*Great job!*" he signed. Sam beamed with pride.

"Paco says that he is getting on great in school. The speech therapist is making some good strides with him."

"They are. Slow progress. But I think being around Paco, Celia, and Xavier helps tremendously. They really are amazing, I tell you. Some of the most talented special education teachers I've ever met," she said.

"Where is Margaret tonight?"

"Playing bingo with the hens from church," Emily said.

Gavin chuckled. "Oh, the hens," he said, and got up to walk around the living room. Emily followed him and they sat on the couch that had never been visible before.

"This is really not a bad house. Nice hardwood floors," he said, tapping them with his boot.

"Margaret always did have an eye for unique beauty. It's too bad most of her most eccentric things are buried below junk. She used to have these fantastic knick-knacks from her travels. She would pick up the most obscure things on the street—a broken fork from a street vendor in Vietnam, a folded origami crane made out of the wrapper of a bottle of Coke, all in Japanese from her trip to Tokyo. Her house in Galveston told these tales just from the knick-knacks."

"Sounds like she has some amazing stories to tell," Gavin said.

"She did. She was always the entertaining one, living life to the fullest. I was the boring housewife. I would call her just to hear her tell the tale of how the newspaper boy had a thing for her and she was thinking of dressing up like Anne Bancroft and reenacting a scene from *The Graduate*." Gavin laughed.

"Seriously. I was like 'Margaret, you will scare that poor kid shitless if you do that,'" Emily said, laughing.

Gavin got a far-off look. It occurred to him just how much he really missed Emily, just talking to her and being around her every day. With Shakes seeing a new woman in Greene County, and Will traveling to Vermont to see the leaves change colors, he was really feeling quite lonely.

"You need to come by more," she told him, reading his thoughts.

"I do," he said.

He looked down and berated himself quietly for not

coming by earlier. Why did he deny himself this simple pleasure of her friendship and company? There was no harm in being her friend. She patted his arm and jumped up to check the chicken.

"This meal reminds me of the day we first met," Gavin said.

Emily smiled. "That's right—I did make you this. Hmmm. How poetic. We should call it 'our meal'." She winked at him. He hated to admit to himself that the silliness of that statement meant so damn much to him.

"All right. I like the sound of that."

The three of them ate dinner around Margaret's small kitchen table. Sam told more tales of school and what he was learning. Gavin told them about movies he watched, the new barn design, how he was thinking of getting another horse and adding an extra acre for more crops to sell at the farmer's market in Dayton. Emily kept filling their plates until Gavin said he was going to pop.

Afterwards, Gavin and Sam drew designs on pumpkins with a Sharpie while sitting in the living room watching *It's the Great Pumpkin Charlie Brown*. Emily toasted pumpkin seeds coated with brown sugar, butter, and pumpkin pie spice while Gavin pulled out his pocketknife and carefully carved out the lopsided faces. At the end of the night, three ghoulishly carved pumpkins greeted Margaret as she came home from bingo. She clapped when she saw them, squealing with delight.

"Gavin Shaw, is there no end to your talents?" Margaret asked.

Gavin blushed. "I think I draw the line at pumpkin carving," he said bashfully.

"Oh, I sincerely doubt that. I suspect you are talented at most things—at least those that count," she said, and winked.

Emily shook her head and smiled at Margaret's attempt to flirt with Gavin. "Careful, I think she's got that Anne Bancroft outfit at easy reach," Emily muttered under her breath.

"You're bad," Gavin muttered.

"I think you're trying to seduce me, Mrs. Rutherford," Emily said in her best Benjamin Braddock impersonation.

Gavin gave Emily a look that made her giggle. "All right, I'll stop. I'll stop. *Sam, come say goodnight to Gavin,*" Emily signed to Sam.

Sam came to the door and hugged Gavin. Gavin patted his head and closed his eyes thinking that there was nothing sweeter than a child's hug.

She walked out with Gavin, carrying a Kroger grocery bag of leftover food and snacks.

"Something for the week. You need to eat more than jerky and eggs. Carbs are your friend. Heat up those meals. Don't make all my hard work go to waste," she said, and handed him the bag. Gavin smiled and put the bag in the backseat of his truck. They looked at each other for a second.

"Don't be a stranger, Gavin Shaw."

Gavin hugged her, despite his best efforts not to. She felt really good in his arms. They pulled away slowly and Emily bowed her head.

"I'll see you soon," she said.

"Count on it," he said, and climbed into his truck.

She waved to him as he drove off and walked back to the house. Margaret was watching her at the window.

"That man has it bad for you," she said.

"Shush."

"Seriously."

"He's a friend, Margaret. A good friend," she said.

"Oh, sweet girl. Good friends make the best lovers." Emily exhaled and walked back to the kitchen to clean up. Margaret followed her. She laughed a short laugh.

"Will you not even consider the possibility?"

"Margaret, Aaron hasn't even been dead a year," Emily said, annoyed.

Margaret leaned against the counters and folded her arms. "Sometimes you can't control when love walks by."

"Are you really doling out relationship advice? You? The one who fell the hell apart when Craig died?"

Margaret's jaw tensed. She lowered her head at the reminder of Craig's passing.

"Has it occurred to you that maybe I am trying to help you avoid the same mistakes I've made?"

"I'm not ready to consider anything other than friendship with another man," Emily announced.

Margaret picked up a couple of roasted pumpkin seeds and popped them in her mouth. She laughed and walked toward the living room.

"Keep telling yourself that, my dear. Maybe you'll believe it."

By November it was bitterly cold, and six inches of snow blanketed everything. It took monumental effort just to get up and get Sam off to school every day. Emily swore it didn't get this cold in New Jersey until at least February, and she was already dreading the winter if this was autumn.

Gavin had kept true to his word and came by to visit Emily and Sam at least weekly, but usually more. Sometimes she cooked, and other times he took everyone, including Margaret, out for dinner to some nice places, where he let Sam order anything from the menu, even two desserts. When he didn't come by, he called. He made excuses at first—he saw a deal at Wal-Mart on flour and sugar; did the heater work okay in the house? He was concerned because of the cold snap; he saw they were hiring at IGA for the holidays.

Gavin showed up shortly after Paco and Celia picked up Sam for school early one November morning. He brought bagels and coffee from Einstein Bagels.

"Someone's up way too early," Emily said when she answered the door. She was wearing black pajama pants with red hearts on them and a long-sleeved red shirt.

"I was in Columbus and decided to stop and get breakfast for you guys," he said.

"God bless you. I miss bagels. Bagels the size of your head with a ridiculous amount of cream cheese, like they serve in New York," she said.

Gavin smiled and handed her the bag as they walked into the kitchen.

"Like your jammies," he said.

"Don't you mean you heart my jammies?" she asked. He made a funny face, and they fake laughed together.

"What kind of bagel do you want?" she asked. She saw he picked out one of everything.

"Surprise me. I don't usually eat those things."

They sat at the table and Emily gratefully sipped the good coffee that Gavin poured her.

"I come here bearing good news and asking several favors," Gavin said.

"I see your game. Bring me carbs to butter me up. Well played, Gavin Shaw. Well played."

"I also came first thing when I knew you'd be too tired to fight me," he countered.

She frowned at him. "So, what's going on?"

"I sold an order for 25 of your various pies to a fellow up in Findlay."

Emily startled awake. "What?"

"One of my buddies up there is hosting a big Thanksgiving party and I bragged about how good your pies were and how you sold them up at the farmer's market this past summer. He said he'd take 25 of them."

"Are you serious?" Emily asked.

Gavin shoved a wad of cash in front of her.

"When?"

"Friday night. I figured you can use the kitchen at the house. The freezer. Whatever you need. I'll help you transport them," he said. There was a giddiness about him that she found endearing.

"Wow. Oh my God. That's amazing. Thank you so much," she said, and hugged him. He laughed and paused, still caught off guard by the feel of her arms around him.

"I have so much to plan. This is so exciting," she said. She counted the cash. "Holy crap, Gavin, what did you sell each pie for?"

"$20 a pie."

"And he agreed to that?"

"He's a multi-millionaire. He breeds champion horses. He can handle $500."

"That's a hell of a profit. Each pie costs between $5-$8," she said.

"I am a hell of a salesman."

"I have no doubts now."

"Well, this is the good news. What are the favors?" she asked.

"I promised ten dozen cookies to the hens at the church for their Thanksgiving dinner week after next. I'll pay you for your time..."

Emily laughed. "That's fine. I can usually do that in an afternoon. Anything else?" she asked.

"What are you doing for Thanksgiving?" he asked.

"Haven't really thought about it just yet."

"I want y'all to come out to the house. Inviting the guys and their families. Josh is coming home. I want to do it up nice and big this year."

"Am I cooking for that, too?" she joked.

"Not all of it. Everyone should bring something—so I just need you to plan who needs to bring what," he said.

Emily leaned back in her chair and smiled. She bit into her bagel and stared out at the dreary sky.

"What?"

"It's always so nice when you come over." Gavin smiled shyly and drank his coffee.

"Do I hear Gavin Shaw in my home?" Margaret called from her bedroom.

Emily crinkled her eyes at Gavin. "You sure do. And he brought us bagels. He's a bang-up guy, that Gavin Shaw," Emily teased.

"If she comes out in lingerie, I swear to Jesus I'm running out the backdoor," he whispered.

Emily laughed. "I'll be right behind you," she whispered back.

Emily spent four days at the farmhouse baking pecan, apple, pumpkin, coconut crème, and lemon meringue pies.

Gavin helped her roll the dough, measure pecans, stir apples, whisk eggs, anything she asked him to do, just to stay close to her in the kitchen. They talked so effortlessly during that time at the house, exchanging tales of early childhood, college days, and favorite bands—Aerosmith for Gavin, Pearl Jam for Emily. Gavin made a Pandora station for Emily to stream through his TV speakers in the living room, and both their favorite tunes played while they prepared the pies. When she thought he was outside feeding the horses, she sang "Black" with a crystal-clear voice as she held her coffee cup and swayed with her memories of college. Aaron had taken her to a Pearl Jam concert when they first started dating, both of them getting swept away in the emotion of Eddie Vedder's sultry voice. Afterwards they went back to his tiny apartment he shared with three other guys in downtown Austin, who were conveniently out of town, and they made love for the first time. She smiled remembering how young they were, and how invincible and alive she felt afterwards, like she could fly.

Aerosmith's "Dream On" came on the channel next, and she started singing while chopping more apples.

She turned and saw Gavin watching her with folded arms. She nearly jumped out of her skin and turned red.

"You have a nice voice," he said. She shook her head, embarrassed.

"I'm serious. Never told you when I heard you this summer...the rare moments I heard you singing," he said.

"Chop those apples and not another word," she ordered.

He laughed at her reaction. "Good Lord, try to pay a girl a compliment, and she puts you to work," he mumbled.

She walked into the pantry to compose herself, taking an extra minute to get the vanilla.

"You can't stay in there all night," he called.

"Shush, Shaw," she yelled back. She walked back out and snapped open the vanilla and poured it into a measuring cup.

They worked quietly as the song continued. She startled when Gavin started singing with his best Steven Tyler impression.

She laughed as he took the wooden spoon and continued to serenade her, just so the embarrassment she felt was surpassed with him completely acting the fool.

"Stop!" she laughed, until her side ached.

He put the spoon down, and with a completely serious expression, continued to stir the cinnamon into the apples like none of it happened.

"Hell, forget the pies. We should take that act on the road. We can be Sonny and Cher," she said. He whistled "I Got You Babe" as he put the pie in the oven but did not respond to her.

She marveled at the sea of pies on every counter and square inch of space on his big oak table. "I can't believe we did this in four days. You and I make a hell of a team," she said.

Gavin stared at her and got quiet. For a moment he imagined that this was his life; talking, singing and baking pies with her, enjoying the simplicity of her hands as she kneaded dough or measured vanilla, with their hard work later rewarded together in his bed. His mind held the fantasy for a moment before his heart and stomach turned on him, making him feel faint and nauseous.

"What are you thinking?" she asked.

"Nothing. Just that I agree," he fibbed.

She went back to filling piecrust. "How does pizza sound tonight? Your oven will be occupied for several hours," she said.

Gavin was grateful for the distraction and went to grab the phone. "Pepperoni okay?"

Friday morning they loaded his truck and drove north to Findlay to deliver the goods. They celebrated her first successful catering gig with breakfast at a dive that he knew just outside of town. She insisted on paying, and he let her because he knew it was something she needed to do, even though the bill was only $15.

She reached into her bag and pulled out a card and slid it across the table to him as they sipped the last of their coffee.

"Don't read it now, but it's just a thank you. For everything," she said. She smiled at him shyly. He was taken aback by her sudden humility, and he gently slid the card in his dark brown duster jacket. She glanced around at the small diner. It had so much kitsch that she mentioned that she loved—old license plates, Elvis memorabilia, Don't Mess with Texas bumper stickers.

"I rather like this dive," she said.

"Figured you would."

"Know me that well, do ya?" she teased.

"A little, perhaps. What you let me see," he said.

"Do you think I'm hiding something?" she asked.

"No. But you keep your cards close. Given what's happened, that's not surprising," he said.

"I don't mean to. I wasn't like that before. Must be a by-product of the grief. Turns you into something you don't intend to be."

"Amen."

"What were you like before? Tell me," she said

"Angry. I was always so damn angry. Illogically so. Angry when people looked at me sideways, bumped my car, spoke in a loud voice, spoke in a soft voice, when my son dropped a foul ball in little league."

"Really? Why?"

"Probably because I didn't like the Air Force life. I didn't like being uprooted. Moving every few years. Part of me hated that I never had a say in my own destiny, really," Gavin said.

"It's a lot of sacrifice. That's for sure. Did you ever talk about it with Natalie?"

"We did at first. She promised twenty years and then she was out. She promised the farm life, the calmness that I was desperately needing so damn bad. But twenty years came, and she got offered the assignment in Dayton, and the chance to make full-bird Colonel. So, I made a deal—buy me the farm to get a jumpstart on things and you can be a Colonel for as long as you want. She commuted an hour every day."

"What did you do for employment when you guys were on the other assignments?"

"High school math teacher."

"Shut up. Are you serious?" Emily laughed.

"Always needed a math teacher in every city we went. Plus, I got summers off with the kids," Gavin said.

Emily grinned at the vision of him in khakis and a tie. Mr. Shaw. "You must have been in hell."

"Wearing a tie did suck. But it wasn't all bad. Not really. I really do like kids and teaching. But the politics. The helicopter parents. I don't miss that."

Emily cocked her head and stared at him.

"What?" Gavin finally asked.

"I'm amazed what I learn about you every time we talk," Emily said.

Gavin agreed. Truth be told, he was amazed what he told her every time they talked. He could not understand how this woman just caused him to open up and spill out every single thought he had in his head; perhaps because she truly cared to hear it and never use it against him for evil, man-eating type of purposes. There was something about Emily that was like a truth serum. He didn't think he could lie to her even if he tried.

"We should be getting back. I still have cookies to bake tomorrow for a certain farmer who is trying hard to impress the hens at a certain church, and I need to go shopping," she joked.

He bit his tongue at the joke, even though it grated on him. He didn't want to impress them at all. He just wanted an excuse to keep her employed and thought her baking for the women at the church would open up other opportunities. He didn't want to tell her that exactly. Not yet.

"They are already impressed with my prowess as a hay farmer, with less than a thousand acres, and a mortgage payment that would make them cry and run the other direction," he said.

"Don't forget the corn. And the four horses of the apocalypse that you own, along with the 32 chickens you affectionately call the Borg," Emily chimed in.

"Resistance is indeed futile."

"Bad *Star Trek* references, horses with water complexes, the hay, the corn, the mortgage payment, and a math teacher to boot! Come on, you got it going on, G."

"Point taken," he said.

"No, I'm serious. You're a hell of a man. I mean that," she said.

He ducked his head at the compliment. "We should get going," he said.

"Try to pay a man a compliment, and he makes you leave before you finish your coffee," she muttered, handing his own words back to him. He frowned then smiled at her.

When he dropped her off a couple of hours later, he put his truck in park, but left it running. She hesitated before opening the door.

"Well, thanks again for everything, Mr. Shaw," she said shyly.

"It was my pleasure," he said. She paused before she leaned over to hug him, cupping her right hand to the back of his head, burying her face in his nook of his neck. His body gave into her embrace, but as it did, she broke away quickly and opened the door.

"I'll see you tomorrow, G."

"Count on it," he said and drove off once she was safely inside the house.

He drove over into the IGA parking lot and pulled out her card before he turned off his engine to walk into the store. The card was white with an orange kitten on the cover that said "Thank Mew." He chuckled.

I know this is a cheesy card, but I also know your affinity for kittens, despite your tough man exterior. I just wanted to say thank you for helping, in too many ways to count. I could write a novel trying to convey my gratitude, but it would be a series of babbling that would probably repeat you are awesome, and I am so lucky to know you. So, imagine me saying that 1,000 times. ☺ But in all seriousness, please know I am so very grateful for the love and compassion you have shown Sam and me, when you really didn't have need to. I close my eyes at night and thank God for you. Always. Love, Emily.

Gavin's hands shook and he swallowed the lump in his throat. He ran his finger along her careful script, put the card to his nose in hopes of smelling her vanilla shampoo, but all he smelled was the ink from her pen. He put the card back in the envelope and placed it back in his coat pocket. He decided he didn't need beer that night, and he drove back home, quietly playing the radio. Every song he heard reminded him of her.

Gavin delivered ten dozen freshly baked chocolate chip, oatmeal raisin, orange cranberry, and peanut butter cookies to Grace Methodist Church the next afternoon. He was praying anyone but Sue Ellen would be there, but unfortunately for him, she was right at the front door and pounced on him the second he walked through.

"Why Gavin Shaw, don't tell me you learned to bake," Sue Ellen teased.

Her blonde hair was teased up in the front in its usual high-to-the-clouds way. She wore a skintight red blouse, amplifying up her doctored size DD cups, and jeans that could have been painted on her. Her perfume made him cough a little.

"No ma'am. Made by my cook, Emily," he said.

Another woman named Jessica Martin came up to rescue Gavin from the grips of Sue Ellen. She was a kind, older woman who didn't think too highly of Sue Ellen and her painted on clothing. She was a woman's literature professor at OSU, distinguished and calm. Gavin always enjoyed talking to her at church functions.

"I'll take those, Gavin. Thank you so much for bringing them. Please give our thanks to Emily for baking them. That must have been quite a feat!"

"Nay. She had these made and baking in no time flat. Took me longer to find out who won the Michigan game," Gavin joked. Jessica smiled and walked back to the donation station. Sue Ellen fumed.

"I thought she wasn't working for you any longer. In fact, I heard she is desperately trying to find work, but no one will hire her," Sue Ellen said. Her voice held an inflection of power and influence. Her eyes gave away her evil ways. Gavin saw red.

"I'm sure as a good, Christian woman you would have nothing to do with that, would you?" Gavin asked carefully.

Sue Ellen raised her palms and shrugged her shoulders. Gavin grabbed her arm and forced her into a small classroom.

"What the hell is the matter with you? She's just trying to support her son," Gavin said.

"I don't like her being around you," Sue Ellen said.

Gavin laughed a short laugh. "Well, genius, since you shot down all her employment opportunities in town, that just made me hire her back. I thought you went to college, or did you just spend all your time at the sorority house giving blow jobs to frat boys?"

Sue Ellen exhaled and crossed her arms in front of her enormous chest. Tears welled up in her blue, heavily outlined eyes.

"Why don't you want me?" Sue Ellen asked.

Gavin exhaled and rubbed his eyes with the palms of his hands.

"I could have any man in this county. Except you. Why?"

Gavin frowned at her and just shook his head in disbelief.

"It's substance, Sue Ellen. You're beautiful, sure. But mean as a snake. Your heart is cold. There is nothing in there but conquest. I swore off women like you years ago. And there is nothing in this world that will make me go back," Gavin said.

She sucked in her breath at his words. Flustered, she walked past him, silently. He heard her high heels clacking all the way down the hall.

He knew there would be consequences for saying that aloud. He prayed they would be minor. But he sure felt good saying it. For the moment.

CHAPTER FIFTEEN

Emily had changed for Thanksgiving dinner after spending all morning and afternoon cooking. A dark green wraparound blouse hugged her bosom and black slacks that she found in the clearance rack at Marshalls completed her new outfit. She decided to apply mascara and chose a deep shade of crimson on her lips. She dabbed a sample of Chloe perfume on her neck that she had been keeping for a special occasion. The green top brought out the green flecks in her hazel eyes and the slacks hugged her hips in all the right and flattering places. She wore open-toed high heels, taking the time to paint her toenails the night before. Black onyx dangling earrings that she borrowed from Margaret almost touched her shoulders. She wanted to dress extra special tonight for reasons that she did not want to readily admit, but when she saw Gavin inhale deeply when he saw her emerge from the guest bedroom, she knew it was in part to see the look on his face when he saw her. They looked at each other and he grinned.

"You sure do clean up nice," he teased. She curtsied.

They walked to the big, oak table set with Gavin and Natalie's wedding china handed down from Gavin's great-grandmother. Emily had asked if he wanted it formal or casual, and he insisted she use it, never remembering a day that Natalie used it in the 21- years they were together.

"Good call on the china," Emily said.

"Table does look nice."

"China should be used. It signifies something special is taking place," Emily said softly.

"I assume you used your wedding china often."

"Um, we didn't have wedding china. Aaron grew up poor, his parents were dead and buried way before we married. His grandma raised him. My parents kept all their earthly possessions with them, even after death. We never

137

even thought to register for it."

Gavin stared at her.

"You can take the girl out of Texas, but you can't take Texas out of the girl," she said, and winked.

He laughed. "Amen to that!"

Her simplicity grounded him. Sometimes he assumed she was well bred and above him. Simple statements like this often reminded him that they were really more alike than he knew.

She walked to the kitchen gracefully, and he thought she looked stunning in a completely understated way. Her perfume lingered by him, and he felt the need to excuse himself, stepping outside for a minute to regain his composure.

People began to arrive a few minutes later. Paco and Celia came with Xavier, Sam, and Margaret. Paco was dressed in a nice, dark blue, button-down shirt and dark jeans, and Celia was wearing a leopard-print long-sleeved blouse and black leggings. Her long, curly hair was pulled back into a French braid. Paco carried in two ice chests full of smoked meat and drinks. Margaret dressed up as well in a long blue jean skirt and a red bulky sweater. Her long, silver hair was piled lazily on her head. She wore a little too much eye makeup, but she was happy to be there. She had followed Emily's instructions and made Sam wear the sweater and button-down shirt Emily laid out. He and Xavier disappeared to Gavin's living room to find something on Netflix.

"I brought the brisket. Now it's Thanksgiving! Where do you want it?" Paco asked.

Will came alone carrying dinner rolls and a cake from a German bakery, his sons deciding to spend Thanksgiving with their respective girlfriends' family. Shakes came with his new friend, Amanda, who was at least fifteen years younger than him and cursed like a sailor. Despite her f-bombs, she was considerate enough and brought a pecan pie and a bottle of rum.

"It's my mom's recipe. It's bomb. I mean, out of your fucking mind good. I hope you like it," she said. Emily smiled, grateful her deaf son couldn't hear the cursing.

Gavin walked in from outside with a tall, young man following closely behind him. Emily marveled on how alike the young man and Gavin looked, sharing dark hair and green eyes. The prodigal son, Josh, was home for Thanksgiving.

Emily had never met him before, but had overheard several conversations Gavin had with him, arguing about something that she could not quite understand from context clues. Today was no different. Josh was full of piss and vinegar, casting a dark cloud on what was supposed to be a jovial occasion. Everyone in the room caught wind of the tension between father and son, yet no one truly knew how to diffuse it.

"Just walk away, like you always do," Josh muttered.

Gavin turned around and hissed, "I refuse to talk to you about this right now in front of our company. I expect you to sit your ass down and be respectful of this occasion."

Josh was conflicted—half kid who looked like he wanted to cry from being told off by his father, half man who wanted to take a swing at Gavin, now that he was old enough to knock him on his ass.

Emily felt a knot in her stomach. She had never seen Gavin angry before. It made her stomach queasy. Celia broke the ice first, always the mediator.

"Food looks great! Let's eat it while it's hot!"

Everyone obediently took seats around the large oak table, and Emily began to move things from the kitchen to the dining room, trying to sneak glances at Gavin, who was sitting like a rocket ready for flight at the head of the table. Daggers shot out at his offspring, who was sitting on the opposite side of the table near Shakes and Amanda.

"How's college, my man?" Shakes asked, shaking his hand.

"Good, good," Josh said. He smiled politely at Shakes and grabbed the bowl of mashed potatoes as it was being passed. He scooped a spoonful and forcefully flicked his wrist, causing a resounding "thwack" when the potatoes hit the plate, all the while daring Gavin to say or do anything. Emily saw

Gavin's jaw tense up.

"Turkey!! Who's cutting the turkey?" Emily asked.

Paco stood up quickly, afraid to put a carving knife in Gavin's hands during this stand-off.

"If you don't mind, G. I've been practicing my mad carving skills since last year," Paco said, smooth as leather. Gavin nodded once, icily staring at Josh.

"Emily, this bird looks fantastic," Paco said.

Emily smiled. "Thanks."

She sat by Sam at Gavin's right side and served Sam some green beans and potatoes as they passed by her. She looked at Gavin, trying to reach through his anger, but he shook his head and gave her a look, as if to warn her to look away from the sun, it was just going to blind her. She suddenly felt Josh's eyes on her, studying what was going on at the table, and judging by his furrowed brow, he was getting it all wrong.

"Dad, you didn't tell me you were fucking the help."

Everyone in the room gasped. Emily's mouth dropped in sheer shock.

"Wow," she said.

Gavin was on Josh in three long strides, grabbing him by his black t-shirt and pushing him against the fireplace in the living room. Shakes and Paco were on Gavin trying to break up the fight.

"You think you can come here, full of bullshit freedom, and disrespect me in my own home?" Gavin growled.

Josh tried to push him back, but Gavin's rage was too much for him. There was genuine fear in his eyes.

"You think you can come here demanding things of me like you're a man? Prove to me you're a man! Tell me this shit to my face, not in some bullshit passive-aggressive way that makes you feel bigger than you really are, you fucking coward. Say it, boy! Say it!" Gavin yelled at him.

Josh cowered by the fireplace as the men pulled Gavin off him.

"I want my money. It's mine. Mom left it to me," Josh yelled. He was crying.

"Your mother left it in trust to you, to be given to you when you're 27. You have not proven you are mature enough to handle the money. Not by far. I'll be damned if you get a dime of it now," Gavin yelled.

"You don't know shit about me. You never have! Never gave a damn what I wanted, or who I was. I'm not like you. I'm not going to be a farmer. I'm like mom. I want to see the world, do something special with my life, not sit around this godforsaken piece of shit little town to wither up and die on a tractor."

Josh's words were like an AK-47 spattering its loathing all around the room. The words ricocheted off Gavin to everyone who had made a conscious choice to stay and live in Champaign County. The mood quickly changed in the room, each person reflecting on their own reasons for staying there and justifying their own self-worth.

Gavin inhaled and raised his hand to strike.

"Gavin, no!" Emily said. The expression on her face realigned him. She truly looked heartsick that he would strike his own son.

He put his hand down. "Go back to Knoxville. Come back when you're ready to apologize," Gavin said, and walked out.

Xavier started to cry and flail his arms from overstimulation. Sam huddled in a corner with Margaret holding him. People fighting terrified him. Paco and Shakes slowly walked back to the table and Emily stood in the living room with Josh and Will.

"I didn't mean any disrespect to you, Will," Josh said.

"Well, you certainly gave it out to everyone. In droves," Will said sadly.

Emily and Josh stared at each other for a second before she exhaled and went to see about Sam. Josh took a few minutes to contemplate his next move, then disappeared quietly out the front door.

"That was fucking awesome! I love a good Thanksgiving fight. Reminds me of home," Amanda said, mouth full of potatoes. Emily wished she could take her fork and stab it in Amanda's eye. Instead, she poured a glass of wine and slumped in the chair.

After the kids were calmed down, everyone ate quietly and tried to pretend nothing happened. Emily had no appetite left, and everything had gone cold.

Later, Shakes, Will, and Amanda were huddled around the TV watching the Cowboys game. Paco had taken the boys and Margaret back into town. Celia stayed to help Emily clean up in the kitchen. She watched Emily quietly washing dishes as she carefully sat more dishes beside her.

"I think he just saw what we all see," Celia began.

"What's that?"

"Josh. He saw how you and Gavin interact and assumed that you were . . . you know," she said

Emily turned off the water. "We're friends, Celia," Emily said through gritted teeth.

"I know. I know. We all know that. But to outsiders it could appear to be more. It's obvious that you two care about each other, that's all I'm saying," Celia said.

"Well to Josh it looked like his father was screwing the help. Isn't that what he said?" Emily said.

"I believe he said 'fucking the help'," Shakes said. He brought in a bowl that he had piled all the desserts in.

"Not helping, Dillon," Celia whispered.

"Well, what part is pissing you off the most, Em? The fucking part or the help part."

"ALL OF IT," Emily yelled.

Shakes startled at her anger. Emily furiously wiped her hands on a kitchen towel.

"All of it pisses me off. That I got dragged into whatever bullshit that was. That I spent six hours cooking just to have the dinner go to crap because bullheaded men can't keep their egos in check. That Josh thinks I am some slut banging his father—sorry, that he thinks I'm a low-life piece of trash banging his father. All of it bothers me!" Emily yelled.

Celia turned and Emily saw Gavin standing at the kitchen

door. Emily exhaled loudly. He was stunned by her outburst.

"I'm going home," she said. She threw down the towel and walked past him.

"Em," Gavin started.

"Don't. Just don't," she whispered.

She fumbled in the dark driveway for her keys, dropping them on the ground not once but three times. When she finally had them in her hands, Gavin was standing by her.

"I'm sorry you witnessed all that. Please believe me that it had absolutely nothing to do with you," Gavin said.

Emily leaned against the car. She felt the tears burn the back of her nose, and she tried desperately to shake them, but they fell anyway.

"It's my fault. I was stupid to think that this would be a normal holiday. That I could somehow pretend I belong here. I don't belong anywhere anymore."

Gavin's mouth turned down. Those words cut him deep. "That's your grief talking. Because you know damn well that's not true," he said, and stomped back inside.

Gavin didn't come calling for over a week after Thanksgiving. Every time the phone rang or she heard a roar of a pickup truck, Emily got her hopes up, and then fell deeper into her funk. Margaret finally had enough and decided to take matters into her own hands.

She spotted Gavin at church that next Sunday, sitting in the back like he usually did, and quietly slid in beside him in the pew. She was dressed in a red pantsuit that would get the devil's attention, with a fantastically large, red, floppy hat. He smiled to acknowledge her, but the music director stood up and started the service with various hymns, preventing him from uttering a word to her.

At the end of the service, which was coincidently about forgiveness, Margaret took his elbow and led him outside to the chilly winter afternoon.

"Haven't seen you around much," Margaret said.

Gavin inhaled and exhaled. "I've been really busy," he lied.

Margaret stared at him, her blue eyes piercing through his green ones. "It's not nice to bullshit an old lady," she said.

She led him to her car, which was parked by a large maple tree, branches barren, waiting for more snow.

"I just think we needed a break. I'm not exactly proud of what happened at Thanksgiving. Or what Josh said. Or how I reacted to it," Gavin said. He shook his head, remembering it.

"Families tend to bring out the worst in us. And the best," Margaret said.

"How is she?"

"Come over and see for yourself," Margaret said. He hesitated.

"A man needs as many friends as he can get, Mr. Shaw," Margaret said.

"Does she want to see me?"

"Are you fishing?" she asked, smiling.

"Maybe," he said.

"I wouldn't be talking to you if I thought she didn't want to see you."

That lit a fire in his belly. "I'll be by in a little bit," he said.

Margaret opened her car door. "Bring lunch. It's the least you can do," she said, and winked.

Gavin knocked on the door about an hour later and Emily sucked in her breath when she saw him. He was carrying a bucket of Lee's Fried Chicken and a brown paper bag.

She didn't speak at first, and he felt panicked that Margaret had lied to him about Emily wanting to see him.

"Whatcha got in the bag, Shaw?" she finally asked, leaning against the door. He exhaled, relieved.

"About a hundred apologies. And some apples." She smiled. It was the sweetest apology she had ever received.

CHAPTER SIXTEEN

Sam, Margaret, Gavin, and Emily were at the local Boy Scout Christmas tree lot next to the IGA early one December evening trying to decide on a Christmas tree. Sam kept jumping up and down, sniffing the pine needles, and pointing out trees he liked to Margaret. Emily slowly walked by Gavin.

"Thanks for letting us use your truck," Emily said. It was a crisp 24-degrees, and the temp was rapidly dropping. She tried to wear her heaviest jeans and a heavy sweater under her dark green Salvation Army pea coat, but even with a wool cap covering her dark hair and a pair of Gavin's heavy gloves she was still freezing. Gavin wore his usual leather duster and showed no signs of the cold getting to him. They both sipped coffee from McDonald's to keep warm.

"Any time," he said.

"Did you get your tree yet?"

Gavin took a long sip of coffee. "I'm not really into Christmas."

Emily understood. It was her initial instinct to keep it low-key and forego all of the traditional Christmas festivities, but Margaret had recently unearthed all her Christmas ornaments and decorations and was eager to display them.

"Is Josh coming home?"

Gavin shook his head. The Thanksgiving blow-up was still a sore subject.

"Tennessee is a lot warmer than Ohio," Emily said. Gavin walked slowly ahead of her.

"Bullheaded to the end," she muttered.

"Let it go, Em," he said.

Margaret came running up with Sam, holding hands.

"We found it. The perfect one," Margaret said, breathless.

She looked young and vibrant with her silver hair recently cut into a stylish bob framing her beautifully lined face.

Emily and Gavin followed both of them to the other side of the lot. It was a 5-foot tree, big and fat, a perfect fit for Margaret's small living room.

"It's perfect," Emily said. Gavin agreed.

He summoned a young kid in uniform and showed him the tree while Margaret took Sam to sample the free apple cider doughnuts and hot chocolate. The boy came back with two older Boy Scouts and an adult to finish the transaction. Gavin's face changed suddenly when he saw the adults coming toward them.

"Why, hello."

Sue Ellen and her husband Darryl slowly walked up to them. Sue Ellen dressed like an Aspen snow bunny completely misplaced in a small Midwest town wearing a white coat with a matching fur collar and white Uggs shoved over her skintight jeans. Darryl was dressed more like Gavin, wearing a heavy, brown leather rancher's jacket and heavy gloves. He was considerably older than Sue Ellen, with a heavily receding hairline, a nice-sized beer gut, and a full salt and pepper beard.

"Evenin', Darryl," Gavin said.

"Found a good one, huh?" Darryl said.

"Yes, sir."

"Darryl Richter," Darryl said, and offered his hand to Emily.

"Emily Mitchell," she said, and shook it.

"Nice to meet you."

"Your boys are growing up fast, Darryl," Gavin said, looking at the three boys who were busy gathering the tree.

"They sure are. Oldest one is starting high school next year," Darryl said.

Sue Ellen looked at Gavin and then glared at Emily. She made no attempt to hide the fact that she was unhappy to see them there together.

"That'll be forty even," Darryl said, pulling the tag off the tree. Emily reached into her pocket and pulled the cash that she and Margaret had taken from the Christmas jar before heading over to the tree lot.

"Damn, Shaw, least you could do is buy your woman her tree," Darryl joked. Gavin's ears turned red. Sue Ellen looked like she was about to spit nails.

"I'm sure he would if I were his woman, sir. He strikes me as being very chivalrous about such things," Emily said, and smiled.

"Oh, I'm sorry, I just assumed. Hell, Gavin ain't set foot in town with no one since the Colonel passed, I just figured..." Darryl said.

"Understood. Understood. But tonight, he was kind enough to loan us his brawn and his truck," Emily assured politely.

"Gotcha. Well, I do appreciate you coming out to support the Boy Scouts tonight. I'll see you both around," Darryl said. Sue Ellen turned on her heels and walked away, never uttering a sound.

"Well, that was fun," Emily joked. Gavin was angry, jaw tense. That surprised her. "Are you mad? Why are you mad?" she asked.

Gavin abruptly walked toward the parking lot, leaving her standing alone by a giant blue spruce. She assumed by setting the record straight that it would diffuse the shock and embarrassment he felt from Darryl's question. She wasn't prepared for it to anger him. She was at a loss for words, and then she was more than a little pissed off about his reaction.

She walked back to the truck and saw Margaret and Sam guiding the loading of the tree. Gavin reached into his pocket and gave the Scouts a tip after it was nestled safely in the back of his Ford. He climbed in the driver's seat and waited for her to get in.

Margaret offered her a doughnut, but she refused and insisted Margaret ride in the front seat with Gavin, preferring not to sit by him as angry as she was. She sat in the back with Sam, who was still hyper from the thrill of Christmas along with God knows how many hot apple cider doughnuts and cups of hot chocolate swimming in his belly.

Gavin pulled up to their house a few minutes later and

silently unloaded the tree into the tree stand Margaret had placed by the front windows.

"Thank you so much, Gavin. I think we got it from here," Margaret said.

"You're welcome," he said, and looked at squarely at Emily. She stood with her arms folded across her chest. Margaret raised an eyebrow.

"Emily, dear, I think I left my purse in the front seat of the truck," Margaret said. Emily sighed and walked to fetch it, with Gavin following behind her. She opened the passenger side door and saw Margaret's silver, sparkly purse on the floorboard and grabbed it. Gavin leaned against the front of the truck.

"So, explain it to me, G. Which part pissed you off—the assumption Darryl made or my response?" she asked and slammed the door.

"It's not what you said."

"So, you're offended he thinks we're dating?" she asked.

Gavin moaned. He was finding that he was terrible at fights with her. She was too quick witted, and her tongue sliced through him like a samurai sword before he could even finish a thought in his head. He stayed quiet.

"You better elaborate, because I am about to get quite the complex over here," she said, near hysterical.

"I would if you let me, dammit. For Chrissakes, Emily! I don't talk as fast as you! Let me get my thoughts together!" he yelled at her. She stood there and waited.

"It doesn't bother me that he thinks we are dating. That's a natural assumption when two single people are out in public together. It bothers me that he assumes to know me at all or assume to tell me what I need to do for my woman, whomever she is. He doesn't know jack shit about me, or the kind of person I am. I don't need him or his fucking wife passing judgment on anything I do or do not do," he said.

Emily was surprised at his tone and his use of profanity. *Damn* was about the strongest word she had ever heard him say.

"Did you sleep with her?" she asked quietly.

He was shocked. "I cannot believe you just asked me that."

"I'm asking because it would explain why she looks at me like she wants to scoop my heart out with a spoon every time I see her, and why she looks at you like you are her property."

"No. God no. Not that she hasn't tried to seduce me in 800 different ways. But hell no. Not ever, no never," he said. Emily raised her eyebrow at him, not fully believing him.

"Okay…"

"I've never lied to you, Emily. I don't see a reason to start now," Gavin said.

"You fibbed once."

"When?"

"When you pulled the wires on my distributor cap to see where I lived." Gavin blushed and stammered.

Emily shook her head. "It's okay. I understand why you did it."

They were quiet for a few minutes while Gavin contemplated how much to really tell her. He finally relented and knew he had to tell her the truth, since she already had a good feeling that something happened. He looked down and Emily saw the change in his face. Her heart sank.

"A couple of months after the funeral Sue Ellen came over. I had been drinking heavily. She came on to me. Hard core, like she tends to do. I let her kiss me, thinking that it would be nice to feel something other than the pain, you know? Screw it. My wife and daughter were dead. Who gives a crap if I bang Darryl Richter's wife? But I couldn't . . . I couldn't respond to her physically. She took great offense to that. It's like her mission from God now to see it through."

Emily felt disappointment of epic proportions, which she knew was ridiculous. But the fact that he even kissed that vile woman hit a sore spot for her that she could not explain. He noticed her disappointment and walked up to her, inches from her face.

"I thank God that my subconscious knew what my damn head was too jacked up to stop. Every. Day. I am grateful I didn't make that mistake with her," he told her. Emily swallowed, always blown away by Gavin's intensity and honesty with her. She could feel his regret, his relief.

She cleared her throat a few times. "So, exactly which head was jacked up? I'm trying to get a visual," she said lightly.

He grinned. "Both, apparently." They both chuckled. She took a deep breath, washing away the Richters and Gavin's past, as they had no place there with them on Avenue B. She grabbed his arm and led him back to the house.

"Let's go eat some doughnuts and decorate this damn tree," she said. He walked with her, arm in arm, the pressure lifted from his chest by the simple touch of her hand and the sound of her laughter.

"Who told you about the wires in your car?" he asked.

"Celia."

"Paco is a damn blabbermouth," he muttered.

"Hell, with a wife who looks like that, wouldn't you tell all your secrets to her if she asked? She's like Cleopatra. Or Helen of Troy."

"Hell, he probably told her that just to get her to stop nagging him," he joked.

Emily giggled. "Probably."

Margaret walked in a week later with tickets in her small hands. "What are you doing Saturday night?" she asked.

Emily poured ladles of hot baked potato soup in three big bowls for their dinner and glanced over her shoulder.

"I suspect you're about to tell me what we're doing."

"I just found out that Gavin has a solo in the Christmas production this weekend," Margaret said.

"Wait, what? He's in the choir? I didn't know that" Emily said.

"It was a last-minute stand in. Apparently, Bill Nelson has the flu and won't be fit to perform. Which is a little disappointing because Bill has a wonderful voice. But I thought Gavin would need our support. I got tickets for everyone," Margaret said.

"I literally just spoke to him an hour ago and he mentioned nothing of this," Emily said.

"Maybe he's hoping you wouldn't find out," Margaret joked. Emily laughed and tried to imagine Gavin performing a solo in front of all of Champaign County—the Methodists, anyways. It was so unlike him. This she had to see!

The production was called "A Night with Jesus" and was a very big to-do. The normal pulpit had been transformed to a theatrical stage, with dramatic black backdrops and all kinds of props. All of Champaign County was there, including Will, Shakes, and Paco and his crew. The Gavin Shaw support club took up an entire pew.

The story was about a drunken man who was out in the cold the night before Christmas who met various angels, akin to *A Christmas Carol*. However, these angels showed very real-life issues of pain and suffering that would lead this main character down the current drunken path he was on. Gavin's solo was at the most dramatic part of the play, where the Future Angel showed the man losing his family because of his behavior and the man discovering the love and forgiveness of Jesus. The spotlight turned on Gavin, looking dapper in a black suit with a white shirt and red tie. He sang "O Holy Night" in a crystal-clear tenor that nearly brought Emily to her knees.

She held her breath as he sang the beautiful words to her favorite Christmas carol, his vibrato resonating through her, finding the pain she had hidden deep, deep down, buried while she did her best to survive the day-to-day. Tears fell as she released the anger of Aaron's transgressions and as she sat with the pain that she missed her husband, her lover, her best friend, and father of her son. Aaron loved Christmas, loved the vibrant lights of Rockefeller Center, skating on the frozen pond near their home, watching the Christmas tree lighting ceremony. He had always played Santa, leaving her small gifts hidden in their Christmas tree for her—a trip to the spa, a small bracelet that reminded him of her hazel eyes, a book of poetry that she loved to read.

Fall on your knees! Oh, hear the angel voices!

151

When his solo was done, tissues came from both directions and Emily graciously accepted them to wipe her tears. She held them to her eyes until the storm of emotion passed, and she glanced up to see a concerned Gavin staring at her from offstage. She smiled gently at him and touched her hand to her chest. He bowed his head back at her.

When the show was over, Paco and Celia invited everyone over to their house for refreshments. Gavin tried to back out of it.

"I'm beat," he said.

"Oh no, sir. You are not backing out of this. Emily baked all the goodies just for you," Celia said. Emily ducked her head, a little embarrassed.

"All right, all right. I'll be over soon," he said. Celia smiled and escorted the kids and Paco out the back door.

"You were phenomenal," Emily said.

Gavin grinned. "Not bad for a Tennessee choir boy."

Not bad at all," she said, and laughed. They lowered their heads in an awkward silence.

"Well, I'll see you all over there," he said.

"Sure. See you in a bit."

He watched her hustle out of the church and smiled. He was feeling very proud of himself as people congratulated him, praising his voice and his performance. His joy was short lived, however, when he saw a blonde in a white coat hanging by his truck.

"Mrs. Richter," Gavin said.

"Mr. Shaw," Sue Ellen said. She smiled a flirtatious smile at him.

He pulled his keys out of his pocket and waited patiently for her to move from his door.

"I just wanted to tell you I was moved by your solo and decided to forgive you for what you said to me before Thanksgiving," she said.

"Um, okay," he said.

"I mean the offer still stands to finish what we started. In fact, Darryl took the boys hunting for the weekend. I'm all alone in my big, 'ole, house," she said.

"Duly noted," Gavin said. Sue Ellen put a hand on her hip and waited. The silence turned awkward.

"I'm running late for an engagement, Mrs. Richter," he said politely.

She closed her eyes in frustration and walked away slowly, clenching her fists into balls.

It was a small gathering at Paco and Celia's. Gavin walked in to cheers from everyone, feeling a little like a rock star. Sam told him he did a good job and that his suit was very nice. Xavier clapped when he saw him then quickly disappeared down to the basement to play video games with Sam.

Emily walked out of the kitchen with a beautiful German chocolate cake and various savory hors d'oeuvres. He noticed she made all his favorites, including cabbage rolls, so he made a point to try to everything.

He walked up to her sitting alone in the living room after he ate. She was drinking a beer.

"Didn't think you liked beer."

"I can take one for the team," she winked. She was a bit tipsy.

He wanted to ask her about her reaction to his singing and was tempted to joke if it was because he sang so badly, but he decided to hold his smart comments and just revel in the fact he touched something deep inside her. He felt empowered he could do that. The beer went straight to his head, making him feel slightly buzzed and a little daring. He sat close enough to her that his knee touched hers. She made no attempt to move.

He admired her black blouse with silver sparkles, dark jeans, and big silver hoop earrings. "You look really nice tonight," he said, feeling bold.

"As do you." He grinned and drank the rest of his beer. Emily shook her head.

"What?" he asked.

"You're kinda cute when you're buzzing," she teased.

"I drank before I ate. Bad combination."

"Will you make it home?" she asked.

"I'm not that gone. Just feeling…good," he emphasized. He wanted to tell her a lot more in that moment, like what else would make him feel good. The beer was about to let him when his cell phone rang.

"Oh, sorry. Excuse me. I should take this," he said when he saw the phone number. He stepped out onto the patio.

"Hey," he said as he pulled his phone up to his ear.

"Last chance for love," a woman's voice purred.

Gavin glanced at Emily on the other side of the sliding glass door and watched her stand to go to the kitchen. He knew to his core that there was no way to be with her tonight, so he heard his favorite Crosby, Stills and Nash song play in his mind, "*if you can't be with the one you love, then love the one you're with.*"

"Meet me at my place in a half hour," he said.

"See you there."

Gavin walked inside and found Emily in the kitchen.

"I'm gonna leave," he said.

"Really? Already?"

"I'm beat. And I should stop while I'm ahead." She nodded, but her eyes showed disappointment.

"Thanks for coming out tonight, and for making the treats. That was very sweet of you," he said.

"Any time."

He hugged her quickly and walked out the front door, shouting good-byes to everyone. He drove out to his place and saw a sleek, black Ford Explorer in his driveway. He pulled up beside it and hopped down from his truck. She stepped down from her vehicle, her blonde hair blowing softly in the wind, her white coat wrapping her body tight.

"Miss me?" she teased.

His answer was a full kiss on the mouth. The whole time he imagined it was Emily.

CHAPTER SEVENTEEN

Emily delivered three fruitcakes and ten dozen cookies to Betty Nelson Christmas Eve morning. Betty, who dared not buy a pie from Emily and Celia under Sue Ellen's watchful eye at the farmer's market last summer, turned out to be one of Emily's regular customers. Emily enjoyed dropping off treats at her house. Betty was a perfect hostess, always offering her a big cup of coffee to go and always tipping her big.

"Emily! Those fruitcakes look divine," Betty said when she opened the door.

"Thanks, Betty. How is Bill feeling?" she asked.

"So much better. That flu bug just stayed forever. But he's up and around. A lot better now. Thank you for asking."

"Big party tonight?" Emily asked. She unloaded everything on Betty's beautiful dark granite counters, noticing the trays of food already being assembled.

"Bill likes to serve the firefighters and law enforcement who are on duty on Christmas Eve. He's an ex-fireman. Did you know that?"

"I didn't. But that's real nice of him to do that," Emily said.

"Yeah, he got injured on call, then decided to retire. He likes the farm life a lot more, as do I, I can tell you. Every time I heard the sirens, it was just so nerve-racking, you know. I still get goose pimples when I hear them."

"I can only imagine," she said. Emily pulled out an invoice to show Betty, and she opened her purse and laid out $100 for the $80 bill.

"Oh, I almost forgot. I picked up something for your little boy," Betty said. She reached behind her sofa and pulled out a medium-sized gift-wrapped box.

"Awww, that's super sweet of you, ma'am. He'll appreciate that so much."

"Please, it was my pleasure. It must be very hard for him.

First Christmas without his daddy."

Emily bowed her head. "He's a trooper."

"Please send our regards to Miss Margaret and Sam. Merry Christmas, Emily!"

Emily waved as she walked out the door. "Merry Christmas, Betty. My best to Bill."

She walked back to the Honda after putting the cash into her purse and decided to forego the last stop before going home to cook Christmas dinner for her, Margaret, and Sam. Paco and Celia were at her sister's the next town over, and Gavin was driving to Knoxville, feeling sentimental when he woke up that morning at not seeing Josh at Christmastime.

"You should just drive there, Gavin. Seriously. It's Christmas," Emily encouraged.

"He'll probably slam the door in my face."

"Well, at least you tried."

Emily noticed Gavin's truck as she pulled up to her house. She walked inside and was surprised to see him sitting on the living room couch watching *It's a Wonderful Life* with Sam and Margaret.

"Hey. I thought you'd left already," she said.

"Canceled the trip. Josh went to Texas to see Natalie's sister," he said.

Emily frowned. "I'm sorry."

He shrugged. "What can you do?"

"Well, you can get this poor old lady some more eggnog, take off your boots and stay awhile," Margaret said. Gavin chuckled and stood to get Margaret's mug.

"Don't skimp on the rum, either" she said. Gavin shook his head and walked with Emily into the kitchen.

"You're more than welcome to stay. I'm making a pot roast. Margaret rented a bunch of movies. Christmas classics such as *The Terminator*, *Transformers I* and *II*, and *RoboCop*," she said sarcastically.

"Nothing says deck them halls y'all like killer robots," Gavin joked.

"Totally."

"I was actually wondering if you'd like to have lunch with me. Unless you have to babysit the roast, then I understand," he asked shyly. He was playing with a dishtowel and looked nervous.

"Just me?"

"Yes."

"I'm just slow cooking the roast. Is there anything open today?"

"A few select places," he said.

"Do I need to change?" she asked. She looked at her dark green sweater and jeans.

"Nope."

"Okay. Let me set up dinner and we can go."

"Okay, great."

Fifteen minutes later Emily was driving out toward the farm in Gavin's truck, curiosity piqued. He drove up to the house and smiled when he parked.

"Best restaurant in town," he said.

She laughed. "Especially if I'm cooking?"

"True, but not today. It's my treat," he said.

They walked in the house and Emily could smell a wonderful smell coming from his kitchen.

"What's this? You are actually cooking me lunch? This is Christmas indeed!" Gavin opened the lid to his slow cooker and stirred a hearty corn chowder that had been kept warm. Emily took off her coat and placed it over a chair and walked up beside him.

"Corn chowder using the corn you squirreled away for me last summer. I am also using one of the loaves of bread you froze to make your 'fantastically cheesy' grilled cheese like you like. Even bought that fancy cheese that you like that I can't hardly pronounce. Phyllis at IGA almost dropped dead when I went in asking for Gouda and Havarti cheese instead of my usual American and pepper jack," he said.

Emily smiled and clapped quietly. "I'm learning, I'm learning," he said.

She pulled out the stool from the island and watched him

assemble the sandwiches. "This is the best Gavin Christmas gift ever," she said with true excitement.

"Well, it's one of them. I actually did buy you something," he said, pointing with his butter knife to a box on the counter wrapped with a big red bow.

"Awww, you didn't have to do that, Gavin," she said.

He looked into her eyes. "Yes, I did," he said.

She smiled shyly and slid off the stool to go see it. She picked up the large box and shook it.

"Can I open it?" she asked.

"Let's wait until after lunch," he said.

She agreed and opened the refrigerator, searching for something to drink. She noticed a FedEx box in the fridge.

"What's in the box?"

"Dessert."

She pulled out the box and saw the New York postmark. She opened it and saw an Eileen's Special Cheesecake box nestled inside. She looked at him.

"You had an Eileen's Special Cheesecake shipped here?" she asked.

"Not just any Eileen's Special Cheesecake. But the salted caramel Eileen's Special Cheesecake," Gavin said.

"Oh. My. God. Gavin Shaw. You didn't," she said. She put the box on the counter and found a knife to open it. There in the box in all its wonder was a New York cheesecake covered in sticky caramel.

"That is a thing of pure beauty," she said. "When did I tell you about this place? I don't even remember . . ."

"You and Will were talking about cheesecake back in July. You mentioned this place on Cleveland in New York."

She remembered that conversation with Will. She was describing how Eileen's cheesecake tasted homemade even though it was from a bakery. The best of both worlds she had called it.

"This must have cost you a fortune to ship," she said.

"I wanted you to have a special Christmas. You've been working so hard since you got here, taking care of everyone, that I wanted you to have a special day today," he said.

"You're going to make me cry," she said.

He put down his spatula. "Don't you dare cry."

"Too late," she said, sniffing.

He wrapped his arms around her and felt her body give into him. "You're such a wimp."

"Yeah, but you love me despite that fatal flaw."

"Yeah, I suppose I do."

She laughed and kissed him quickly on the cheek and walked back to the counter. He paused, caught off guard by her show of affection, but caught the sandwich just before it burned.

They ate their soup and sandwiches at the table, set by Gavin. He put out red placemats with Santa on them, poured their iced tea into wine glasses, and served their lunch on fine china. She smiled big when she saw the spread.

"Some girl I know told me that using china signified something special was occurring," he winked.

"Do you remember everything I have ever said?"

"Pretty much," he admitted.

The corn chowder was probably the best she had ever eaten. And so was the grilled cheese for that matter. Gavin served them an enormously large piece of cheesecake with coffee. She was so stuffed after the meal she could hardly move.

"I'm going to have to take a walk," she joked.

"Why don't we go to the living room? You can open up your gift," he said. She had almost forgotten about the box on the counter. She stood and started to clear the dishes.

"Leave them. It's your day," he reminded her.

She smiled and went to sit on Gavin's leather couch. He brought her the box and sat next to her. She fingered the red bow and slowly opened it. Inside there was a green apron and a white chef's jacket. Emily looked puzzled. She pulled them out and saw that each was embroidered with Emily's logo that she designed for Shaw Farm and Bakery last summer. At the bottom of the box was a letter from the State of Ohio registering that name as a business. She looked at him, eyes questioning.

"I want this to be a partnership. You run the bakery, I run the farm. I want to invest in more land for produce, more hens, whatever you need. I think we could handle production from the house for the first few years, but then we can think about a brick-and-mortar place if needed."

Emily was floored. "I . . . wow. Wow. I'm so overwhelmed by this," she said.

He studied her closely. "I'm having a hard time reading your reaction right now," he said.

She shook her head. "I'm sorry. This is really such an amazing thing you're offering. I just feel like I'm not worthy of such an offer." Gavin cocked his head to the side. He had never seen her doubt her abilities before. He was taken aback by her insecurity.

"Emily, you brought in nearly ten grand in 12 visits to the Dayton farmer's market. That was working a couple of days a week. Imagine what you could bring in if you worked more, had a small staff, and devoted the time you needed to it? Plus, the work in the fall and winter with holidays. How much did you gross from your holiday sales?"

"About $2000," she said.

"Exactly."

"I've been out of this business for almost nine years. It's a big gamble on me, Gavin. A big gamble on the unknown. I'm a horse in the race that you've only seen run one season," she said.

"I trust my gut above all else. I believe in you. I know we can make this work."

She fingered the lettering on the apron. "I really would like to think about this."

He was disappointed. She grabbed his hands. They were warm and comforting, like they always were.

"I don't want to do this unless I can be successful for you. For us. Please understand that," she explained.

He paused. "All right. Take some time to think about it,"

he said. He leaned back against the couch.

"And for the record, the gift that I got you looks really, really tacky and cheap now," she said. He leaned his head back and laughed.

"Thank you for believing in me," she said. He bowed his head.

Gavin dropped her off an hour later and came inside to exchange gifts. He bought Sam several things—a few toys, some clothes including a new coat and winter boots, and a few books about hiking and the Appalachian Trail. He bought Margaret an old, framed picture of Galveston Island. It may as well have been a Tiffany diamond the way she reacted to it. She hugged him and kissed him on the lips, much to Gavin's chagrin. Emily laughed while feeling a little envious that Margaret beat her to it. Sam bought Gavin some new leather working gloves, signing to him that he saw he had a hole in his last pair. Gavin smiled big when he saw them and told Sam they were perfect. Margaret gave him a nice burgundy sweater to wear to church. Emily handed him a flat present. He opened it slowly.

It was a photo book she designed with one of those on-line photo places. She used Celia's good camera and new laptop and snapped several artsy pictures of Gavin's farm, including the Borg, the cats, the horses, and the hay that was dormant during the fall. Gavin thumbed through it, impressed with her photography skills and the way she captured the aspects of life on his property. Bob looking defiant out in the sun. The chickens gathering together when the feed was dropped. The mass of eggs piled high in a metal cage where he gathered them. It was a beautiful masterpiece.

"Thank you. This is—so beautiful," he said. He touched the cover gingerly.

"You're very welcome."

She and Margaret gathered the wrapping paper and Sam sat near Gavin and started thumbing through the books. Margaret helped Emily carry the trash to the kitchen and out to the back porch.

"So, did he give you his gift earlier?" Margaret's eyes were raised in a scandalous pose.

"You are such a dirty old woman," Emily mumbled.

"You were gone a few hours. I was hoping . . ."

"You were hoping what?"

Margaret raised her eyebrows again. "That he was showing you little Gavin."

"Holy hell, Margaret," Emily said.

"All right then, Ms. Prude. What did he give you?"

"He made me a nice lunch, shipped in a cheesecake all the way from New York . . . and he asked me to be his business partner." Margaret was quiet.

"What?" Emily asked.

"That's really amazing!"

Emily's smile radiated from her head to her toes. "It was."

"And incredibly romantic," Margaret said.

Emily sighed. "The only romance going on over here is you sticking your tongue down his throat," she mumbled.

"He's a good kisser. You should get on that ASAP," Margaret laughed. Emily shook her head and walked back inside.

Gavin stood when he saw her and gathered his hat and gifts. He walked slowly toward the front door.

"You sure you don't want to stay? I hate the idea of you being alone tonight," Emily said softly.

He was about to open his mouth to give her an excuse, but he paused. She saw the sadness in his eyes; it mirrored her own.

"Please don't go," she whispered.

Gavin dropped his hat on the side table and took off his coat. Emily was so relieved that a tear escaped her eye.

"So, are we watching *RoboCop* or *Transformers II* next?" he asked.

Emily smiled gratefully. "Thank you," she said.

He gently ran his fingers on her face to remove the tear.

CHAPTER EIGHTEEN

Emily hung black and white streamers from Paco and Celia's living room ceiling early afternoon on New Years' Eve. She was carefully trying to balance on a ladder when Paco walked up and pretended to shake the ladder.

"EARTHQUAKE!!" he yelled.

"NO! NO! PACO! DON'T!" Emily screamed. Paco laughed.

"You're a little shit."

"Yep," he laughed, and walked to the back yard.

Celia buzzed around from the kitchen and outside trying to set up for the party. She had obsessively planned a masquerade party for weeks with the help of Pinterest. Paco was sent into Columbus four different times for decorations and special trinkets. He finally put his foot down on the fifth request and threatened to call Time Warner Cable to disconnect their Internet service.

Everything was done in black and white, and everyone was instructed to wear black and white. Celia wanted sleek and elegant, which was a stretch for small town Ohio, but by 7 p.m., the Ortiz house in that small cul-de-sac in Champaign County could have been any penthouse on Fifth Avenue hosting an elegant party.

Celia was dressed in a skin-tight black and white dress, accentuating all her curves. Her long, curly hair was piled on her head, with soft ringlets framing her black cat-masked face. Emily felt a bit plain in her white button-down "boyfriend" shirt tucked into a thin, black pencil skirt. Her mask was a simple black lace one that she picked up at the Dollar Store. After seeing Celia, she slowly undid two more buttons in her shirt to reveal just a bit more cleavage.

"Is Gavin coming tonight?" Celia asked, as she rearranged her centerpieces.

"He didn't commit to it. College Bowl games are on. You know men and their football."

"That's just silly. He knows that the men will be downstairs watching it tonight."

Emily shrugged. She half hoped Gavin would make an appearance, but then half hoped he wouldn't. The intensity of Christmas and Gavin's offer still burned fresh in her mind, and she was worried that their friendship was too strong, too fast. In what reasonable world would a man offer to fund her business only after knowing her for six months?

The guests started arriving by 7:30. By 8:00, the place was packed with Celia's family, co-workers, and neighbors. Margaret was there dressed as a flapper, in an outfit she claimed belong to her grandmother. She sat on the couch with a captive audience and told the story about how she survived a volcano eruption in the middle of her trip to Italy back in 2001. Margaret talked with her hands, in big, grandiose movements. Emily laughed to herself, as she did not recall the escapade as being at all life-threatening, rather a huge annoyance that Margaret had to leave Italy early because of a "godforsaken volcano of all things." Nevertheless, she was pleased that Margaret was back in full form enjoying life once again.

Emily served Sam some dinner and handed him a Sprite, when a man dressed to the nines in a tuxedo and a Phantom of the Opera half mask smiled and asked if she had tried the crab dip. "It really is spectacular," the man said.

"I know. I made it."

"You made it?"

"I made all the food—except the brisket. That is Paco's turf."

"I'm Gil O'Leary. I live next door." He held out his hand and Emily shook it.

"Emily. I am a friend of Paco and Celia's."

"Nice to meet you, Emily."

Gil was a smaller man, but fit. She guessed he was a distance runner, knowing the body type, even in his tuxedo.

She saw her fair share of men like him while walking through Central Park.

"All of the food is really fantastic. Do you cater?"

"I do," she said, and fished a card out of her pocket.

"Emily Mitchell of Shaw Farms." He grinned at her. He had nice brown eyes and a dimple.

"So, Gil, is that short for Gilbert?"

"No, Gilligan. Because my parents hated me and wanted me to get my ass kicked repeatedly in school."

Emily laughed.

"It's my mother's maiden name. But I wish she had thought a little harder and named me Bob, because getting asked about the Skipper and the Professor got really old, just sayin' . . ."

Emily laughed even harder, not exactly sure why the whole conversation just tickled her, but it did.

Gil smiled and his eyes crinkled. "I should take offense that you are laughing at my childhood trauma."

"I'm sorry. But it's really funny trauma," she said.

"It's all right. I don't mind being laughed at by a beautiful woman," Gil teased. Emily shook her head at the pickup line. As she turned her head, she caught sight of Will and Gavin walking back out the front door.

"Sorry, Gil. Can you excuse me for a second? A couple of friends just walked in." She squeezed her way through the crowd to the front door. She walked to the packed driveway and down the street to look around for them, confused about where they went. Just as she was about to turn back to walk to the house, she saw Gavin's truck parked on the side street about a block down. He was leaned up against it and Will was talking to him. Emily walked up slowly.

"Then take what is yours," Will said, before he saw Emily. He was surprised to see her.

"Emily."

Gavin stood up straight, startled to hear her name and to see her standing there.

"Hey, what's going on? Are you okay?" she asked.

Will looked at Gavin and then at her. He was fed up.

"I'm going to go get some food and a beer. Maybe she can talk some sense into you," he muttered. Gavin looked away.

"What's going on?"

He leaned back against the truck again and exhaled. He was dressed in a nice white shirt and black jeans. A mask was tucked into his front pocket of his jacket.

"I just don't do parties well. Natalie dragged me to plenty of them. Seeing everyone there kinda brought up some ugliness again," he said.

"Do you think you can try? Maybe stay for a few minutes at least? Get some food? Hell, I made most of it," she said lightly.

He shook his head. His eyes were sad, and she thought she saw the formation of tears.

"Hey. Hey. It's okay. It's not your cup of tea. You tried, right? Why don't you head on back home, watch the game? If you wait here, I can make you a plate to take with you," she said.

"Nah. I mean I have leftovers at home. Snacks and beer. I'll be all right. Just tell them I'm sorry and I'll see them later on, okay?"

"Sure, G."

He made a move to get in the truck and she grabbed his hand.

"Hey. Happy New Year," she said.

He dropped his head, closed the door and hugged her tightly. He was so warm. She didn't realize how cold she was until his arms were wrapped around her. He pulled away gently and she moved to kiss him on the cheek, but he deliberately moved his head, so she caught him square on the lips.

It was only a small flutter, a simple peck, a gentle grazing, but the night sky lit up for a moment before her eyes. She stepped back from him then shyly bowed her head.

"Well, since you won't be here at midnight, there you go," she joked.

Before she could even process what had just happened, he climbed in his truck and started it.

"Happy New Year," he said quietly, and drove off. She thought she saw him banging the steering wheel with his fist as he drove down the street, but she could not be sure.

She ran back to the house, shivering from the cold and rubbing her lips together compulsively over and over again. She made a beeline for Celia, who was talking to a small group of people.

"Where have you been? Did you go outside without a coat? Your hands are freezing," Celia said, as Emily led her to the back bedroom, which was their guest room. Emily closed the door.

"What?" Celia asked, as she removed her mask.

"Gavin and I kissed."

Celia's eyes grew wide, and she jumped up and down.

"Oh my God! Yay! Yay! Yay!"

"No, no, no, it wasn't planned. It was an accident."

"An accident? What, did you fall onto his lips?"

"Oh, Jesus, Celia," she moaned.

Emily paced and shook her hands as a feeble attempt to shake off what had just happened.

"Okay, just please calm down, and start from the beginning," she said.

So, Emily told her what happened, emphasizing that Gavin moved his face toward her, and watched as Celia took it in, chewing on her bottom lip.

Celia sighed. "Why does that man have to be so damn difficult?" she finally said.

"What do I do?" Emily asked.

"Nothing. Tonight, you do nothing. He had the chance to come here and be your man, but he ran away like a scared little boy. So, I say you do nothing. You come outside with me, eat and be merry tonight," Celia suggested.

Emily sighed and ran her hands through her hair. Celia went up and hugged her and adjusted Emily's mask.

"You look fabulous. Everyone is raving about the food. Men are curious about you. It's really his loss, Em," Celia said.

Emily took a deep breath and realigned her thoughts.

"Okay, okay."

Emily followed Celia back to the living room and walked back to the kitchen to check on the food. She filled bowls and platters that were low on food and then checked on Sam before she finally served herself, making a sandwich out of Paco's brisket with white bread and pickles. She sat on the counter by the stove.

"Simplicity. That's what I love about you," Will said, as he walked up to her.

"Simple Emily. That's me."

Will tossed his beer bottle into the trash and opened up two more with his own bottle opener, handing one to her. He leaned against the counter and watched her drink it.

"You know he saw you talking to that short fellow, laughing, and got pissed off. He was all set to come to this shindig," Will said.

Emily coughed, the beer going down the wrong pipe. Will handed her a napkin and she wiped the beer off her chin.

"He didn't want you to know that . . . but he's not here to stop me from telling you."

"Fantastic," Emily said. She wiped the BBQ sauce off her hands and shook her head. "Never took him for a man who would be so jealous to see me laughing at a man named Gilligan."

"I'm not sure it was jealousy. Fear and insecurity, I think."

Emily drank a long swig of beer. "If I had a lifetime I could never figure that man out, Will."

"It's quite easy, really. There are two kinds of men in the world. Those who are all cards in and bet all the time on love, and those who hold their cards close and pass every round because they won big one round and they never feel they will be that fortunate again."

Emily wondered if the same held true for women—and which woman she was. "Why *did* you tell me this?" she asked.

"Because he needs to play his damn hand! I think he may actually win big this round," Will said and folded his arms. His blue eyes were focused on her.

She looked away, unable to answer the questions behind his stare.

"Well, enough about Gavin. Let's talk about me," Will said, smacking his hand on her thigh, and grinned.

Emily exhaled, relieved. "Yes, let's."

"So, I took your advice. Decided to go abroad."

"Really? Oh my goodness, Will! That's fantastic! When? Where?"

"I leave in a couple of weeks. Taking about a month. Fifteen countries. France, Switzerland, Italy, Vatican City, Slovenia, Austria, Slovakia, Czech Republic, Netherlands, Liechtenstein, Luxembourg, Germany, Spain, Monaco, and Belgium. I have them all memorized," he said sheepishly.

"You will have the best time. I'm so excited for you!"

Will smiled shyly. "You know I owe you a great deal of gratitude. I would have never done this if you hadn't been so insistent. But you're right. The boys are grown and settled. I can get away for a little bit and see the world. I'm really looking forward to it."

Emily hopped down and hugged him. Will patted her on the back.

"Emily! Em! Emma-LEE. It's your turn for karaoke!" Paco yelled, walking into the kitchen. He was red-eyed and more than a little drunk.

"What? No way. I never agreed to sing!"

Paco grabbed her hand and led her to the living room. "Everyone has to do it."

"Everyone? I haven't even heard a single person sing yet!"

"Well, everyone after you start it," Paco said. He thumbed through the selections until he found one that he thought was appropriate.

"No, Paco. I don't want to do this," Emily said. She hated singing in front of people.

"Come on, I'll do this with you."

"No!"

"I'll give you my brisket rub recipe…" Paco tempted. She frowned. She had asked him for that damn recipe all summer and he would never give it to her. She relented. She chugged the rest of her beer to give her some courage.

Paco picked Des'ree's "You Gotta Be" for their duet. Emily laughed, embarrassed as Paco began to sing with a microphone in one hand and a beer in the other. She managed to overcome her shyness and began to belt out the song, tilting her head a little bit, performing. The crowd cheered her on and even joined her on the chorus.

"All I know, all I know, love will save the day."

"See I told ya'll. She's good, ain't she? I've heard you singing when you were cooking."

They fumbled through the rest of the song, and people who were on the verge of drunkenness found an inner groove and started singing along, beers in the air, with this anthem about loving each other. After the song ended, people clapped, causing her cheeks to flood crimson. She took a bow and handed the microphone to the next person who suddenly felt empowered by her performance. Paco hugged her and people she didn't know gave her high fives.

"A new year, my friend. A new beginning," Paco whispered in her ear.

Emily hugged him tighter and patted his back. He was right. Regardless of her relationship with Gavin, she knew this would be a better year. Sam was in a good school. Margaret was on the upswing, dancing with two men half her age in the corner of the living room. She was grateful for friends and for opportunities.

They sang and drank until midnight, when Celia flashed the lights, and everyone counted down. She hugged everyone in the room and dodged a few men trying to kiss her. When the cheers and confetti finally fell, she wondered if Gavin was still awake.

Margaret stumbled to her a half hour later while she was helping Paco and Celia clean up in the kitchen.

"Well, this old woman has partied her fair share," she said.

"We can get going in a few minutes," Emily said.

"The boys fell asleep in Xavier's room," Celia said. She had taken off her heels and let her hair down. She looked exhausted, but beautiful.

"Why don't y'all just stay here? Not that many people left. You both can share the spare bed," Paco suggested. He took Celia's arm and spun her around, half asleep and still very drunk. He sang Smokey Robinson's "Cruisin" as it played on the stereo. He rested his head on Celia's ample chest and smiled. She giggled.

"What do you think?" Emily asked Margaret.

"Hey, Mark," Margaret called to one of the men she danced with. "Want to come have a night cap with an old woman? I'll show you my stamp collection," she teased.

Mark, a tall, slightly overweight 40-something man with a goatee, laughed.

"Wild horses couldn't keep me from your stamp collection, Margaret," he said.

Margaret looked at Emily. "I think Mark and I will head on home. The keys, please."

Emily laughed and shook her head. "You are the horniest old woman I know. Are you okay to drive?"

Margaret hugged her and kissed her cheek. "Yes. Get some rest. I sure hope I won't."

When Margaret and Mark were safely in the Honda, Paco closed the door to the last of the guests.

Emily checked on Sam and Xavier, who were sleeping quietly next to each other on the full-sized bed. She kissed them both and fell asleep with her clothes on as soon as her head hit the pillow. All she remembered before she fell asleep was how warm Gavin's lips were and how he shivered when his lips touched hers.

CHAPTER NINETEEN

Gavin had fallen asleep in his recliner watching the Virginia/Auburn bowl game when his home phone rang to bring him the news. He pulled on his boots and heavy coat and was speeding down his driveway in two minutes flat, skidding on sleet that threatened to turn to ice.

He could see the thick smoke in the early morning dawn as he drove into town. Will did not tell him much detail, only that Margaret's house was on fire, with flames that could be seen over in Union County. Gavin said a prayer to every god, demi-god, and saint he ever read about, over and over again, as he drove the torturous eight miles into town at 100 mph.

Police cars and two fire trucks blocked off Avenue B. Gavin drove up to the Dollar General, threw the truck into park, and ran down the street past two cops who called his name to stop, as fast as he could until the cold air burned like battery acid in his lungs, making him slow down.

"Jesus, please, please, please, please," Gavin said, as he caught sight of the thick black smoke coming from the front windows of Margaret's house. The sight of the smoke brought him right back to that awful night five years ago as he watched his life burn up before his eyes. Two officers held him back from running into the burning house.

"Gavin, no! You can't go in there," one officer said to him.

"EMILY! SAM! MARGARET!!" he yelled.

"We don't know who's in there yet," they said.

Gavin walked back to the gathering crowd and watched helplessly as the fire crew doused the flames with water. He paced back and forth, heart beating wildly in his chest, the bile from too much beer and too little food that day burning his throat.

"GAVIN! GAVIN!"

Gavin turned and saw Paco waving his hands wildly from behind a barricade on the opposite side of the street. Gavin pushed by the crowd and ran toward his friend.

"Where are they?" Gavin asked frantically.

"Emily and Sam are safe," Paco said. Gavin's knees almost buckled from sheer relief.

"She and Sam spent the night last night at our house. But Margaret," Paco paused, then looked sadly towards the house.

They walked quickly past the barricade and Gavin saw Emily standing in a neighbor's yard staring at the smoke with silent tears running down her face and her hands cupping her mouth, like she was trying to suppress her screams. They locked eyes, and the look on her face was a punch to his gut. She was about to say something when they heard one of the fireman call "WATCH OUT!!!"

The explosion knocked out every window in the house and rattled the windows of all the houses up and down Avenue B. Any chance that Margaret was alive went up in the massive flames that raged out of every corner.

Emily let out a wail and covered her face with her hands. Gavin caught her before she fell. The last thing she remembered was Gavin muttering, "I got you," and smelling his familiar Brut aftershave before everything faded to black.

***

Emily woke up and heard Gavin and Will talking to Celia and Paco in their living room. She was lying in Paco and Celia's bed. The pillow smelled like Celia, warm and comforting. Someone had taken off her boots and coat and put a tall glass of water on the nightstand. Emily blinked in the dim room and saw a small TV and a large dresser with an even larger mirror that had miniature saint statues in cubbies that framed the mirror. A white doily that was probably thirty years old sat underneath a lamp. The bedside clock read noon.

"Fire Department said that it was probably started from the garage. Paint and fumes. Maybe oily rags. It burned quick and hot. Burned right through the sunroom. And the kitchen. They assume Margaret and Mark died from the smoke inhalation from all the clutter before the flames . . ." Will said.

Poor Mark was with Margaret. Emily closed her eyes at that news.

"God bless them. May their souls be at peace," Celia said. Emily could imagine Celia doing the sign of the cross like she did whenever she heard awful news.

"Thank God Emily and Sam were here. The garage was right by the sunroom where they slept," Paco said.

"They were so damn lucky they were not home last night," Gavin said.

Emily lay back down. Now, she had no one. She closed her eyes and cried softly. She wished she and Sam were in the sunroom. At least the hell they called life would be over.

When she woke up again the clock read 2:00 p.m. and Celia was sitting on the edge of the bed with a plate of food of leftover brisket in a sandwich and some Fritos.

"I thought you might be hungry," she said.

Emily sat up, groggy from too much sleep. "Where's Sam?"

"Paco took him and Xavier to my sister's house to go see their new puppies. Their dog had puppies at Christmas," Celia said cheerfully. She handed Emily a plate and a Coke.

"Thank you," Emily said.

She picked up the sandwich and tried to eat it, but it vibrated from her hands shaking so badly. Celia took the plate and put it on the end table. She held Emily as she cried.

"It's gonna be all right, sweetie. I promise you, it's gonna be alright," Celia murmured.

Gavin came to the door as short while later. Emily was sitting in the kitchen and heard him knock before walking in.

"Is she awake?" he asked Celia.

"She's in the kitchen," Celia said.

Gavin walked in and saw Emily at the table stirring honey into a cup of tea that had turned cold.

"Hey," she said.

"Hey."

She found it hard to keep his gaze and went back to stirring her tea. He sat across from her at the small table.

"How are you doing?" he asked. She shrugged. Talking would just cause her to cry again.

"Sam?" he asked.

"At Lupe and Miguel's house. Petting puppies," she said. Gavin nodded. His cheeks were pink from the cold. Emily thought he looked good—healthy and alive.

"I was having a really good time last night. We were singing and laughing. The kids were playing video games, and I was feeling so good. Like this year was going to be the best year yet—a fresh start. I felt the hell was behind me. Now I feel like we are right back where we started. I can't believe I have to tell my son another person he loved is dead. I mean how many times can I break his heart? How many times do I have to remind him about how unfair life is? I'm his mother. I'm supposed to shield him from this."

Gavin sat silent and just listened.

"I just wanted to fall asleep with that good feeling. Wake up with that feeling. Not trek back to that goddamn house that reminded me that I have so much left to do . . . I should have gone home. Margaret went home. I should have gone home. She would be alive if I wasn't so selfish wanting to hold on to that ridiculous feeling," Emily said.

"If you'd gone home, you'd be dead too," Gavin said.

Emily shook her head—in part to argue, in part to relent to defeat.

"This is horrible, Gavin," she said. Tears fell down her cheeks like rain. He reached across and put his warm hands over hers. She hung her head in gratitude at the simple gesture.

"You're not alone," he said. She shook her head and took her hands out of his grasp. She wanted to believe him, but she didn't think she was capable of it. Not anymore.

Margaret was laid to rest on a Thursday afternoon in a small ceremony held at the Grace Methodist church. Mark's remains were sent back to his family in Wisconsin, and his cousins, Celia and Paco's neighbors, drove back for the funeral to be held later that weekend.

Sam sat with Emily in the front row in the small church in a blue suit that Celia found on clearance at JC Penney. She wore a black dress from Celia's closet that was too big in the chest and bottom, with black flats she pulled from Payless Shoe Source clearance rack. She and Sam stared at the small white coffin holding Margaret's charred remains. Sam was inherently sad, his spirit crushed, and Emily feared this would be the final blow, the blow that would fundamentally change who Sam would become in the future. Too much death. Too much change. Too much hope lost, never to be regained.

The ceremony was low-key. Margaret had pre-planned and pre-paid her funeral. She wanted white roses, a white casket, with no burial. She would be cremated and placed with Craig near Wright-Patterson AFB in Dayton. The song selections were a combination of her favorite hymns and her favorite kitschy show tunes including Evita's "Don't Cry for Me Argentina." The ceremony was all Margaret, simple, elegant, yet quirky.

"Don't cry for me, baby. Just put me in the ground and get on with your lives!" she had told Emily when she was a little girl listening to this song with her one summer.

Gavin, Shakes, and Will sat a few rows behind Emily and Sam. Celia had stayed home with Xavier, not wanting to upset him or expose him to death this close up. Paco sat on the other side of Emily, dressed in a dark blue suit, acting as her surrogate brother that she never had but always wanted.

After the service, Shakes took Sam to the small courtyard to get some air while Emily went to the ladies' room. While sitting in the stall, she heard a racket as multiple women walked into the small bathroom.

"I don't know how a decent man like Gavin Shaw got tangled up with the likes of Margaret Rutherford and her skanky niece," said a voice Emily didn't recognize.

"It's like they put a spell on him or something. Did you hear how frantic he was at the fire scene? He about knocked out the fire chief to rush into that house to save them," another voice said.

"I blame the niece. She has put some sort of spell on him, I swear. Did you know her husband was a Wall Street thief? Like one of those Potsie schemers," another woman said.

"What's a Potsie schemer?"

"You know, Potsie. Where they take money and give it to someone else and say they are investing it."

Emily shook her head and put her head in her hands.

"Oh my God. What if she is like telling Gavin all these things to take his farm away? Like using her cookie to get him all hot and bothered where he will sign away the deed to his land? That is just horrifying. He's just a fool."

Emily had enough and flushed.

"Who's in here?" a voice asked no one.

Emily opened the door and a group of women she had never laid eyes on before stood speechless by the sinks. Emily casually washed her hands and reached around one of them to get a paper towel.

"It's Ponzi scheme. PAWN-ZEE. Not Potsie schemes. Potsie was a character on *Happy Days*. I suggest that when you decide to talk crap about a woman who just buried her kin you at least use the right terminology to spew your evil and hate," Emily said.

All of the women looked down.

"God bless you all, have a wonderful day," she said sarcastically and walked out of the bathroom. She went straight to Paco and Celia's spare room and slept on their futon for two solid days.

Paco, Celia, Sam, and even Xavier took turns checking in on her during that time. Most of the time she kept her eyes closed to avoid conversation. Sam would crawl into bed with her at night and she would hug him tight to her. She knew she was being a terrible mother, but she was too exhausted to care.

On Monday morning, after Sam left with Celia, Paco, and Xavier for school, Emily fell back into a deep sleep and had a vivid dream. She could hear a waltz in the background, and there was a sea of people on a ballroom floor dressed in beautiful, elaborate gowns and tuxedos, the type with flaps. Emily was fighting her way to get to the center, as a group of people gathered in a circle around a couple that was dancing.

Emily finally reached the center and saw that the couple was a young Margaret and a young Craig. Margaret's dark hair was in luxurious curls around her shoulders, and she was wearing a white gown with an empire waist. She had a crown of white roses on her head. Craig looked dashing in his formal military uniform. He twirled Margaret with so much love in his eyes. Margaret's head was tilted back in pure joy and happiness. Emily lifted her hand to wave to her, and Margaret spun by her, pulling a white rose out of her hair and handing it to her, smiling that special smile she always gave her when she was a young girl. Emily cradled the flower in her hands, and she smiled as she saw the two of them dancing around and around in a circle.

Emily opened her eyes and sat up. She swore she could smell roses. She felt a peace about her she hadn't felt in weeks and decided then and there that the crazed mourning period was over. Margaret was happy and safe. It was time to reconnect with the world.

She walked to the guest bathroom and turned on the hot water in the shower and began to strip out of her clothes. She stepped in and let the water loosen the tight muscles in her shoulders. She soaped up with Celia's Bath and Body fruity smelling body wash and shampoo and let all the agony of the last few days run down the drain.

She walked back from the bathroom with a dark purple towel wrapped around her and screamed when she saw Gavin, Shakes, and Paco in the living room.

"Oh my God! What are y'all doing here?" she yelled, as she ran to the guest room.

"I live here!" Paco yelled in her direction.

She pulled on clean underwear and threw on one of Paco's old sweatshirts and sweatpants. She ran a comb through her hair and walked out to the living room.

They were all in the kitchen talking while Gavin was

making eggs and toast.

"Looking good, Em," Shakes said, and whistled when he saw her.

"Shut it, Dillon. I thought you left for school," she told Paco.

"I took the day off. We were finishing up with Margaret's house," Paco said.

The mention of Margaret's name made Emily lower her head. Gavin quietly finished scrambling eggs and pulled down four plates from the cabinet closest to him. He refused to make eye contact with her for fear she would be able to read his face and know he would be taking that image of her in a purple towel to bed with him that night.

Shakes poured her a cup of coffee and Emily sat down at the table and poured half and half in it. Shakes sat with her.

"We found something at the house," he said.

Emily stopped stirring her coffee. "What?"

"A fire safe. A small one. It's the only thing that survived the blaze."

Emily swallowed. "Did you open it?" she asked.

We thought it should be you," he said.

Gavin walked in with four plates of eggs and toast and set them down on the table. Everyone started to eat except for her. She had no appetite these days. She passed her plate to Shakes. She could feel Gavin's eyes on her as she moved to the living room with her coffee. She tried to focus on how good the dream made her feel, but now she was dreading learning what was in that safe.

Gavin and Shakes walked out to the garage after they finished eating and brought in the safe, putting it on the table with a thud. She felt tears well up in her eyes as she saw the charred marks around the safe. Poor Margaret. Poor Mark.

"Shakes busted the code," Paco said.

"It helps having a former locksmith for a friend. This brand has a default code to open it," Shakes said. He entered the 6-number code on the keypad and heard the door pop open. Inside were documents. Emily started to leaf through them.

"Craig's insurance papers, her insurance papers. She had a life insurance policy for $50,000. Benefits for widows of fallen vets . . ." Emily stopped and looked at the top shelf of the safe.

She pulled out Aaron's watch and her small bag of her heirloom jewelry. She exhaled slowly and felt a small cry get caught in her throat. Margaret must have stashed it when Emily was working out at Gavin's last summer.

"This was my husband's watch. And this was my mother and grandmother's jewelry," she told them.

Emily breathed in and out a few times to suppress her emotions and continued to search the safe. Margaret had a few pictures in the safe—her wedding picture with Craig, a few of her family pictures including Emily's father when he was just a boy, and Sam's school picture taken in the fall. He was wearing a red polo and smiling his shy grin. On the back Margaret had scribbled "my precious Sam—8 years old."

The last picture was of her and Margaret on the beach in Galveston when Emily was 16 or 17 and Margaret was pushing 40. Both of them were in modest black swimsuits posing with their arms around each other, the sun setting behind them on the Gulf. On the back Margaret had written "my sweet girl Emily—16 years old."

Emily showed Gavin the picture. "She looks like she could be your mother."

"In a lot of ways, she was my mother. More than my actual mother was. I don't think my mother ever wanted children. My dad was 30 and she was 28. They had been married for about eight years when I arrived, unexpected and unannounced."

Gavin handed her the picture back. She studied it closely. "This was back before I discovered the wonders of flour and butter. I can't believe that was almost twenty years ago," she chuckled.

"You look the exact same," he said. Shakes and Paco looked at it.

"Yeah, you look the same," they agreed.

"Young and hot? Hardly," she joked.

Emily leafed through more documents and found a will.

"Her will. Updated before Christmas," she said. In the will Margaret stated that she wanted to leave her assets to Emily, including her wedding rings, her insurance policy, and the house.

Emily looked in another small bag and saw four diamond rings that were Margaret's. The prettiest was the one Craig gave her—a 1-carat princess cut diamond. A princess diamond for his princess he had told her.

Emily put the diamond on her left hand, but it didn't make it past her second knuckle. "Always so petite," she said.

Emily stared at all that remained of sixty years of life and covered her eyes, taken with emotion again. Gavin, tired of being a bystander, hugged her like he wanted to for the last week. Paco hugged her from behind and Shakes hugged all of them.

"You smell good," Shakes said, after a few minutes.

"Don't be a freak, man," Paco said.

"Not you, her."

"But you're hugging me. A little too close, I may add."

She laughed. She pulled away and wiped her tears. She sat with the bag of jewelry and examined the pieces.

"I know a good man if you want to get cash for the jewelry," Shakes told her. She looked at the diamonds and thought about Margaret over the years as she wore each of them.

"Not just yet, okay?" she told him.

Shakes looked at Gavin and Gavin looked at her.

"I think that's best," he said.

Two days later she stood with Will and watched the bulldozers take the last of the charred remains of the house. When the last scrap was placed in the huge dumpsters, she exhaled loudly, and Will hugged her. All that remained was an empty lot and a charred concrete slab. Will put a sign in the front that read "LOT FOR SALE." His phone number was listed as the contact number. He agreed to handle the transaction for her while he was still in town and arranged for a friend to handle the business while he was in Europe. Up until then she never knew that Will had his real estate license for close to ten years, but hardly used it.

"Now's as good a time as any to get back into it," he told her.

Everyone had been extremely kind and helpful, above and beyond any friendship that Emily had ever had with anyone in her entire life. Paco and Celia had the Academy's psychologist, Dr. Gina Gibson meet with Sam twice a week to talk about the fire.

"She's excellent, Emily. I know you think she's young, but I would not recommend it if I didn't think she was a great shrink," Paco said.

Dr. Gibson called Emily once a week and gave her an update and recommended discussions to have with Sam, or things to focus on. Sam became very concerned that others he loved would die, and he started forming separation anxiety with Emily when he left for school. Dr. Gibson suggested a phone for text messaging to allow him to text her during lunch and their sessions. Gavin quickly picked up two phones at Cricket, one for each of them, and Sam's screaming fits subsided as quickly as they began.

Celia and Emily walked around the Goodwill in Columbus the next weekend trying to restock some clothing lost in the fire. She enjoyed shopping with Celia because she had a good eye for what fit and what was in style, but she was frugal.

"These jeans are 10s, but we can use a belt on him," Celia said.

Emily put them on a pile of shirts, socks, and underwear. Celia continued to walk until she reached the woman's section and scavenged the racks until she found a few sweaters that were acceptable for Emily, and she added them to the pile.

"So, what's the plan now, Em?" Celia asked.

"I thought we'd grab a coffee after this."

"No. I mean what's next for you?"

"I'm not quite sure yet. Still trying to get my bearings on most days."

The life insurance was finally paid out, but it was barely enough to survive for a year, if she was very, very careful.

"Gavin came by the Academy to talk to us yesterday," Celia said, her eyebrows raised.

"About?"

"About you moving out to the farm with him."

Emily was floored by the suggestion. "And what did you guys say?"

"We told him that would be up to you, of course."

Emily walked around and got lost in her thoughts. She fingered the polyester material of a truly gaudy blouse.

"What were his reasons for us moving out there?"

Celia kept flipping through the racks. "Space mostly. He said he had the empty rooms. And the business partnership that he proposed to you at Christmas. He said it made sense for you to be at the farm. Closer to work."

"I'm sure that would look fantastic to Champaign County if we moved in with him," Emily muttered.

"Girl, there will always be talk. Small towns talk, that's what they do. You have to do what you think is best and say screw it to the rest of the people."

"Do you want us to move out?" she asked.

Celia looked at her. "As far as we're concerned, you can live with us forever. We love you and Sam. You are our family and Paco is ready to convert part of the basement to another room, to give you some privacy. But Gavin told Paco about the business and threw in this other plan . . ."

Emily thought about those awful women in the bathroom after Margaret's funeral. She imagined Sue Ellen spontaneously combusting at the news she and Sam lived with Gavin. She envisioned the stares in town, the business suffering because of the gossip and of Sue Ellen's retribution in the form of her influence over the humble and meek women of Champaign County.

"I think it would be best to stay put for a little while."

"Then it's settled. I think we have picked this place clean, girl. Let's go get that coffee," Celia said.

CHAPTER TWENTY

Gavin navigated slowly on the slushy highway to the next town over and drove Emily to Bob Evans, away from the wandering eyes of their neighbors, and away from interruptions. Emily didn't bother to open the menu when they sat down.

"Order something," he said.

"Coffee is fine," she mumbled.

"Bring her a cheeseburger. No onion. She hates onions. And some fries," Gavin told the waitress. He handed the menus back and watched as the blonde woman walked away.

"Hope you're hungry. You'll be eating two burgers tonight," she said. They sat in silence until the waitress returned with their drinks. Emily poured creamer into the coffee and stirred. Gavin watched her and tried to frame his next sentences in a way that wouldn't cause her to shut down like she had the few times before.

"I want to know the real reason you keep saying no to moving out to the farm. I mean, the *real* reason. Is it me? Did I do something to offend you?" Gavin asked.

Emily looked up, startled. "No."

"Then please explain it to me," Gavin said.

"Gavin . . ."

"Whatever it is, I can take it, as long as it's the truth," he said. Emily rubbed her hands over her eyes and let them rest under her chin for a moment, thinking. She placed her hands palm side down on the table.

"I won't have anyone trash talk you because of me. And I won't let your hard work that you've done since Natalie and Sissy passed suffer because of me. You're too decent of a man to be the fodder for hateful rumors and bad mouthing," Emily said.

Gavin leaned back in the booth; his eyes narrowed.

"What are you hearing?" he asked.

"Oh, just that I started that fire so I can get my hands on the Shaw farm, and that I cast some wicked spell on you because you hardly know me but are willing to go into business with me. Oh, and my favorite, that I am carrying out Aaron's evil work, secretly using my vagina to influence your investment strategies, and that you're a fool and will lose the farm to the likes of me," Emily said. Gavin chuckled.

"It's not funny, Shaw," Emily said.

"I'm sorry. I was not aware your vagina gave investment advice. We should take that act on the road," he said. He took a long sip of Coke and smiled at her.

"I'm serious, Gavin. Why should you have to endure this crap? It's not worth it," Emily said.

"Who are you hearing this pile of crap from? Sue Ellen? Those hens at the church?" Gavin asked.

Emily bit her lip and refused to answer. Gavin shook his head, disgusted.

"Let me tell you about those *good, Christian* women at the church. They came over after my girls died, brought their casserole dishes, their pies, gave condolences. Cried tears for my loss. Then a few weeks later, kept bringing over the dishes, but would linger. Touch my arm and say that a man like me must get lonely without a woman around. Offered me other pie, if you get my drift, all while their husbands were driving on a tractor all day and night to pay for their Range Rovers and trips to Columbus to go to the fancy malls. It's like becoming a widower turned me into George Clooney or something. Let me make myself perfectly clear when I say I can give two shits what those bitches at the church have to say about you, Sam, and me. My conscience is clear. And my conscience is all I give a damn about anymore," he said.

They stared at each other for a long time, a million conversations held with just their gazes. The blonde waitress brought back their order and Gavin smiled politely and thanked her. He assembled his burger, pulling the tomatoes off his plate and putting them on Emily's plate.

"I don't have a lot of people I call friend, Emily. Paco, Will, Shakes. That's about it. I have a lot of people who are acquaintances, neighbors, business contacts. But I can name on both hands who I call friend," Gavin said.

"And I make the cut?"

"Damn straight," he said. He looked at her so seriously it took her breath away. "And I always help out my friends, come hell or high water . . ." he said.

Emily put Gavin's tomatoes on her burger and slowly squeezed mustard on the bun.

"Then I think we should make a gentleman's wager," Emily finally said.

"About what?"

She dipped a fry in the mustard, chewed on it slowly. "About the time it will take for you to tire of us when you are around us 24/7 and how long it takes before we get kicked off the illustrious Gavin Shaw friendship list," Emily said. Gavin smiled.

"I say six weeks," Emily said.

"It doesn't matter. You're a life member when you're put on the list," he said.

Emily was quiet, mulling her choices. "Ok. I'm in," she said. Gavin grinned into his Coke, so proud of himself and his powers of persuasion.

Emily took a bite of a burger. "Now . . . *George*, tell me about this pie that the hens offered you," Emily said with a wicked smile.

Gavin coughed, Coke spilling down the wrong pipe, and Emily laughed. "Oh, God. You do NOT want to know," he said.

They moved in later that night. Sam and Xavier were sad to leave each other, but both parents reminded the boys that they would see each other the next day at school, and there was always the weekend. Paco was a little sad, too, but Emily also reminded him that she would see him every morning, and she would bring him muffins.

"The banana nut ones. Those are my favorite," he said

sadly.

"I know, I know . . ."

Paco hugged her and Sam and Celia put on a brave face trying not to cry.

It was almost 9 p.m. when Gavin finally drove them up his driveway. Snow started to fall down in light white flakes. Sam had fallen asleep between them, and when Gavin turned off the engine he glanced over at Emily. She stared at the farmhouse and then she looked over at him.

"What are you thinking?" he asked.

"It's going to be nice to sleep in a real bed tonight," she said.

Gavin carried Sam up the stairs, and Emily brought in the two gym bags that held their meager possessions. He opened the door and let Emily walk in first. She welcomed the familiarity of this house and allowed it to calm her soul.

"I set up the rooms upstairs for you. I gave you the guest room. I put Sam in the room next to yours," Gavin said.

"He probably will want to sleep close tonight. Why don't you just put him in my bed?" she asked.

"Okay," Gavin said, and walked upstairs, turning on lights.

The guest bed had fresh blue sheets and a nice red, white, and blue patchwork quilt on it. Emily dropped her bags beside the dresser and pulled back the covers, slowly removing Sam's shoes and coat. Gavin gently placed Sam in the bed and pulled up the covers. He rested his hand on the boy's dark hair for a second before turning to Emily.

"Is it warm enough for you?" he asked.

"It's perfect," she said.

"Good. Well, help yourself to whatever you need. Towels are in the hall closet, toiletries in the bathroom. Just holler if you need anything," he said.

Emily walked up to him and hugged him, resting her head on his chest. He exhaled and placed his hand on the back of her head.

"Thank you," she whispered.

"You don't ever have to thank me," he said. They broke

away and stared at each other for what seemed like an eternity until Sam stirred, breaking the spell.

"Get some rest, Em. I'll see you both in the morning," Gavin said and left the room.

Emily turned toward the welcoming bed that beckoned her. She peeled off her boots and coat and turned off the lights. She climbed into bed with Sam, held him in her arms, and fell into a deep sleep knowing she was safe with Gavin keeping watch downstairs.

When Emily opened her eyes in the morning, she knew something was wrong. Her throat hurt badly, and her body ached, like she'd been hit by a bus. She sat up slowly and the room started to spin. She walked with sock feet to the stairs and sat on the landing, afraid she may fall down them.

Gavin saw her from the first floor. "You all right?"

"I think I have the flu," she said.

"Oh, damn."

He climbed up the stairs and offered his hand to lift her up and brushed a rough hand to her forehead.

"You're burning up. Back to bed," he ordered.

"Sam needs to get ready for school."

"He's eating cereal. I'll make sure he gets to the meeting point to meet Paco and Celia," he said. He pulled back the covers and set her down in the bed.

"I'm freezing," she said, her teeth chattering.

"Your body is burning up. I'm going to bring you some ibuprofen and some water. Hang tight," he said. Emily shivered under the covers and closed her eyes, listening to Gavin talking to Sam slowly, making sure Sam could read his lips. A few minutes later she heard Sam's footsteps in the room.

"Are you sick?" he asked.

"I think it's the flu."

"You didn't get your shot like me. You said you would," he scolded.

"I know. I know," she mumbled. She had taken full advantage of the state program to ensure Sam was getting all his medical coverage, but in true mom fashion, she neglected to get her flu shot, unable to squeeze the $30 she needed to get it done at CVS at the time. One of the many repercussions of being poor. Poverty—the gift that kept on giving.

Gavin walked in with a bottle of Advil, a large glass of ice water, some crackers, and a plate with lightly buttered toast. He was flustered. Emily sat up to grab some items off him.

"Take two and we'll take your temperature. I brought you crackers and toast, because Nat used to not be able to take these on an empty stomach. Didn't know if you were the same," he mumbled.

She opened the bottle and shook out some pills. She drank them down and handed him back the glass. He placed the crackers and toast on the end table. He fidgeted nervously.

"It's the flu, G. In five days I will wish for death, then I will be good as new," she joked. He didn't even muster a smile. He walked out of the room; thumbs hooked heavily into the belt loops of his Wranglers.

"Do you want me to stay home and take care of you?" Sam signed.

"That's really sweet of you, but you should go to school and have fun. Gavin will be around, and I am just going to sleep most of the day."

Sam thought about it. *"Okay. I will be home at 4:30."*

"Okay. I'll be waiting for you. And I will want to hear about your day."

Sam leaned in and hugged Emily and she patted his head and kissed his cheek. *"I love you."*

"I love you more," she signed.

She heard Sam walk down the stairs, the shuffling of gathering coats and backpacks, and the door closing. The silence calmed her, and she fell back asleep quickly.

She stood on the top of the Rockefeller building, shivering on a cold February day. The view of Central Park was depressing with all the leaves gone from the trees.

"What's colder? Winter in Ohio or winter in New York?"

Aaron stood by her, wearing the blue suit she had him buried in. He had just bought it, never having a chance to wear it. She thought it looked great on him when he paraded out of the dressing room in Macy's wearing it.

"I'm freezing. Why did you bring me up here?" she asked. She wore her Salvation Army heavy coat over her nightgown and boots that she used to muck stalls.

"You used to like it up here," he said.

"I never liked it up here. I never liked high places. You liked them. Loved to walk on the rooftops and see the people below," she said.

"They look like ants," he smiled. He always used to say that. He had a slight overbite in his smile that made him more adorable. It was that smile that got her to go out with him after persistent asking.

"I like the farmer. What's his name, Fred?" he said.

"Gavin. His name is Gavin, for the hundredth time," she mumbled.

Aaron climbed to the top of the railing of the observation deck. The safety glass that was usually there was gone.

"Get down, Aaron, you're scaring me," she said.

"It's like you're flying, Em," he said.

"Don't do it, Aaron. Please. Please don't!" she yelled.

Every time she pleaded with him to get down. Every time he jumped.

She startled awake to find Gavin sitting at the foot of her bed. She was groggy and confused.

"What time is it?" she whispered. She had tears in her eyes. Gavin gently pushed her back on the pillow.

"Noon. Your fever is spiking. I have a call into a family friend, Doc Thomas," he said. He placed a cool, wet compress to her head. She jumped at the temperature difference.

"You're at 103. Don't want it to get up anymore," he said softly.

"I feel hot," she mumbled.

"You were having a nightmare," he said.

She rolled to her stomach, pushing her face into the pillow to erase the vision of Aaron flying through the air to his death.

"Aaron jumped. He always jumps even when I beg him not

to," she mumbled. She sat up pulling her sweater and her t-shirt over her head. Gavin averted his eyes as he saw her belly and realized pretty quickly that she was not wearing a bra.

"I'm hot," she mumbled, eyes still half-closed, trapped in her sweater.

"Let me help you," he said. He separated her sweater from the black t-shirt and gently pulled it back down over her stomach, his fingers grazing the soft, smooth flesh. She lay back on the pillow and looked at him.

"He calls you Fred. Farmer Fred," she said.

Gavin smiled. "I had an uncle named Fred. But he was an insurance agent." He wrung out the compress and placed it back on her forehead.

"You're a good nurse," she said, eyes half closed and smiling.

"You're a chatty patient," he mumbled.

"You're grumpy."

"I don't like fevers."

"Me neither."

"Doc Thomas will be here in a bit. Hopefully give you a shot of something to bring this fever down," Gavin said matter-of-factly.

"Grumpy Gavin," she said, and closed her eyes. Gavin exhaled. He heard her softly breathing when she fell back asleep. He put his hands to his eyes and left them there.

She awoke a few hours later to a pair of warm, brown eyes staring at her.

"Hi, Emily. I'm Doug Thomas. I'm going to check you out to see if you're okay," he said.

Dr. Thomas looked like he was only a few years older than her, with brown hair and eyes, but she knew that he was at least ten to fifteen years older based on his demeanor. He was in his green Air Force Reserves flight suit. He had an eagle on the left side of his chest.

He peered into her eyes and ears. He asked her to show him her throat. He took his warm hands and felt on the sides of her throat. He was methodical in his evaluation, yet kind.

"Just woke up feeling bad?" he asked.

"Yes, sir," she said.

"Throat hurt?"

"And my body."

"Yeah, it sounds like flu. Good news is that the strains going around respond to Tamiflu. I'm going to leave you a script for that to hopefully lessen the symptoms. I know you know that it's only supportive therapy. I'm going to give you some medicine to treat your symptoms. It just has to run its awful course," he said.

She shook her head yes. "Did you work with Colonel Shaw?"

The mention of Natalie's name pained the good doctor. The hurt fluttered across his brow.

"I did. We knew each other for a long, long time. Hadn't been stationed together for a while until we both were here. She was a flight nurse. A damn good one," he said.

"I'm sorry for your loss," she said softly. Dr. Thomas paused while he wrote.

"Are you a surgeon?"

"I am. Trauma. I actually operated on Gavin the night of the accident. Saved his leg."

"His leg?"

"Ever wonder where the scar came from?"

"I've never seen a scar. He usually wears jeans," Emily said. Dr. Thomas looked surprised and then shook his head. She could tell he assumed that she was Gavin's lover and was shocked when he was proven wrong.

"Gavin's leg was severed from the knee down. A first responder put a tourniquet on the leg, preventing him from bleeding to death. I sewed it back on," he said simply. That explained the limp, and a whole lot more.

"Well, Emily. I think with a little rest, hydration, and pills we can get you going again," he said.

"Thank you for making a house call. Those are rare in this day and age."

"It's my pleasure. Please take care of yourself," he said. Doug walked downstairs and saw Gavin sitting at the table waiting for him.

"What can I say, Gavin? It's the flu. I have a couple of scripts that can lessen the symptoms, but she's going to be out for a few days. But her lungs are clear, her fever is responding to meds. She looks okay," he said.

Gavin shook his head and looked relieved. "That's good news. Coffee?" Gavin asked.

"I got to head back in a bit, but I'd take some water," he said. Doug followed Gavin to the kitchen and took a glass of ice water from him. "Who is this woman to you, Gavin?"

"A friend."

"Just a friend? Who lives with you?"

"Doug . . ." Gavin warned.

"Look. I'm not judging you. If you found someone, I'm happy for you. I think Natalie would be happy for you. It's been almost six years."

"I know how long it's been," Gavin growled.

Doug drank the water quietly. "You weren't the only one who loved her, who misses her," Doug said softly.

"But I am the only one who was married to her," Gavin said sternly.

"Nothing ever happened between us, you know that."

"Not that you didn't want it to."

Doug put the glass down on the island and dropped the prescriptions by the glass. He shook his head in disbelief.

"She always wanted you. I never understood why. I still don't. I only saved your life that night because she would have wanted me to."

"Sometimes I wish you had let me die. Then I wouldn't have to be grateful to a man who was in love with my wife for saving my damn life!" Gavin yelled.

Doug bowed his head and walked out of the house. Gavin exhaled deeply when he heard his car drive away. He walked toward the staircase and saw Emily sitting at the top of the stairs, looking at him. He stopped short and she leaned against the banister looking sad. He walked up slowly and sat a couple stairs lower than her. He leaned against the wall and sat in silence with her.

"Nat and Doug were deployed in Iraq together, went through a lot together. War tends to bring out the rawest of emotions in people. Doug developed feelings for her, but Nat always put him in his place. Gratefully they weren't stationed together for a while, until here. He got her the position here, encouraged her to take it. Part of the reason I hated that we ended up here. I knew that he was trying to get close to her again."

"But she was faithful to you. She chose you," Emily said.

"I don't know why. Hard to believe she preferred a retired math teacher turned farmer to a surgeon."

Emily looked at him sleepily. "She chose her husband and children. Her family. Her home. Nothing hard to believe about that."

Gavin stood and held out his hand. She grabbed it and hoisted herself up and walked back to bed still holding his hand. She climbed in and lay on her side facing him. She held on to his hand as he sat by her on the bed and he did not let go, feeling it nice to be connected to her, even if it was with this simple gesture.

"Do you remember the accident?" she asked. Gavin stared at her intently, his green eyes slowly turned teary and red.

"Every detail," he whispered.

"I'm sorry."

Gavin let go of her hand and cleared his throat a couple of times to regain his composure.

"I'm going to go to the pharmacy and then I'm going to pick up Sam," he said. She touched his face and he paused, feeling so much but saying nothing. He touched her hand with his, slowly stood up and left the room.

"Sissy! Your cute little tush better be in that damn car in two minutes or there'll be hell to pay!" Gavin yelled from the porch. He fiddled with a tie that he didn't want to wear. Natalie insisted that he

should wear it, as it was an awards ceremony and a big deal for the Girl Scouts.

"Why are they not doing this in town? Why are we driving all the way the hell to Columbus on a Friday night? Her troop is here," Gavin complained, as he was pulling back on a nice shirt and tie that he had just taken off to do his afternoon chores.

"They wanted it to be nice, Gavin. Have a nice dinner and awards at a nice restaurant. You don't find a lot of those here," Natalie said.

She was out of her fatigues and into a nice black, knee-length skirt, knee-high boots, and brown sweater. It was still 40 degrees in early March. Her short blonde hair was tucked neatly behind her ears. She lined her blue eyes with brown eyeliner, then applied mascara and a neutral lipstick.

She smacked her lips together. "Your attitude needs to improve. I told you about this over a month ago and reminded you last week. You knew this was happening, so I don't need to hear your pissy crap all night, you hear?" Natalie was only 5 feet 2 inches, but she ran that house like a squadron commander. He didn't particularly appreciate being barked at like he was an Airman on most days, and definitely not after the day he had at school. All he wanted to do was finish his chores and curl up with the TV and a cold beer.

Gavin shoved his feet back into his brown loafers and grabbed his blue sports coat in a huff. Walking away was better than dealing with repercussions of a smartass comment.

Josh was on the couch with a bag of Cheetos watching college basketball, eagerly preparing his brackets for March Madness.

"Have you done your homework?" Gavin asked.

"Yep."

"I don't want anyone over tonight while we're gone. I don't care if it's Friday."

"All right."

"And finish gathering the eggs."

"Yep."

Gavin sighed and walked out to the porch. He wished he could beat the 16-year-old defiance out of that boy, but then reminded himself he was way worse at that age. He'd take smugness over the crazy, hair-brained things he did while he was in high school. At least Josh stayed

195

home most nights and got good grades.

The storm clouds were blowing in. It was going to be a crappy drive to Columbus, he thought.

"Sissy! Get in this car!"

Sissy walked out in her Girl Scout uniform. She had just made Junior that fall and was so excited to be in the green uniform instead of the brown one from the Brownies. She wore her sash with her badges proudly. Her blonde hair was pulled back into a nice French braid, resting down the middle of her back.

"No need to yell, Daddy-O" she said, and smiled. He grinned despite his annoyance at going to this function. He opened the back passenger door to Natalie's Ford Focus for her. With gas being so expensive he hated taking his truck much further than work and to pick up supplies. Sissy climbed in and buckled herself in. Gavin slid the driver's seat back to accommodate his long legs.

Natalie came down the steps. "Are you driving?"

"I'm in the driver's side, aren't I?" he said, annoyed.

She sighed and walked over to the passenger side. She saw Sissy through the window. "Are you chewing gum? You need to spit that out. With your braces? Are you kidding me with that?" Sissy rolled down the window and spit the gum out.

Natalie climbed into the car and put on her seatbelt.

"Great weather for a drive to Columbus," he muttered.

"Can't control the weather, Shaw. Zip it."

The traffic and rain were light on OH-29, but when Gavin hit I-70, the rain really came down. He could hardly see five feet in front of him.

"Take your time. So what if we're late," Natalie said.

"Don't tell me how to drive," he muttered. She rolled her eyes. Gavin ignored her as he was getting more and more frustrated with the rain and the slow speed.

When they were about five miles from the I-270 loop, traffic eased, even though the rain did not let up. In the rearview mirror he saw a black BMW riding his bumper.

"What's this asshole's problem?" Gavin muttered.

The BMW swerved and went around Gavin on the right side of traffic, cutting him off to get in the middle lane where he was driving.

Gavin stepped on his brakes and narrowly avoided hitting him. Both Natalie and Sissy gasped.

"That son-of-a-bitch," Gavin yelled. "Hell no. I'm going to teach that frat boy a lesson. See how he likes me riding his ass all the way to downtown," Gavin said, picking up the speed.

"Leave it alone, Gavin. Slow it down," Natalie yelled.

Gavin ignored her and put the speedometer to almost 80 mph in the pouring rain.

"SLOW DOWN!" Natalie yelled louder. Gavin was almost touching that BMW's bumper with his.

The sound of the tire blowing snapped him back to reality. He panicked as the Focus hit a counterclockwise tailspin, catching the BMW in the twirl, throwing it into oncoming traffic on the opposite side of the median.

Gavin heard Natalie screaming "OH MY GOD!!!!!!!" and Sissy screaming "DADDY!!!!" in her ultra-high-pitched 9-year-old voice.

He white knuckled the steering wheel, trying in vain to gain control of the vehicle. They ended up spinning into another car in their lane, throwing it into the path of a tractor-trailer in the right lane and landing upside down and perpendicular to traffic in the left lane. The tanker tried to stop, but all Gavin could see were the headlights coming directly toward Natalie and Sissy in slow motion.

"Gavin," Natalie whimpered, right before the impact. Her face was bloody from the broken glass. He could not hear Sissy.

The sound of steel hitting steel at high impact sounded like an explosion. As the tanker T-boned the small Focus, spilling its contents all over the highway, the real explosion came in a fiery inferno.

Gavin was knocked out for a few seconds after the initial impact and came to watching a fireball coming toward him in a straight line. The tanker truck driver had narrowly escaped the flames unscathed and was trying desperately to pull Gavin out what was left of the car. Natalie's blue eyes had gone cold, but he could hear Sissy moaning in the backseat. The rain was freezing cold.

"OH JESUS, MOTHER MARY, PLEASE HELP ME!!" the driver screamed over and over again. He was a young man, probably 23. It wasn't until Gavin felt the tightening of the belt around his thigh that he realized his leg was gone.

The small man dragged Gavin and his leg to the median, but Gavin fought him as he saw the flames coming toward Natalie and Sissy.

"NO! NO! NO!" Gavin screamed, hysterical. The tanker truck driver ran back to try to get the girls, but the flames exploded and had engulfed the car. Gavin felt the heat from the fire and watched as the Ford burned before his eyes, helpless to stop it.

"I'm so sorry! I tried to stop! I tried to stop! Jesus why couldn't I stop!" the young driver sobbed. Gavin heard later that the driver never recovered from that accident. He took a loaded pistol to his temple a year later to end the instant replay of that horrible night. Gavin was downright jealous of the man's courage to pull the trigger when he read the obituary.

"Gavin, I have Ms. Mitchell's prescription for you," John Lovelace, the local pharmacist, said. He was an older gentleman with a very round belly and white hair that went wild in every direction. He wore heavy, black-rimmed eyeglasses. Gavin snapped out of his recollection nightmare.

"No insurance?"

"No, sir."

"These are a little steep. Let's see what I can do for her," he said, and typed on the keyboard.

"I can go as low as $90 for the Tamiflu. The others are generic. Still brings you to about $110."

The firemen and paramedics reached him within a few minutes, which was a miracle since both lanes of traffic were stopped on I-70. He watched the firemen stand in a row of three and douse the car with water.

"SIR!! SIR, CAN YOU HEAR ME?" the young paramedic yelled. "TELL ME YOUR NAME."

"Gavin Shaw," he mumbled.

"ARE YOU ALLERGIC TO ANYTHING MR. SHAW?"

"No."

"Starting the line," a female paramedic said.

"SIR, WE ARE GOING TO GIVE YOU SOMETHING FOR THE

PAIN."

Gavin felt the prick of a needle for the IV and then the warmth of a narcotic that made him drowsy and sick to his stomach. He allowed sleep to finally take him.

He woke up two days later at Ohio State University Medical Center in ICU. Josh was asleep in the chair at the end of the bed. His sister-in-law Nancy, Natalie's fraternal twin, was standing over him.

"Gavin?" she asked.

Josh startled awake and jumped up to stand by his father. He looked scared and sick. Nancy had tears in her eyes.

Gavin blinked a few times and looked around the room.

"Gavin, we lost Nat and Sissy," Nancy said slowly.

Josh started bawling, consumed by big, heavy grief. Gavin lifted a hand to his son, and Josh grabbed it and tried to calm himself down, trying so hard to be brave for his father.

Gavin met Paco, Xavier, and Sam at the Kroger parking lot, which was the designated meeting spot, as it was directly off the main road into town. Gavin got down from the truck. Paco and Sam did the same.

"How's Emily?" Paco asked, shaking Gavin's hand and patting him on the shoulder.

"Doc said she should be okay. I picked up some meds for her to lessen the flu." Paco signed what Gavin said to Sam. Sam smiled and was relieved.

"All right. Give my best to her. Celia was worried sick. Said she'd be by tomorrow after school. She had a school board meeting she was prepping for today," Paco said, and walked back to the driver's seat. Xavier waved to Sam from the backseat.

"Will do. You guys drive safe," Gavin said.

"Roger that," Paco said and winked, driving away.

Gavin pulled the backpack off Sam's shoulders. Sam pointed to Kroger. "You need something?" Gavin asked. Sam nodded. Gavin pointed to Sam to lead the way.

Once inside Sam found a small bunch of daffodils near the front checkout. He reached into his pocket and pulled out his

Star Wars wallet and came up with three ones and a couple of quarters. The bunch of flowers was $2.99. Gavin smiled, extremely taken by the gesture of the boy giving flowers to his sick momma.

Sam walked through the checkout and Cyndi, the woman who had checked him and Emily out every week, smiled at Sam.

"Hi Sam! Are these for your mom?" Sam nodded.

"She's under the weather," Gavin told her.

"Oh, that's too bad. Please tell her Ms. Cyndi said to feel better."

Sam handed her his money and his Kroger card to get the discount. Cyndi smiled, "just like his momma, always getting the savings."

Gavin walked out with Sam carrying the flowers and led him to the truck. They drove silently back to the house.

Gavin was in ICU for close to a week. Colonel Doug Thomas, who was in the Reserves and was privileged at OSU, prepared all the paperwork for Gavin to stay in Columbus for treatment so TRICARE would cover the hospital stay. Gavin was not able to attend the funeral. Nancy and Josh stood there in place for him along with Nancy's husband David and their two teenaged boys, Dustin and Dex.

Gavin could not imagine the kind of pressure and pain that not being there caused Josh. How brave his son was. Nancy told Gavin that he would be proud. The military service was beautiful, and hundreds of people attended.

"The police report came back," Nancy said, when she came to visit him a few days after the funeral. She brought him daffodils and arranged them in a water cup. "They said that the weather and the debris left in the road contributed to the accident, causing your tire to blow. They also said that witnesses saw the black BMW cut you off, starting the chain reaction accident. Do you remember any of this?" she asked.

"Did he die?" Gavin asked in a hoarse voice.

"Yes. An 18-wheeler hit him. He died at the scene."

Good, Gavin thought.

"The other car the Focus hit in the tailspin had two college girls from Dayton. They were going to a concert. They didn't make it either," Nancy said softly.

Gavin closed his eyes. He didn't know there were others.

Gavin pulled up to the house and Sam quickly ran into the house with the flowers for Emily. He carried in Sam's backpack and went to the kitchen to make Sam and Emily something to eat.

It took almost a month of physical therapy for Gavin to be released home. By that time Nancy had returned to Texas, and it was just him and Josh left in the house. When Gavin walked in with the aid of Will and Josh, the house was just as he left it that fateful day. Everything was frozen in time like Miss Havisham's house from Great Expectations. Dishes were done, the table wiped clean of Sissy's homework, but overall, there was an imprint that was left on the house that could never be erased. His bedroom was still in disarray from the rush to get ready for the ceremony in Columbus that awful night. Nat's clothing was in a pile on the bed. Gavin fell onto the bed and buried his face in her blouses and skirts, hoping to smell what was left of her. That first night he sobbed for the first time since he woke up from the accident, buried beneath a pile of fabric.

Gavin was a mess physically. He had three discs blown in his back and his left arm had a nice, clean compound fracture along with twenty-seven stiches from when it went through the window at impact. His leg was reattached below the knee, and even though he felt sensations and blood supposedly flowed well, it still felt like dead weight most days, and he fell more times than he stood until he got used it.

It took him about three months to not groan in writhing pain for day-to-day movement. By that time, he knew he was starting to depend on the pain pills too much. He picked up the phone and called Shakes, who took the next bus out from Memphis, where he was living at the time, to come and help. Shakes walked up the stairs to the farmhouse, threw out all of Gavin's pills, and replaced them with Tylenol and Advil, and a month later made Gavin get focused on getting back to the fields to get his hands busy doing something again.

Gavin brought a tray of crackers with peanut butter, cut up Pink Lady apples, and the medicine Doug prescribed to Emily a short while later. He also brought a small vase for the daffodils.

Sam was lying next to Emily, in the crook of her bent arm, with his eyes closed. Emily was sleeping soundly as well. Gavin put the tray on the dresser and pulled the daffodils gently from Emily's hands and placed them in the water. He walked out, closing the door.

He ran to the barn and instinctively saddled up Lily. He rode her to the backfields, feeling the cold air in his lungs burning a little, making him feel alive. Lily took him to the stream with the fallen trees. He got off the horse and walked toward the water, watching it slowly move. He felt the emotion stuck in his chest, the pain of his stupidity for trying to teach a kid a lesson in the pouring rain, the guilt of the lives sacrificed to teach a lesson of humility. He cursed God, cursed the devil, and cursed himself. He wished he were dead.

"Did you ever think there was a reason you answered that request in the church bulletin?"

He could see the apparition of Nat sitting on a fallen tree, wearing her faded Levis and long-sleeved faded flannel shirt, left over from her grunge phase in the early 90s.

"What do you mean?"

The apparition stood and walked over to him. *"I mean, that you never volunteered to help anyone out before. You've been going to that church for eight years."*

Gavin shrugged. "So?"

Nat's apparition walked up to him. *"She's good for you."*

"Doesn't matter if she is. It isn't worth the trouble of finding out. Someday I'll lose her just like I lost you," Gavin said sadly.

Nat's face was neutral. *"Not necessarily."*

"It's best just to be friends."

"You already love her, Shaw. It's done. Better to ride the wave than to fight it like you tend to do."

"I loved you. To a fault. And look what happened to me when you died. I fell apart and all I'm left with are ghosts," he said. He rubbed his eyes and when he looked up, she was gone.

He rode back to the house as it was getting dark. When he walked into the kitchen, he saw Sam had made a simple meal of mashed potatoes, leftover roast covered in barbeque sauce, and a tossed salad. Gavin wasn't aware that Sam even knew how to work the stove. He was impressed.

Sam motioned him to the kitchen island to sit for dinner. Sam had set up three plates. He served Gavin the biggest serving and then split the servings between him and the plate he assumed was for Emily.

Gavin washed his hands and sat down. "Looks great."

They ate in silence for a few minutes. Sam had pulled down a small dry erase board that Celia had bought back in the summer to help Sam communicate with Gavin easier and scribbled a note down on it: Thank you for getting a doctor here & the medicine.

"*You're welcome*," Gavin signed, then tousled the boy's hair.

He washed the dishes and checked on Emily while Sam was in the bathtub. She was sleeping peacefully. He touched her forehead and felt it was cooler. He exhaled with small relief. He watched the slow rise and fall of her chest. He heard Nat's voice in his head, *"You already love her, Shaw."*

It was a mistake bringing her out here. He thought he could keep her at arm's length, have her around without feeling more than he already did. But he was wrong. So very wrong.

CHAPTER TWENTY-ONE

Emily slept for almost four days, and on the fifth, she woke up at her usual time of 5:30 and walked down to the kitchen feeling weak, but much better. Gavin was sitting in the dining room with his paper, sipping coffee.

"Morning," she said. He jumped at the sound of her voice. His reaction made her laugh. "Sorry."

"Quite all right," he said. He went back to reading his paper. He did not ask her how she was feeling. He didn't ask her about anything. Emily noticed the slight.

She walked to the kitchen and poured herself a cup of coffee. She went to sit by him in the dining room, but no sooner than she sat down, he stood up.

"I'll be in Columbus most of the day. No need to hold dinner for me," he announced.

"Okay. Are you all right?" she asked. He folded his paper into a tight tube and swallowed the last of his coffee. He did not make eye contact with her.

"Yep. Just running late. Talk to you later."

But they never really talked later. Something had dramatically changed in their relationship. At first, she assumed he was busy, and that he was just running normal pre-season errands. But when the days turned into almost two weeks of missing dinners, and hardly any conversation, Emily was starting to question what went wrong, and started to seriously regret moving out there.

The day before Valentine's Day, Shakes took Emily out for lunch at Golden Corral while everyone was either working or at school. Huge paper hearts hung in every corner of the restaurant, making her feel more awful about being alone this Valentine's Day and making her realize that she was nearing the 1-year mark of Aaron's death.

She had been spending more and more time with Shakes

since he was the only one around. Between caring for Will's animals while he was in Europe, and Gavin's animals while Gavin was making himself scarce, Shakes was always nearby. She found herself making lunch for them every day and running errands with him, just to have some sort of human contact during the day.

Emily reached into her purse to pay for her meal and Shakes clicked his tongue at her.

"No ma'am. No woman I take out pays," he said. Emily smiled, appreciating the gesture.

Shakes visited the buffet four times to her one time, eating, as always, like he'd been starving for months.

"Are your parents alive, Shakes?"

"My momma died when I was 4 giving birth to my baby sister. I have no idea if my father is alive. He walked out on us when I was born."

"I never understood men who did that. Or women," Emily sighed, thinking of Will.

"Me neither."

"So, it was you and your sister?"

"Beth," he said.

"Where is Beth now?"

Shakes got sad and put down his fork. "Lubbock. I think. She cut me out of her life a while ago," he said.

"I'm sorry."

Shakes pushed his plate to the side. He fiddled with the straw in his glass of Coke.

"Beth and I were living in Biloxi at the same time Gavin and Nat were stationed there. Josh was just a toddler. Sissy wasn't even a thought yet. Beth was working at the bowling alley, and I was on a shrimping boat for a good man named Pat Michaels. Beth had a son around Sam's age. Noah. She had gotten into some trouble with a boy when she was 16, but she kept the baby, and I helped raise him. Together we were able to do right by him."

"Beth was attracted to these hard-ass, gangster drug dealers. Drove me fucking crazy that she would allow Noah around these assholes. Well then one day she meets Trey. He's white-collared. Seems upstanding. Has a 9-5 job. He's perfect." Emily waited patiently as Shakes took a drink of Coke and continued.

"Well, he ain't perfect. He was messing with Noah. We didn't know what was goin' on, but Noah started acting out at school, at Little League. Depressed. I didn't know what the hell was going on. I got back from a 2-week fishing gig and my nephew was a different kid."

"Gavin was Noah's teacher. He called me and Beth in to talk about Noah. Told us that he was concerned with Noah's behavior. Then he started asking if there had been changes at the house. That this behavior sometimes could be a result of abuse. Beth denied it all. Was offended that Gavin would think such a thing. But it fucking clicked like a light bulb. Beth always left Noah alone with Trey. They had moved into his house. She was starting to take college classes, and she was never home. It made perfect sense."

Emily sat riveted.

"So, I drove out to Trey's house to confront this asshole when she was in class. I made a copy of her key and let myself in. When I walked in . . ." Shakes cleared his throat a couple of times.

Emily felt her stomach turn. "What did you see, Shakes?"

Shakes paused, the memory bringing fury into his eyes. He spoke slowly, as if he was recalling a bad dream.

"He had Noah pinned down. He was recording that shit, too, so he could share with his other deviant buddies. I flew into a rage. I was carrying that day. I unloaded my 357 in him. Uncle Dillon took care of that son of a bitch," he whispered.

Emily felt the hairs in the back of her neck stand up. She closed her eyes at the horror of it all. She swallowed and slowly opened her eyes. "Then what happened?"

"I was arrested, Noah was put into a home until they could figure out if Beth was involved at all. By the time they figured out she wasn't, Noah tried to end it—hung himself in the shower at the boys' home. The rod snapped, but he fell and hit his head. Had serious brain damage from the lack of oxygen and head injury. He was never the same after that."

"Beth blamed me. For everything. Even though it was her fucking boyfriend who did this to her. To Noah. To all of us. After she was released from police custody, she never spoke to me again."

Emily shook her head. "Did you go to trial?"

"No. Gavin was there for me through the whole thing. Hired me a really good lawyer, was a key witness about Noah's behavior to the cops. It helped that they found enough in that sick bastard's house to confirm my story. They never charged me. I think Gavin felt really guilty about telling me, but then again, I think he would've done the same thing had someone gone after Josh. He understood. There wasn't a man alive who wouldn't have done what I did," Shakes said.

She thought about someone doing that to Sam. She would have done the exact same thing. "So, what became of Noah?"

"He was in a rehab center for a long time. I would send him gifts and cards. But I don't think he really remembered me or understood who I was. He didn't even know his own mother. He was that far gone. He works with a gardener in St. Louis. Real decent man. Asian. Hardly speaks English. But Noah trusts him, and Mr. Chang is really kind. Noah lives at a home that helps him pay his bills and looks out for him. I try to go out there every three months or so to visit him. I send letters and help with the bills for the home."

Emily sat back and played with the straw in her glass, thinking about all that Shakes had revealed. What he said about Gavin just solidified what she knew to be true about Gavin— his honor and his integrity was unparalleled. She really, really missed him.

"Some people called me a murderer," Shakes baited.

Emily looked him in the eye. "Not me." He nodded, satisfied, and stood to get more dessert.

"You coming?" he asked.

Emily stood. Until she could get a hold of some hard liquor to process that story further, ice cream would have to suffice.

Gavin walked in late after Emily and Sam had gone to bed. On the kitchen counter was a note on top of two red envelopes. She had taken to leaving notes for him like a pen pal, and he felt guilty every time he saw one, knowing full well that he was being a coward avoiding her, but it was safer this way.

G—leftovers in the fridge. Meatloaf. Yum. P.S. Happy Valentine's Day.

Gavin looked at the cards. One was from Emily, and one was from Sam. Sam had written out Gavin's name very carefully on the envelope in his little boy script. Gavin opened that one and saw Snoopy holding a heart. On the inside Sam signed his name perfectly. He smiled. He really did love that kid.

Gavin stared at Emily's card and felt both a pull to and from it. He left it on the counter unopened and opened the fridge to get a beer and pull out the plate of food.

When the meal was heating up in the microwave, he summoned up the courage to open Emily's card.

There was a little stick man holding up a sign that said "Hi." When he opened it up the man was holding up another sign, "So how's the weather over there?" She wrote, "You are missed around here—Love, E."

He closed the card, returned it to the envelope, and left it on the counter. He took his meal and beer to the living room to watch the news. He pretended to care about Whitney Houston's death, watching CNN announce the horrible details of how they found her in the bathroom. It was a good distraction from the card. He chewed on a piece of meatloaf and swallowed it. She was right. It was yummy.

Emily awoke on Valentine's Day and went downstairs. Gavin was nowhere to be seen. She saw the cards were not where she left them, and the plate she saved his dinner on was washed and neatly placed in the drying rack. There was no sign of a card or anything from him. She was disappointed, and she hated that she was disappointed.

That evening Sam came home from school feeling warm

like the beginnings of a cold. Emily made him a big pot of chicken soup with stars and sent him to bed to rest. She was in the kitchen wrapping up the remaining whoopie pies that she sold and delivered earlier that day for Valentine's Day, setting aside two for Gavin, out of habit, even though she was still annoyed with him. Betty and some of her friends had ordered a dozen of them for their respective husbands and boyfriends. As Emily delivered them to each home, she caught sight of red roses and balloons delivered from the local florist. Betty showed Emily a James Avery locket, still nestled in the orange box, next to the cream-colored bag. Emily smiled kindly but felt like a jealous, unpopular teenager as she drove the Honda back to the farm.

She was about to put the soup away when she saw headlights of an unfamiliar car drive up. She felt her pulse quicken at the thought of a stranger on the land, and quickly remembered the shotgun in the hall closet that Gavin had resting on the top shelf. She was just deciding to move to grab it when she saw Josh step out of the driver's seat of the black Mustang. She breathed a sigh of relief.

He walked up to the porch and knocked while he used his key to enter.

"Dad? You here?" he called.

Emily came out of the kitchen wiping her hands.

"Hi, Josh," she said. He stopped when he saw her, surprised.

"Oh, hello. I'm looking for my father." He dug his hands in the pockets of his leather coat, and he looked uncomfortable.

"He's out running errands. He's been getting back really late. Not sure what time he will be back tonight. Did he know you were coming?" she asked.

"No. I . . . no," Josh stammered.

"Did you drive all the way from Tennessee today?" He nodded.

"Come on in. Take your coat off. You must be hungry. I made some chicken soup," she offered.

"If he's not here, I should just try back later," he said,

making a move back to the door.

"Please, Josh. Please. Please come in," she begged softly. They looked at each other for a few seconds and Josh bowed his dark head, relenting to her request. He took off his black leather jacket and slung it against a chair in the dining room. He followed her to the kitchen.

Emily pulled down a big bowl and poured Josh some soup. He sat at the island and waited. "Where's your son?" he asked.

"Sam. He wasn't feeling good today. He's upstairs resting."

"I'm sorry to hear that," he said, accepting the bowl from her. She pulled a few yeast rolls out from the breadbox and put them on a plate next to him.

"There is iced tea and Dr. Pepper to drink. And beer," she offered.

"Water is good," he said. She poured him a glass of ice water and leaned against the counter with her big cup of hot tea.

Josh bent over and blew at the hot soup to cool it down. He tasted it, then paused. "Wow, this is really good," he said.

"Thanks," she said. She continued to sip while she sized him up. She was amazed how much he really favored Gavin with his dark hair and green eyes. He was on the slender side. In true maternal fashion, she wondered if he was eating properly in Tennessee.

"Will told me you were a really good cook. You know, when you were cooking for the crew back in the summer," Josh said.

"Will is a good man. I haven't seen much of him since he's been travelling. He's been missed," she said.

"Where is he now?"

"The last I heard he was supposed to be in Ireland this week."

"I never thought that old man would ever leave Ohio. Then I get a postcard from England of all places," Josh said, and smiled.

"He's really loving it, the history buff that he is. He sends Sam long letters of all the things he has seen and little treasures he finds along the way. He has loved getting the mail," Emily said. Josh continued to eat slowly.

"Your dad said you're graduating this May. Any plans afterwards?" she asked.

"Well, that's kind of the reason that I'm here. This *thing* that we keep going round and round about."

"And what is that?"

Josh looked at her. "He hasn't told you? I figured he told you everything."

Emily laughed a short laugh. "No. There are some things he holds private and sacred. Like when he's being bullheaded and irrational."

Josh exhaled and contemplated. He pushed the soup to the side and reached down to pull out a backpack that he had brought in with him. Emily walked over to him on the island and sat by him. He pulled out an iPad and showed her a folder of drawings, pictures, and designs of motorcycles. He scrolled through them for Emily. There were about fifteen in all. Most were low-riders, some with high handlebars, some with sissy bars, and some without. All of them had amazing paint jobs.

"Did you design these?"

"Yep. And did the artwork on them. I work with a local fabricator. He owns a shop—a series of shops that help put them all together, but he wants to retire. I would like to buy him out. I have enough money if I get what my mom left me in trust."

Emily smiled and handed him the iPad. "You are very talented, Josh. Truly," Emily said, drinking her hot tea.

"But . . .?"

Emily sighed. "Your father reminds me a lot of my father. My father was a government contractor in Saudi—made like $300,000 a year, all expenses paid. And when my husband and I were living in squalor in a piece-of-shit apartment in New York City, he never ever helped out, even though he could. Not one cent. I mean this place was so bad we stored all our food in the fridge, even the flour and bread, because the rats would get into everything, even plastic containers. And when I wanted to start my first bakery, I asked him for a loan, and he said no. He never gave a reason, really. Just no. Hell, even when he died, he left most of his money to charity. My son, his only grandchild, got like one percent of his estate. I got nothing."

"That's some bullshit."

"Yep."

"How did you manage it?"

"Well, we worked hard, and we caught a break. We managed because we had no other choice. Everyone always has these ideas about how to be, or what's best, or how to execute things. But if you believe you are good enough, then it will happen. But on your terms."

Josh frowned. "The money belongs to me. It's my money."

"But it's controlled by your dad. I wouldn't count on changing that man's mind. He's set in his ways."

Josh frowned, defeated. "So, what would you do if you were me?"

"You took business courses in college, right? Learned how to write a business plan? I would go to banks to get the money. Use your trust as collateral if you can. If not, try to talk to your boss to take you on as a true apprentice, buying into the company by free labor." Josh bit his lower lip, thinking.

"And if you ever told your father that I gave you these ideas, I'll kill you," she said.

Josh went back to eating, thinking. "So, what's in those whoopie pies?"

"Red velvet cakes and cream cheese frosting. Would you like to try one? It's a new recipe. I sold them for Valentine's Day."

"Oh, man, totally."

Gavin walked in about an hour later to Josh and Emily watching old episodes of *American Chopper*. Josh was explaining the different styles to Emily and educating her on the pieces of the fabrication that his boss currently had. She asked several questions, and he eagerly told her all he knew, grateful that someone was interested in his passion. Gavin's eyebrows raised and he struggled to grasp what he was witnessing.

"Hey, Dad," Josh said, and stood to hug him. Gavin inhaled deeply at the feel of his boy's arms around him. He missed him so much.

"Hey. Wish you called. I would've been here earlier."

"Emily was kind enough to feed me and entertain me while we waited. She said you were pulling some long hours. I thought this was the slow time for you. I half expected you to be on the couch catching up on Netflix movies from the summer. What are you working on?"

Gavin glanced sideways at Emily and fumbled to find his words.

"Different things, you know—getting the barn ready, the seed for planting."

Emily knew then that he was lying. She stood up, disgusted.

"Goodnight, all. It's been a long day. I should go check on Sam."

"I hope he feels better, Emily. Hey, thanks for dinner and listening," Josh said, hugging her. Emily smiled and patted his back.

"Is Sam sick?"

"Just a cold, I think. He has a low-grade fever." She was annoyed that Gavin suddenly gave a damn.

"Well, let me know if he needs to go in and see the doc in the morning."

"I can drive him if that's the case. I don't want to keep you from whatever you've been working on," she said, and glared at him. Gavin lowered his head.

"Goodnight," she said again.

"Night, Emily. Sleep well," Josh said.

Josh watched his father's face and smiled. "Maybe someday you'll explain this whole arrangement to me."

"Nothing to explain, just helping out a friend and her son," he said simply.

"Well, I like her. For what it's worth."

Gavin walked to the kitchen in search of food, and Josh

followed him. He saw the big bowl of soup, rolls, and red velvet whoopie pies.

Josh popped open another beer while Gavin unwrapped the dessert first.

"Whoopie pies. Maybe it's a hint?" Josh winked.

"Joshua."

"It is Valentine's Day."

"Boy . . ."

"I can sleep at Will's if you'd like." Gavin put the dessert down and gave him a stern look.

"Fine. Okay. You're not interested. I get it."

Gavin went back to eating, nearly inhaling the soft cake and cream cheese filling, it was so damn good.

"She's pretty hot. So, if you're not interested, do you mind if I make a move?"

The sheer horror on Gavin's face, his mouth half open with red cake falling out, made Josh double over in laughter.

"Wow. I guess that answers that."

"You are a punk-ass kid. To the end," Gavin said, annoyed that he lost a battle of wits with his 22-year-old.

"I am. Totally. I learned from the best."

"Did you come here to talk money again?" Gavin asked, licking his fingers, gearing up for a fight.

"Nah. I'm done with that. I came here to visit. It's been too long, old man," Josh said, slapping Gavin on the back. Gavin raised an eyebrow.

"Stop looking so damn surprised. But I better head up to bed if I'm going to get up and help you with chores tomorrow," he said, finishing off his beer.

"Who are you and what have you done with my son?"

Josh laughed and winked. "Night, Daddy-O."

Gavin smiled sadly at Josh's use of Sissy's name for him. He watched his son bound up the stairs to his old bedroom and felt happy. That happiness turned into panic when Emily reappeared a few minutes later in the kitchen.

"I left the thermometer down here," she said. She was in her nightclothes, a long-sleeved t-shirt and flannel pants. He tried to find some words, any words. She waited and saw that he was coming up empty. She rolled her eyes and opened the junk drawer near the sink and fumbled around the nuts, bolts, batteries, and wine openers until she found the thermometer.

"I never thought we'd be at a point where you would purposefully avoid me. I wish I knew what the hell I did wrong to cause you to be so damn nervous around me," she said.

"Nothing. I've just been . . ."

"Busy? Busy?" He looked down and played nervously with the label on his beer bottle.

"You're a terrible liar, Gavin Shaw. Just plain awful," she said. Her voice caught with emotion. She walked away before he could see her tears. She wouldn't give him the satisfaction.

Gavin rubbed his eyes, covered in guilt. He paced a few minutes before he grabbed his coat and headed outside to try to make this right.

Emily woke, dressed, and walked downstairs just before 6 a.m. Gavin had already made breakfast and was reading the paper at the table. Josh was still half-asleep sucking down coffee next to him.

"Morning. How's Sam?" Josh asked, perking up.

"Better. I think it was a 24-hour thing. He'll be down shortly," she said. Gavin took note and went back to his paper, not daring to make eye contact after she shredded him the night before.

"So, what did your father feed you?" she asked Josh, walking over to the kitchen.

"Runny eggs and burnt toast. A Gavin Shaw specialty. Bet you would've made something amazing," Josh said.

"You didn't bellyache when you ate two platefuls," Gavin grumbled, annoyed. He didn't like this sudden friendship that Josh and Emily had one bit. That was his woman his son was attempting to flirt with. Badly.

"Well, if you guys are around, I'll make a good dinner tonight," she said, and smiled at Josh.

She emerged from the kitchen with a cup of coffee. She sat across from Josh and chose to ignore Gavin.

"Get your long johns on, boy. We will be hitting that back fence near Will's today."

Josh grumbled and stood up. He walked slowly up the stairs. Emily sipped on her hot coffee and then stared at Gavin, challenging him to a fight with her gaze. He slowly reached into his coat pocket and slid a red envelope and small box of Whitman's chocolate with Snoopy on it across the table, the only thing left in the small section of Kroger when he got there ten minutes before it closed last night.

She debated about whether or not she should open it in front of him, but decided she wanted to see his face when she did. He had drawn a comedic picture of a donkey on the front of a white piece of printer paper. On the inside he wrote, "I'm sorry I'm such an ass." She smiled and then looked at him.

"Hey, Dad, these long johns are crushing my junk and only go down to my calves. I need to borrow a pair of yours," Josh yelled down.

"That boy is all charm."

"Takes after his Daddy. Self-portrait?" she asked, pointing to the card. Gavin grinned.

"By the way—you owe me a bigger box of chocolates. Lindt. Truffles. Milk, but I like peanut butter and caramel. File it away wherever you file such things. And be home for dinner. I'm tired of making plates for you. We have a business to run," she said, walking back to the kitchen.

"Yes ma'am."

CHAPTER TWENTY-TWO

When March began the weather had the usual flip-flop between sunny days with 45-degree weather and four inches of snow. Emily began to feel more comfortable driving the Honda into town for errands instead of hitching a ride with Shakes. On the way back from delivering two birthday cakes to Mrs. Edison on 5th Street, she saw a black Ford Explorer in her rearview mirror, parked on the side of the road. In it she saw the piled high, wild blonde hair of Sue Ellen Richter.

Confused about why Sue Ellen would even be on that side of town, Emily slowly started the car and made a U-turn to drive by the SUV. Sue Ellen pulled down her visor when she saw Emily's car approach hers.

"What the hell," Emily muttered out loud as she drove by her. She noticed the SUV didn't follow her back to the farm. For this she was grateful.

"What's the plan for this Saturday?" Gavin asked at dinner that night. He was thumbing through his mail and sipping on his beer. Emily didn't mention the Sue Ellen sighting. She didn't want to upset him.

She served Sam more mashed potatoes and turned somber.

"I think Sam and I are going to take the day off. It's the day Aaron . . . passed. Sam said he wanted to go to a park or something."

Gavin's mouth curved into a frown. "On March 10th?"

Emily nodded and went back to focusing on her meatloaf. She took a bite and saw that Gavin was holding his breath, troubled.

"What?" she asked.

"That's the date of the accident," he said. Emily's fork lingered above her plate, and they looked at each other for a long time. Gavin took a long drink from his beer, and she pushed her plate away from her.

As much as she was dreading the day, March 10th ended up being a quiet but nice day, sunny with clear blue skies and pushing 50 degrees. She packed up a picnic lunch and headed to a local park that had some hiking trails. Sam asked Emily to stop to pick up two balloons at Kroger and he wrote a message on one of them with a Sharpie. He didn't let Emily see what it said. Emily stared at the blue balloon, not sure what to write or say. In the end she wrote Aaron's name and the dates he was on this Earth. Then she kissed it and sent the balloon to the heavens along with Sam's.

"*I love you, Daddy*," Sam signed. Emily hugged him and wiped the tears from both their eyes.

Emily's serene and calm demeanor was short-lived when she saw a black Explorer turning left out of Gavin's road, just as she slowed to turn left onto it. She couldn't make out Sue Ellen's face, but she saw the back of a blonde driving it. Her pulse quickened. She sped down the driveway and nearly bolted out of the car, running toward the door. She had an awful feeling in her gut.

"Gavin?" she called, running into the house.

"Hey, how was the hike?"

He was sitting in the living room watching a show and eating a bowl of cereal. She stared at him and then searched around the place. Something felt off to her.

"Have you been here the whole time?" she asked. She paced to the kitchen and back to the living room where he was seated in his recliner like she was trying to find something.

"Yeah. What's wrong, you seem edgy?" he asked, arching an eyebrow at her.

"Nothing. Nothing," she said. She tried to shake off the feeling she had. "What are you watching?" she asked. She walked back to the kitchen and saw Sam run to the living room. When she went to close the door that Sam left open, she saw Gavin's boots by the door.

Gavin never took off his boots unless he was going to bed. It was a thing with him that she teased him about constantly. He never liked to walk around with sock feet. He stepped on too many scorpions as a kid, he said. He had to wear shoes.

She slowly walked back to the living room and saw Sam sitting on the armrest of Gavin's recliner scrolling through Netflix to find something. Gavin's white-socked feet were sticking out in front of him. He smiled kindly at her.

"Beer?" Gavin offered from the mini fridge that Shakes recently installed in the living room.

She accepted it, letting the alcohol burn away the thought that Gavin had just been in bed with Sue Ellen Richter.

"I need a favor," Gavin said to her about a week later.

Emily was making lemon curd on the stove, which required stirring liquid in the pot for nearly half an hour. Spring was in the air, daffodils and tulips were poking their colorful heads through the thawed earth, and she was baking more with citrus, dreaming of sunny beaches and picnics in the park.

"I already do your laundry, what more you could you possibly want?" she joked.

He bit his tongue, careful to not let a sexual innuendo slip out of his mouth.

"This has to do with the bakery. I met a fellow named Trevor Stevens a few months ago through a mutual friend. He runs a fudge shop in Dayton. He said he was willing to talk trade and maybe showcase some of your goods in his shop."

"Wow. That's great."

Gavin winced. "Well, it's great, but I have a problem. He wanted to have dinner this Friday, but I have to meet to sign the final paperwork for the barn raising in Columbus."

"So . . . what are you asking me?"

"What do you think about having dinner with him on Friday night? Try your hand at sales?"

Emily frowned a little and stirred. She hated sales pitches. She did her fair share when she was running her catering business in New York, but she was never comfortable telling a client how fantastic she was and that they should choose her over everyone else. She was grateful for people like Celia and Gavin who could speak to her work, so she never had to.

"I wouldn't ask you to do this unless I was in a pinch. You know that," Gavin said. Emily moaned quietly.

"Please. This could be a really good thing for the shop," Gavin said. She stirred and stirred, contemplating his request. She was such an ungrateful wench. Of course, she should do this. Gavin would do this for her.

"Sure. Okay."

"Great. You do own a dress, right?"

"Wait, I have to wear a dress?"

She decided on a black skirt and red blouse for dinner, thanks to the help of Celia.

"A dress makes it look like a date. A skirt and shirt look more like business," Celia said.

The shoes Celia picked out, however, were these torturous sling backs with a very pointy toe. As soon as Emily stepped down the stairs in them, she knew they were going to be giving her feet trouble all night long, but it was already late, and she had nothing else to change into.

Gavin left for his meeting with the bank people earlier in the day, and Sam was at an overnight retreat with Celia, Xavier, and Paco. She was alone in the house.

She caught sight of herself in the hallway mirror, and thought she looked nice. The shirt and coloring were flattering. She put on a nice neutral shade of lipstick and fluffed her hair. She felt confident. She could do this.

Dinner was at one of the nicer restaurants in town called Fusion Grille. She parked the Honda and walked into the trendy place with her bag filled with information and samples.

Emily was escorted by a blonde hostess to meet Trevor Stevens, who was sitting with a martini at one of the smaller tables. He was an older man, in his mid-50s with darker hair and blue eyes. He wore black-rimmed eyeglasses that accentuated his blue eyes and a very nice suit. Emily was almost positive it was Armani. He stood to greet her.

"Hello, Mr. Stevens. I'm Emily Mitchell of Shaw Farms and Bakery. I'm Gavin's business partner and head baker," she said, full of confidence.

"Where's Gavin?" he asked.

"Gavin couldn't make it tonight. I'm sorry. I thought he informed you it would just be me tonight."

Trevor did not hide his disappointment. In fact, he was full on pouty about the news, flopping down on his seat and focusing back on his drink. Emily raised an eyebrow and took her seat.

"You know this is the fifth time he has stood me up. I should just stop bothering," Trevor said.

"Again, I apologize. He had some paperwork to sign for his new barn tonight."

"On a Friday night? Honey, please."

Emily suddenly realized that Trevor was hoping this was a date. Alone. With Gavin.

"Hello, I'm Paul and I'll be serving you tonight. Can I get you a drink?" the waiter said.

"Yes. Vodka tonic, please," Emily said. This was going to be a long night, and she needed the alcohol. They sat in silence until the drinks came.

"Do you even want to order or hear about this business?" Emily offered. She was praying for an out.

"I suppose so. I mean, I put on the Armani, and you wore your church clothes, so why not?" Trevor said.

Emily smiled a tight smile and signaled to the waiter. She wanted to hurry this up, and with any luck, she would make it back home in an hour.

They both ordered steaks only after Trevor complained about the prices.

"Please, at this price, you know it will be a half step up from Outback Steakhouse. That's all you can get here in the sticks," he muttered.

Paul, the poor waiter, tried to convince him the beef was local and delicious, but Trevor waved him away and started in on his third martini. Then he looked at her.

"Well, show me what you brought. Let's get this over with," he said.

Emily reached beside her and grabbed her bag, dreading even opening it.

"Why don't I just send you home with it? There is no need to add to your disappointment of the evening," she said.

"Shit, girlie, you are a terrible saleswoman! How do you expect to ever make it in this business if you can't even handle a pissy queen like me?"

Emily exhaled and handed him a plastic container that contained smaller plastic containers. "In here is a sampling of what we have been offering locally in Champaign and Union County. Pies, cookies, and some cakes. We are staying out of the cupcake business and the wedding cake business because there are two companies in town who offer those services. The idea is to offer small individual treats or to take a dessert home for dinner."

"How quaint. Are your cakes better than the cupcakes in town?"

"Depends on your preference . . ."

"Bullshit, you know whose cakes are better."

"Ours are."

"Then you should offer cupcakes. Fuck the competition." Emily exhaled and drank her iced tea, smartly switching from cocktails the previous round for fear of being too drunk to drive home. If she drank every time Trevor made her feel small and insignificant, she'd been passed out cold by now.

He opened up one of the containers. "What's this?"

"Fudge," she said, regretfully. That was Trevor's domain, and she was not prepared for more critique.

He bit into it and spat it out. "Too much butter. This is not fudge. Fudge should not have butter in it. Only sweetened condensed milk and sugar."

"That's your opinion," Emily said.

"It's the right opinion. I sold a million-five last year in fudge."

"Mostly due to your corporate account with the Dragons. Your individual stores only brought in a quarter million."

Trevor arched an eyebrow. She could not tell if he was

impressed or annoyed with her knowing his financial background. For once she was grateful that Aaron taught her how to look into a person's company and finances through the Internet.

The salads came. Trevor sent his back because he swore something was crawling on it. Paul looked like he wanted to turn it over on Trevor's head.

"So, tell me, Emily. Are you married?"

"Widowed."

"Ah, like the poor Gavin. So heartbreaking, isn't it? All that man wasted on a woman. Tragic." Emily poked at her salad.

"So, are you banging him? Is that what's going on here?"

"Nope. We are friends and business colleagues," she said matter-of-factly.

"But you're interested. I can tell. How can you not be? He's a saint. And damn fine." Emily reached for her tea glass again. She was going to have to pee all the way home.

"Have you been with a man since your poor husband died?"

"Why do you care to know that information, Trevor? So, you can exploit it? Tell me the ways of the world, when you obviously haven't lived anywhere other than the State of Ohio?"

Trevor finished his fifth martini. "Exploit it? No, but I would offer you something. As charity. As friends. You are a very attractive woman. You deserve to be laid properly."

"I thought you were gay," she said.

"Sweetie. Such labels. I'm all about the pleasure. And a mouth is a mouth and a hole, a hole. Doesn't matter to me as long as the packaged attached to it is reasonably attractive."

Emily put down her glass and grabbed her purse. "Excuse me, sweetie. I have to pee," she said. She walked toward the bathrooms but passed by the kitchen and saw her young waiter.

"Do you have a back door out of this joint?"

"Oh my God, that guy is a total dickhead," Paul said.

"Totally."

"Yeah, come through the kitchen. We have the door to the alley."

"Wait," he said and grabbed a plate with her steak and potato on it. He quickly wrapped it in a container and threw in a piece of apple pie.

"I'll tell him he still has to pay for it, since it was ordered," he said, and grinned.

"You're awesome," she said, and handed him a $10. "Just in case he skips out on the tip," she grinned back.

She walked over to her Honda and closed the door, placing her dinner on the driver's seat. When she went to start the car, it would not turn over.

"Oh no," she muttered. The car whined and moaned but would not catch. "Shit, shit, shit, shit," she said. She didn't want to be in the parking lot when Trevor realized she was missing, so she looked around to come up with a plan.

Panicked, she slammed her car door and crossed the street to the United Dairy Farmers parking lot, high heels squeezing her baby toes mercilessly. She walked inside and smiled at the attendant and tried to gather her thoughts. Who could she call? Gavin was still probably signing paperwork. Paco and Celia were at the camping jamboree all the way in Springfield with the boys. Shakes was on a date.

"Hey, Miss Emily."

Ian had changed a lot since he worked at the farm last summer. His hair was cut shorter, showing off the blue eyes he and Will shared, and he had trimmed down a lot. He wore a blue and red Domino's Pizza shirt and had two Mt. Dews in his hand. She had never been so glad to see a person in her entire life.

"Ian! Thank God. Can I have a ride back to Gavin's?" she asked.

"I would, Miss Em, but I'm working tonight—delivering. The normal driver is out sick tonight."

Dammit, she thought. She was going to have to break down and call Gavin. The thought of doing that nearly brought her to frustrated tears.

"Are you okay?"

"No. Yes. I'm just stuck, Ian. I have no way back home. I

224

just had the worst dinner of my life, and now I'm stuck," she said, and exhaled.

"Well, what if you place an order for a pizza? I can deliver it out to Gavin's place," Ian suggested.

"Do you deliver out that far?"

"Sure. I mean, most people live in the boonies around here."

Emily opened up her phone and dialed the phone number that Ian punched in. "Yes, hello. I'd like to order a large pepperoni and mushroom pizza . . ." She grinned at Ian as he gave her two thumbs up.

Thirty minutes later, Ian drove Emily back to the farm in his beat-up Chevy Cavalier, a car that made her Honda feel like a brand-new Buick. As he made the turn to Gavin's gravel road, she saw an unfamiliar vehicle in the distance, parked by the house. A black Ford Explorer.

"Stop the car," she said.

"I can drive you up to the house," Ian said.

"Stop the car now!" Ian slammed on his brakes.

She took several deep breaths to get her battle plan. Should she run from the house? Should she run to the house?

"What are we doing?" he asked quietly.

It finally dawned on her that this business dinner date from hell was actually a ploy to get her out of the house to allow him the privacy to carry on his affair with Sue Ellen. And once that realization came to her mind, she was livid.

"Ian, I thank you for the ride. And the pizza." She handed him $20 and opened the car door.

"Are you sure?"

"Thanks, Ian," she said firmly, and closed the door quietly.

Every pebble that she felt through her too-tight high heels as she walked up that driveway, carrying an oversized pizza, brought her closer to a rage that she had never felt before in her entire life.

The farmhouse was quiet and dark when she walked in. Her heart was beating loudly in her ears as she stood there for a full minute listening for unusual sounds. Thankfully, she heard nothing.

She pulled off her horrible heels and walked to the kitchen barefoot. She was startled to see a young, blonde woman sitting at the kitchen island, dressed in one of Gavin's white buttoned-down shirts and nothing else, drinking water. Thankfully, it was not Sue Ellen. But who the hell was she?

"Hello," the woman said. She did not seem surprised at all to see Emily in the house.

Emily walked cautiously to her. "Hello."

She put down the pizza on the counter next to the stove and stood awkwardly near the half-naked woman.

"I'm Caitlin."

"I'm Emily."

"I know. Gavin talks about you."

"Oh? Can't say the same about you." Emily said. Caitlin smiled. She had perfect white teeth, making her even more attractive and radiant. Emily felt faint.

"Bad date?"

Emily stared at her.

"When I have a bad date, I usually bring home a pizza and call it an early night," Caitlin explained.

Emily opened the pizza box and pulled down a plate. "Bad does not even begin to describe it. Are you hungry?"

"What kind is it?"

"Pepperoni and mushroom."

"Yeah, I'll take a slice," Caitlin said. Emily pulled down an extra plate and handed the blonde goddess a piece of pizza, shaking her head at the scene that was unfolding in the kitchen. *I'm serving Gavin's girlfriend, that I didn't know he had, a piece of pizza in the dark. How in the hell is this happening?* she thought.

"This is good. Domino's? I usually don't order Domino's pizza," Caitlin said. Emily continued to stare and her and drank a long drink from her beer.

Gavin snapped on the kitchen light, making the women squint. The look on his face was sheer, unadulterated horror.

"Evening, Gavin. Would you like some pizza?" Emily said in a high-pitched voice he that had never heard before.

"No thanks. Caitlin, I think it's about that time," he said.

Caitlin smiled and took her plate to the sink. "It was nice to meet you," she told Emily, and walked back to his bedroom.

Gavin followed her to the bedroom and three minutes later Caitlin walked out of the house, wearing a white, puffy coat, skin-tight jeans, and thigh-high boots. She didn't say anything, but gracefully and casually walked out the door, Gavin right on her heels.

Emily opened the freezer and pulled out the Stoli vodka that Shakes stashed in there. She poured about three fingers worth in a small glass and took the entire shot in one gulp and poured another.

She suddenly felt like she didn't know Gavin at all, and the last seven months of assuming she knew everything about him seemed like a joke. How did she not know he was *dating* someone?

She nearly jumped out of her skin when he stormed into the kitchen after slamming the front door. He was furious.

"What the hell are you doing back so early? Are you simply incapable of making it through a dinner with a man?" he growled through gritted teeth.

She was floored by his anger. "Sorry. If you had told me you were going to be getting laid by a teenager tonight, I would have made sure to stay out longer. Next time hang a tie on your freakin' doorknob!" she snapped back.

"A teenager? She's 25 years-old," Gavin said. Emily saw red. She was younger than her!

"Whatever. Sorry I interrupted you. Please, don't forego your sexual escapades on my behalf. But I see that you were already finished when I walked in. I hear that's common for men your age—you know, premature ejaculation," Emily jabbed.

"Is that a challenge? Maybe you just want to find out for yourself if that statement is true," Gavin said. His Tennessee twang was getting stronger the angrier he became. His jaw was clenched in a tight line and fire danced behind those green eyes.

Emily paused and felt the buzz of too much vodka hit her head.

"Maybe I do."

She stared at him and took a long drink from her glass. She continued to look him square in the eyes while she crossed her arms in front of her chest. He looked shocked that she called his bluff. Any fire that was left in him was completely doused by the very thought that Emily was serious. He exhaled and locked his thumbs on the front hoops of his faded Wranglers.

"Emily, I don't think . . ."

She put her hand up to stop him. "Please spare me the bumbling, Gavin. I just don't think I can bear it, okay? One horribly, awkward sexual innuendo a night is my limit," she said. She felt the burn of tears behind her eyes. She blinked and cleared her throat in an attempt to make it go away and hide her disappointment and anger from him. She focused on pouring more vodka. But he saw it. He saw all of it.

"What happen with Trevor?" Gavin asked carefully.

"He's a real charmer that one. I'd rank him right up there with Saddam Hussein and a rectal exam," she grumbled, and drank some more. She glanced at Gavin and saw his strong, tanned arms were crossed across his chest. His eyes were fixed on her. She looked everywhere but directly at him.

"What happened, Emily?" She always liked the way her name sounded in his voice. Deep and meaningful. She didn't answer him right away.

"Did he try something with you?" His jaw tensed.

"With me? Ha. Apparently, he was disappointed that you did not show up, because you were the one he was interested in."

Gavin's eyes grew wide.

"But after he slammed his fifth martini down, he made it a point to say that he knew I was hard up being a widow and all, so if I was so inclined, I could have dessert on my knees, because a mouth was a mouth," she said.

Gavin's eyes clouded with fury. "That son of a bitch," he breathed.

"Why in the hell did you send me into that situation? What the hell is the matter with you?" Emily demanded.

"I honestly did not know that was the kind of man he was! I didn't know any of that. He has always been kind and respectful when I met him."

"Yeah, because he was trying to land you in bed."

"I also thought that maybe you two had something in common and would hit it off," Gavin said.

"Except for being human, and I would need a DNA test to prove that we had nothing in common! You sent me there to broker a deal just so you could be alone to get laid by your girlfriend tonight! Admit it! Do you have any idea how awful I felt when I thought I was going in to try to land a deal for the shop, and I had to fend off that asshole? What the hell did I ever do to you to make you think that I deserved a night out with a man like that? What the hell, Gavin!" Emily yelled.

Gavin shook his head. Emily frowned and looked away. She exhaled and picked up her glass and fingered the handle.

"I know that I come off like I'm doing okay with all that has happened to me, G. Like I've moved on. But you need to know that on most days I'm hanging on by a thread. I had a good life and was deeply loved and adored by my husband. And I don't sleep around. I never did, even when I was younger. Making love is a big deal for me. It has to mean something to me. At a minimum, the man has to have my heart. This is something you need to know in case you ever try something stupid, like setting me up again," she said quietly.

He bowed his head, guilty. She paused and finished her drink, feeling good and drunk. She took a minute to compose herself, clearing her throat.

"Look, I'm sorry that I interrupted your night. Hell, one of us should be moving on. You deserve to have at least a special someone in your life, seeing how I have invaded all other aspects of it," she said, and laughed a short laugh. "But you should've just told me. Told me you have a new girlfriend, and you wanted some time alone with her. I would have gone to the movies, stayed at Paco and Celia's or Will's house. You don't have to lie to me to meet up with her," Emily said.

He stared at her, trying to figure out what to say.

"What?" she finally asked. "Jesus, say something! I hate when you're so damn quiet," she said.

"Caitlin is not my girlfriend."

Emily looked confused. "Then what is she?"

"She is someone I hire for the purpose of release," Gavin said.

Emily cocked her head to the side. "Um, what?"

"She's a professional," he said.

Emily blinked a few million times. "A professional? As in prostitute?" she asked.

"Yes," he said. He licked his lips, not sure how she was going to react to his revelation.

"So, you pay her for sex?" she asked.

"Yes," he said. He wanted to run away. His leg shook nervously, and he jingled the change in his jean pockets.

"Interesting," she said. The alcohol was not letting her react much more than quiet pensiveness.

"You see, unlike you, I do not need nor want someone to have what's left of my heart. I'm not exactly proud of it, but it's better than the alternative," he said.

"Which is what, an actual relationship with a real human being?" Emily asked.

"Yes."

"Jesus Christ, Gavin . . ." Emily shook her head.

"I'm not good with women. Never have been. It's still a miracle to me that I snagged Natalie. And after she died, I just decided that I didn't even want to bother with it anymore. It's just easier this way," Gavin practically shouted at her.

Emily walked up to him and looked him in the eyes. He fidgeted and closed his eyes, unable to meet her stare.

"That's complete and utter bullshit. You don't fool me, Gavin Shaw. Every wall you throw up, every boundary you set, every rule you establish—none of it will stop you from feeling for another woman again. You can try, but one day, someday, someone will get in," she said.

His jaw tightened. He just stood there and shifted his feet nervously.

"I'm tired. I'm drunk. I'm going to bed. Put up the pizza. Oh, and the Honda is still at the restaurant. Wouldn't start," she said. Gavin watched her climb up the stairs, and he hung his head.

The next evening Shakes walked in to find Emily making hot chocolate on the stove. She had been absentmindedly stirring the pot for close to 20 minutes.

"Howdy," he said.

"He's not here. Haven't seen him all day. He didn't leave a note. He's not returning text messages," she mumbled. She made no attempt to hide the frustration that Gavin had been AWOL after last night's spectacle.

Shakes leaned against the counter and pulled down an extra cup for himself. Emily smiled at his lack of subtlety and started pouring the gleaming hot liquid into the mugs.

"Marshmallows?" she asked.

"Yes, please," he said.

She loaded them up with tiny marshmallows and walked a cup over to Sam, who was watching TV in the living room.

He signed "*thank you*" and gave her a peck on the cheek. She smiled and touched his nose. She came back and took a hot mug in her hand.

"Gavin told me that you met Caitlin last night." Emily felt a marshmallow get stuck in her throat. She coughed slightly.

"Do you want to talk about it?" Shakes asked.

"Nope."

"Are you sure?"

"You obviously want to talk about it. Why else would you still be standing here?" Emily asked, annoyed.

"Well, for the excellent hot chocolate, of course."

Emily gave glared at him. He put down his cup, reached into his coat pocket, and pulled out his flask. He offered the flask to Emily, who decided that whiskey would aid in the execution of this awkward conversation and handed him her cup.

"He thinks that you think badly of him now," he said, pouring a shot of alcohol in the mug.

"I don't. Really, I don't. I just don't understand why . . . why he chooses to go this route." She had a hard time finding the right words.

Shakes hopped up on the counter. "A man has needs."

"I get that. Really, I do. But there are women around here," she offered.

Shakes raised his eyebrows and laughed. "Not really. You've lived here long enough. Who?" Emily shook her head. He had a point.

"Look, Em, I've known Gavin a long, long time. And something happened to him when Nat and Sissy died. He shut down. Darkness like I'd never seen set in." A lump formed in Emily's throat.

"I offered Caitlin as a solution to prevent him from being sucked completely into oblivion," Shakes said. He sipped his hot chocolate and glanced at Emily.

"You found her for him?"

"Yes."

"Where?"

"I have my connections."

Emily drank from the mug and let the chocolaty whiskey burn her throat. "I'm not judging him . . . I'm just sad for him, if that makes any sense," she said.

"He's getting laid! Don't be too sad for him!"

"Well, there is that. Lucky for him. She's beautiful. You chose well," Emily said. She thought of Caitlin's flawless skin, her long, silky blonde hair, her size 2 waist. She wondered how it was that Gavin wasn't completely in love with her.

Shakes stared at her for a long time. "He doesn't love her. He's incapable of it," he said.

Emily sighed, cursing the voodoo intuition that this man possessed, reading her thoughts like a damn message on her forehead.

"It's not my business," she said.

"I know you care for him, and that's the only reason I'm

here. The only reason I am telling you any of this. Gavin cares a great deal for you, and he is convinced that you are disgusted by him now. He's pretty low," Shakes said.

Emily put the cup down and rubbed her eyes.

"You know, he's like a brother to me, saved my ass more times than I can count. And I don't like to see him like this. So, if you could find a way to reassure him that this is not the case, well, I'd appreciate it," Shakes said.

"Where is he?"

"Will's house."

"Can you watch Sam?"

"Yep. Go."

Gavin opened the door and rolled his eyes. "So much for Shakes going to get beer," he said.

"May I come in?" she asked. Gavin opened the door wider. Emily walked in and pulled off her black gloves.

Will's house was a lot like Gavin's, but without the woman's touch. A small couch and recliner were in a vast living room. A small table with three mismatched chairs was in the dining room.

"I think you mistook what I said last night, and I wanted to come here to clarify some things." Gavin crossed his arms in front of his chest and refused to make real eye contact with her.

"Just because I didn't understand about Caitlin doesn't mean I am appalled by it. I'm not. At all."

Gavin remained quiet.

"You are a wonderful person. And even if you became a homicidal killer tomorrow, I don't think I could ever utter bad about you. Ever," she said. He shook his head. She walked up close to him. "Please believe me," she whispered.

He was overwhelmed by his embarrassment and from relief. She reached out her hand to him. "Come home."

He stuck his hands deep in his pockets, afraid that if he touched her, he wouldn't be able to stop himself from doing something drastic, like scooping her up in his arms. She took the gesture as defiance.

"Gavin, please."

"No, I heard what you said. And I do appreciate it. I just need to clear up a few things here, and I'll be back to the house shortly," he said.

She touched his arm and he felt panicked. He walked away from her touch.

"You should leave," he said softly. She tried to grab his other arm and he forcefully grabbed her by the shoulders.

"Please don't touch me," he said through gritted teeth. His anger scared her and brought tears to her eyes.

"Gavin, please," she pleaded. She looked at him with so much concern and care he felt physically ill.

"DON'T! I don't deserve your understanding!! I'm a horrible man who can't get close to anyone! Can't you see that? I have to sleep with whores. I don't deserve anything but your contempt and disgust!" he yelled.

"Stop it. Stop it!" she yelled. She grabbed his face and overtook him, holding on to him for dear life, shaking him until he came to his senses.

He crumpled in her arms, the disgust and self-loathing he felt was palpable. Tears fell down her face as she cradled him in her arms as they slumped to the floor. A storm that had been brewing for years was finally freed, as Gavin finally released the tears, he held in about the life that was taken so brutally from him. He cried for the injustice of all of it, and the fear that he had most days that his heart was really dead. Emily stroked his dark hair and became the strong anchor that he so desperately needed.

After the storm passed, Gavin sat up and moved next to her. They held hands like little children, cupping palms instead of intertwining their fingers, staring out into space, both in their own version of grief and release. They didn't look at each other for a long time, both knowing that one look would send them down a path that they both were still afraid to take.

He studied her small hand in his, put it to his lips and graced it with a gentle kiss. Emily closed her eyes. It was in that moment that she finally admitted to herself that she was in love with him. Completely and achingly in love.

She opened her eyes and looked at him. She leaned her head against his shoulder and felt Gavin's arm wrap around her. They were quiet.

"Will needs more furniture. Why does he live like a hobo?" she suddenly announced.

Gavin laughed. "I've been telling him that for years."

A mail truck drove up to the farmhouse while Emily was washing the dishes after lunch a few days later. Odd, she thought. The mail was never delivered there. Gavin had a post office box that he checked twice a week when he ran into town for supplies. She wiped her hands on the dishtowel that was tucked into the band of her jeans and walked to the front door.

Gavin beat her to the truck, walking slowly up to the driver, shaking hands and exchanging pleasantries. A few minutes later, both men looked at the direction of the house and Gavin nodded and pointed. He whistled for Shakes who was in the barn as the driver opened the side door of the mail truck. Shakes appeared, grabbed a couple of boxes and brought them to the front porch. Emily finally walked outside.

"What is all this?" she asked.

"They're addressed to you," Gavin said.

"To me?" The only mail she ever got was the occasional post card from Mary, who was now living in Paris, having only found dengue fever in Bali, not true love. Emily looked at the address label of one of the smaller boxes and saw the postmark from Watchung. All in all there were 17 boxes of various sizes.

"What are they, Em?" Shakes asked.

"Not sure," she said. Gavin pulled his knife from his boot and sliced one open. Inside were Sam's toys from his room in their old house. Sam appeared from the barn carrying one of the newest kittens when he saw his Transformers. He gasped with glee and dropped the kitten who thankfully landed on her feet with an aggravated "mew."

Sam clapped at the sight of his old toys, diving into the box

235

like it was Christmas all over again. Shakes smiled at the sight of the little boy's joy and took out his knife and began to slice open boxes too. One was filled with books that Emily had collected over the years, including cookbooks, fiction, and poetry anthologies. She saw some of her clothes, her wedding gown, a box filled with photo albums, and the initial three boxes that she had packed of Sam's baby mementos, her journals, and her photos that she wanted to keep of her family. In the last box, there was an envelope with her name on it.

"Emily—I just heard about the fire, and your Aunt Margaret. I wanted to say I was sorry for your loss. I know you only packed three boxes, but I thought you may want some of your other belongings now as they were excluded as assets for the investigation. I want you to know I believe you when you said you had nothing to do with any of it. But I want to give you a heads up that Stanton is still hell bent on trying to link you to all of it. He is planning on subpoenaing you for your testimony in the near future. I hope that you are doing all right. Please know that I am praying for you and your little boy every night and hoping you are doing well. Take care of yourselves. Respectfully, Erica Barnes."

Gavin read over her shoulder. "Who is Erica Barnes?" he asked.

Emily folded the letter and dropped it back in the box.

"One of the agents who let me pack some clothes before the feds kicked us out of the house," she said.

"It couldn't come at a better time," he said.

Emily stared at the sea of boxes, unsure how to take the Agent's gesture.

"I never gave them my address, Gavin. They're obviously still watching me."

CHAPTER TWENTY-THREE

On April 7th, Emily turned 36. That Saturday started out like normal, Gavin got up early to tend to the animals with Sam and Shakes as his helpers, and Emily started to stir around 7:00. As she walked down to the kitchen after taking a shower, she noticed that fresh coffee was being brewed, the smell wafting up the stairs. She walked into the kitchen and saw Will fixing breakfast.

"Hey!! When did you get back?" she asked, hugging him.

"Last night. I'm still on UK time," he said, hugging her tightly. He had shaved his beard and looked like a Cambridge-educated professor now, wearing khakis and a dark blue buttoned-down Polo shirt.

"You look so different without your beard!" Emily said, laughing.

"Well, I was tired of being asked if I was Santa Claus by the children in the village," Will said.

Emily giggled and sat down at the island. Will poured her a cup of coffee.

"So, tell me all about it. Was it fantastic?" she asked.

"It really was. I can't thank you enough for encouraging me to go and do this. It really was life changing," he said. He pushed sausage around a cast iron skillet and got lost in thought.

"I'm so glad," she said.

"Did Sam get my letters?"

"He did. He loved reading them and receiving all the wonderful gifts you sent. That was really thoughtful of you to keep in touch with him that way," she said.

Will put a plate of eggs and sausage in front of her and poured a cup of coffee for himself, joining her at the island.

"How's business?"

"Good. Really good. I'm almost too busy. I may need to hire some help soon."

"That's excellent!"

"Did you meet any hot English broads?" Emily joked and smiled as she ate. Will smiled a slow smile and drank his coffee. "Oh yeah? Do tell," she said.

"Well, I met a history professor named Evangeline Jones. Doctor Jones," he said, and raised his eyebrows. Emily raised her eyebrows, too.

"She's almost 50 years old. Marathon runner, has more energy than I could ever hope to have."

"Well, that was probably a good thing," she said, and winked.

"I'm not complaining," he said. "She wants to come visit me in a few months," he said.

"So, it's sorta serious?" Emily asked.

Will had a look of whimsy on his face. "Sorta."

"Can't wait to meet her," she said. She stood to take her plate to the kitchen sink.

"Well, I've told her all about you and Sam. And of course, the rest of the gang. Speaking of. I have something for you." He walked back into the living room and came back with white roses and a small black box covered with a white ribbon.

"Happy birthday," he said.

Emily felt giddy as she took his gifts. She hugged him and he planted a kiss up high, near her ear.

"Thank you. These are beautiful." She opened the box and saw a bracelet that was composed of small cubes of glass that were etched with small purple flowers.

"Oh, Will. This is so beautiful."

"I picked it up in Florence. It reminded me of you."

There was a knock on the door while Emily was trying on the bracelet, and she heard Celia's voice.

"Where's my birthday girl?" Celia sang.

"In the kitchen."

Celia walked in carrying a massive amount of pink balloons.

"Oh, wow," Emily said when she saw her.

"Thirty-seven. For each year and one to grow on," Celia said proudly. She tied the balloons on the back of the chair and let them float to the top of Gavin's kitchen ceiling.

"Don't you ever pull that stunt on my birthday, ya hear? With so many balloons I'd might float away," Will joked.

Celia shook her head and hugged him hello. "Oh William. How we missed you around here. I'm here to steal you for the day. I have made us appointments for a cut, manicure, and massage in Columbus, and then we'll do lunch. Go on. Get dressed."

"Yes, ma'am," Emily said, and disappeared.

"The plans all set for this afternoon?" Will asked.

Celia picked up a piece of uneaten toast and nibbled on it.

"It's going to be the best birthday ever in the history of birthdays," she said confidently.

The trip to Grandview took about an hour and Celia chatted the whole time about how beautiful the weather was and how long it had been since she'd gotten a proper haircut. It was a beautiful April day, with clear blue skies and highs in the high 60s. Emily was so grateful that the miserable winter was finally behind them, and spring was finally here.

The salon was new and modern. The receptionist took Celia's information and led them both to a large round table with white chairs. From that view you could see all the stylists working with their clients. Emily accepted the offer of coffee and was impressed it was served in a real mug with real cream.

"Where did you find this place?" Emily asked.

"Actually, Gavin made all the arrangements. Said he looked it up on-line," Celia said, eyes wide. She smiled a wicked little smiled at Emily.

Emily felt her cheeks blush as she sipped her coffee. Celia dug in her purse and passed her a small box wrapped in gold paper. "He also told me to give this to you when we got here. That you would understand what it meant."

Emily opened the box and saw it stuffed with Lindt truffles, milk chocolate and peanut butter. She laughed and shook her head.

"Damn, that man does remember everything," she mumbled. She offered Celia a chocolate and popped one in her mouth and sipped her coffee.

"Ms. Emily. Bryan is ready for you," the receptionist said.

Bryan was the owner of the salon and had been styling hair for 20 years. He was wonderfully warm but matter of fact about styles of hair.

"When's the last time you've had a cut?" he asked.

"Over a year," Emily admitted. "I just pull it back with I'm working."

"And what do you do, love?"

"I'm a baker. Have a small business in Champaign County." It felt strange for Emily to say that out loud. It made it real, even after several months of baking, advertising, and delivering to various clients.

"I think you look better with shorter hair." He pulled the long strands up to just below her jawline and showed her how beautiful less hair accentuated her jaw and neckline.

"You're the expert," she said.

"And we are getting rid of these damn grays. You're 36. You should not have this much gray hair."

She sat back and watched him mix a color in his bowl and a young apprentice helped him with the foil strips. Emily looked around and saw that Celia was getting her nails done, chatting up the nail technician.

Bryan was quick, adding the color to her head and setting a timer. The young apprentice washed Emily's hair and gave it a good towel rub. Bryan reappeared when Emily sat back down in his chair, took his stainless-steel scissors and cut Emily's hair a good six inches. She had never felt such liberation in her life as the hair dropped. He rubbed a product in her hair that smelled like cherries and blow-dried her hair until it was just right.

When he swung her around, she was taken aback. The girl staring back at her looked ten years younger. The color Bryan chose was four darker shades of brown, and it made her hazel eyes look green.

"You're beautiful," Bryan said.

"Thank you," she whispered. She was amazed how a single haircut could bring back the person she was over a year ago, and how Gavin knew that it would.

After getting her nails painted a deep purple color, and after a wonderfully relaxing massage, Celia and Emily ate sandwiches at Panera and sipped on iced tea.

"So, any other surprises coming my way that I should know about?" Emily teased.

"Girl, I have no idea what you're talking about," Celia winked. "But I will tell you Gavin is going to flip seeing this new you. You are stunning. I almost want to come across the table and kiss you myself." Emily laughed and threw a napkin at her. They split a gigantic chocolate chip cookie and carried their teas to go, driving back to Gavin's house singing old 80s tunes at the top of their lungs.

She was greeted back home with a beautiful cake placed in the center of Gavin's dining room table, decorated in Tiffany blue with tiny white flowers. Will's white roses and another dozen red roses from Gavin surrounded the cake. As Celia predicted, Gavin stopped dead in his tracks when he saw her, unable to speak until Shakes whistled that she looked amazing, speaking Gavin's thoughts. He did manage to smile at her and said she looked lovely. She hated to admit that she loved everything about that day and the care that everyone was taking to make sure it was wonderful.

Paco had been watching the meat smoker, babysitting seven whole chickens all day, and between checking the meat and drinking beer, he and Shakes managed to make potato salad, baked beans, and deviled eggs. Emily could hardly wait for dinnertime.

When Paco pulled the chickens from the smoker to "rest," Celia gathered everyone on the porch to officially exchange gifts. She looked giddy with anticipation as she held Xavier and Sam's hands.

"All right, well, as you all know we are here to celebrate the lovely Emily. We have a couple of gifts to show how much we love and appreciate you. We'll start with Shakes."

Shakes threw down his cigarette and then cleared his throat.

"Well, Em, it isn't any secret that you drive a gigantic jalopy of a car, and well, we got to thinking with the new business and the need to carry more product, you needed an upgrade. So, here you go," Shakes said, and threw her a ring of keys.

"So much for fanfare, Dillon," Celia mumbled. Shakes shrugged.

"You bought me a car?" Emily asked stunned.

"Well, sorta. Took it off a man's hands that really needed some cash and some help, so it was more like a trade. It's not like it's a Lexus. I mean, it'll get you where you need to go with a little more comfort. Go see it, it's around the corner."

Emily walked around the wraparound porch to Gavin's side driveway and saw a silver Honda CRV parked there.

"Oh my God," she said, and hopped over the railing to get to the car, with Shakes following her.

"It's a 2005. Has like 150,000 miles. It'll probably go another 200,000 if you're careful. These cars are hard to kill," he said.

Emily opened the door and felt like she had won the lottery. The interior was clean and in perfect condition. No more duct tape on a shaky steering wheel, exhaust fumes, and dying in the heat with no AC.

"You're amazing. Thank you, Shakes," she said, and hugged him. He patted her back affectionately.
"You're welcome. Happy birthday," he said, and smiled.

Gavin watched her carefully from afar, gauging her reaction to everything.

"All right, well, we also pitched in and decided to help you upgrade somewhere else, too. So, ta-da!" Celia said, opening the back of the Honda. There was a new KitchenAid mixer with a big red bow on it.

"You guys, this is too much!" Emily said. She had tears in her eyes, overcome with so much emotion.

"Well, just you wait. We saved the best for last," Celia said, giddy. Celia looked at Sam and he walked up to his mother and handed her a card that he made. Emily knelt down by him and read it.

"Thank you, Sam," she signed, and smiled.

Sam held up his hand and signed, *"wait."* He took the card back from her. She waited, confused.

Sam opened the card and cleared his throat. "H-h-h-app-y b-b-b-irth-day, Mom-Mom-Mommy. I l-lo-ve you," he said softly.

Emily felt the air get knocked out of her and she covered her mouth.

"Oh my God," Emily said, as she grabbed Sam and hugged him. She held on to him and wept in earnest, burying her face into his head. He spoke! Sam spoke!

Everyone wiped their eyes, taken by the sweet emotion. Celia hugged Sam and told him she was so proud of him, and the men all gave him high fives, even Xavier as Emily tried to compose herself. She felt Gavin walk up behind her and slide an arm around her shoulders. She held on to it for a moment and leaned against him before she turned around and hugged him.

"This is the best day that I have had in a long, long while," he told her. He kissed the top of her head and hugged her a while longer.

"Me too," she whispered.

"Let's eat! I'm starving!" Shakes said and clapped.

They broke away from their embrace and Gavin held her hand as they walked around to the front door. Sam ran up and held her free hand, and for a split second, everything felt right and normal in her world. She prayed for the millionth time that nothing would change it but knew better to wish for such a thing.

CHAPTER TWENTY-FOUR

Two weeks later Emily walked up to Gavin in the new barn clutching a certified letter. They had installed the final hay awning and the horses were getting to know the new stable area, which was twice the size of the old one. Gavin spent a lot of time there, walking around, inspecting and admiring.

He was brushing Lily, taking his time, and getting lost in a daydream. In those rare moments when he did not immediately sense Emily's presence, she could see how they connected, horse and owner. He patted her strong hind muscles and she snorted. "Need to run a little more, girl. You're getting a little soft there," he teased.

Lily snorted in retort. Emily smiled. The horse whisperer at work.

Lily noticed Emily and turned her head in Emily's direction. She instinctively rubbed the horse's muzzle, and Lily nuzzled her, and snorted.

"Never seen her take to anyone else but me and Sissy," Gavin said.

"I read once horses know your true heart," Emily said. Lily nuzzled her again. Gavin smiled and continued brushing the horse. He paused when he noticed the envelope.

"Whatcha got there?" he asked.

Emily exhaled. "A summons. I need to book a flight back to New York. I have some money for a ticket, but it's cheaper to go on-line to book. Any chance I can give you the cash for use of your credit card?" Emily asked. Gavin stopped mid-brush and looked shocked.

"So, the son of a bitch did it, eh? Summoned you back," Gavin shook his head, angry.

Emily took the brush from Gavin and started brushing the mare.

"I don't think you should go," he said. "I mean, what's the worst they can do? They already took everything you had."

"I don't have anything to hide. By not going, it implies I knew what Aaron was doing," she said.

"They've been investigating for almost a year. If they had found anything of substance, they wouldn't have waited a year. They are looking to trap you into saying something," Gavin said.

"I have to go, Gavin. Please. I just want this to be over already so I can fully go on with my life. Can I pretty please use your credit card? I already hate that I have to spend money on a damn plane ticket. I just want to spend as little as possible," she said.

"All right. Let me finish up here and we'll look on the computer," he said.

"Thank you," she said. She handed him back his brush. She walked out of the barn; hands deep in her jean pockets. It was her worried pose. He knew it all too well lately.

She was in the kitchen mindlessly scrubbing a pot when he walked back into the house. She quickly rinsed her hands and poured him some coffee. She sat at the dining room table next to the opened laptop.

"I already priced a ticket. Columbus to Newark," she said.

"Okay," he said.

"I found one leaving on the 1st, coming back on the 3rd," she said.

"Next week?"

"Yes. Can you watch Sam?"

"Absolutely," he said. He walked to the kitchen, looking for something sweet to go with the coffee. "Did we finish all those cranberry orange cookies from two days ago?" he asked.

"I saved you two. Check the pantry. Behind the flour," she called back to him. He opened the pantry and saw it neat and organized. He pulled the cookies out of their hiding space.

Gavin pulled up a chair beside her and looked over her shoulder. He put the cookies and coffee down by her and she instinctively pulled off a piece and ate it. The familiarity of her small action made him stop and take notice. She was so close that her hair tickled his nose. She mindlessly picked up his coffee cup and took a sip to wash down the cookie. Sharing a snack, like he had done with Natalie a million times, made him ache a little. He stood up to shake the sadness off.

"It's $210. That's not terrible," she said.

"Where will you stay?" Gavin asked.

"The YMCA. Cheap rooms. Clean. It'll do," she said.

"This will do," she said. She slid the computer over to him to purchase the ticket. He reached into his pocket for his wallet and credit card and pulled out his reading glasses. He filled out the passenger and billing information.

"What's your middle initial?" he asked.

"R," she said.

"And what does that stand for?" he asked.

"Rachel." Gavin smiled.

"What's your middle name?" she countered.

"Merrick. After my grandfather. Meanest son of a bitch you ever met," he said, while he typed.

"Well, that's why your momma called you Gavin, I'm sure," Emily said, and laughed.

"She did call me Gavin Merrick when she was about to put a pounding on me, though," he said.

"Of course she did."

She walked back to the kitchen, taking Gavin's empty coffee cup with her. He watched her rinse it and place it on the drying rack. She dried her hands and took a moment to smell the tulips that Celia sent over a few days earlier, resting in a blue willow vase that belonged to his grandmother. In a rare moment of spontaneity, Gavin changed the number of passengers from "1" to "2" and typed in his name. His hands shook so badly he could hardly type in his credit card number.

What the hell are you doing? he thought.

Doing what he did best. Protecting her. There was no way in hell she was going to New York without him.

"She'll be mad as hell when she finds out."

Gavin looked at the blinking button. *Book now?* It asked. He clicked on it.

"All set?" she asked.

"Yes, ma'am," he said, closing the laptop. He'd find another time to mention it to her.

Emily hugged Sam tight while Gavin loaded up her bag in the back of his truck. It was the first time that she had left him in a year, and she was not dealing well with it, acting like Celia did when she left Xavier back in the summer.

"You can text me any time. If I don't answer, it means I'm on the plane," she signed.

"Mom, I'll be fine. I promise. We have school today and the zoo tomorrow. You'll be home the next day," Sam signed.

"I love you, you crazy kid," she said.

"I love you more," he said back and hugged her. She kissed him a hundred more times and Sam finally pushed her to the truck.

Paco and Xavier were waiting by Paco's truck to take Sam to school while Gavin took Emily to Columbus to the airport.

"If you need anything . . ." Emily told Paco.

"Em—I'll guard him with my life," Paco told her, and she nodded.

She went to the truck and tried hard not to cry. Gavin waited patiently as she finally climbed into the passenger side. Paco, Xavier, and Sam all waved at them as Gavin drove off. She looked out the window and quietly took the bandana that Gavin handed her.

"He'll be fine," Gavin said.

"I know. Just sucks that I have to do this. Go back. Deal with this. Leave Sam. It all just sucks," she said.

Gavin quietly drove to Columbus. Emily eventually composed herself about ten minutes into the drive, but she was still silently reflecting on the impact of this trip.

"I need you to promise me that if they try to do something stupid like arrest me that you will look after Sam," she said.

"Emily, that will never happen."

"Promise me, Gavin."

"That will never happen."

"Promise me!"

Gavin looked at her. "I promise," he said. She relaxed.

Gavin shook his head, even more convinced of his plan to go with her to New York. Because, if God forbid something like that happened, he would need a lawyer for himself—to bail him out of jail for kicking some special agent's ass.

Gavin navigated his truck around the airport and Emily noticed he was parking. "You can just drop me at the gate," she said.

He didn't answer her. Instead, he pulled into long-term parking.

"This is long-term parking, Gavin. It'll cost you a fortune for an hour," she said.

He still ignored her. It wasn't until he finally parked, and she saw two suitcases in the backseat that she finally understood what was going on. She looked at him. "I should've known," she said.

He turned off the engine and looked at her. "Are you mad?" he asked.

"Does it matter?"

"Maybe a little."

"Tell me why you decided to come, and I will tell you if I'm mad," she said.

"You really need me to tell you why?" Gavin challenged.

"Yes."

"There is no way in hell I'd let you meet a son of a bitch like Stanton alone. Hell no. Not on my watch," Gavin said.

Emily exhaled. "All right," she said, and grabbed her bag.

"Are you mad?" he asked.

"Mildly annoyed."

"I can live with that," Gavin said.

"Better stick close. Because if you really piss me off, I'll just leave you in Times Square and make you fend for yourself, like Crocodile Dundee," she mumbled.

"Should've brought my big knife then," he joked. She tried to hide her smile. She didn't want to admit it, but the idea of

Gavin in New York with was a gigantic relief. She felt empowered and ready to face whatever her fate was.

After they landed, they took a shuttle to the Westside YMCA where they both stood in a long line with young tourists waiting for a room. Most of them spoke different languages, and some definitely could have invested in some deodorant. They were given rooms right next to each other, each with a small twin bed, small TV, and barely any room to hang up clothes in a makeshift clothesline that acted as a closet.

"Well, it's clean and it's only for a day or two," Emily said.

"I've stayed in worse," Gavin reassured her. "Are you hungry? I can run out and get us some food."

He watched Emily sit nervously on the bed. She pulled out her phone and dug in her purse for the paperwork for the Stanton meeting.

"I just want to get this over with. I want to see if he can see me now," she said.

Gavin glanced at his watch. It was already after noon. He sat quietly next to her on the bed as she dialed the number.

"Agent Marcus Stanton, please. This is Emily Mitchell."

Emily waited a few minutes and paced around the small room nervously, waiting for him to come to the phone. "Agent Stanton. I'm in town. Where shall I meet you?" Her voice was calm, and somewhat defiant. Gavin squinted as he caught glimpse of pre-tragedy Emily, full of confidence and fearlessness. She jotted down an address on an old envelope.

"I'll be there in a half hour," she said, and hung up.

The Jacob K. Javits Federal Office Building downtown was around 40-stories high and housed DHS, FBI, and other federal agencies. The building reminded her of Aaron's old office building on Wall Street, and her stomach turned at the sight of the skyscraper. They rode the elevator after going through security to the FBI offices and told the woman at the front office that they were here for Agent Stanton.

"I'm sorry, Agent Stanton had to leave suddenly. He left you a message," the young woman said, handing a white piece of paper to her.

In barely legible writing, Emily was able to make out "Subpoena is canceled. Your testimony is not necessary. Case is closed. Will call if we need you."

"Is he serious? He no longer needs me? The case is suddenly closed? Why didn't he tell me this on the phone when I called less than an hour ago? Or before I flew out here?" Emily demanded.

"I'm sorry, Mrs. Mitchell. He did not tell me any more details. And he really was in a rush when he left."

Emily turned the paper over and wrote a note back to him. "*Agent Stanton. Your assholiness knows no bounds. Thanks for wasting my time. Sincerely, Emily Mitchell*." Gavin smiled and turned his head to prevent from laughing out loud. She folded the note and handed it back to the receptionist, but Gavin intercepted it, not wanting her to tempt the good fortune that had smiled on her that afternoon.

"Can you believe that man?" Emily said in the elevator. "I mean I fly out all this way and then come all the way downtown and then he cancels everything and says the case is closed. What the hell?"

"Em."

"He is such a human ball of slime. What a piece of work, I mean really."

"Em."

"What?"

"You're missing the bigger picture here. It's over. The case is closed. It's all over," Gavin said, holding her by her shoulders.

Emily exhaled. "Oh my God," she said. Relief flooded from her, and she hugged him until the door of the elevator opened.

He walked them outside into the warm, bright sunshine, and held her hand until the cab that he hailed pulled up to the curb. When they returned to the YMCA, Gavin ordered her to pack her bags while he made a phone call. He carried both bags downstairs twenty minutes later and hailed another cab after paying for the rooms that they were not going to stay in.

"Where are we going?" she asked.

"Occasions like this deserve stupidly, ridiculous celebrations," Gavin said, as he helped her climb into the cab. The cabby was a large, older black man.

"Where to?" he asked them in a deep voice.

"The Ritz Carlton," Gavin said. Emily raised her eyebrows.

"I said stupidly celebrate. I meant it," he said.

They drove the short ten-minute drive south around Central Park and stopped at the iconic Ritz, with its two flags, the American flag and their blue and gold flag, flapping in the warm May breeze. Two men in tuxedos and black top hats greeted them and opened the door for her while Gavin paid the fare and carried their bags into the luxurious lobby. They were greeted warmly as Gavin walked up to the receptionist.

"Welcome to the Ritz-Carlton. Checking in?"

"Yes, sir. Last name is Shaw," Gavin said.

"I see you are staying with us for two nights, Mr. Shaw. I have you down for the city view room. But I apologize, that is not quite ready for you. Could you please pardon me while I look into something?"

"Sure."

The young man continued to type while Emily looked around and instinctively touched the cold, marble counters and admired the old-fashioned décor in the lobby.

"I apologize for that wait. It looks like I don't have another one of those rooms ready for you just yet. We would be happy to extend to you the city view suite at no extra charge for your inconvenience."

"Sounds perfect," Gavin said grinning, laying down his platinum Visa card on the counter.

"Are you sure?" Emily asked.

"Never been so sure about anything in my life."

The city view suite was bigger than Emily's first apartment in the city, with extravagant linens on the king-sized bed, two marble bathrooms, and a living room with a pullout sofa bed. Outside of their living area they saw a fantastic view of the city.

"You can have the bedroom," Gavin said. Emily smiled to hide her disappointment. She half hoped that "stupidly celebrate" meant something different altogether.

He took her shopping at the Shops of Columbus Circle just a few blocks away. She couldn't remember the last time she had been in a mall like that, with high-end boutiques dominating the real estate.

"I think we should buy some fancy clothes for dinner," Gavin said.

"Here? Did you recently rob a bank that I don't know about? A dress in that shop over there will cost you $500, easily," Emily said, pointing to Eileen Fisher.

"Let's go look," he said.

"I'm more a J Crew kind of girl—even when the money was no object," she said. "They have one of those in this mall, too."

"You've never really treated yourself properly, have you? Always sacrificing yourself for the betterment of others," Gavin said, looking at her. She bowed her head. "You just got your life and freedom back from the freakin' feds. I have five credit cards, and I don't care if I max them all out. We are celebrating it right tonight," he said.

Emily laughed. "Okay! Okay!"

The wandered in the shop and were systematically ignored by the sleek saleswomen. Emily looked around and saw that most of these dresses looked like her t-shirt dresses from the 1990s, but with a much steeper price tag.

"Pass. Let's try another store," she said. They gazed at the white linen fashion at Armani and the 20-something fashion at H&M. They finally wandered into Hugo Boss, and she saw a plum dress that she particularly liked. It reminded her of one of Andromeda's gowns in *Clash of the Titans*, long and flowing, with a crisscross pattern at the mid-section. All that were missing were lace up sandals. Gavin watched her finger the material.

"Try it on," he encouraged.

She relented and motioned for the saleswoman, who was watching from afar.

"I would like to try this in a 10, and the gentleman needs to be fitted for a suit. The 110 or the 120 Italian, I think," she said.

The saleswoman looked surprised that Emily knew their suit line, and her attitude toward them completely changed.

"Yes, ma'am," she said, motioning to another gentleman to help Gavin while she worked with Emily to get her fitted.

In the vast dressing room, Emily pulled off her blue shirt and cardigan and felt the silkiness of the dress as it slid down her sides. The color complemented her pale skin and dark hair. Her breasts, which barely filled out most dresses, fit perfectly in the deep V-neck. She laughed to herself trying to imagine Celia getting her chest into a gown like this.

The saleswoman knocked and walked in. "You look amazing." Emily felt amazing. She moved her hips slowly from side to side to see every angle of her body in the dress. She felt like a Greek goddess. She walked out into the store and saw Gavin wearing a black suit. His broad shoulders fit expertly in the fabric and accentuated his trim waist. She snuck back into the dressing room and decided to buy it without Gavin seeing her in it. After Hugo Boss, Emily made a quick stop in Aveda for makeup, and they rushed back to the hotel to get ready for dinner.

At the hotel, Gavin paced in the small living room wearing his black suit with a brand-new white shirt. His tie was gray with hints of purple. He was clean-shaven and ready to see Emily's big reveal.

She stepped out of the bedroom wearing her beautiful plum dress, flowing and showing off more skin than he had ever seen before. Her dark hair was wavy, and her makeup was impeccable, almost professional. Emily had been out of practice for a while for dressing up for fancy affairs, but like riding a bicycle, the techniques for putting on a smoky eye and contouring and shading came back to her.

"Gorgeous," he whispered.

"I do love to leave you speechless," she teased.

"Not speechless. You look amazing," he said.

"As do you, Mr. Shaw. Shall we hit the town?" she asked

and grabbed his arm.

"Yes, we shall," he said.

The concierge recommended a place atop the Kimberly Hotel called Upstairs. It was a modern lounge with a 360-degree view of midtown. The hostess led them to a back corner to a small table with the Chrysler Building as their backdrop.

Gavin opened the menu. "What sounds good?"

Emily sighed. "It all does. I'm starving. The drinks sound delicious, too," she said.

"You order. I'll just sit here and take in the view," he said.

"Well, there is plenty to look at up here," she said. Gavin drank a sip of water. "I wasn't talking about the buildings." Emily looked up from the menu and smiled at him.

The waiter came back, and Emily ordered an assortment of items such as lump crab cakes, crispy artichokes, mac and cheese made with truffles, and braised short ribs. She ordered a drink made of rye whiskey for her and one made of bourbon for Gavin.

"The lady has impeccable taste," the waiter told Gavin.

"Present company excluded, that she does," he said.

"I rather like this spry, confident Gavin. Where's he been the last year?"

"Oh around. Trying desperately not to make a horse's ass out of himself on most days."

"And now?" The waiter placed their drinks down in front of them.

"Now, he just wants to put down his guard and have a good time tonight," he said.

Emily raised her glass. "To tonight," she said.

"To freedom," he said, and they clinked their glasses. They both drank and paused.

"Damn, you do have good taste," he said.

"Present company included, yes I do."

They drank and they ate, and they talked effortlessly like they did at most meals, but tonight was special, and they both knew it. It was Emily's freedom and Gavin's enthusiasm for life like she had never seen before that magnified their easy rapport. They shared sips of drinks and bites of food with each other. They laughed at stories and felt a connection deeper than they ever imagined in those five hours they sat there, closing the place down by 1 a.m.

They caught a cab back to the Ritz and Emily held and fell against Gavin's strong arm. They walked through the extravagant lobby and up the elevator ride holding hands, hanging on to the night before they walked into the hotel room.

The lights were on in their room when they walked in, and Emily saw the twinkling lights of the city. She snapped off the lights to really see the view outside their windows.

"It's amazing how beautiful the city can be at night," Emily said.

They stood there for a few minutes in the dark when she finally looked at him. Gavin continued to stare at the scenery, not quite knowing what to do next, feeling the familiar sense of anxiety and fear that he felt whenever a possible moment of intimacy could come with her. He felt almost faint.

Emily reached for his hand and tried to bring him closer to look at her. Gavin exhaled and seemed to be wrestling internally with what to say, what to do. The night had been so perfect. Why did this pause always have to linger between them? She wanted him. That was obvious. But in a moment of panic, he finally spoke.

"Em, I don't think I can do this . . ." he whispered, and immediately hated himself for saying it. Emily's head lowered in defeat. She swallowed a few times to get the disappointment down.

"Very well then. Good night, sir," she whispered, walked through the bedroom door, and closed it.

Gavin walked to his sad, lonely couch and tossed his tie on the desk. He kept feeling that pecking in his head from the look on her face. Such disappointment. He wished that he could just walk into that room and do what he'd imagined doing since she drove up on his property nearly a year ago, but there was always something that forced him to stop, and he hated it. It was as if the pain he felt when Natalie died immediately saturated his senses when he considered life with Emily, and he felt sick with panic. He would never put himself in a position to feel that kind of loss again. He didn't know how he survived it, but he did know that there was no way he could do it again.

He kicked off his nice boots, threw his suit jacket over the back of a chair, untucked his white shirt, and sat on the couch, staring at the wall that separated them. He wondered what she was doing, prayed she wasn't crying or upset. God, how he hated himself.

He heard the bedroom door open and suddenly she was standing there, defiant. She was barefoot and her purple gown was sliding off one shoulder. She walked right up to him without allowing him to utter a word.

"I have to know, for my own personal edification, if I am out of my mind when I think that you have some sort of feelings toward me. And the reason I am asking this is because I think that you do, then you end up slamming me down in some sort of, pardon my French, 'cock block.' Am I crazy? Do you not want me?" Emily asked. She was near hysterical and the look in her eyes was enough to light a fire in him that only she could do.

"You're not wrong," he finally muttered.

"Great. Fantastic. Thank you for being honest. And screw you for being a coward, always making me look like the desperate female needing to get laid," she said.

"I don't expect you to understand . . ."

"Then talk slowly," she challenged.

"I swore to myself I wouldn't fall for another woman after Natalie died, swore I wouldn't go through the pain of losing another person I loved," he said.

She shook her head sadly. His green eyes were so desperate. So gone. So lonely. "And look, you went and did it anyway," she said. "Don't you know you can't control this? You either run from it or ride the wave, Gavin. Life is too short and precious. Haven't you learned that by now?"

He hung his head in desperation. She walked to him and held his hands. They were trembling. "Look at me." He looked up.

"Tonight. For one night. No guilt. No excuses. No worries about the future. No demons. Tonight. Can we just do what we both desperately want to do?" she said to him. She placed a hand on the side of his face. He pushed the small of her back toward him. When her body touched his, he no longer wanted to fight it anymore.

Her hands dropped to grab his back, sliding slowly up his clean, white shirt, until she felt his bare skin. His eyes closed at her touch, and he exhaled like he had been holding his breath for a year. She placed her head on his chest, heard his heartbeat. He lifted her chin with his strong hand and licked his lips slightly before he kissed her. He tasted the saltiness of the hot May sun on her skin, and a mix of wine and a sensualness that was all her. He placed both hands on the side of her face and looked at her. His hands were shaking. She placed her hands over his. His shaking worsened.

"I love you," she said. His eyes widened. She was no longer afraid to let him know her true heart, even if she risked him running for the door at that moment. "I just wanted to let you know," she said softly. His shaking stopped. That was all he needed to hear.

The early morning light peeked through the curtains of the hotel room, and Emily already knew that Gavin was not in bed with her before she opened her eyes. She expected that. She closed her eyes and remembered the intensity of his face, the forcefulness of his kisses. He wanted her to know what it meant to him to make love to her. It was not an action he took lightly. There was so much he didn't say, but when it was over, he called her 'my Emily.' She knew that he would never leave her, always love her, and die for her. She felt comforted and scared out of her mind from the realization and intensity of that moment.

She heard a rustling and smelled hot bread. She pulled on

257

her underwear and his white shirt before going to investigate. She walked into the living room and saw Gavin setting up breakfast by the windows. "Did you really leave the hotel room unescorted?" she asked.

"I did," he said, and smiled.

"I'm impressed. See, I told you New York was more afraid of you than you of it," she said.

"You said you missed bagels. Big bagels with the ridiculous amounts of cream cheese, I believe you described it. Lucky for me and for New York City, there was a place that sold them down the block. I didn't have to travel far," he said.

Emily smiled at the gesture. She walked up to him and hugged him. "Thank you."

He exhaled deeply, holding her tight. She looked up at him and he kissed her. He looked so happy that she felt compelled to kiss him again.

"You better eat this bagel while I can contain myself," he said. She laughed and sat on the couch.

"Because I look so appealing first thing in the morning." She took the lid off the coffee and poured a few creamers in the liquid black mixture. He picked up a coffee cup as he sat down on the couch. He stared at her; green eyes locked on her hazel eyes.

"You're the most beautiful thing I've ever seen," he said, with so much sincerity that her stomach flipped. Her cheeks turned pink.

"Are you blushing?" he asked.

"Maybe," she said. She bit into her bagel and hid her smile.

"Wow. So maybe I should forego talking about your beautiful breasts for fear that you'll pass out on the floor," Gavin joked. Emily shook her head and drank her coffee.

"And your . . ."

"STOP!"

Gavin full-on belly laughed then. Emily stopped and marveled at the sound of it. She had never seen him so relaxed, so happy before. She put down her coffee and bagel and went and held his hands. "It's so nice to hear you laugh like that," she said.

He pulled her close. "It's you. It's all you. I never told you this, but I would go to church every Sunday and pray to a God I didn't really believe in anymore to remove this pain, this pressure in my chest. Hell, I prayed for death, just to take the pain away. And then I answered the call to help a mom and her son. Who knew that would change everything? Maybe the old man took pity on me, threw me a bone when I least expected it," he said.

She kissed his hands, his big strong hands. His thumbs grazed her cheeks. Her eyes lowered from his gentle touch.

"I'm crazy about you," he whispered.

"Me, too," she said softly.

Just as he slid his hands inside his shirt that she wore so well, the phone rang. Gavin moaned then leaned over to answer it. "Hello? Yes, this is Mr. Shaw . . ."

Emily recognized Special Agent Barnes the second she stepped out of the elevator of the federal building. She stopped in her tracks, causing Gavin to run into her. She had a terrible feeling in her gut. Agent Barnes reached out her hand and smiled.

"Emily, so nice to see you again. Thank you for coming in."

Agent Barnes was dressed as a typical FBI agent, in a black suit, but she wore a light blue top underneath, showing off her blue eyes. She smiled a gentle smile at Emily, trying hard to make her feel at ease. Emily appreciated the effort but could not shake the feeling something awful was about to happen to her.

"What's going on?" Emily asked.

"Please follow me, there is a lot to explain," she said.

Agent Barnes led her and Gavin into a small conference room where two other people were already waiting. "This is Agent Lopez and Agent Fritz from the SEC. They were assisting me with the case." Barnes waited patiently for Emily and Gavin to take a seat.

"I thought the case was closed. Stanton called off the

subpoena," Emily said. Agent Barnes sat at the small table close to Emily and Gavin and crossed her long legs.

"I asked Stanton to call off your subpoena, because it was unnecessary. I think what we have uncovered bolsters what we, here at this table, have known all along—that you were unaware of your husband's dealings, and your lifestyle and spending habits corroborated that," she began.

"So, why did you call me back?" Emily asked.

"The problem is that this case never made much sense to me as an investigator. I have been working in this unit of the FBI for over ten years. There are classic cases of fraud, schemes, stealing, and they all follow a particular *modus operandi*. It bothered me that Mr. Mitchell's case never made sense in the classical sense. He was an upstanding broker, did well, followed all the rules, then in a period of about two or three months prior to his death, he just randomly stole $30 million from his clients. Quite sloppily, I might add. In addition, there were really no trails of where the money went. Usually you see extravagant spending or opened accounts offshore, for example, but we could not find any of this. Stanton was convinced Aaron had a person he handed the money to, an accomplice. For the last year, he was hell bent it was you and has tried unsuccessfully to prove that."

Emily sat stiff as a board.

"I began to look internally at his work colleagues. And I was struck by one of the conversations I had with his colleagues, Dan Reynolds. Do you know him?"

"Yes. He was Aaron's best friend. They met in college. Our families vacationed together sometimes," Emily said.

"When I first interviewed Dan, he was showing classic signs of lying, with hand gestures, facial cues. I was really starting to wonder what he was hiding. After a lot of persuasion, I managed to get the warrants to tap his calls, look into his records, and he was starting to emerge as a person who would be in the traditional profile of stealing from clients. He had a huge gambling problem. Mostly on-line, but it spilled over into poker games, racetracks. His bank account was in the negative, yet he was still making payments for his expensive house, his new cars. From an offshore account," she said.

Emily sucked in her breath. She had dinner in that expensive house countless times and saw Evelyn Reynolds show off her newest model of Mercedes Benz, the latest Tiffany diamond jewelry that Dan lavished upon her and had to listen to Evelyn brag about the most expensive private school she had her children attend. Emily also remembered that Aaron was baffled how Dan was doing so well and confessed that he wished he could give Emily the same things.

"I just want you and Sam," she had told him, hugged his blonde head close to her chest. She never cared about the money but was grateful that he made enough money that she could concentrate on Sam to ensure that he could function well in the hearing world. How many times did she tell him that? Did he ever really *hear* her?

"What are you saying, Agent Barnes?" Emily asked.

"We have been collecting evidence on Dan for about six months. We finally brought him in for questioning yesterday for several hours and showed him the evidence. He finally confessed to his part in the scheme. He told Aaron that he was going to be murdered by gangsters if he didn't repay $250,000. Aaron, wanting to save his best friend, worked out a plan to float money between ten accounts to pay off the gangsters. Dan admitted having access to the accounts made him greedy, and he continued to steal past the agreed-upon amount. He said Aaron didn't know the extent of it until someone had filed an investigation with the SEC. He said Aaron was a wreck when he found out, said he was going to confess, explain what had happened."

Emily remembered the days leading up the day that he died. He was a mess— not sleeping, not eating, drinking several drinks a night. God how she wished that she could go back in time and reach out to him. How scared he must have been.

"There's more, unfortunately. He told us more. And that is the reason we called you in . . ."

"What?" Emily said.

"Dan said he panicked when Aaron said he was going to confess, that he didn't want the money to be shut off just yet because of some gambling debts he had. So, he and Aaron argued in the early morning of March 10th," Barnes said.

Emily stopped breathing. "And?"

"Dan confessed to us that he pushed your husband off the roof of their office building in anger, and scribbled a suicide note to leave in his office. Our forensic analysts examined the note and concluded that it was most likely written by Dan Reynolds," Barnes said sadly.

Emily's breath left in a straight line as she processed it all. Dan Reynolds. Aaron's best friend of 15 years. Best man at their wedding. Over 6 feet 5 inches, 250 pounds, towering, broad shoulders, pushed her 5-foot 9-inch, 175-pound husband off a 40-story building to his death. Angry tears welled up in Emily's eyes.

"Jesus," Gavin whispered. She turned to see Gavin's stark white expression. She had completely forgotten he was there. "What happens now?" Gavin asked.

"Mr. Reynolds will be charged with murder and conspiracy in the morning. We have managed to recover about $10 million that was stolen, plus more when we seize his assets. Emily's property is to be returned including her house in Watchung. Her bank accounts unfrozen. Aaron's life insurance will be released to his son and held in trust, as his will specified."

Emily's thoughts turned to Evelyn and her two, spoiled rotten children. Beautiful Evelyn, tall, blonde, and thin. Evelyn, who refused to offer a safe haven to Emily and Sam those early weeks after everything had been taken away, scared of what the neighbors would think.

"I want to see Dan," Emily announced.

Agent Barnes looked surprised. "I'm not sure…"

"Why, Emily?" Gavin asked. Emily looked at Gavin. He looked heartsick for her after hearing this terrible news.

"I want to look him in the eye. I want him to know what he

has taken from me. From Sam," she said.

"I'll see what I can do," Agent Barnes said and gave a signal to the other two agents. They stood up, gave Emily a sorrowful look, and left them alone in the room.

"Are you okay?" Gavin asked. He reached for her hand, and she recoiled at his touch.

"No," she said, and stood. She could not meet his gaze. She looked out the window of the federal building. Clouds were blowing in, turning the cool spring day into a cold, dreary mess. Appropriate, she thought.

"You know Dan would not return my phone calls. Didn't even show up to the funeral. Said it was too much for him. Guess if you murder you best friend, you would have a hard time paying your last respects, no?" Emily said.

"Yes," Gavin said softly.

"And Evelyn. Said that she couldn't 'harbor' us, me and Sam, because we could be in on it. I mean she didn't say that to my face, but she told every other friend of ours in Watchung. She was like a virus. Her words planted in everyone's ear, and the women who knew me for ten years suddenly thought they didn't know me, or Aaron, at all. That we were liars and thieves. Wrote us all off, even Sam, who didn't know anything and was innocent. Evelyn and Dan. The ringmasters of our demise," Emily whispered.

"And you know what's worse? I actually believed the lies, too. I believed when they said that my husband was a thief and a monster. The man I had been with for fifteen years, who knew me inside and out, who I knew inside and out. They made me believe that he was capable of doing this. How could I believe those lies?" she said. She put her face in her hands and cried. Gavin held her as her cries turned into sobs. For the first time in a year, Emily grieved properly for her dead husband, the blonde-haired jokester, the one who made her laugh and smile with a simple wink.

"I'm so sorry, Aaron," she whimpered. Gavin held on tight to the woman he loved as she mourned the man she loved.

CHAPTER TWENTY-FIVE

Emily was sipping her first Starbucks in almost a year waiting outside a door on the 4th floor. Gavin brought them back coffee after stepping out to get some air and make a few phone calls to Will to hastily explain the horrible situation and to Paco to check on Sam.

He handed her a vanilla latte, which was also one of the things on the list of things that Emily missed about NYC that Gavin had memorized, and drank his own Café Americano that he drowned with half-and-half to stomach the burnt taste. He told her that Sam was doing well with Paco and Celia and wanted her to text him later that night.

"Thank you for the coffee," Emily said.

"You're quite welcome."

She held his hand and he exhaled in relief. All he wanted in that moment was to be relevant. He felt like an outsider, and even though he was an educated man, he felt so ass-backward and simple in this world that Emily lived in before she stumbled on his wraparound porch.

Agent Barnes managed to convince her superiors to let Emily see Dan Reynolds, as a means for emotional closure, she stated. She asked Emily not to speak to him too much, as it could jeopardize the criminal case against him. Emily really didn't want to speak. Just to see him. Her stomach was in knots.

"You don't have to do this," Gavin said.

"Yes, I do."

Agent Barnes reappeared from the door.

"Emily, we're ready for you," she said. Emily stood and handed Gavin her purse. She exhaled loudly a few times and walked with Barnes through double glass doors.

"Did you tell him that I wanted to see him?" Emily asked.

"Yes."

Barnes brought her to a heavy metal door and used her badge to scan access into the section. There were corridors with a lot of gray, metal doors with small windows.

"Who do you usually keep here?" Emily asked.

"Varies, but usually criminals in transit to the federal penitentiary in Ray Brook. We put him in the last room," Barnes said, and unlocked a door.

Emily's nervousness made her belly physically shake. She was freezing cold. She inhaled and walked in.

Dan was sitting behind a table, handcuffed but still wearing a blue dress shirt and blue slacks. Armani. Probably bought by Evelyn at Saks Fifth Avenue because she didn't shop anywhere else. His dark hair looked dirty and unkempt. She took heart that he looked like hell. Good.

"Emily," Dan said. His hands shook nervously on the table, causing the handcuffs to make a slight tapping sound. She sat down across the table from him and took a hard look at a man that she knew for over a decade, a decade of sitting across the table at countless dinners, hearing his boisterous laughter as Aaron recalled numerous stories from their college days, holding his children in her arms hours after they were born, consoling him after the death of his mother. So much of her life was intertwined with this man only to have him take the one thing that mattered most to her, the man they both loved. It was utterly unforgiveable. Emily stared at him.

"Aaron loved you so much," she finally said. Dan's bottom lip quivered, and his brown eyes quickly filled up with tears.

"I'm garbage, Emily. I know that. If I could take it back and it be me, Jesus knows I wish I could. He was always the better man. Always. He had the better life, the better kid, the better wife. He deserved good things because he was good. I was just the piece of shit who was lucky enough to have him for a friend."

Emily wanted to scream at him, blast him for putting her and Sam through hell the last year, but she looked at her coffee cup in her hand and thought of Gavin in the waiting room, of Sam eating one of Paco's creations from the grill surrounded by people who genuinely cared for his well-being, of Will, who brought her a bracelet all the way back from Italy, of Shakes, who found her a newer car so she could succeed at her business, and even Margaret, who was so lost and found her way back before her death. She landed far from Watchung, but she landed on a bed of feathers when it could have been worse...so much worse.

"May you come to learn the depth of what you've taken from us, Danny," she said. Dan shook his head sadly and wiped his tears from his eyes. She got up and knocked on the door. She didn't look back as she left. She had nothing more to say.

It was raining hard on the cab ride back to the hotel. Emily fingered the brown envelope that contained her old life in the form of house keys, car keys, and a cashier's check for what was taken from their bank accounts. Gavin glanced at the amount and swallowed his pride. That check had more zeros than he had ever seen in any check written to him in his entire life. The cab finally made its way to midtown and Emily stepped out of the cab toward the hotel entrance. They rode up the elevator in silence. He wanted to say something but was at a complete utter loss of words. He opened the hotel room door and Emily walked in.

"Did you want some food?" he offered.

"Not right now," she said. She had been quiet all evening. Gavin was feeling more desperate as the hours went on.

"Do you want to be alone?" he finally asked.

"No."

Gavin exhaled. "You have to guide me, Em. I don't know what I need to do for you here," he said. He ran his hands through his hair and left them at the back of his neck. Emily felt tears well up in her eyes for the hundredth time.

"Just hang on tight," she whispered.

"That I can do," he said, and took her into his arms. He felt her body release, and the storm clouds come again. She cried for a solid fifteen minutes as he held on tight to her.

He left her lying on the bed and walked to the bathroom and began to draw a warm bath for her in the marble bathtub.

He came back and reached for her. She took his hand and followed him into the bath where he slowly undressed her with so much kindness and so much tenderness that she started to cry silently. She climbed in and sat down in the warm water, feeling instantly more relaxed and calmer.

"My momma used to say that when people were upset you should put them in a tub."

She smiled sadly. He sat on the floor beside the tub holding her hand as she sat in the tub. "It's like he just died all over again," she said softly.

"In a way he did."

"And I have to start all over with this horrible process." She shook her head at the unfairness of it all.

"I'm going to order some food. You take some time in here," he said. He leaned over and kissed her hand and then her cheek. Her eyes closed.

He was so lost. He had no idea what to do next, how to feel, what to say—nothing. He quickly ordered dinner and waited on the bed, praying a plan to help her would come to him. After a few minutes someone knocked on the door. Gavin exchanged pleasantries with the room service gentleman. Emily walked out wearing a white robe after the young man left.

Gavin ordered a little of everything—fruits, salads, two burgers, two desserts, iced tea, and a Coke.

"I want you to eat something. It's important to keep your strength up," he said. He was all too familiar with her tendency to fast when she was stressed or upset. She stood still and quiet, watching him pull lids off the plates. He met her gaze and stopped the process.

She walked over to him and kissed him full on the lips. Her mouth opened to his, aggressively asking for his kiss in return. He knew that he should not do this, that the timing was wrong, and it was just sex to dull the pain. But he could not say no to her. He feared that he would never get another chance after tonight. He slid his hands to untie her robe. His reasons for complying with her wishes were all selfish. If this was the last time she wanted him, he was going to give it his all.

"When did it happen for you?" she asked. It was a half hour later and they were both semi-dressed eating the room service food like they had been starving to death.

"How I felt? I think it was always there. From the first day. It grew. Like a flower." She chuckled and scooped the last of the bread pudding with her spoon.

"What?"

"A flower? Seriously? Don't get all poetic on me now, Shaw," she teased. He leaned back against the headboard of the bed and smiled. "Give me a break. I think you about killed me. It's unfair asking any sort of questions given my current state." He bent his knee up. She saw the large pink scar below his right kneecap.

"Does it hurt you?" she asked, touching it.

"Sometimes. When it's cold. It mostly feels strange. Nerves never quite grew back right," he said. She took off her robe and crawled in the bed belly down next to him, wearing only her underwear. Her legs were lifted up at a 90-degree angle, and her ankles crossed. She rested her chin on her hands.

"When did it happen for you?" he asked.

"I admitted it to myself when we were at Will's that night. But it happened way before that. Around the time I could call you Gavin," she said. He placed a piece of stray hair behind her ear, and let his fingers linger on her face.

"I meant what I said," she said.

"Which part?" he asked.

"That my feelings haven't changed for you because of this."

He slid down and laid on his side to face her. She leaned over and kissed him. He wanted so much to believe her, but the doubt rested in the shadows of their content. He held her in his arms, heard her gently breathing, felt the warmth of her body, and saw the calmness in her face. For tonight he would slay the thoughts of doubt down. Tonight, all he wanted to think about was her finally being his, even if it was only until the morning.

Emily was dressed and patiently waiting for him to wake up in the morning. Gavin sat up, trying to shake off sleep.

"What time is it?" he asked.

"8:30. I didn't want to wake you. I think you needed the sleep," she said.

He could not believe he had slept almost ten hours straight. He felt out of it and slightly hung over.

"Are you going somewhere?" he asked, noticing her clothes.

"I need to go to Watchung and get some things in order," she said.

"Our flight is this afternoon," Gavin said.

Emily was quiet. Gavin closed his eyes. He knew it. He knew that she would be pulling away from him once light came. "I can change the flight," he offered.

"I think you should go back. You are about to close the window for the corn to get in the ground."

Gavin threw off the covers, angry. He pulled on his black boxer briefs. "The goddamn corn can wait," he said.

"I just need a few days, Gavin. I need to shut things down here, for good," she said.

"Without me?"

Emily sighed. "What do you think will happen in these few days? I'm still coming back to Ohio. My son is there for Chrissakes."

"So, you are only going back for Sam?"

"No! What's gotten into you?" she yelled.

Gavin pulled on clothes and said nothing. Emily bowed her head and felt the tears start to well up again. He exhaled and put his hands on top of his head. He paced the hotel room like he had just finished a sprint and was trying to catch his breath.

"I knew this would happen. I knew it would. I screwed things up by making love to you," he said. Emily sucked in her breath. Tears fell freely from her tightly closed eyes.

"I wish to God you could just tell me that you're afraid of what's going to happen in the future. But no, you put up the walls again and bring out claws just to prevent yourself from getting hurt, not caring what that does to me," she cried. Gavin crossed his arms in front of his chest and looked away.

"I have no regrets about crossing that line with you. I love you. That has not changed. I can't believe you are feeling so damn scared that you will pull back from me when I need you the most!" she yelled.

"I'll always be your friend, Emily," Gavin said softly.

She pounded his chest then she wept. He bit his lip until he tasted blood. He felt the emotion swell in his chest, but he kept it contained. He could do this. He could just walk away and still be intact. He would be just fine without her in his life. He didn't go to hug and comfort her. Instead, he slowly pulled down his suitcase and began to pack. She grabbed onto him from behind. He could feel her hot tears soaking the back of his t-shirt. The more he heard her sobs, the more he felt his resolve start to crack.

"Please don't do this again," she cried.

He could be heartless. It was easy. Sever all ties. Go back to just him and women who made him feel nothing.

She wedged in between him and the suitcase and made him look at her hysterical face. Her tears did him in and cut him so deep. His brow furrowed at the pain in her face and she kissed him. He resisted her at first, but as his eyes closed, he could see her serving him coffee in the mornings, see her beautiful smile, hear her infectious laugh. She was embedded in every nook of his subconscious. His lips softened, then parted. He kissed her with all that he had in him.

"Stay," she whispered.

"Gladly," he said, and pulled her onto the bed, pulling off his t-shirt.

They lay facing each other when it was over, as quickly as it had begun, the storm clouds passing. "I'm afraid of what will happen in the future," he whispered.

She touched his face. "I'm not leaving you," she said. He breathed a sigh of relief.

"You're too good in bed," she joked. He grinned.

Emily hired a car to drive them out to Watchung. She reasoned that the taxi ride would cost the same, but it would be a more pleasant ride. The driver was named Nick, and he was from Brooklyn. He sounded almost exactly like Rocky Balboa.

"Watchung, huh? Yeah, I drive out there about six or seven times a month. Nice little drive. I'll get you there, no problem."

Nick was a friendly soul and liked to ask questions. "Where are you from, sir? Ohio? Yeah, I like those Buckeyes. Except for that tattoo, Tressel thing. Kinda crappy if you ask me. But if you paid those players some money, they wouldn't have to be selling their jerseys. All I'm sayin' . . ."

Gavin noticed the lush trees once they moved off the Jersey turnpike and onto 78. With spring in full bloom, he could see the appeal of the small New Jersey community. He could hardly believe he was 30 miles from Manhattan.

Emily gave the driver instructions and the young man turned down Hill Hollow Road, where the space between houses grew and the price tag of the property rose. The driver navigated up a long driveway until a nice-sized white colonial house came into view. The driver whistled. "Nice pad. Yours?"

"Yes," Emily said.

"Nice. I hope one day to make it. Have a family in the burbs. The American dream, I tells ya."

Emily paid the man and added in a large tip while Gavin grabbed their suitcases. They both walked up to the front door as the cab drove away. Emily noticed the grass had been recently cut and that there was no for sale sign on the property. She half expected an abandoned mess with boarded up windows when she walked up. She was confused about who was taking care of the property if there was no listing to sell it. She turned the key in the lock and was met with a beeping followed by an alarm.

"What's the code?" Gavin yelled, looking at the pad by the door.

"We never had an alarm system. I don't know who installed

271

this," Emily said frantically, as the alarm got louder. She looked in vain through the envelope for a code but saw nothing. She started punching in numbers to try to get the alarm to stop.

"Get your hands where I can see them!" a male voice boomed.

Emily and Gavin both put their hands in the air and slowly turned toward the front porch. An older man with a deer rifle and a rather large beer belly was standing on the porch in front of them.

"Emily?" the man whispered.

Emily put her hands down and exhaled loudly from relief.

"Stuart!" she gasped.

The older man slung his rifle behind his back and went to hug Emily.

"Oh, my goodness. My goodness. Emily! I can't believe it's you. I knew you'd be back; I just knew it."

Gavin put his hands down and watched confused.

"Stuart, please shut off the alarm," Emily said

"Right. Right. I'm sorry. I had it installed when the first for sale sign came up. Damn feds. Thought they could just seize your property with no burden of proof. Over my dead body. This is still America, goddammit. We have laws to protect us from that bullshit," he mumbled while entering the code. The alarm went silent. Gavin looked at Emily and she shook her head, still filled with adrenaline.

"Stuart Jamison, this is my friend Gavin Shaw. Stuart is my neighbor," Emily said.

Stuart pumped Gavin's hand. "Gavin, damn fine to meet you. Please, come over to the house. Judith will be so thrilled. This is a fantastic day! We have lots to catch up on," he said, already walking back to his side of the property line.

Gavin quietly drank black coffee from a white bone china cup decorated with a large blue owl in the large kitchen that belonged to Stuart and Judith Jamison, Esquires. Judith was so thrilled to see Emily that it took her ten minutes to stop crying and hugging both her and Gavin like lost, prodigal children.

Judith was a larger woman, pear shaped with white hair cut

short. She brought over a cinnamon coffee cake and fruit to the table in front of Gavin and filled his cup after three sips. She straightened out her glasses as she set the coffee carafe down, patting Gavin affectionately on the back.

"We had just missed seeing you. We took an extra week in Florida that winter because Jenny came with the grandkids to Disney World during their spring break. We got back and heard the news about Aaron, about this mess. We tried to find you for months. Stuart even hired a private detective. We were so scared for you after we found out what they did to you and Sam. Kicking you out of your house like that, with no legal representation. Despicable!" Judith said.

"They had no right to kick you out of your house. That house was paid for, and the case was still not solved. All circumstantial! I marched right up to that office and served them with a cease-and-desist order. That Agent. Stanton. What a piece of work. Thought he was above the law," Stuart said.

"And taking Aaron's life insurance policy. That was taken out years before he started that job. Despicable," Judith repeated.

Emily shook her head, still speechless about the turn of events. "I am grateful to you both, really. Truly," Emily said. She drank her coffee, still in a daze.

"Ohio. We couldn't remember where your aunt lived. We remembered Galveston. We drove to Galveston, asked around. No one had heard of Margaret or you."

"I was going to try the W-2s. I was hoping that you found employment and that I could track you down that way. But my guy at the IRS said that I had to wait until summer, after the initial returns were processed before he could help," Judith said.

Emily drank quietly. Judith and Stuart both paused and sipped on their coffee.

"We came to the city because they were going to subpoena me for the grand jury," Emily said.

"Not without your lawyer you will not!" Stuart said. His big chest puffed up, ready for another fight. Emily shook her head and felt the tears fall, unable to speak. Gavin cleared his throat several times.

"They dropped the charges against Aaron. Found that his friend Dan was stealing with Aaron's passcodes. And . . . they found that Dan pushed . . . that Aaron did not commit suicide," Gavin explained. The story still sounded horrible and surreal, even as the words spilled from his mouth.

Judith's eyes welled up and she went to hug Emily. Stuart's jaw tensed and he stood to look out the window.

"I just knew it. I knew it was all a big mistake. Not our Aaron. Didn't we know it, Stuart?" Judith wept.

Stuart nodded. He swallowed several times and regained his composure. Aaron was like the son the Jamisons never had, stopping by every day to talk, playing golf on the weekends, mowing their lawns in the summer. In her grief and mourning, and then followed by her need to implement quick survival tactics, Emily was ashamed that the Jamisons never crossed her mind. How different the outcome would have been had she been able to just think clearly. She looked at Gavin, quiet and stiff, and then felt horrible for wishing him and the farm away.

"Well, you're home now," Judith said, and patted Emily's hands. She took off her glasses and wiped her eyes.

"Yes. You're home. When will Sam follow? After the school year?" Stuart asked.

Gavin felt lightheaded and sick. He instinctively stood up.

"Excuse me. I need to get some air," he said. He stepped down the multi-tiered deck until he reached the Jamison's backyard. Tulips of every color of the rainbow surrounded the perimeter of the yard. He could see Emily's house an acre over. Tall cherry trees were blooming pink, petals falling to the green grass below. He imagined Sam running in the backyard and a younger Emily watching Aaron fire up the grill.

Two basset hounds that looked to be 100 years old slowly walked up to him. He bent down and scratched them both behind their ears. They closed their eyes, appreciating the affection.

He heard Emily walk up behind him. "Hey," she said.

"Hey."

"Chuck and Barry. Brothers. They have had these dogs for years," Emily said, and patted the dogs.

"Good mutts," he said, and sat down. Chuck instinctively sat in Gavin's lap and licked his chin.

"I know it's hard to hear all this," Emily began.

"You had a life here. You had a good life here before Dan took your husband away." Emily nodded.

"You can have this life back. Stuart and Judith stood guard for you to have what was rightfully yours. Damn nice to have friends like that," he baited.

"It's damn nice to have friends who would employ you when you had nothing, to offer to go into business with you when you have no collateral to invest yourself, to teach your son life skills that could sustain him a lifetime . . ."

He shook his head. "This is hard to pass up."

"It's real estate. It's not my soul. It's not my life," she assured. He didn't believe her. She could see it in his eyes.

They were quiet for a while. "I think I should go back to Ohio. The window on the corn is about to close."

Emily closed her eyes. *Dammit*, she thought.

"You do what you need to do here, and I will see you in about a week. I'll go in and pick up Sam after I land," he said.

Emily opened her eyes and stood up. She was tired of fighting him, but she was more disappointed that he would not fight for her. For them. Instinctively, she turned numb.

"I think he should stay with Paco and Celia."

Gavin bit his lip. This was backfiring on him.

"You'll be on the tractor for a week solid. It's best that he stays with them. To be out of your hair," she reasoned. They both knew that was not the only reason.

"I'll keep my flight, then," he said.

She swallowed her disappointment and walked back to Stuart's house to give Gavin some privacy. And to cry for the millionth time that day.

She drove him to Newark airport later that afternoon in her Mazda CR-9 after he spent most of the morning in her old house, walking aimlessly through the near empty rooms attempting to capture who she was before she ended up on his porch a year ago. He liked her choice of art, random and colorful. He could tell she bought pieces that moved her, not pieces that were meant to fit together. There were pictures of fall leaves, oceans, canvases of red with a single black dot. He couldn't describe it; separately the pieces did not make sense, but together they were all her.

Her kitchen could hold his entire ground floor of the farmhouse. He secretly wished he had a kitchen this big for her to cook in. He was a little sad that he would never see her cooking in that space.

He gazed at the family pictures hanging on the walls. Aaron was young, handsome, and confident. He did not look like someone who took his family for granted. He looked like a decent, hardworking man. He had to be, he reasoned, for someone like Emily to love him. They might have been friends had they been introduced. Aaron's eyes were hopeful. His smile was genuine. He was not jaded. Gavin knew that in pictures he happened to be in after the accident, he looked old and worn, and the light was gone. He would stare at recent pictures and wonder who the hell that man was that was staring back at him. That man was old and haggard. That man was not him.

Gavin grew jealous of the place the longer he stayed. As the hours ticked by, the more he felt that he had nothing to offer Emily and Sam. A farm that he still had twenty years to pay on. No real wealth to speak of. A man who had ghosts chasing him daily. A man who didn't know how to fight for what he wanted anymore. A man who would let her go, just because there was a chance that she would let him go first.

"How long is your layover in Philly?" she asked as she took the airport exit.

"Not long. Less than an hour," he said.

She moved to the lane to park. "Don't park, Em," he said.

"I want to."

"No. Please. I can't bear it . . ."

She conceded and switched lanes to drop him off at the American Airlines terminal. She put the car into park and walked over to him. She smiled sadly at him while he grabbed his suitcase.

He looked at her, stoic, with fear in his eyes. He didn't say anything. He couldn't.

"Safe flight, okay?" she said.

He dropped his bags and kissed her; grabbing the back of her t-shirt with both of his hands and holding her so tight that she could hardly breathe. He gently pulled her away and walked toward the terminal with his bag, never looking back.

She ordered Chinese food from China Chef, out on Hwy 22 that night and brought it back to eat at the house. She sat alone at the long dining room table and felt the vast loneliness of that table deep in her soul. She got up and moved her meal to the backyard.

She looked at the pool that was still covered and the flowerbeds that desperately needed tending. Ten years of memories danced on her eyelashes like firecrackers. She closed her eyes at the setting sun and willed herself to feel the love that once resided at that house. She thought she could smell the charcoal-cooked burgers and the laughter of her friends as they teased Aaron about his meticulous methods for grilling meat. But the memories were so far away and so long gone, that they could not stay more than a few seconds. When she closed her eyes, all she could see was Sam in a vastness of green hay, chasing kittens with the hum of a tractor in the background. She knew that this was no longer her home. It was time to move on.

She walked back to Judith and Stuart's house later that night and knocked on the door. Judith answered in her housecoat. She could hear *Law and Order* on the TV in the background. Emily bowed her head. She didn't even know why she was there. Judith reached out her hands to her and nodded. Judith was a mother. She knew what Emily knew—it was time to go home.

CHAPTER TWENTY-SIX

Emily pulled into the PNC Bank parking lot just after 1 p.m., having met with Stuart's friend and realtor, James Lin, for most of the morning. James was a younger man but had been selling real estate in Watchung for five years and knew the area and the market well. He walked through the house and took ample notes.

"What did you pay for this house?" he asked.

"Four hundred thousand, twelve years ago."

"It's easily doubled now. You are sitting on a goldmine," he said. Emily sighed. She didn't know if she was sad or happy that her beloved home was worth a goldmine.

"We need to do some cosmetic things, but it will be minor. Landscaping. I work with a team."

"Whatever you need to do," Emily said, and walked out to the patio. Details were too overwhelming right now.

She gathered her checks and paperwork to reinstate her bank accounts. She purposefully picked this bank because there was a branch in Ohio, although she wondered if she even had a life worth going back to there now. There was no word from Gavin last night or in the morning. She went back and forth from being devastated by his lack of contact with being downright enraged. Celia called her while she was driving to the bank and said that Paco saw him at IGA, and he looked terrible.

"It was his decision to go back," Emily said.

"He obviously regrets it," Celia said.

"He hasn't even called me, Celia," Emily said.

"You know men like Gavin. They give you too much space. You should call him," Celia urged. Emily didn't respond. She didn't tell Celia that she was testing Gavin and he was failing miserably.

Emily worked with a young woman at PNC named Lois to

become a legitimate account holder again, re-depositing her savings accounts, checking account, and Sam's college fund back into the bank, waiting through various phone calls and verifications. It took almost three hours to get her financial life back together. At ten after four, Emily walked into the lobby of the bank with a few thousand in cash, a bankcard, and temporary checks. She was putting all of the paperwork into her bag when she heard the familiar screech of a woman's voice.

"I don't understand how you can't cash this check! It's only for a $100!"

"I'm sorry, ma'am. But we cannot cash checks from other accounts from other banks," a young teller responded.

Two unruly, blonde-haired children ran around the kiosk where people wrote their deposit slips, running into a few older people trying to get their last-minute transactions completed. Emily put her hands out and stopped the boy, Ethan, and his older sister, Amy.

"Oh, hey, Aunt Emily, where have you been?" Ethan said.

"You need to go and sit down, now," Emily said firmly. The children saw the look in her eyes and went back to sit with a pile of Louis Vuitton suitcases. Evelyn turned when she noticed the silence and sucked in her breath when she saw Emily.

Evelyn looked awful. Her long, blonde hair was pulled into a sloppy ponytail, and she wore black yoga pants and a hot pink sweater and tank top set. She had on mismatched Burberry flats; one tan checkered and one dark brown checkered.

"Emily. Oh my God," she said. She put her small, boney hands to her face and wept.

Emily drove them all to the park after picking up some sandwiches for them to eat. The kids ran around after inhaling their food, leaving Emily to watch Evelyn pick at the food.

"You need to eat," Emily said.

"I'm not very hungry."

"You are responsible for these children now, Evelyn. You need to keep your strength up. Eat."

279

Evelyn picked up the sandwich and picked off small pieces like a bird, drinking her Coke Zero nervously in-between bites.

"He wouldn't let me call you when Aaron died. Said that it would look too suspicious. It didn't make any sense to me. How could taking you in look suspicious? To whom? We had a horrible fight about it. He walked out and was gone for two whole days. I thought he left me for good. I was so scared. I should have known. I should have figured it out sooner."

"We see what we want to see, Evelyn." Evelyn nodded. They were quiet for a while.

"Where will you go?" Emily asked.

"I haven't thought that far ahead."

"You have to! You have to think and be prepared to do what you need to do to protect Ethan and Amy. Dan is gone! Your names are mud now. No one will help you here. You have to find a way to start over somewhere else," Emily barked.

Evelyn exhaled deeply. "My sister is in Delaware. She doesn't like me very much. Of course, I think I am responsible for that. I have always been a bitch to her. To everyone," she whispered. Emily drank her Coke and said nothing.

"Have you been ok? Is Sam ok?" Evelyn asked. She truly looked concerned.

"We've been good."

"Good. I'm so glad."

"You'll be all right too," Emily reassured. Evelyn smiled sadly and nodded.

The next morning, she drove the Reynolds to Penn Station in the city to board the 9 a.m. Amtrak to Wilmington, Delaware, after they spent the night at her house. She handed Evelyn a little bit of cash for the road and allowed her to hug her gratefully. She knew people would never understand why she helped them. It wasn't for sainthood, that's for certain, but rather for the understanding about the horror of the unknown and knowing that she would not wish that fear of the unknown on her worst enemy. Her conscience was now clear.

"I don't know how you could even sleep with that woman in your house. I'd be afraid that she'd slit my throat and steal my car," Celia said when she called later that morning.

"Aaron would have helped her. I did it for Aaron."

"You're a good woman, Emily."

Gavin still had not called her. She wasn't about to be the one to break radio silence. At that point, she was so angry at his silence that she'd rather die than give him the satisfaction.

The next morning, she packed her Mazda with her family photos that were on the walls and various mementos that she wanted to keep including cuttings from her garden that she wanted to replant wherever she landed next, including her Mother's Day *Euonymus fortunei* and a Liriope that they planted when Sam was born. The rest she was leaving for Stuart and Judith to mail when she was ready for them. Her house was officially on the market as of 1 p.m. that day, and James Lin said that he already had two showings planned for 2:00 and 3:00 p.m. Stuart, Judith, and Emily all said their tearful goodbyes, but instead of true sadness, there was hope restored as they each knew that they would keep in touch this time. Judith packed her a brown bag lunch of turkey and cheese sandwiches on fresh croissants, chips, and several bottles of water and Coke. Stuart checked her engine and tires and made sure that she knew the way back to Champaign County.

"I know you're planning on driving through, but promise me you'll stop if you get tired," Stuart said.

Judith hugged her and took her time letting Emily go.

"I promise. I should be there by dinnertime. I'll call you when I get there." She hugged them both again and waved tearfully at them until they were nothing but specs in her rearview mirror.

CHAPTER TWENTY-SEVEN

Nothing was the same when Gavin got back to Ohio. The house was too quiet, too dark, and too damn cold. The cold spring rain made the air damp in the house, especially in the bedroom and living room. He wouldn't step foot upstairs, refusing to be reminded that Emily and Sam were not there. He remained a prisoner on the first floor, walking back and forth in every room, freezing, unable to get warm. He tried desperately to push down the dreadful feelings of déjà vu that he had. He constantly reminded himself Sam was in town with Paco and Celia, and she was coming back. She was not gone for good. *Yet.*

When she didn't call him that first night, or the second, he couldn't stop his anger from spilling over to everyone he came into contact. He yelled at the pimply-faced kid at McDonald's for serving him old coffee, and he made a service clerk at the IGA cry when his beer was not in stock. A manager came out to try to calm him down, and he got a bit of his wrath, too. The manager who knew Gavin for several years, politely asked him to leave and come back when he was in a better mood, and made it be known that he would not accept Gavin making his employees cry because of a bad day, or he could take his business to Kroger.

Shakes and Will quietly worked beside him on the tractors, finishing the last of the corn planting, fighting with the weather that was so damn unpredictable that time of year. Twice a tractor got stuck in a bit of mud due to poor drainage of the previous day's rain. Shakes and Will got the tractor out, all the while having to endure Gavin's misplaced wrath. The men looked at each other sideways as they were called every name in the book, daring not engage. But on the third morning, the last day of the planting, Gavin took a look at the rows that had been planted and decidedly lost his mind.

"How far apart did you set the rows?" he asked Shakes.

"Thirty."

"Goddammit!" Gavin yelled and threw his coffee mug clear across to where Shakes and Will were standing.

"Why in the hell would you plant 30? We have been talking about 20 for the better part of a year!" Gavin shouted. Will bit his lip and shook his head.

"What the hell are you talking about? I have put this godforsaken corn in the ground for six damn years and this is the first I have heard about switching the spacing," Shakes yelled back.

"You just don't listen. Only do what you want to, hear what you want to hear," Gavin mumbled. Shakes had had enough. He threw down his cigarette and stomped it furiously. Will grabbed his sleeve and shook his head to try to stop him, but it was too late.

"I do what I want to do?!? Oh, bullshit! Let me tell you something. Sitting on this fucking tractor is not what I want to do. I'd rather be in Tennessee working my last job with the locksmith. I was happy there before I came to this cold fucking state to pull your sorry ass out of the pit!"

"So leave! Who fucking needs you anymore?" Gavin said angrily.

"Oh, fuck you and your empty threats."

"I'm dead serious. Get your shit out of my quarters and leave. I don't need you here."

Will looked at Shakes and Shakes exhaled, furious. "Man, I don't get you. Every Sunday you go to that church of yours and pray to your God for a miracle. Something to change, to make you believe, to make life worth living. And what does your God do? Drop her on your fucking doorstep. And what do you do? You run like a fucking coward from her. You should have stayed your ass in Jersey. Stepped up and been the man she needed!" Shakes yelled.

Gavin came after him, knocking him into the ground in a dust of fury. Shakes kicked him off with his surprisingly powerful legs, flipping Gavin over and throwing him down hard on his shoulder, knocking the wind out of him. Will grabbed Shakes before he could go after Gavin again, who was turned over, defeated and coughing.

"I'm out of here," Shakes said, and spat on the ground.

Will went to offer Gavin a hand, but he turned his head, embarrassed and still angry.

"You're losing friends left and right here. I suggest you keep the few you have," Will warned.

Gavin swallowed his pride and let Will help him up. He wiped blood from his lip. They leaned against the tractor while Gavin shook off the pain in his shoulder from where Shakes tossed him. That was going to hurt for a couple of weeks.

"I have some news," Will said. "I'm moving to London."

Gavin felt the breath being knocked out of him again. "What? When?"

"As soon as I can arrange it. Evangeline and I want to travel. Spend the summer together."

"Chasing the tail again, Will. Always chasing that goddamn tail," Gavin said, and spit blood, angry.

"No. Not tail. Not by a long shot."

"You don't even know this woman. And you are up and moving to a foreign country for her?"

"I know enough. I know how she makes me feel. I know how I make her feel. It's enough."

Gavin shook his head. Will stood up and reiterated Shakes' disgust.

"You're going to lose her, and you don't care. Or maybe you do care, but God forbid you allow yourself a break from the role of the martyr. Best hold up that pride and die alone, right? Well, not me. No, sir. I'd rather take a chance."

Will walked to his truck and left Gavin sitting by his tractor, staring at the rows they just planted. For the first time in his life, he didn't care if the rains came and washed it all away. Bring the rain, he thought. A moment later, he felt the drops fall from the sky.

***

Emily drove until she stopped at a rest stop/welcome center in Wheeling, West Virginia, on a little stretch of land that crept up on you after Maryland on I-70 before hitting the state line for Ohio. She found a table out in an open area and decided to eat one of the many sandwiches that Judith packed. As she pulled apart her croissant, she watched people pull in and out of that area—older couples, young couples with small children, and a few loners like herself. She willed herself to focus on the strangers, because it took her mind off the decisions she knew she'd have to make as soon as she rolled into town a few hours later.

Celia texted her while she was eating, asking for her location, competing with Judith for the most maternal award of the day. She decided to call her instead of texting back.

"Girl...Shakes came by to say goodbye," Celia said, voice full of fear and warning.

"Goodbye? Where's he going?"

"Back to Tennessee he said. He and Gavin had a huge fight and Gavin kicked him off the property. He's really upset about it. Paco took him for a drink to talk him out of it."

Emily closed her eyes. *Gavin, what are you doing?*

"You need to come back and get that man's head on straight. He's losing it."

"I don't think I can, Celia. I don't think I have that power."

"We all think you do."

"I don't think I want that power, then. I'm just . . . tired, Celia. I wish I could tell you in words how tired I am."

"I know, sweetie. I know. Let's just get you home, okay? Everything else will work itself out, you'll see," Celia said, always, always playing the role of Molly Sunshine.

Emily threw out her trash and used the bathroom before she got back on the road. When she saw the welcome sign for Ohio a few miles later, she felt tears roll down her face.

CHAPTER TWENTY-EIGHT

It was late when Emily drove up to Paco and Celia's house. Before she could even turn off the ignition, both of them were standing on the porch, waiting patiently for her to get out of the car. The simple act of them waiting for her, wanting her to come back, caring so much about her and Sam, made her emotional again. When she opened the car door, they walked up to her, both taking turns hugging her and breathing her in, like their long-lost sister.

"Are you hungry?" Celia asked.

"No. Just tired. Leave the stuff in the car, Paco," Emily called to him. He looked hopeful that maybe she would be going to Gavin's.

"We can unload them in the morning," she said. He nodded and followed them inside.

The familiar sights and smells of the house made her finally exhale. Celia had painted the bright red wall light blue and was burning a tropical candle in the middle of the coffee table where they were watching a movie, waiting up for her. Celia's decorating motif that summer was beach shabby chic. Paco groaned when he saw fifty pounds of seashells come in a box from Amazon.com, but obediently painted the accent wall with two coats of primer and two coats of Tidal Wave, a blue-green color from Valspar.

Emily saw Sam on one side of the sectional on a pillow, wrapped in a Teenaged Mutant Ninja Turtle comforter. She felt her heart ache in her chest. How she missed her son. Five days felt like an eternity.

"Poor baby tried to stay up for you," Celia said.

Emily kneeled in front of Sam and touched his hair, lightened by his time in the sun. He looked like a miniature version of Aaron sleeping there. He opened his eyes and smiled. She took him in her arms and smelled his familiar smell and knew that come tomorrow, everything would be okay in the world, even if she did not have Gavin anymore.

After Sam had been put to bed, Paco, Celia and Emily sat quietly around the dining room table drinking wine, letting the stories that Emily retold sit with them.

"Damn, Em. I'm so sorry," Paco said after a while.

Emily didn't know which part he was offering condolences about—the part where Aaron's best friend murdered him or the part where Gavin took off like a chicken shit in the middle of it all. She finished her glass of wine, and Paco poured her another one, emptying the bottle. He stood to get another one, sensing the night was young and the wine needed to keep flowing.

"I'm sure he thought that you needed some space to make up your mind after being bombarded with so much new information," Celia reasoned.

"No, I think he was scared I already made my choice to come back with him and didn't know what to do with me," Emily said.

Paco sat down. "I'm with Celia on this one, Em. Gavin goes the hell out of his way to not be in the way, you know?"

"How could he think he was in the way? Especially after we'd . . ." Emily paused and drank. She closed her eyes and willed away the sight of him towering over her when they made love from her mind.

Paco looked at Celia, questioning. Celia shook her head to let him know she'd explain the details to him later.

"So now what, Em? You have your money back. Are you done with the business? Done with Ohio?" Paco asked. Celia looked sad.

"I don't know yet. I don't want to be. But I can't very well be partners with a man who can't be in a room with me."

"We did contact Dr. Gibson, like you asked. She said she'd meet with you and Sam as soon as you were ready to explain what you learned in New York, and to help you both deal with it," Celia said.

Emily laughed a short laugh. Could anyone help her truly deal with this, except maybe Gavin? "The sooner the better. Sam has a right to know the truth about his father."

That night in bed, Celia placed her head on Paco's chest.

"We have to fix this, babe. They are too stubborn to fix it themselves."

"Babe, you have to learn to let people take care of their own lives," Paco said, half asleep.

"They belong together. We have to help them," Celia said. Paco groaned.

"Babe. Babe. Are you listening to me?" Paco sighed heavily. He knew she was right, as always.

"What do you want me to do?"

CHAPTER TWENTY-NINE

Gavin woke up to the sun spilling on his face, peeking through from the lacy white curtains in his living room. He sat his recliner to the up position and groaned as he moved his neck that had a crick in it from passing out drunk sometime after midnight. An empty bottle of Jack Daniels was by him, and he scurried out of the chair and barely made it to his bathroom, where he threw up for a solid ten minutes. The whiskey coming back up reminded him of too many nights after Nat died. He'd grown to hate the taste of Jack Daniels and his tears after too many drunken nights with both of them. He sat on the tile and used a wet washcloth to try to calm the nausea, but it was not working well. A few minutes later his phone buzzed. It was a text message from Paco.

"She's back home at our house. She still wants to be with you. She still loves you. Thought you should know . . ."

Gavin held the phone for a long time then forced himself up with the help of his bathroom wall. Enough was enough.

Paco slid his phone into his pocket and gave a thumbs up sign to Celia before heading back to class. Celia was sitting next to Emily in the small conference room waiting for Dr. Gibson. She winked at him and slightly puckered her lips at him. How she loved that man of hers.

Emily sat in Dr. Gibson's office waiting for Sam to meet them. She had spent an hour talking to Dr. Gibson in the conference room to prepare for the talk with Sam. He looked surprised to see them there. "Are you okay?" he asked. His voice was getting stronger every day.

"I am. I just was talking to Dr. Gibson, and I wanted to talk a little about my trip to New York," Emily signed and spoke.

Sam sat down on the small couch in Dr. Gibson's office.

Emily sat next to him and Dr. Gibson and Celia, who was there to help translate Sam's sign language if needed, remained seated by the desk to allow them some space.

Emily looked at her hands and exhaled. She willed them to convey the complicated emotions that she had going through her. Sam looked at her patiently.

"It is very hard for me to tell you what I am about to tell you. I know I was not very open and honest with you about when Daddy died, and for that I hope you can forgive me someday . . ." she signed.

Sam looked confused. *"Why do I have to forgive you? I don't understand."*

"When the police came to tell me that Daddy was dead, they told me that he jumped off the roof of his office building because he did not want to live anymore. He and I had a very bad fight the night before because he was not acting like himself. He was staying away from home, from us, and I was upset about that. He was upset, too, and he left. I thought that our fight caused him to do that," she explained.

Sam looked shocked but didn't say anything.

"After the funeral, the police came back to the house and told me that Daddy stole $30 million from people he worked for, and that is why he jumped off the roof. Because he was scared that he was going to go to jail. They also said that everything we owned had to be used to pay back the people that Daddy stole from. That's why we had to leave New Jersey."

"Daddy would never steal! He hated thieves. Remember when someone stole my bike at the park? He was so mad and said he hated thieves!"

Emily felt a pang of guilt that she did not defend Aaron during that time, and here was his son defiant that his father could do no such thing.

"You're right, Sam. Daddy didn't steal that money. Uncle Dan stole the money and said that Daddy did."

Sam's face looked crestfallen.

"Why would Uncle Dan say that? He and Daddy were friends," Sam signed. Sam looked so heartbroken that a friend could say such a thing about another friend.

Emily shook her head sadly. *"I know they were, sweetie.*

Sometimes people do bad things to the people they love." Emily thought to Gavin and felt a pain in her chest.

"Sam, Uncle Dan also told another lie. Uncle Dan hurt Daddy and made it look like Daddy hurt himself. He's the reason that Daddy died," Emily whispered while she signed.

Sam bowed his head and had angry tears in his eyes. "Why?" he squeaked out.

"I wish I knew why, Sam. Daddy was such a good friend to him and tried to help Uncle Dan . . ."

Emily held on to Sam's shoulder and tried to calm herself down enough to answer more of Sam's questions.

"Did they catch Uncle Dan? Will he go to prison?"

"Yes, he will."

Sam nodded and wiped his eyes with a tissue. *"Gavin told me that I should forgive people that have hurt me. That that is a sign that you are truly becoming a man, when you can forgive."*

"That's right."

"Mommy?"

"Yes, Sam?"

"I'm not going to be a man today. I'm not ready to forgive Uncle Dan yet."

"Me neither. Maybe with time we both can."

"Do you think Gavin will be disappointed in me because I couldn't forgive yet?" he signed.

Emily choked up with emotion. "Gavin loves you. He would never be disappointed in you. Ever." She hugged him and looked at Celia. Celia gave her a sorrowful look.

Sam nodded and Emily could sense his relief. *"I miss him. When can we go back to the house?"*

"Soon, baby. Soon," she said, and hugged him again.

Emily felt bone-tired from so much emotional turmoil but allowed Celia to drag her out to Fusion Grille for a drink and late dinner that night when Sam decided to go to bed early. Emily had not been to that restaurant since her disastrous dinner with Trevor months ago. The place was crowded with regulars, which included a few of Emily's customers. Many people waved to her and asked about Gavin. The constant uttering of his name, plus the memory of meeting Caitlin that fateful night a few months ago, was putting her into a deeper funk. She couldn't sit still or concentrate.

"Maybe we should've grabbed McDonald's and chilled at the house," Emily said. Her tolerance for crowds was waning with the passage of time waiting for a table. They were stuck at the bar waiting for one to come open for the last half hour.

"Girl, you are worse than Xavier tonight," Celia said, her voice even and kind.

"I know. I know. I'm just crappy company right now. I warned you."

"Order another drink, please."

Emily finished her pink cosmopolitan and asked for a shot of Johnnie Walker Blue Label. Fruity drinks would just not do that night.

A young waiter set down a plate of hot Brie wrapped in puff pastry surrounded by crackers. "Sorry for the wait, ladies. Compliments of the house. We should be able to get you seated in ten minutes," he said.

Emily watched Celia eat with the intricate balance of delicacy and voracity. "How's that Johnny Walker treating you?" Celia asked and winked.

Emily felt the burn of the whiskey and the calmness of the alcohol soothe her. She smiled and gave a thumbs up.

Celia laughed. "Good."

Emily exhaled deeply and took a cracker of hot Brie and bit into it. The salty, mushroom creaminess melted in her mouth.

"So, Gavin came by to see you this afternoon while we were in Columbus."

Emily felt her pulse quicken. "And?"

"He was disappointed you were not there. He wants to see you. Said you were still his girl. Sent Paco a text that he wanted to see his girl."

Emily felt conflicted with those words. She was angry at him for abandoning her in Watchung, but the thought of her still being his made her feel weepy.

At that moment she saw him walk into the restaurant, dressed in the same suit they bought in New York to celebrate her freedom. He wore no tie but wore a black Stetson hat, looking like a true cowboy. The restaurant suddenly went silent as they realized that handsome man was their very own Gavin Shaw.

Celia smiled and slid off the barstool, winking at Gavin. He touched her arm in appreciation and walked up to Emily, who was sitting there stunned.

His green eyes only focused on her. They showed intense love and intense sorrow.

"Hey, beautiful," he whispered.

Emily burst into tears, crying a hysterical, ugly cry filled with so much relief. He took her into his arms, and she buried her face in the curve of his neck. He grabbed the back of her head with his strong hand.

"I love you. So very much. Please forgive me," he whispered. His words made her knees weak, and he held her tighter in his embrace.

She found his lips through her blurry tears, and the audience be damned, he kissed her like he meant every word that he uttered. The restaurant broke out into thunderous applause.

Emily smiled and wiped her tears away with the tissue that Celia provided. Celia had black streaks of mascara going down her own eyes. Celia loved love. All people did. The congratulations and well wishes from the townsfolk who knew Gavin and experienced his tragedy from afar were genuine. Women swooned at Gavin's grand act of romance, and men became nostalgic for younger days of conquest and the memory of when they finally got their girl.

"Take me home," Emily said. Gavin gently wiped her last tears with his thumbs and kissed her ten more times before he escorted her of the restaurant.

They walked through the door of the farmhouse and saw Paco and the boys watching *SpongeBob SquarePants* in closed caption. Sam ran up to Gavin and hugged him tightly. Gavin hugged him back and kissed his head, and Paco smiled a knowing look full of pride and conquest.

"All righty, my work here is done!" Paco said.

Emily hugged him. "Thank you."

"Any time, sis. You both deserve to be happy together," he said. Paco and Xavier made their way to Paco's truck and quickly drove away.

Gavin was patient as Emily got Sam settled back into the house, unpacking his belongings and chatting with him after he took a bath. Sam bolted down the stairs to say goodnight, and Gavin lingered on the couch in silence waiting for Emily to come downstairs after he hugged him goodnight. When she finally did come down, dressed in a black nightgown, he stood quickly and kissed her, his patience completely gone. She felt weak in her knees and broke away gently.

"What's wrong?" he breathed.

"I'm just nervous—I know, it's silly, all things considered," she said. He smiled and walked her to his bedroom.

She walked in and slowly took in the changes that she saw as she maneuvered in the space. He rearranged the furniture, moving the bed to face the doorway. He removed the tall dresser and placed the wide dresser where that had been. The curtains were changed to neutral beige colors with no frilly lace. He purchased a new quilt, more masculine, with greens and blues in a handsome pattern. She saw he had new red-striped sheets on the mattress.

The biggest change was the pictures—all but three remained on a small corner of the dresser. They were of Gavin's family of four, out near the falling down barn, smiling radiantly by a bonfire; one of Sissy riding Lily; and one of Natalie in her Iraqi war fatigues in front of a helicopter with her air evacuation team, looking beautifully proud and strong.

"I wanted this room to be for us. A fresh start," he said. Emily felt a lump in her throat.

"You didn't have to put away their pictures, Gavin."

"Yes, I did. I kept the ones up that meant the most to me," he said softly. "The rest are out of sight, but close by. Maybe you want to put up one of Aaron and Sam. A reminder of where we came from. How we came to find each other . . ." Emily squeezed his hand.

"Do you like it?"

"I do," she said. This place felt like she had crossed the finish line of a marathon. She felt a mixture of relief, exhaustion, and some pride for getting there.

"Will you stay here with me tonight?" He touched the side of her face and placed his forehead on hers.

She closed her eyes. "Yes."

And with a kiss, Gavin's wish of her being in his bed finally came true.

CHAPTER THIRTY

Gavin was 22 when he married Natalie, against every odd that could surround a couple. He was a poor kid with little family who worked on her father's cattle ranch. She was the beautiful, blonde debutant whose penchant for bad boys just to get under daddy's skin became an anecdote among the ranch hands.

But it was different when Natalie Wentworth locked eyes on the tanned, redneck that was Gavin Shaw. On the surface he was a bad boy, rough around the edges, but deep down to his bones he was deeply kindhearted, and that made the rebel Natalie take pause. He was quiet as a mouse around her, taking in every detail of her existence, as he tended to do with most people, he found intriguing. He did not fall for her usual flip-of-her-hair-and-grin techniques. With him she had to work. She took him riding out in the back forty of her daddy's land and got him talking about his life and his dreams. In those horse rides where Gavin became transparent, she felt compelled to do the same, and they fell deeply in love. To the other ranch hands, it simply looked like Gavin snuck off to get some action with the boss' daughter, earning him the title of badass among the group. When he up and ran off with her to elope, everyone assumed a little Gavin was soon to arrive. Little did they know that he never had touched her with more than his soft lips grazing hers.

They were married a hundred miles away from Tucker Wentworth's ranch by a justice of the peace who was nearly 80 years old. The old man's hands shook as he read them their vows and as he signed the piece of paper that made Natalie Wentworth officially Natalie Wentworth Shaw. Natalie wore a white eyelet dress with her blonde hair lying loosely around her shoulders and little makeup, showing off her spattering of freckles on the bridge of her nose, just like Gavin liked to see her. Gavin wore clean Wranglers, his work boots, and an oversized, clean white shirt stuffed deeply into his Wranglers that he borrowed from his wonderfully large friend, Flacco Sanchez, who worked alongside him on the ranch. Flacco agreed to bear witness to the event, primarily because he was a sucker for a good love story, despite his large and tough exterior.

The three of them celebrated the nuptials at a local Whataburger that night, compliments of the best man, dining on cheeseburgers and crossing their arms in ceremony to feed each other French fries and chocolate malts. They spent the night at a La Quinta Inn somewhere off I-35 en route to Dallas for their honeymoon. Gavin watched his bride emerge from the bathroom, where she had been preparing for their wedding night, and stare at him with so much love and adoration. He would consider that moment the happiest day of his life for years to come, despite the unknown wrath that was yet to come from Tucker for stealing away one of his daughters, or the unknown reality of how to support his new bride in the coming months. He had gotten his girl and the future was a bright, blank canvas, ready to be painted. He had never been so content, or experienced joy like that in his entire life.

When Gavin opened his eyes and saw Emily lying beside him in his bed, in his own house, together as a couple, he realized that happiest days and contentment were not devoted to just one major milestone event. He wished he realized this years ago when his heart broke at the loss of his bride and daughter, but then reasoned it took someone like Emily to make him understand this. There was happiness still to be had, and one look at Emily's face as she slept soundly beside him proved it. One story ended tragically, but another was still waiting to be written. The realization that he was granted another story to write suddenly became the happiest moment of his life.

He held on to her until the morning chores were calling to him. He climbed out of bed, quickly showered, dressed, and walked out to the kitchen to drink a strong cup of coffee. Sam was waiting at the kitchen counter with a glass of milk and Gavin's coffee already poured.

"Morning," Sam said, and smiled.

"Morning, Sam."

"Is mom in there with you? She wasn't upstairs," Sam asked.

Gavin's ears turned pink. He did not know how to handle that question. He stammered before he decided to tell him the truth.

"Yes."

"Good," Sam said. "About time," he mumbled, and drank his milk.

Gavin was shocked and laughed. He tousled the boy's hair and motioned for him to move over to let him sit. They drank quietly until Gavin felt compelled to talk.

"Are you okay with your mom and I being together?"

"Do you love her?"

"Very much. And I love you, Sam," he said.

"Then yes," Sam said, and smiled sweetly.

They walked out to the barn after a quick breakfast of Rice Krispies and bananas. Gavin stopped short when he saw Shakes already there mucking out the stalls.

"Whoever you have doing this for you does a shitty job," Shakes said.

Gavin smiled and closed his eyes, grateful that Shakes was always the better man and knew how to deal with his hothead temperament. He walked up to Shakes and offered him his hand. Shakes shook it, gave him a quick pat on the shoulder, and quickly retreated back to his chores.

"So, I heard you have your woman back," Shakes said.

Gavin started to fill buckets with water. "That's a fact."

"You're a lucky bastard, you know that?"

"Yes, I do."

Elliot and Grace, Gavin's other two Quarter Horses, quickly moved out to pasture when Sam opened their stall. Sam dragged a bale of hay toward them while Gavin quietly cleaned out their stalls. Will walked into the barn a few minutes later. "Looks like rain today."

"Yeah, the week looks terrible," Gavin said.

"We may want to think about alternate draining for the southeast lot or we may lose it all," Will said.

"You say that every damn year, and every damn year it's fine," Shakes said.

"Well, at least let's go look at it before you tell me I'm full of shit," Will said.

"Fair enough—let's ride out there. I'll follow you," Gavin said. They all piled in two different trucks and drove down the road to the second half of Gavin's land that was closest to Will's house.

Emily slept later than she intended to that morning, and it was closer to 8 a.m. when she walked into the kitchen to make some coffee. She saw a note underneath her yellow mug and the coffee already set for her to push "start."

Mornin' beautiful. Call me when you wake up, the note said. It was written in Gavin's slanted script. She smiled as she put a slice of toast in the toaster and waited patiently for the coffee to finish brewing.

As she poured cream into her coffee, she looked out the kitchen window and saw that dark clouds were rolling in and the wind was picking up. She also saw that the horses were still in the pasture, probably still unsure about bringing themselves into the new barn. She pulled on her boots and called Gavin as she walked to the barn.

"Hello?" he said, breathless.

"Hey. Why are you out of breath?"

"I was running to get my phone. I left it on the bed of Will's truck. Sorry," he said.

"That's okay, I like you breathless," she teased. He laughed.

"Good. I'm old. That's the way I roll," he joked.

"Is Sam with you?"

"Yes. We are about to head back to pick up his boots

because there is some serious mud out here and his tennis shoes are not cutting it."

"Well, it looks like rain. If you all head back, I can whip up a second breakfast. And maybe first lunch," she joked.

Gavin chuckled. "Well, we could definitely eat. Plus, with this storm, I don't know how much we'll get done today. Do you have any orders today?"

"No. Day is free."

"Okay. We're headed back. I love you. See you soon."

"I love you, too," she said, and hung up.

She slid open the barn door to let the horses back in, confused why the door was shut in the first place. She felt an odd sensation on her right cheek, and it took a few seconds to realize that it was metal from the barrel of a gun being pressed there, and the person holding the gun was Sue Ellen Richter.

CHAPTER THIRTY-ONE

"Don't you move, you man-stealing whore," Sue Ellen hissed and pointed a .38 caliber pistol at Emily. Emily was frozen with fear and disbelief that this was happening.

Sue Ellen looked deranged, with her blonde hair in four different directions and black mascara smeared around her eyes, making her look like a raccoon. Her clothes looked more like Darryl's than hers—baggy blue jeans and an oversized brown jacket.

"It took me a while to realize it. But it's you. You're the reason that he doesn't want me. You're the reason that I can't get him to understand how we belong together."

Emily didn't say or move much as she watched Sue Ellen twitch nervously, sniff, and rub her runny nose. Emily saw her fair share of addicts in New York on the subway that looked the same way as she did, and started thinking of a plan of escape, more fearful that drugs were causing this standoff. The thunder started to rumble in the distance. Emily could hear the horses starting to neigh and make their way back to the barn.

"I don't know what he could possibly see in you. Your small tits, dirty hair, dirty hands. You know how he wanted me, right? How he was all gunning for me. I just needed more time with him. Just another chance and he would have been mine forever."

Emily stepped backward as Elliot charged past Sue Ellen, the 1,000- pound animal uncaring about a stranger with a firearm blocking his way. Rain had started to fall, making a spattering sound on the roof, and that horse did not like water at all.

"These damn horses," Sue Ellen mumbled, and rubbed her nose again. "And you decided to rub it in my face with that showing downtown last night, right? Flaunting your love for the whole town to see? No one makes a fool of me. No one!"

Emily knew it took about fifteen minutes, give or take, to drive back from Will's house. She prayed that they were not that far out.

Bob walked in from the outside and charged passed the women to his stall, with Grace and Lily following behind him. Grace and Lily's stall doors were shut, causing the two horses to walk back and forth impatiently. Sue Ellen grew more agitated with the two large animals obstructing her view of Emily and began to scream at them to move.

"Let me open their stalls," Emily said calmly. She watched Sue Ellen hold her gun with a shaky hand and wipe her nose.

"Open them!" she conceded.

Emily walked behind the horses and slid open Grace's stall and then walked carefully to open Lily's stall. Grace gladly walked into the safety of her stall as another clap of thunder rang out, but Lily hesitated.

Lily, whose stall was near the eastern part of the barn closest to the door leading to the pasture, refused to go in her stall. She neighed and stepped backward until Emily was boxed in the corner between Lily's stall and the wall to where the door went to the pasture.

"Move this horse, bitch!" Sue Ellen yelled.

"She won't move," Emily said, as she pushed with all her might. The horses were not bridled, so there was nothing to grab onto to move her. Lily would not budge.

Sue Ellen started punching the horse with her closed fists, screaming at her to move, causing Lily to neigh loudly and lift her hooves at Sue Ellen, pushing Emily back further into the corner. Emily scrambled to move away from Lily's hind legs, fearful she would be kicked to death by the horse, and she found herself almost pinned to the wall by Lily's hindquarters. Emily tried to squirm out of the crushing weight of the horse and started to panic as she felt the tightness of the horse on her chest as Sue Ellen smacked Lily on the opposite side.

"Sue Ellen!" Gavin's voice boomed. Sue Ellen stopped screaming at the horse and Emily heard a clap of thunder. Lily released Emily and she stumbled to the ground coughing, trying to catch her breath.

Gavin stood at the opposite end of the barn, on the west end by the door that faced the farmhouse. He was unarmed and walked slowly toward Sue Ellen with his palms facing out by his sides.

"What are you doing, Sue Ellen? This is madness," Gavin said carefully.

"Madness. I know a little about madness. Madness is waiting for you to realize that we belong together. Madness is waiting for you to realize this so you can come rescue me from my fat-ass, balding husband and my ungrateful children, like you promised you would."

"I never said I'd take you from Darryl and the boys," Gavin said.

"You said it with your kisses. When you pinned me to the wall that night. When we were finally going to make the dream come true after all these years of wanting each other."

"I never . . ."

"YES YOU DID!!" she screamed. Emily crouched against the wall, watching the horror in Gavin's face, and the regret.

"All we needed was another try. But then you hired this bitch with her retarded son. They got in the way. So, I tried to get rid of them. New Year's Eve. I saw you kiss her in the alleyway that night. And I followed you home to change your mind. But your damn farm hand showed up. So, I went back to take care of her once and for all. I saw the car in the driveway. Threw a match in that cesspool of a garage and let it burn. But she fooled me, this one. She wasn't in the house. YOU WERE SUPPOSED TO BE IN THE HOUSE. YOU WERE ALL SUPPOSED TO DIE!" Sue Ellen screamed and turned the gun to Emily again.

Emily felt sick. Margaret and Mark. Dear God.

"There was never a chance with us, Sue Ellen. You were a drunken mistake. You were the town whore, coming on to me with my wife and daughter's bodies not even cold in the grave. I could taste your desperation. You'd do anything to anyone if they promised you a chance to get out of this town and away from Darryl. I knew this and I used you. And that's all I wanted that night. Your desperation," Gavin growled. Emily looked at him, alarmed, but knew full well he was diverting Sue Ellen's attention away from her.

It worked. Sue Ellen turned her gun back on him and looked like she had been slapped.

"What did you say to me?"

"You heard me, whore. How many men have you slept with to try to get out of Champaign County, out from under that pig of a man you married? How many of them would ever want a stupid woman like you? Falling for his lines. What did he promise you? A Lexus and a diamond ring the size of Texas? What a line he must have fed you. He promised you the world and only gave you a life on a tractor and three unruly boys who are the spitting image of him," Gavin continued.

Emily saw something out of the corner of her eye and was horrified to see Sam standing behind Sue Ellen in the doorway leading out to the pasture. Gavin saw him, too, and his eyes showed fear that only Emily could see. She waved her hands at Sam and signed *"Get help! 911! Run! Run! Run!"* before she ran for the door, pushing him out into the rain before Sue Ellen could turn around and see him.

Will turned on his windshield wipers to high as he pulled up Gavin's driveway. "Yeah, definitely not figuring out the draining issue today," Will said.

"Is that Sam?" Shakes asked, squinting. Will slammed on his brakes right before he hit Gavin's driveway and threw the truck into park, both opening their doors to see what the problem was.

Sam ran frantically to them and screamed in a high-pitched voice "HELP ME!!!!" The sound sent shivers down Will's spine.

"GUN! GUN! GUN!" he yelled. Will and Shakes looked at each other, and in an instant Shakes snatched up Sam and pulled him back behind to the passenger side door, opening the glove box to grab his .357 magnum. Will instinctively opened his toolbox to grab his hunting rifle and ran for the barn. As Will ran, Shakes called 911 and asked for backup and an ambulance. His voice shook on every word.

Will ran to the west entrance of the barn facing the farmhouse and slowly peeked in. He could hear Gavin talking to someone. He could see that everyone in the barn was at the east end, facing the pasture, so he ran quickly to the south entrance, where the hay was stored. From that angle, Will saw Sue Ellen Richter with a small handgun with her back against Grace's stall. She was going back and forth pointing to Gavin and then pointing to Emily, who were standing about 20 feet apart near the east entrance. Will climbed onto a few bales of hay for a better shot and used his scope to get Sue Ellen into the crosshairs of the rifle. Once she was in his crosshairs, he was ready to put a bullet in her head when a massive flash of lightning flashed and a loud crack of thunder crashed, startling Grace. Her back hooves kicked Sue Ellen in the ribcage, injuring her badly, but not enough to prevent her from pulling her trigger a half second before Will pulled his. He saw Emily stumble into Gavin's arms just as Sue Ellen fell to her death.

"EM! EM! NO! NO! NO!" Gavin cried, as he held her limp body. Will was immediately by his side.

"LAY HER DOWN! GAVIN, LAY HER DOWN!" Will searched for the wound and felt a cry escape from his lips when he saw it was a chest wound. There was so much blood coming from the hole in her chest and out of the corners of her mouth. He put pressure on the chest wound to slow the bleeding and prayed that it would help. In the distance he heard sirens in-between the claps of thunder.

Gavin's tears were so thick that all he could see was Emily behind a waterfall.

"Stay with us, Em!" Will screamed. Uniformed sheriff's deputies charged into the barn and cleared the area, allowing the paramedics to rush in. They tried to pull Gavin away from her side.

"Sir! Sir! You have to move so we can help her!" the male

paramedic yelled. It took the force of three men to pull Gavin away from her.

"I can't find a pulse."

Gavin crumpled against Will and sobbed.

CHAPTER THIRTY-TWO

Emily's eyes fluttered open, then closed from the bright light of the sun. All she could hear was noise. What was that noise? It sounded like muffled gunfire and air whooshing.

A pair of sky-blue eyes looked intently at her. "She's responsive!" the woman yelled above the noise. She was in military fatigues with "USAF" on the chest and an American flag on her right arm. She had on a camouflaged helmet with a small black microphone.

"That extra bag did it. ETA to the trauma center?" asked a male military nurse.

"Fifteen minutes."

"You're very lucky, ma'am. We thought you were a goner," he yelled.

Emily fought to refocus her vision. She finally realized that she was on the floor of a helicopter. The man looked exactly like Aaron, and the blue-eyed woman was a dead ringer for Natalie.

"Oh my God, I'm dead. Sue Ellen actually killed me," Emily thought.

"She looks terrified," Natalie yelled.

"Em, you're safe. It's okay," Aaron yelled.

"You didn't think we'd let her kill you, did you? Not on our watch," Natalie said, and winked.

"Plus, poor Gavin. If you died, we think he would have joined you a few weeks later, right Nat?"

"Definitely. That man has a tender heart. One of the reasons I loved him so much."

"And we didn't want to leave Sam alone. So, the big man let us have a pass on you. But you have to die twice and then you'll come back, okay?" Aaron said.

"What?" Emily croaked.

"It'll only hurt for a minute; I promise you. I love you, Em.

Take care of our boy. You're both so precious to me. I'll always be watching. . " Aaron yelled.

Emily saw the light get brighter and she felt the pain in her chest get unbearable until she heard herself screaming.

CHAPTER THIRTY-THREE

Emily was in surgery when Will and Gavin arrived at the trauma center in Columbus. The MedFlight team arrived almost an hour before they rushed in. It was a miracle that MedFlight was able to land at all, but the storm clouds miraculously parted and the sun shone for a full twenty minutes, which allowed them to take off and land safely on Gavin's property. When the helicopter lifted Emily off, the clouds rolled back in just as quickly as they had parted, making the drive to Columbus agonizingly slow.

Shakes stayed behind with Sam, who had fallen asleep in his arms from overwhelming fear and exhaustion. Shakes rocked him back and forth in Natalie's old rocking chair until he fell asleep, like his momma used to do for him, and like he used to do with Noah when he went through his night terrors as a toddler. Sam fell asleep before he knew that Emily was hurt, and Shakes intended to let him sleep until he knew for sure if she was alive or dead.

Gavin and Will sat in a waiting room that was running non-stop *Fox News* on two TV screens. Surgical patients were given a number, and the number on the electronic board told the status of the surgery. Gavin sat and stared at that board until his eyes blurred at the "in surgery" green highlighted area by her number.

Celia and Paco walked in a few minutes later and Gavin stood and hugged them, grateful to have another set of people there who loved her just as much as he did. Celia was quiet and mournful, unable to muster any positivity in this situation. She was completely inconsolable at the thought of losing her best friend, sitting with her elbows on her knees and crying softly as Paco rubbed her back, stoic yet terrified.

During the agonizing four-hour wait, Gavin waxed and

waned between hope and utter despair. In his positive moments he would assure himself of her recovery and make intricate plans about the life they would start. He would sell the farm and buy a piece of land anywhere she wanted to live. They would take long rides on Lily and Bob and talk for hours until the sun went down. They would raise Sam and maybe have another baby, if she was willing. He could see that future. He wanted it so much he could taste it, feel it.

As the surgery went on, he started coaching himself about the reality of her dying and never coming back to him. Who would take Sam? Paco and Celia or him? Could he raise him without crying hysterical tears seeing her eyes looking back at him every day? He had decided Paco and Celia would be best to raise him. He would set up a trust for Sam, then walk to the stream where he first took her into his arms and end the madness that Sue Ellen had started.

The board switched and read "in post-operation" and Gavin felt his pulse quicken and his breathing labored. His name was paged and all four of them stood up and walked to the check-in desk. He was surprised when he saw Doug Thomas come out from the doublewide doors. Doug was equally surprised to see Gavin, and he pointed to a small counseling room where they could talk in private.

"It was bad, Gavin. Hollow-point bullet. Lots of damage to the lung that we had to repair. Lot of blood loss. She coded twice, but we got her back. She's a hell of a fighter. We'll know more in 24 hours. They will transfer her to ICU in a bit," Doug said.

Celia and Paco both looked at Gavin, waiting for his reaction. Gavin finally took a deep breath and reached out to shake Doug's hand, and Doug's head bowed as he shook it. It was a painful cease-fire between two men who had dueled for the love of the same woman for over a decade. Both were exhausted from the fight, and both finally seemed to understand that they lost what they were fighting for in the first place.

"Thank you," Gavin said. Doug nodded to him and to the

rest of the room. He exited quietly, leaving them to regroup.

No one wanted to exhale or feel relief just yet, it seemed too premature. Celia finally spoke after an hour of silence. "I'm going to call Shakes," she said. She wiped her tears and left the room.

It was another hour before they could go see her, one at a time and only for a few minutes. Gavin went last and was not prepared to see her intubated, with a tube sticking out of her chest. She looked frail, like she could fade away at any minute. His heart lurched in in his chest.

He sat by her and grabbed her hand, listening to the sounds of the machines that were monitoring her and helping her breathe.

"Em," he said.

He placed her hand on his face and kissed her palm. He left her hand there and closed his eyes.

"I won't leave this damn hospital without you; do you hear me?" he said. He waited for a sign that she could hear him, but she just laid there, still.

"I tried so hard not to love you," he whispered. Emotion caught in his throat and tears welled up in his eyes. His head bowed at all the memories, the happiness, the love that the past year brought him. He wiped the tears away and cleared his throat.

"But I don't regret it. Even if this all goes to hell. I don't regret a single moment I had with you," he whispered.

He didn't know if it was a reflex or if it was real, but Emily's hand grasped his. He kissed her hand several more times.

A few minutes later a nurse came in with two blankets and pointed to the chair in the corner.

"Dr. Thomas said you could stay as long as you follow our instructions to leave when we need to work with her."

"Thank you," he said, gratefully.

He held Emily's hand for a few more hours, praying so hard that the words ran together and made little sense. He was so scared and so exhausted but sleep finally took him. The night nurse gently urged him to move to his recliner and he relented, falling asleep to the rhythmic beep, beep, beep of Emily's heart rate on the monitor.

Just before he fell asleep, he saw her. His baby girl. Sissy. She always visited him when he was in his most desperate hour.

The first time Sissy came to visit him was when he was in ICU after the accident. She sat on the bed, smiled and told him that she loved him and would always be there with him. He blamed the vision on his drugged-induced coma, even though it felt so real to him. Every time that he contemplated ending it, throwing his life away, or giving up, she came to him and gave him the strength to carry on for a little while longer.

"I think you both should have a baby girl. She'll have your dark hair and Emily's hazel eyes," Sissy said. *"I always wanted a sister."*

"I think we're still a little early to be thinking this way, baby girl. She's been hurt real bad. Docs don't know if she'll make it or not," he said.

Sissy came and sat on his lap on the recliner like she did when she was a little girl. She placed her head on his chest and her hand on his heart. Gavin smiled and hugged his daughter and felt himself rocking her, her blonde hair tickling his nose.

"I think it's a perfect time to plan a wedding, Daddy. In the summer when everything is green and in bloom. Then we can talk about my baby sister. I like the name Autumn. Maybe she'll be born in the fall."

"You'd be a great big sister," he said.

"Bet your ass, Daddy-O."

EPILOUGUE

It was just after 9 a.m. Thanksgiving Day and the smell of turkey wafted through the entire house. Celia, Paco, and Xavier had arrived late the night before from Ohio and were just starting to appear in the kitchen in search of food and coffee. Celia poured coffee in a big brown cup and passed it to Paco, who grabbed her by the waist and kissed her. Sam and Xavier climbed on chairs surrounding the large island and grabbed a cinnamon roll and a banana before running off to spend time together exploring outside. Three-month stretches were getting too long for them, and every time that Paco and Celia drove back to Ohio, they would spend the first three hours seriously considering moving to Gatlinburg to be closer to their friends. Ohio just wasn't the same without them.

Gavin walked in from outside with an arm full of firewood.

"Think we may get a few inches of snow tonight," he said. He dropped the logs by the fireplace and walked into the kitchen, taking the cup of coffee that Emily handed him. She kissed him and turned to finish kneading bread for dinner. Gavin slid his arms around her, stopping to rest his hands on her very pregnant belly and waited to see if his baby girl would delight him with a kick.

"She's sleepy this morning," Emily said. She closed her eyes as Gavin grazed the nook of her neck with a kiss. The baby kicked and she laughed.

"I know how to get her to respond to me," he grinned.

"Girl, I don't know how you managed to make a turkey being this close to your due date," Celia said. She pulled out a chair and motioned for Emily to sit down.

"I still have a few weeks. She won't be here until New Years, mark my words," Emily said, and sat down.

Emily's recovery from the gunshot wound had been slow and painful. The scandal that surrounded Sue Ellen's psychotic episode was too much for Darryl Richter. He sold his land and moved to Indiana with his boys a few weeks after Sue Ellen was buried, just before Emily was released from the hospital. Gavin's reputation was equally tarnished, as the hens from church turned on him and suddenly exalted Sue Ellen to martyrdom—after all, she was just a woman who was in love. Who could blame her for being pushed to the edge for the man she loved? It was a betrayal that he could not forgive, picking Sue Ellen over Emily, the real victim, and it made saying goodbye to Champaign County so much easier for him.

Josh was the one who suggested they move to Gatlinburg, near Gavin's childhood stomping ground in Sevier County. Josh spent a whole month at the farm after his graduation helping Gavin out while Emily recuperated. He took over for Will, who followed through with his desire to move to London permanently with Evangeline. When Josh got back to Knoxville to begin his apprenticeship, he e-mailed farm listings to them almost daily. When Gavin and Emily opened up the listing of a log cabin on almost 100 acres on Huskey Grove, they both knew that was their new home. They put the farmhouse on the market and decided to not mess with the corn harvest when it sold a week later. They packed all their possessions, the horses, the Borg, the cats, Shakes and left town.

Gavin felt no rush to start planting right away in Tennessee. He spent that autumn exploring his new land and his new bride. They were married late October in a small ceremony on the property with only close family and friends. Six months later Emily was pregnant with a girl. Sissy had been right.

Shakes walked into the kitchen just as another batch of cinnamon rolls came from the oven and made a beeline for them. He lived in town and worked for a locksmith, but still came to the house almost daily for dinner. Emily would not have it any other way.

Will and Evangeline had just woken up, still on London time, and were searching for hot tea in the pantry.

"Save me some sponge. Don't let that prat devour it all,"

Evangeline called from the pantry. Her British accent was a delight to Emily, who smiled and hung on every word that woman said more than Will did.

"So, who are you bringing to dinner tonight?" Paco asked Shakes.

"No one. Thought I'd just keep it to family," Shakes said. He smiled at the shocked faces in the room. Since moving back to Tennessee he was calmer, less lonely, and less critical of his life and the choices he had made. He didn't drink every night, and he smiled a lot more. It was a peace that Gavin was downright jealous of, but tried to emulate every day he got to spend with Emily and Sam.

Gavin led Emily to the front porch and sat with her in their porch swing, looking at the pond. Laughter boomed from the kitchen.

"What time is Josh coming?" she asked.

"Around noon," Gavin said. She put her head on his shoulder and he moved his arm to keep her close to him. They moved slowly back and forth, lost in the moment and their memories.

"Good. It's all good," she said.

ABOUT THE AUTHOR

Clarise Rivera has been writing short stories and fiction since she was a young girl, growing up in South Texas. She lives in Dayton, OH with her husband and two children. This is her first novel.

Made in the USA
Coppell, TX
09 November 2024